MW00441155

OLD GROWTH & IVY

Jayne Menard

OLD GROWTH AND IVY

By Jayne Menard

www.jaynemenard.com

International Standard Book Number ISBN: 978-0692476376

This is a work of fiction. Names, characters, cases, places, events and incidents are either the products of the author's imagination or used in a fictitious manner. Any resemblance to actual persons, living or dead, or actual events is purely coincidental.

Acknowledgement

My appreciation to my friends and family who supported my endeavors in writing this book, through encouragement, inputs and editing. My special gratitude to my niece, Cindy, for her never-failing enthusiasm for this project and for her insightful editing.

Prologue

If you think a career as an FBI agent is like watching a Hollywood action movie with lots of gadgets, spicy seduction scenes, and constant field action, then you should think again. In our electronic age, an FBI field agent can spend hours, days, weeks, and even months of desk time seeking the hard evidence that will break a case open. The work is often tedious, stressful, and intellectually frustrating. You spend years building your skills, only to find that your reputation is based on the results of your last case. Your life is on the line when you make an arrest or a vindictive perpetrator sends his hit men after you. Mostly your life as an agent is so demanding that you have little time for a personal life, not if you want to be the best at what you do.

The Bureau gives you a place to belong, although it can also become a place to hide from yourself and your emotions. I know because I was a federal agent for over 35 years. I have heard it said that my case success rate was exemplary. Working on Bureau matters damn near took my life now and again, both physically and personally. Don't get me wrong -- the FBI is the best. My career was challenging and satisfying. However it was not enough. This story is about finding the neglected parts of my life.

Steven J. Nielsen
Executive Field Director, Retired
Complex International Cases
Federal Bureau of Investigation
March 1, 2014

PART I

Chapter 1

At 7:15 in the morning Ivy Littleton tore out of the driveway of her home nestled in the hills over Portland, Oregon, turned left and zoomed along the street towards downtown where the offices of her company were located. She did not own the company but she ran her business unit of 100 people as if she did. She had been finishing up her usual morning routine when their receptionist called sounding rattled. Three FBI agents were in the lobby waiting to see her. Ivy knew this could not be good. Usually she liked Mondays. It was the one day of the work week when she felt recharged. She had just three more months of work ahead. Her replacement has been identified and by the end of the year, Ivy would be retired. Soon this sort of panic at the office would be some other executive's problem.

As her SUV sped down the long hill where trees were beginning to show the golden edges of warming fall colors, she checked her appearance in the mirror. She knew that despite her advancing years, she was still an attractive woman, well-toned, with a vast amount of silver-streaked black hair that curled and twined no matter how she fought to tame it. Her hair was the one part of her that still had the energy to bounce along through her long days at the office. Ivy was 62 with a long, creditable career, working her way up from a college student with a load of student loans to her executive position.

Ivy pushed a tendril of hair back that escaped the quick upsweep she attempted that morning, turned into the underground parking lot at her office building with a squeal of tires and parked, bouncing against the curb. Grabbing her briefcase, she jumped out of the car and ran to the elevator to the main lobby. As she strode past the building security desk, the guard told her that she had three visitors waiting upstairs. She thanked him, hurrying to the main elevator and frowning.

Part of what kept her motivated was that on any day when she opened the door to their large suite of offices, she never knew what might happen, between clients, prospects, employees and their corporate owners. She was unsure what would be worse: a visit from the IRS, the DEA or the FBI. The CIA might be worse. She forced her shoulders down and back, tilted her head up, and assumed a calm expression. Whatever happened, she knew of nothing wrong that their company might have done in assisting companies and banks to comply with government regulations. In any case, she would not let the FBI agents see that she was flustered. Clearly they wanted to catch her off-guard by arriving unannounced so early in the day.

Ivy stepped out of the elevator, smoothed down her jacket, walked briskly over and opened the glass door to their reception area where three men in ominously dark suits were waiting. One was pacing and swung mid-stride to face her. Even though Ivy was six feet tall, she had to tilt her head up to look him in the eyes. He had to be six and a half feet and substantial, yet he looked trim, fit and about her age, with broad shoulders, a flat stomach and strong hips. He reminded her of a mighty giant sequoia which had needles with thick, sharp points and rough, stringy bark. Ivy tended to classify men as trees and the results were only sometimes flattering. Ivy sucked in her abs, resettled her shoulders and forced herself to retain a calm, friendly smile.

"Steve Nielsen. FBI," the big man said without preamble. "You run this operation?"

"Ivy Littleton, the executive in charge." She held out her hand.

He reached out and took it. His handshake was firm and brisk and his skin was dry, but not rough. His fingers lingered on hers for a moment causing an unexpected sense of warmth. She kept her eyes fixed on his. No way was she losing a stare-down with this brusque man. If he wanted to intimidate her, he would find that she did not give ground easily.

"May I see some ID?" Ivy forced her voice to be crisp and professional.

She looked at the big man's badge – Nielsen, she said to herself. Steve Nielsen. Then she met the other two agents, checking their credentials also -- Agents Brian Tovey and Michael O'Leary, although he called himself Moll.

"What brings you here?"

2

"A court order for certain banking information in your possession."

Nielsen had such a deep voice that the words came out in a low feral rumble as a warning not to mess with him. Three federal agents and a court order. Ivy knew this was going to be one heck of a day.

"Let's go to my office," she said, turning towards the door to enter their suite of offices. As she ushered the men down the hallway, her mind was racing to devise a plan to handle the situation. She settled the agents in her office and then buzzed her assistant for a coffee tray.

Nielsen looked impatient. "This is not a social call."

She smiled at him, feeling that errant curl slide against her cheek. "I am sure we all will work better if properly fueled. Now, could I please see this court order?"

He clicked open his briefcase, took out a folder and handed a short document to her. Ivy read it quickly. The order requested that all data and any related documents received from three of her banking clients be turned over immediately to the FBI for analysis in conjunction with a case related to human trafficking.

"Why come here? We only examine specific time periods of data for our clients to assess compliance with banking regulations. You could obtain a much broader spectrum of data from each bank."

Nielsen glared at her. "The why is not important. We have a court order and we want the data now."

She glanced down at the business card he had tossed on her desk, looking for his title. "Director Nielsen."

"Just Agent Nielsen, Ms. Littleton."

"Agent Nielsen, you must understand that we take care to safeguard the client information entrusted with us. I must verify that you are indeed FBI. I need to confer with our legal counsel and obtain a certified copy of this document directly from the Court to ensure it is bona fide. You have clearly given me a copy. We also must examine this request in the context of our contractual obligations to our clients, where we are required to protect the confidentiality of their data."

3

"We need the data now. The court order specifies the immediacy of the timeline."

"I will call our Internal Counsel to start the ball rolling," Ivy said firmly.

Her assistant came in with a tray of coffee, cutely supplying the three federal agents with bright white corporate logo coffee mugs, and asking if they would rather have tea, water or soft drinks. She included a plate of buttery shortbread cookies from the stash they always kept for guests. Ivy thanked her and requested that she clear a meeting room for the three visitors, then she swiveled in her chair, put the court order in her desktop printer/scanner and emailed a copy to Corporate.

Ivy invited the agents to have coffee while she dialed the phone, luckily reaching the man who served as their internal counsel after only a short delay. She explained the situation and asked how to verify that the men were federal agents. Their three cards were spread out on her desk. As she talked, she scanned in the agents' cards and sent them off to the attorney. While the attorney read through the emailed court order, Ivy watched the three agents.

The two younger men were good-looking, in their late thirties, fit and well-dressed. Each seemed more agreeable than their big, pushy friend, who was clearly the hard-driver of the group. She noticed that none of them wore wedding rings. Ivy would never call the one named Nielsen handsome, although he did have a rugged appeal, silvered hair that was only slightly thinning, and intense, gray-blue eyes. Despite his demanding manner, Ivy felt a physical reaction to him that tingled along her torso. She noticed that notwithstanding his grumblings, he quickly tucked into the cookies and coffee, lacing his with sugar and cream.

The attorney came back on. "How long will it take to give them a working copy of the data and files?"

"Just a few hours."

"That all? Here's the way I see it. We could go to the Court and delay the process and then wind up in the same place we are now or we can comply at this time. I would prefer that we get it done while you are still there."

"Understand. What's next?"

"To be safe, I have to consult with our external attorney firm that has more experience with these situations than I do. Send me a copy of the contracts for each of the banks and any other agreements we have with them, particularly as related to safeguarding their data."

"How long will that take? The agents have impressed upon me the urgency of this request." Ivy was tucking the wayward lock of her hair back again when another one popped out on the other side.

"Gathered time was of the essence from the Court Order. I will call you back later this morning. In the meantime, keep them away from your staff, see if they will sign our standard confidentiality agreement, and have your folks prep the data. Don't let them take any data or files offsite or even download them. Setup server space for them and demand they work onsite. I'll draw up a quick agreement. They may not sign any documents. After all, they are the Feds."

"Got it."

"What a way to start the week. I hope they are at least good eye candy."

Ivy had to smile. "Yes, I am lucky there."

"Wish I were in Portland today to have a look -- back to you as soon as I can."

Ivy put the phone back in its charging slot, stood up from her desk and went to pour herself some coffee.

"It will take some time to do the necessary research on our obligations and conflicts."

"Time we don't have," Nielsen barked at her. He jumped up and moved closer, as if to coerce her into faster action by his sheer size.

Ivy put her hands on her hips, but she did not step back. "Agent Nielsen. I have dropped everything to address you and your court order. I am being cooperative, not obstructive."

One of the other agents nodded. Ivy thought he was the one named Brian. He had warm brown eyes that showed a hint of amusement at the confrontation in front of him.

"Is there someplace we can work in the meantime?" he asked.

5

The big agent looked over his shoulder and glared at him.

"My assistant will show you to a room."

"I am not leaving your office until we have the data," said Agent Nielsen.

"For all three of you, please do not talk to my staff. I do not want them rattled."

"And we do not want the banks tipped off."

"Now, Mr., I mean Agent Nielsen, I am going to meet with a couple of my technicians."

"Great. I will listen in."

Ivy inhaled deeply. "I am going to tell them that you are here at my request to perform an audit of our data handling practices. The FBI is offering this new service to companies handling sensitive information. Got it?"

He regarded her for a moment. "Works for me. We don't want the real reason getting back to the banks."

For the next half-hour, Ivy met with her technicians, spelling out what data she wanted, its exact source and how she wanted access set up for the three agents. Nielsen listened intently but stayed quiet.

After they left, she said to him, "You will only access the data on-site for analytical purposes. You will not download it or take a copy."

"If we find what we're after, we will need to produce evidence in Court."

"At that point, I suggest that you obtain the data directly from the banks."

"And if for some reason, we can't. Then what?"

"We will make a secure copy. It will be turned over to our legal counsel for safekeeping and your requests may go there directly."

She watched the big agent considering that option and let out a sigh of relief at finding that he had a reasonable side, when he said, "We can live with that."

She pulled out a big chart and placed it on the table in her office. It showed how the data flowed from clients into her company. She explained where the original source data from the banks was stored and then began to explain how they did their analysis work.

Nielsen leaned over closer and pointed about a dozen steps down in the chart. "I want copies of this version too."

While Ivy was impressed by his quick comprehension of the complex chart, what he was requesting was outside the scope of the Court Order. His closeness was unnerving, especially as he seemed to be sniffing her perfume. She stepped a little to the side.

"That data has been manipulated by my staff. There is a risk it could have been altered."

"I'm interested in the notes on their findings."

"Some of which are speculative – interim thoughts."

"It may give us some pointers. Shortcut our time here. And the physical files?"

"All electronic. PDFs."

"Notes from your team there too?"

Ivy rolled her eyes at him. "Yes."

"I want your workpapers, reports and so on. Give me anything on these banks that will tell us what your staff has found."

"The court order only specifies data and files from the banks. Provided I receive the clearance from our counsel that is exactly what we will give you."

The big agent regarded her steadily, as if assessing her character. He went to speak, then stopped. He tilted his head to one side and then the other, as if debating with himself. After a few moments he said, "Let me tell you a little more about this case and maybe you will understand why time is so important."

Ivy nodded. While she did not expect what he had to say would change her stance, she was curious.

"The humans trafficked in this case are children sold into sexual slavery. From what we have learned so far, they range in age from five to fifteen and are from Eastern Europe, the former Soviet Union and Turkey. Boys and girls.

Every day that goes by, more kids are abducted, sold, and then go through disgusting experiences that ruin their lives. Every day the kids already sold are going through terrors you and I can only begin to imagine – they are drugged and abused in every way possible."

Ivy knew her faced registered her horror. She had an expressive face and her emotions could sneak up on her. Agent Nielsen was focused and intent. Even though she might disagree with his approach, she could see that he was a good man -- a demanding man who was driven to fulfill the FBI's role.

"How many children are involved?"

"The operations are veiled in secrecy. We only know what we have found from two places here in the States that local police shut down. We think the operation is big and runs on an international scale. That's why I have the case. My teams and I only pursue complex, high-impact multinational matters."

"Are there really that many men who are so twisted they want," she hesitated to say it.

"Children. Yeah. And not only men. Women can be twisted in that way too. There are likely many of these places in major cities in the U.S. and in Europe. We have inquiries out to all our counterparts around the world and to local police in the U.S., searching for more information – anything that will lead us to the perps who supply the children."

He leaned closer to her again, his eyes fastened on hers. "Ms. Littleton, we have to stop this travesty. We need your help. So if your team has found anything at all that could move this case along faster and help us to identify the perps, we want it. We will find the information anyway, but you might be able to speed this process along."

She moved back behind her desk, turned her back to the agent and gazed out her window at the sunny October day. Way down below, the Willamette River reflected the morning light, forming a silvery blue strip that flowed serenely, cutting the city down the middle and crossed by the many bridges of Portland. All around the city, children were on their way to school, living in relative safety and freedom. The very thought of children enslaved as Agent Nielsen described was chillingly disturbing. Her priorities were always clear – do what is in the best interests of the Company, their clients, and their employees and do it in a legal and ethical manner. They would have to comply with the court order, sooner or later. However, what Agent Nielsen was asking for now went beyond that. Still the disclosure of her team's preliminary findings would cause no direct harm to her Company or its employees, even if any issues were there to be found. At some point, any problems that surfaced would have to be disclosed to the bank owning the data or documents. Despite her misgivings, she felt she had an obligation to act in a way that was best for the larger community. She turned to face the big agent.

"If you find anything based on my staff's notes or work papers, I want to review it."

"And you won't tip the banks off."

"If we find something suspicious, we have to include it in our report."

"How long can you give us?"

"The reports are due out in November on a staggered basis, however for any major finding, we typically give a heads-up as we go along."

"Look, we're not after the banks here, not unless their involvement is egregious. Let me know a few days before any issues related to this case are disclosed to the banks. Agreed?"

"Yes, but Agent Nielsen," Ivy began.

"Call me Steve."

She regarded at him for a moment, uncertain if she wanted to drop formality in their communications. The aggressive posturing was no longer in his body language or in his expression. "Okay Steve, I still do not understand why you are here and not going directly to the banks."

"We think someone at one or more banks may be involved in the money movement from the child brothels to the mastermind behind this operation. A person in some position of authority at each bank is doing the approvals and keeping the transactions of sizeable amounts of cash from coming under scrutiny. We don't want to sound any alarms that could tip off the perps."

"How do you know it is these banks that we have as clients?"

"Certain records from the two operations in the U.S. that were shut down indicated doing business with those three banks."

9

"How did you find out about us?" Ivy knew she was grilling the big agent, but he didn't seem to mind.

"You can thank another agent on my team, Harvard, er, Mathew Heylen for that. He searched for other companies that could have access to bank data. He found your website and then made a few calls."

"Why not go to the Federal Reserve? That data is in their Fed Wire System, right? Or in the private banking CHIPS system?"

Steve shook his head. "They each move with the speed of a dung beetle. We have the requests out. Our pace of haste is not in their vocabulary. We have been shaking them up, but no results so far. Besides they only have the electronic files. You have copies of the supporting documents."

"My clients can't learn that we are the source of your findings. It will end our business. If you go after the banks in addition to this perp, you must get the data from another source."

"Understand. We can handle it without reference to your company."

Her assistant interrupted with a call from their internal counsel. Ivy smiled at Steve, who for first time that morning smiled back, just a little smile that curled up the edges of his lips. Ivy noticed that his eyes had lost that piercing hard gray-blue. She liked the changes.

***

That evening at home, Ivy Littleton reclined on a couch in her living room for a few minutes, enjoying a cold glass of spring water with a translucently thin slice of lemon. While it was already dark outside, the air was unseasonably warm for October in Portland, and Ivy was enjoying a little breeze that came in through the long casement windows. Her two corgis were nearby, with her tri-colored Harry dog stretched out flat on his side. The other corgi, Cleo, had tucked her plump yet still elegant body up against the couch to enjoy having Ivy reach down and cuddle her ears. Druid, her aging grey-striped cat, was taking his after dinner bath on the corner of the dining room carpet. Her pets were her guardians -- little fluffs of soldiers faithfully on duty, even at rest.

Ivy felt tiredness hovering over her like a specter pressing on her chest, weighing her down. She breathed deeply and concentrated on thinking about her life and her future. Sometimes Ivy viewed her world as a farce -- all gilded success and happiness on the outside; parched and barren within. If she had to pick a color for her life, it would be a dull brown, the color of dried mud, at least as she saw it these days. While retirement would be a welcome change for her after all the stress at the office, she worried about filling the hours. She needed to dramatically change her life, regain a sound degree of physical fitness, find some fascinating new challenges and soar off the cliff that marked retirement. Most importantly, she wanted to avoid the safe path down to obscurity.

Her mind wandered on the breeze in the way it did these days, scuttling away from serious thoughts. Her days at work had so many demands that her ability to concentrate had waned. While she still loved her career and its challenges, her nervous system was sidling towards breakdown territory.

A few years before, Ivy sublimated all her energies into work, putting up walls of no interest with prospective suitors. Two failed marriages, along with too many affairs and dates, had led her to that decision. Now with retirement looming, she would have time for a relationship. How would she find someone different and yet suitable? She used to be attracted to the delusionary charms of dreamers. Now more mature and independent, she wanted a man who would make good on his dreams. She thought then about Agent Nielsen. He was a man of action and she was attracted to him. At the same time, he was at the extreme end of the spectrum. She could not imagine how any romantic liaison could work with him, given his demanding nature. She needed to find a middle ground between a man like him and men who were dreamers.

He had woken something in her. She had to acknowledge that. While annoyed with his manner and demands, she had been challenged in good ways too. She found herself disappointed when he told her late in the afternoon that he was flying out that night to work on a different case, leaving the other two agents there – Brian with the nice manners and smile and the offbeat agent called Moll. Steve's eyes lingered on hers when he added that he would return at the end of the week for a briefing.

With her retirement date set, Ivy wanted to consider dating again, although dating at 62 sounded ridiculous. How would she have the patience to sift through all the misfits, the losers, the bores, the men with peculiar habits, or the fellows who only wanted a share of her comfortable retirement? At a gathering last week after work, one woman talked about having 85 Internet first dates, which seemed like an excessive number of cups of coffee to find one man. Ivy doubted she would have the patience, much less the fortitude.

The timing was premature anyway. The overload of her nervous system made her question her ability to handle the complexities of a relationship. Ivy was a driven achiever and a leader, pulling away from a mediocre upbringing to define herself and her life. Her ambition gave her success. On the flip side, it also over-stressed her. Meeting client expectations, the financial pressures from Corporate and the demands of her staff combined to leave her spirit sapped of its characteristic spunk. Without a balanced personal life, not enough tipped the scales in her favor. The root problem went on with each passing week, month and year, leaving her less and less of herself.

Her work cell rang. Years of habit had her check who was calling. It was her boss at Corporate. If he was calling at this hour, it could not be good.

"Hello, David," she said, trying to inject some cheer into her voice.

"Hi, Ivy," he said in a voice shaky with fatigue. "I heard you had an interesting day. Were you able to meet the FBI's demands and comply with the Court Order?"

"Yes, though likely they will be on-site all week."

"Lucky you. Let us know if they become unreasonably demanding. Well, I have yet another favor to ask of you. The guy we tagged as your replacement took another job where he lives in Chicago."

She listened, her mouth turning down at the corners while her shoulders rose another inch as the muscles tightened in self-defense.

"He what?" Long years of practice allowed Ivy to keep her voice level, even when she wanted to scream the words out.

"Yeah. Just called me. Claims he got more money. Wouldn't listen to a counter offer from us. Between you and me, I think our job was going to be a filler. He needed income and never planned to move to Portland."

"That just sucks." Ivy tried not to swear very often, but sometimes cursing was the best shorthand around.

"Almost my precise words. Look, I appreciate that you want to retire but we need you to stay on. We have no one we can patch in until we find a new replacement.

"Let me think about it," Ivy said. "I really was planning to retire."

They talked a little longer and then Ivy clicked her cell phone off. The calm she maintained on the call vanished. She fought the urge to scream out her frustration. She imagined herself chained to a boat that was pulled deeper and deeper into a wide, bottomless vortex. She bowed her head and let out a low moan. Her Harry dog came over to lick her hand out of concern. Cleo stirred near her feet and pressed against her legs. Old Druid jumped up on her lap, instantly purring when she stroked his back. Each of her little protectors rallied to comfort her.

She felt she had no reserves left to continue working. She could feel an all too familiar clutch of hot pain at the top of her throat, spreading from her jaw down into the muscles of her neck, tensing the already tight ligaments into bowstrings. She raised her head, swallowing to relieve the grip her muscles had on her windpipe. The room around her jumped the way her surroundings did sometimes, giving her a feeling of unreality as if for a few seconds, she had not been there and the world had moved on without her. Ivy grappled for the glass beside her, desperate for a drink of water, which she learned could calm these episodes.

She sipped some water and pulled Druid closer, holding him the way a child might hold onto a teddy bear for security. She thought about all the people at the office who were dependent on her company for their livelihoods, their careers and even their self-respect. She could not leave them adrift. They would function well for a month or two. Then the lack of local leadership would allow the painstakingly built bonds between them to erode. Jealousies, resentments and ambitions, never far from the surface, would break loose and the business she had single-mindedly worked to foster would start to crack and crumble.

Ivy could see that she owed the people six months to see them through the executive transition. She had to leave knowing she fulfilled her duty. Somewhere she had the grit to hold herself together until the end of March

2013. Her depleted reserves had sunk below strength, resilience and fortitude. She only had the elemental grit that she envisioned as a layer under the marrow in her bones. She leaned back on the couch, drained the glass of spring water and made of mental list of how to handle the delay in her retirement. After all she was Ivy Littleton. She had pulled herself up by her bootstraps her whole life. She could and would scrape together enough vestiges of herself to struggle through.

Resolutely she stood up and for about the tenth time that day, squared her shoulders, forcing them down and into place. She sent a quick text to her boss, telling him she would sign on for another six months so they could find a new replacement. Now it was time to make a late dinner, have a glass of calming wine and sink into whatever degree of sleep would come to her.

Chapter 2

Much further south in Guadalajara at 3.00 a.m. on Thursday, Steve was already showered, shaved and dressed for the day. He was reviewing his team's plans for the arrest of a major Colombian drug lord. He went over the evidence again from the FBI's money laundering case that led them to this perpetrator, along with their proof of drug-related activities from the Drug Enforcement Agency. Steve's team had the meaty evidence, although it bugged him that they lacked a real name for this drug lord. All they uncovered was a nickname and a number of fictitious names. El Zorro Astuto, or the Sly Fox, was his self-given designation. The DEA claimed on Monday to have located him proceeding on his yacht to Manzanillo, less than 200 miles to the south on the western coast of Mexico. Steve had flown into Guadalajara via Mexico City, meeting up with his agent Mathew Heylen on the way. They planned to fly down to Manzanillo by helicopter if all was ready for the sting.

Other than having to trust another agency's work, their evidence was reasonable. Steve already knew that it was. However before each sting, he had a punch down list that he methodically went through. Thus far in his 35-year career, he had never an issue over insufficient or faulty evidence when he brought perpetrators, or perps as they called them, to justice. He expected that record to remain unbroken.

He shifted his six and a half foot frame uneasily in the undersized hotel desk chair, and proceeded to review their plans for the sting operation, including each identified scenario of how it could go down. This process took nearly an hour, even though he had all the details in his head. He wanted to be certain that the action would go as smoothly as possible.

With that step done, he stood up, stretched, straightened the creases in his trousers, walked over to his nightstand, took a long drink from a bottle of water and checked the time -- just after four in the morning. He stepped out on the small balcony overlooking an internal courtyard filled with plush plantings in many shades of green and scented with aromatic tropical flowers. He breathed in deeply and leaned against the railing. The air floated against his cheeks like a whispered caress, bringing the scents of the small city laced with a whiff of flowered perfume. He inhaled to draw the early morning air deep into his lungs. Five years ago the subtle scents would have been lost on him. Outside of his work for the FBI, he failed to notice much of anything back then.

Beyond the hotel, it sounded as if the city lay in predawn tranquility below him. He wanted to learn more about the places he flew into and their histories, but he wanted that knowledge to come from experiencing it and not as it did now, from books or websites. Even though he was committed to his work at the Bureau, he found as he grew older he wanted more in his life and he wanted to stop living it alone.

That Ivy Littleton was sure a firecracker – full of fight yet alluring too. She was intelligent and capable, and she was simply lovely to look at. On the other hand, he bet life with her would be a roller coaster ride. If he was going to risk his heart at this late date, he wanted someone level-headed, didn't he?

He shook his head at himself. He had to stay focused on the upcoming operation. This was not the time to let his thoughts wander. He inhaled the scented air once more, pushed the dreamy thoughts away and went back to the desk. For the next hour, Steve reviewed the details of logistics, equipment and schedule, and then he closed his laptop. He checked his watch. It was nearly 5:15. He tapped his forefinger on the desk as he quickly ran through the preparations once more in his mind. Then he unplugged his cell phone from the charger and pressed a shorthand number to call his second in command.

"Harvard?" Although Steve spoke quietly into the phone, his low voice carried authority and a sense of urgency. "Get the team ready. Be in the lobby before six. We are going in now. Can't risk having this perp sail out of here. Next call is to the DEA."

As abruptly as he had dialed Senior Special Agent Mathew Heylen who Steve nicknamed "Harvard" after where he earned his law degree, he dialed the head of the DEA team.

"You up? We're going in now. Get your guys ready." He listened to some grumbling, but he was used to hearing himself called various names. Steve cared about results -- ending crime, catching perps, making charges stick and keeping his teams and the public as safe as possible. "Six at the heliport. Get the lead out."

Steve hung up, checked his gear and pulled on his lightweight suit jacket. No matter what the temperature was, Steve had his standards for how an FBI agent should appear just as the Bureau did. He checked his appearance in the mirror, straightened his tie, smoothed down his white shirt and shook out the creases in his trousers. While not a vain man, he did believe he should be presentable and in his mind that meant crisp, neat and clean. He rechecked his gun, or roscoe in FBI lingo, felt for his cell phone in his pocket, grabbed his protective vest and exited the hotel room, striding down to the elevator to meet his team in the lobby. From there, they would jump into a waiting car and head to the heliport. He had that familiar tightening in his abs that always happened before an operation. Everything checked out. It was time.

His core squad, or team as he preferred to think of them, were Mathew, Brian and Moll. With the other two agents combing through the data up in Portland on the child trafficking case, he and Mathew were working with a couple of agents out of Los Angeles. He was glad to see that they were already in the lobby. Each one was on his cell phone re-verifying last minute arrangements. The call to Harvard put a whole procedure in motion. He nodded, acknowledging Mathew and the two LA agents, and hustled out to the waiting car, not wanting to waste time getting to the helicopters.

Luckily Manzanillo was large enough to have its own heliport and conducted tourist flights. Having a chopper or two coming in from Guadalajara would not be out of the ordinary to the perps. Steve planned to alert their surveillance agent on the ground only when they arrived at the docks so as not to risk a tip off.

Once they were heading to the heliport, he watched the agents. They looked sharp and ready to go. Each of them climbed quickly into the chopper, settled in, pulled on the seat harnesses and positioned their headsets. A full fifteen minutes behind them, the DEA team piled into the second, larger helicopter, along with a six member Mexican SWAT team. Each one of these international operations or ops was different, depending on how the local authorities wanted to participate. The Mexicans agreed to supply a SWAT team, which had performed well when they observed them running drills the afternoon before.

They took off and rose quickly above Guadalajara. As they flew south to southwest, the small city lay below them imbued with a rich glow from the slanted rays of the early morning sun, reminding Steve again of his longing to see the world as a tourist. He would like to learn about regional histories, appreciate each country's culture, and taste more of their local foods and drinks.

"Hey Mathew, any words of wisdom applicable to today?" Steve asked, knowing that Mathew was keen on quoting Latin phrases to sum up his thoughts or recap a discussion or argument.

"*Audaces Fortuna Iuvat,*" Mathew quoted quickly.

"Fortune favors the bold," Steve muttered. "Jeez Mathew. You get that out of a fortune cookie?"

Even the pilot laughed. About fifteen minutes later, the chopper started descending as they neared the Manzanillo Heliport. From there they would drive down to waiting police boats not far from where the perp's yacht was docked in the sheltered harbor. The plan was for the SWAT team to go in first, followed by Steve's team, then the DEA. Holding back was always hard. He liked to lead, but sometimes he had to work in joint actions like this one. However this was his case and he intended to make the arrest, no matter how bristling the DEA team leader was. While they may have located the perp, the FBI's research made up the bulk of the evidence.

After quietly boarding the police boats, the three teams squatted on the deck in silence as they made their way into the harbor of *Bahia de Manzanillo,* one police boat heading towards the bow of the suspect yacht and the other to the stern to cutoff any sudden moves to escape. The Bay shone a remarkable deep blue in the early morning sunlight, serving as a benign backdrop to their grim operation.

The SWAT team boarded the yacht first, moving soundlessly from one boat to the other. Steve and his team halted. He signaled for the DEA agents to

18

hold where they were on the other police boat. The SWAT team ran stealthily across the deserted deck towards the stairs to head below. Some shouts came as the team made their way into the cabin. No gunshots rang out. Steve and his team stepped cautiously onto the yacht, moving towards the stairs to the lower cabin. Four men filed onto the deck, hands on their heads, eyes wide with surprise and fear. Two appeared to be crewmembers, one was a cook, judging by his apron, and the last one might be the perp, still chewing his breakfast like cud that refused to be swallowed.

The SWAT team located identification for each man. The crew was from the Veracruz area on the Caribbean side of Mexico. The fourth man carried a U. S. passport and claimed to be an actor hired to impersonate a man he knew only as El Zorro Astuto. Only the actor had been armed. They would verify his identity and they might hold him for minor charges, but Steve doubted that this man was the big money laundering and drug-dealing perp they were after.

He glowered at the DEA team leader, who had turned red in the face and stood shaking his head in disbelief as he examined the actor's passport. They might learn a little more during the interrogation of the actor and the crew, but likely the DEA would have a black eye on this operation for leading the FBI here based on misinformation. Steve turned away, signaling his team that he was leaving. He left the two LA agents to stay with the DEA and the perps. He would not bother to point out the obvious botch-up to the DEA leader. His immediate departure with Mathew would deliver the message he wanted.

This failure by the DEA to have accurate information was one of the reasons that Steve disliked joint operations. He was annoyed at the waste of time and resources. They would take the four men back to Guadalajara for questioning, however the sting itself was a flop. El Zorro Astuto had named himself well. He was a clever and elusive fox of the drug world.

Once they were heading back to the heliport, Steve exchanged a look with Mathew, who appeared as taken aback as he was. The facts of the day were clear enough. They had been duped and they felt foolish. On the return trip to Guadalajara, they would devise their interrogation strategy for the four men from the yacht. Steve doubted they would learn much but he had never missed apprehending a perp in his career. He would run this Astuto character to ground. It might take some time, but Steve had no intention of letting a major drug dealer and money launderer evade the FBI for very long.

Once back in Guadalajara, he would leave Mathew in charge and head back to Portland. He wanted a thorough briefing on the data analysis that London and Stanford were doing on the child trafficking case and he would get another chance to see the lovely but prickly, Ivy Littleton.

***

As her eighth meeting of the day finished up just before four, Ivy took advantage of the break to stop in and make sure the two FBI agents, Brian and Moll, were doing okay. While they were easy-going guys, they were so motivated, focused and intelligent as they worked methodically through the data that she would be glad to have them as employees. Brian would be a wonder with clients, while Moll was one of those half technical/half data guys who would be a real asset to her analytical team.

"Hey you two – checking to make sure you don't have any questions."

Brian glanced up and smiled. The agent was tall and slender, with a delightfully friendly personality and he was altogether good-looking enough to be a male model. Instead he was an attorney, an FBI agent and a data hound. Ivy thought of him as an aspen, a tall and attractive tree with year round interest in its nearly white bark and whispery leaves that turned brilliantly yellow in the autumn.

"I think we are progressing along nicely – should soon have this nailed. Thank goodness too. The big guy is due back tomorrow."

Ivy was curious to learn more about Steve Nielsen. "Isn't he a bit old to be an agent?"

"Steve's not really an agent. He's an FBI HBO."

"A what?"

"High Bureau Official. Only one level between him and the Director of the Bureau and that doesn't really count because Steve has the Director's ear."

"And he is here, working on this case?"

"He lives for solving cases, catching the bad guys and putting a stop to crime. When we are on the hunt, he does whatever work is required, no matter how tedious it is. He wants this case solved and he will do what it takes to break it open. The man is a walking legend at the Bureau. He has a record of always getting the perp he is after. He never forgets a case, a perp or anything. In a word, he is the best."

"Yeah well, I thought at one point he might put a gun to my head to get the data."

The agents shifted uneasily in their chairs. "He would never do that," Brian said softly. "Not to any civilian, and certainly not to you. He has strict rules of operation and standards for performance."

The curly-headed agent took over, saying in the soft, pleasant way he had, "Thanks to your team for all the ground work. They were honing in on a likely issue."

"Tell me more," Ivy said, pulling out a chair to join them at the table. Moll was definitely like a noble fir which grew with its sometimes sparse limbs springing out at odd lengths, making it an attractive, if somewhat odd tree to decorate for Christmas. If left to its natural ways, it often had a little whirl of branches at the top, almost like a propeller.

"Well this Terry guy who works for you left a great trail of possible issues. Cryptic pointers here and there. He noticed little patterns that might have taken us weeks to find or maybe that we would have missed. Do you have some special software or something?"

"Yes, we do, but Terry is a talent of his own. He never focuses on the obvious issues. He is one of those rare analysts who hones right in on the more abstruse ones. We make sure he is on the team for every bank we handle."

"He's a techno-miracle. If I could be allowed to meet him, it would be an honor."

"We'll see. Give me an example."

"Well here," Moll switched on a tiny portable projector attached to his laptop. He thumbed his way around and brought up a bank approval document with a little note on it. "See it says. 'ap/ac fmlr. X√√.'"

"And you think that means?"

"Approver and account are familiar. Cross-check it. This Terry guy has like a table in his head or something of approver names, accounts, and account owners. We followed that trail and it led us to . . . ." Moll stopped, looking up behind Ivy.

She could feel a presence and knew that the big agent must be back. She swiveled in her chair and tilted her head up, pulling her hair away from her face as she turned. Today she wore it down and it was making the most of its freedom by curling out in every direction. There he was, standing right behind her, staring at the Moll guy with a mixture of annoyance and curiosity.

"Not giving away confidential case information, I hope," he said sternly.

"No, sir. Nothing our Ivy Vine hasn't seen before."

Steve raised an eyebrow at the moniker. Moll was famous for his humorous comments. He was one of the few people who could make Steve laugh.

"Moll was kind enough to compliment the work of one of my senior analysts." Ivy quickly jumped to Moll's defense. "I just came in to make sure all was going well and to see if . . ."

"If?" Steve echoed.

"If they would be interested in joining me for dinner. Great couple of agents you have here."

"Have they earned it?"

Brian said quietly. "We think we have, thanks to leads from Ivy's team that we found in the notes."

"Let's hit it then." Steve sat down, opened his briefcase and dealt out energy bars like cards around the table. He looked over at Ivy. "You have time to sit in?"

"I will make time." He dealt her a crunchy Cliff bar with white chocolate and macadamia nuts in a whole grain base. The man knew something about energy bars.

Ivy spent the next hour watching Moll and Brian zoom their way around the data and electronic documents. Out of the ten million records from two of the three banks in question, they had isolated twenty transactions, all winding up in two banks in Sofia, Bulgaria in accounts under the cryptic translated name of "Adjunct Resources International" and totaling nearly two million dollars. Steve watched, listened and questioned. The analysis stood up to his intense scrutiny. Ivy could see that all three of the agents were fully focused on finding the trail that would lead them to the bad guys or perps, as they called them.

"And the third bank?" Steve asked at the end.

"Unfortunately, we are not finding any notes from our friend Terry. We'll have to slog through it on our own, unless Ivy will lend us his brain."

Steve turned to face her. "Well, Ms. Ivy Vine. You with us on this? Will you throw in the talent?"

She considered the request while keeping her eye contact with Steve. Sooner or later Terry would find the pattern at that third bank if one existed. It may as well be sooner. She walked over to the phone on a side table, dialed and asked Terry if he could work that night. Terry was a free spirit and tended to start his days late, then worked past midnight or worked weekends when a project really interested him, and Terry found a good deal about data that intrigued him. He was like a curly willow tree, right down to his soft blond hair that he wore about mid length in barely brushed ringlets.

Ivy was uneasy about how much support she was giving the FBI that was not required by the Court Order, including direct contact with one of her best analysts. She was a loyal executive who was protective of her company's best interests. Surely even from a corporate viewpoint, cooperating in a critical federal investigation had to be the best option. Yet she knew if she went back to their Internal Counsel, the answer would be to stick to the strict interpretation of the Court Order. This would be one more responsibility she would have to shoulder alone. It was what she did – took risks when needed. They weighed heavily on her shoulders. Ivy knew there would be no dinner out tonight. She would order in for the agents, Terry and herself.

Although Terry planned to work through the night, Ivy shooed the agents out of the building just before 9. The big agent was looking like he might go to sleep on the floor. Only Moll refused to leave, wanting to learn what methods Terry used. They agreed to start at 7 the next morning, going over the notes Terry and Moll would leave.

***

Around 4:30 a.m. Ivy's home phone rang, waking her up. She answered sleepily – the long days that week had hit her hard the night before. On the other end of the line, Terry was full of excitement. "Ivy, I think we found something, but I can't be sure about it."

"What?"

"On transactions going to accounts in Bulgaria for this third bank, sometimes one guy at the bank approves it; sometimes a woman does and sometimes a couple of other guys do."

"And?"

"I think one of them is forging signatures. I'm not a handwriting expert, however the writing looks almost traced, without those little variations signatures usually have."

Ivy pushed herself up further in bed. "How many?"

"Fifteen in total. The transactions originate in various cities and are from different companies and source accounts."

"Dollars?"

"Over five million."

"Wow. All going to Sofia?"

"Uh-huh, spread over the months we have."

"This will be delicate, but the FBI can have signature analysis done."

"Ivy, I have a question."

"Yes, Terry?"

"Those agents aren't here to give an opinion on our practices, are they?"

24

Ivy thought for a moment. She avoided directly lying to her employees, although she might shade the truth a bit or tell them she was not at liberty to disclose information. However Terry was tight-lipped.

"The FBI is here on a critical humanitarian case. You cannot tell anyone. For right now, this cannot get back to the banks. The case they are pursuing is both very sensitive and important."

"Got it."

"Did Moll say something to you?"

"Nothing, but what a guy! He was great help last night until he fell asleep curled up on the floor about an hour ago. I didn't want to wake him. He is the smartest guy I ever met and the first one who thinks like me."

"Good to know. I'm going to call Agent Nielsen. In all likelihood, you can expect us to arrive within the hour. You okay to hang around until then?"

"Yeah. Might need a ride home. All of a sudden, I'll just crash."

"No worries. Terry, I've said it before -- you are a great asset to us. Thank you."

Ivy hung up the phone, grabbed her cell and searched for the big agent's phone number in her contacts. She dialed and waited. When she heard a gruff, "Neilson" on her phone, she thought she heard a shower running in the background.

"Steve? Ivy Littleton."

"Give me a minute." She heard the shower turn off and after a few moments Steve came back on. "Sorry about that. Just finished my morning swim and shower. What's up?"

Ivy tried not to think of him standing dripping wet in his hotel room. She hoped he had a towel on. She explained what Terry had found.

"We'll want copies of the signatures."

"Signatures, yes. Not the docs. We'll assign a cross-reference code."

"Yeah okay. I'll call London, er Brian, and we'll be at the site in a half hour. You be there?"

"Yes. See you."

Ivy jumped out of bed and into the shower, planning a mad scramble to let the dogs out, feed them, get dressed and drive to the office. She would phone in a quick order to a nearby Starbucks for coffee and breakfast sandwiches to shore the team up.

Three hours later, Terry had explained his findings to the team, shown them the documents and been driven home by Ivy's assistant to get some sleep. The three agents carefully examined each transaction and were running searches to try to find more. Ivy now had her assistant electronically cutting and pasting signatures into an indexed document, while she was in her office handling her other work. Steve rang her phone and asked her to join them in the conference room.

"Ms. Ivy Vine," he said. She noticed that sometimes his voice had a slight drawl and she wondered where he had grown up.

She had to laugh at the nickname. It was one she used herself sometimes.

"We need one more thing."

"Only one?"

"We need you to request a larger set of data over a longer date range. Now, for each of the three banks, we need . . ."

Whether from the long hours or the stress of the situation, Ivy had reached her limits. "No."

"Think about it. We have a trail here. We need to scope how big these operations are."

She stood stiffly. Ivy rarely became angry. She could argue heatedly, but real anger was something else. When it hit, it was immediate, white-hot and impossible to control. The agent was pushing her too far.

"I have stuck my neck out sharing as much as I have. No way can I go back to the banks and ask for more data. It would create all sorts of concerns. You must realize that."

"Then I'll go for another court order and we'll come back."

"You do that."

Ivy glared at him, marched over and stood next to Steve where he sat at the head of the meeting table. "I may not be some high-powered FBI attorney, Agent Nielsen, however I do not believe any judge can or will force a service organization like this one to ask a client to supply more data."

It was then that Steve broke into a big grin, turning his severe face into that of an impudent boy. "Got you!" he said, breaking out in laughter.

Right then Ivy was too tired and too fired up to be the butt of a joke. She turned on her heel and marched out of the room. She stomped down the hall, took the elevator to ground level and went out the front door, seeking fresh air to get her temper to settle back down. That big agent was totally exasperating. She marched down the street and around the block, annoyed at herself for having lost her cool, irritated with Steve for embarrassing her in front of the other agents and particularly aggravated that he had gotten the better of her. She kept moving for a few blocks, stopped, breathed in and out about twenty times to bring herself back together, turned and walked back. Once on her floor, she saw the damned big agent in the reception area to her offices. Ivy gritted her teeth and lectured herself to keep calm. She was 62 and this man had her acting like a crazy person. He waited until she walked up, looked at her contritely and held the door open to their office suite.

"Bad timing on my part," he said quietly by way of apology.

She nodded stiffly, knowing she should laugh it off but she wasn't quite back in command of herself. He walked closely behind her to her office, watched her go to her desk, and then turned back to the meeting room.

Two hours later, the three agents filed in to Ivy's office as she finished a conference call. She forced a smile, doing her best to appear like her usual self. Steve hovered near the doorway.

Brian said quietly. "We left our working models on your server. Please have them archived along with the data."

Moll joined in, "And we checked each other's laptops to be sure we didn't have any copies or residual files. Be seeing you. Uh, you've been great, helping us. Thank Terry for me – he's like my brain-twinner."

Brian smiled his sweet smile. "Thank you. Ivy, you're the best."

"Glad to be of help. Call me if either of you are back in Portland. Should you need anything more, you have my business card."

The two agents filed out. Steve walked into her office to stand staring out the window. He turned to face her. "Mt. Hood is unbelievable, isn't it? Almost like a fantasy mountain."

"Even to those of us who see the mountain every day, well every day she is out, the view provides inspiration."

"She?"

"Yes, that is the way us locals refer to the Mountain. Not sure why. Perhaps because she is so graceful. Or perhaps because somewhere underneath that beauty lies a powerful earth force that could erupt without warning, the way Mt. St. Helens did."

"Reminds me of someone I recently met – elegantly attractive but potentially volatile."

"I assume you mean me. Well, I'll take part of it as a compliment," Ivy said with a smile, back in command of her temper.

Steve walked closer to her. "Thank you, Ms. Littleton. Your cooperation has given us a place to start digging, which is far more than we had before. It also has given us some indicators on how large this operation might be."

Despite her annoyance with him, Ivy could not help asking, "How do you know that? Apply experience?"

"Guesses. Never handled a matter quite like this one. Just in case I need to follow-up on something in a hurry, could I have your home phone and personal cell?"

"Seems like I am always working or checking my work cell," she said grudgingly. "Oh well, you probably can find them out anyway."

She pulled out another business card and wrote down the two numbers, then added her personal email. "Let me know how the case turns out."

Surprised by her request, Steve nodded and moved towards the door, then stopped and turned back.

"Goodbye Ivy. You really are the best," he said softly.

Chapter 3

While he waited for takeoff on the FBI plane, nicknamed the "Bubird" at the Bureau that Friday afternoon, Steve realized it was his birthday -- October 5th, 1952. He turned 60 that day almost without realizing it. They were heading to New York to drop off Brian and Moll who worked out of that office, and then he would take the short hop down to D.C. where he was based. Using the Bubird allowed them to work in privacy and reduced their travel time. The complex cases they handled meant that dedication and long hours were critical to their success, and they were always successful, no matter how long it took. He smiled a bit dourly to himself at their failure in Manzanillo, yet he was proud of their overall record. They would apprehend that evasive drug lord who eluded them in Mexico and they sure as hell were going to nail this child trafficking perp.

Putting his laptop aside, Steve leaned his head back and thought about the importance of this milestone birthday. Sixty years of his life were now behind him, along with most of his career. He wondered how long he could hold on with the Bureau. For sure as long as the Chief stayed, although the President was overdue on appointing a replacement. The Chief, Robert Mueller (or Mule as Steve sometimes called him), had been appointed by George W. Bush and had stayed on under President Obama. Sooner or later when that changed, Steve would likely be forced to retire. Every year their Human Resources folks reviewed agents over 57, the mandatory retirement age for those in field work. Every year the Chief stepped in and extended him. While the FBI had been his home for Steve's adult life, age was catching up with him. Without the Bureau, how would he spend the next 10, 20, or even 30 years?

When his career was over, Steve worried that he would be empty, bereft and alone, with nothing to occupy his days, challenge his mind or get his adrenaline running. Without the Bureau, how would his life have value? For the last few years, he had been searching for more inside himself, trying to find additional facets of his personality and character. To enrich his mind, search for his heart and reach out towards his soul, he had read the classics and more contemporary literature. He pondered the precepts of Confucius and Buddha. Still he wondered, how does a man find his heart, much less his soul?

His mind drifted back to his boyhood when each day seemed to glisten with promise. He saw himself with his Dad early on a Saturday morning fishing in a nearby stream. They never caught much other than some sunnies. Being out there together was the important part. His Dad, tall with thinning blonde hair, had been a serious man, somewhat strict, yet always supportive. When he spoke, he carried a lilting Norwegian accent. A small-town lawyer by trade, his Dad inspired confidence and dedicated himself to making things right for people. One day Steve wanted to learn more about the Norwegian life philosophy that formed his parents' thinking and contributed to his own.

Steve thought about a quote he had seen recently, *"In the end these things matter most: How well did you love? How fully did you live? How deeply did you learn to let go?"* He knew he lacked good responses to those questions of the heart. Inside he had a great emptiness. While he believed he could find the depth to answer each question within himself, his life thus far had been emotionally shallow and not overly broad. He assumed he was capable of deep feelings, even though he had never fully tested that belief, making him keenly aware of his narrowness as a man. What happened to that boy out catching sunnies with his Dad, back when life seemed as dazzling as the sun sparkling on the currents in the stream? He closed his eyes and pictured the stream as it wove through farmland and into the woods where dappled light played on the rippling water and the time-rounded stones. He could still remember the fresh morning breeze ruffling his shirt and the scent of newly mown timothy in the nearby field with its sweet, yet pungent tang.

Reluctantly he picked up his laptop, postponing once again dwelling on his solitary personal life, thus deferring a confrontation with his inner barrenness. For now his focus had to be on the child trafficking case. He preferred to pursue one active case at a time and go after it with single-minded intensity, even though he was skilled at juggling multiple cases. For the next few weeks this critical humanitarian case would be their primary focus. He had started some agents in the D. C. office examining email traffic in and out of Sofia, as well as pursuing more information about the company identified in the bank transfers. They would work through the weekend, updating him on progress a couple of times each day.

Although Moll was looking exhausted from his night at the office, he was busily checking emails. He glanced up from his laptop. "Say Chief, how did you get into technology? I mean it's like unusual for someone your age."

Steve raised an eyebrow at him. Things were so different for Moll's generation and all the ones after him, where technology wove itself into their day-to-day activities. "My Dad enrolled me in a special summer program sponsored by IBM. When I was eight years old, I developed my first computer program, which was some rudimentary batch job written in an early version of FORTRAN."

"That would be like the early '60s, right? Man, how did you do that? Did they even have dumb terminals back then?"

Steve laughed and shook his head. "No, Stanford, I had to make my own punched cards on this clunky machine with a keyboard and no screen, stack them up in order and physically run them through an IBM 704. Crude, huh? The program performed calculations and produced a result on a printed report. Sounds like no big deal today, but back then it was considered miraculous." His parents were so proud of their young son that they framed that report and put it on the wall in their den. He still had it stored away as a memory of how his parents supported him. Sadly they were long gone, dying about ten years ago within a year of each other.

"What was next?" asked Moll, clearly intrigued by this bit of living history.

"My Dad was always seeking special educational programs for me because he was convinced I was a computer whiz."

"Wow, you were like the original techno kid."

Steve said, "More like the Geek of the Week."

Moll chuckled at the remark, closed his laptop, cranked his seat back and closed his eyes, drifting off into a much needed sleep. He was a Californian with his undergrad degree in mathematical theory from Stanford who carried a big student loan burden that he was still working to pay off. He was the creative thinker on Steve's team. He brought lightness to their cases with his outlandish ideas and talented ability to mimic others, yet he was perceptive, logical and dedicated. When Moll first worked for Steve, he had been disorganized and looked like he lived a ramshackle life, judging by his wrinkled shirts and rumpled suits, but after Steve gave a morning lecture on how neatness and organization contributed to solving cases and to leaving a good impression on the public, Moll changed both his work habits and his appearance, although he lost none of his originality.

Steve glanced over at London, aka Brian, documenting their findings in Portland in that painstaking way he had. He was the analytical talent. His research and investigative work were always meticulous. Like Mathew and Moll, his law degree was from Harvard. Before that he had spent a year at the London School of Economics -- hence his nickname. He was the scholarship fellow, having made his way through by hard work and determination, as well as by his likeable, upbeat personality.

Mathew, now making his way back to D.C. from Mexico, was the strongest performer of the three senior agents, although each one was intelligent and talented. Mathew had brought the other two agents with him on the first case he was on with Steve. Even though Steve knew that Mathew was independently wealthy, he appeared only to live on what he made as an agent. He could be persnickety, but never snobbish. Over the years, Steve had worked the most with him and Mathew had become like a son to him.

In combination, they were the three best agents Steve had on his teams at the FBI and he always went out of his way to work with the best agents he could. Even though he was at the senior executive level, he functioned as a field agent and he attributed his success to the quality of his team members. He had worked with agents from all different backgrounds and out of universities and colleges across the United States. All he cared about were their abilities, their commitment to the Bureau and the way they worked on a team.

Steve pulled his mind back to the child trafficking case. He wanted to bring the case to conclusion rapidly and stop this perverse ring of kidnapping and abuse. The tragic reality of children sold into sexual slavery affected him more deeply than any other case had. Getting the court order to obtain data

32

from Ivy's company had been a chance initiative -- one that had paid off big time. Some companies would have stonewalled them, filed a brief disputing the FBI's right to access data in their custody or at least demanding more time. It said a good deal about her company that they were prepared to act quickly and do the right thing. More than that, it said a whole lot about Ivy Littleton.

He was wrong to have baited her that morning, but she was so damn attractive when she was riled. Still in all, it was typical of him that he had little idea of how to build a relationship with a woman. Casual sex he could handle, but how to actually relate was something else. Ivy was a woman to remember. She had the nerve to stand up to him and yet she would bend to a logical argument. She struck him as a woman of deep passions, a strong sense of justice and loyal commitments. She was fast on the uptake, intelligent and highly conversant technically. Her attraction was more than her lovely looks – her good qualities shone through her whole being. He thought about her hair which was so full of life, streaked with silver and soft-looking despite its springy buoyancy. When he saw it twining around her shoulders the day before, he wanted to bury his face in it.

She was feisty or at least he brought out that quality in her. Even though her mercurial reactions worried him, he needed a woman who would challenge him. Ivy was a captivating combination of logic, charm and courage. He had known a number of career women during his lifetime, but they had lost much of the freshness and femininity that he saw this week in Ivy. She had a certain intense verve about her that even years of working had not dulled.

He would check in with her next week to be sure the data and files were securely in the hands of their corporate counsel. That could mark the end of their FBI business relationship. During that call, he would try to assess whether she thought he was the greatest jerk around or if he might stand a chance with her. While she was on a different coast and he was on the road most of the time, Ivy sparked his interest.

***

Mathew was glad to be the first one in the D.C. office on Sunday morning. He figured Steve was doing his usual weekend morning routine -- work out and swim, an hour at the firing range and then a long walk around the city.

That would put him in around 11. The rest of the team had worked late the night before and he figured they would regroup around noon.

He needed time alone to think. He had taken a run at dawn because his thoughts had been jumping all over the place. Now he felt calmer. His condo that morning seemed like one more sterile place where he dropped his luggage. Here at the office, he felt more at home. The J. Edgar Hoover Building had its own sounds, noticeable now when it was quiet, like birds that settling into shrubs with little rustles and creaks here and there. He found it soothing.

Here he was almost forty and still single. Like Steve, he traveled and worked long hours – six or seven days a week. Would he ever find the time to share his life with a special someone? Was he doomed to muddle along, occasionally venturing out, then retreating feeling disappointed, mismatched, or even downright unadventurous? How many years would he continue to ask himself these questions before he gave up? He pulled his thoughts back -- never would he give up his search for his true life-partner, whoever she may be. Yet how could he find her with the work schedule he had? He was at an age when he needed to infuse his search with a sense of urgency.

Sitting alone there in his office, Mathew decided to think back over his more serious relationships and see if there were any common reasons why they failed. True to his nature, he would take an analytical approach. He pulled a pad of paper out of his briefcase and wrote the names of the women he had dated down the side of the page, planning to list the reasons the relationship had not worked out by each one. Even before he got started, failure bounced off the page at him.

He pushed back in his chair, thinking about how to make the exercise feel more productive. Instead of listing why the relationships ended, he would examine how each relationship might have succeeded and then decide if he would want to be that person. The list of women was depressingly short and not because the relationships had been very long ones. Six in all. He had dated and or gone to bed with other women, but those liaisons were casual. Even that list wouldn't have made the total more than 20. He realized that was not even two a year, for chrissakes. His life as a federal agent was full of work, not sex. On the other hand, a revolving door to bed was not what he wanted. He wanted love, a warm home and a connected family – three things his own boyhood lacked.

Mathew considered and discarded several quotes he remembered from his Latin studies to describe his situation until he settled on Virgil's simple *Fugit Irreparabile Tempus,* Time is Irretrievably Flying. That was it exactly. He had to change his life before he wound up like Steve, alone at 60 with nothing except his life as an agent. Mathew started with the latest relationship first, listing down what would have been required to make it work, then he went on to the second. At the end, he reviewed the list and felt some of the home truths it represented. Then he enumerated the top five changes he needed to make in his life and in himself. He needed more personal time. He had to open up his feelings. He had to learn how to be joyful and to spread that joy. He had to define a life with space for a mate where they had common interests, goals and understandings. Perhaps most importantly, he needed to look forward to a warm future and not backward to his cold childhood. On the surface, those changes sounded easy, but he knew himself well enough to understand they would be a struggle.

The door to their office suite opened and in came Steve, uncharacteristically smiling to himself and jeez-louise, he was humming some tune or other. He raised a hand in greeting and made his way into his office, still humming. Something was up for sure. Then it hit Mathew – Brian and Moll had come back praising that woman they dealt with in Portland. Steve hustled back to Portland after the failed capture attempt in Manzanillo and today he was smiling and humming.

Now Mathew was really depressed over his own life. Even Steve had someone he was dreaming about. He had known Steve a long time and had seen him go through a period of one night stands, followed by apparent abstinence, and now perhaps interested in forging a relationship. Brian and Moll dated whenever they could, although Mathew was never sure that Moll's heart was in it. Moll was a bit of an island. Brian played the field, taking care not to get serious, wanting to avoid becoming stifled in the way his mother had suffocated him. Still in all, he knew that when Brian was ready, he would have no trouble finding a mate. Mathew reviewed the five things he needed to change within himself to have a chance at a good relationship. If he did not get moving soon, then the man reputed to have bedroom eyes would never be more than a member of their sometimes four-man FBI monkhood.

***

A week later, Steve and Mathew flew to Los Angeles on the child trafficking case. They received word from the local FBI office that the undercover drug unit of the Los Angeles Police Department followed a lead and raided the operation of an alleged local pimp. The man ran women out of an upscale duplex and dispensed CNS stimulants to their clients, including cocaine and ecstasy. Secreted away in the basement, they found four children forced to work as part of the prostitution ring. All four spoke limited accented English and were from the Ukraine. Steve scheduled a Bubird as soon as the call came in, alerted Mathew and then grabbed the suitcase he always kept packed in his office to take off immediately for LA.

Working with the local authorities, they reviewed the evidence and questioned the perps. Then they talked with the prostitutes and the four girls who ranged in age from eleven to sixteen. Seasoned agents though they were, both Mathew and Steve had trouble seeing those kids already hardened into a life of drugs and sex. They could go from innocent and fearful to cocky and aggressive, or to withdrawn and silent as if all they could do was play a role. That made a sort of sick sense, since the pimp was a failed movie director and some of the adult women working for him had once aspired to careers in Hollywood.

Mathew was combing through the pimp's texts and emails, hitting some that were encrypted and likely in one or more foreign languages. Steve estimated how much work they had yet to do and decided to leave on Friday. How he went back east would be determined by the phone call he was about to make to Ivy Littleton. When he talked with her early the week before at work, she had been, if not encouraging, at least not hostile. Early this week he called her again ostensibly to find out what other banks they might have data on, although he had no intention of using it. On the second call they talked about the case for a short time, then he asked about what she was doing at work and what Portland was like in the fall. While she was a little distant with him, he was encouraged enough to ask her to dinner Friday night.

Steve selected her work phone even though it was after seven on Thursday evening. The call went to voice mail. He dialed her home phone. She picked up after three rings.

"Ivy Vine? Steve Nielsen here."

"Steve? Are you calling to terrorize me into giving you more data?" she said, but she laughed after asking the question.

"No, I'm down in L.A."

"You do get around, don't you?"

"Uh, yeah. Same case. Say, I could be in Portland late tomorrow afternoon and wondered if you would have dinner with me."

Ivy was silent. Steve waited for her to respond. Was she thinking up a reason to say no? Did she have another date? Was she in a relationship?

"Steve, I don't like to cross the line between business and personal lives."

"Understand. As far as I'm concerned, any future dealings with your company will be through your attorney at Corporate." He paused to let that sink in, then said, "Look Ivy, I was a real jerk with you at times. It is my way to get what is needed for a case as quickly as possible. That is what I do, not who I am. Hopefully there were also times when you saw that I could be a reasonable guy."

"Maybe so. Still in all, you seem to bring out the worst in me."

"Ivy, give me a chance. Won't you give me one dinner to prove myself?"

Ivy was silent again. In the background, he could hear classical music playing. He waited. He could be good at waiting when he thought it would advance his cause. He watched the minute change on his laptop clock.

"Seven. At a restaurant called Urban Farmer upstairs in the Nines Hotel. I will meet you there."

"I'll make a reservation."

"I'll be the woman sipping a Manhattan at the bar wondering why she is crazy enough to be there."

"Correction. You will be the lovely tall woman with the amazing hair wondering . . . "

"See you tomorrow," she said in a voice that sounded a little warmer than it had before.

"Goodbye, Ivy."

Steve clicked off his phone. If the ceilings were higher, he might have jumped up in the air to release the tension from fearing he would be turned down. Tomorrow at 7. He opened the browser on his laptop to book the restaurant. He would take a commercial flight to Portland on his own nickel. Mathew could wrap things up here tomorrow, take the Bubird up to meet him in Portland early Saturday, pick him up and they would then fly back to D.C. together while Mathew briefed him on new findings.

He stopped for a moment, reconsidering. Was he ready for the emotional ups and downs of getting to know someone? Did he have time? Was the mercurial Ivy a wise choice? The answer to each of those questions was 'no'. Should he call her back and cancel? He sat back, trying to think rationally. It was only dinner. Nothing more. Was he so fearful emotionally that he could not risk having dinner with an intelligent, feisty woman with delicious curves, expressive eyes, and a mouth that . . .? Just dinner – who was he kidding? This was about a whole lot more than dinner. Com'on Nielsen. If you won't take a risk now that you are 60, when the heck will you? He found the website for the restaurant, checked out its menu and then clicked the booking option.

***

On Saturday afternoon, Ivy was out in her yard, cutting back spent perennials, deadheading the fall bloomers, and doing some pruning. She always found it a bit sad when the gardening season was over. The asters were still bravely showing off sapphire-blue flowers in a brilliant shade that only nature could have produced. Around their base, a deep pink hardy geranium bloomed playfully. They looked so happy and cheerful that she decided to leave them to enjoy any remaining sunny fall days.

The garden needed to be tidied up before winter and a life-long Portlander like Ivy knew that the rains would soon hamper working outside. Around the neighborhood, other folks were mowing grass, working in the garden, caulking, doing repairs – all taking advantage of the still pleasant weather. The corgis were on the other side of the yard raising a ruckus at any passing dog,

38

person, or squirrel. They were protective and territorial, making them the neighborhood busy-bodies. Soon Ivy would have to bring them to sit near her before they became too much of an irritant.

While she worked, gradually filling up the gardening recycle bin, she was thinking over her time with Steve. Dinner the night before had gone better than she expected. After a little stumbling conversation at the beginning, they were soon chatting over appetizers, laughing when their entrees arrived and feeding each other tastes of dessert. Actually Steve fed her tastes of his dessert. He would take a taste of each course she was served, eat his food and then bide his time until he could finish off whatever she had ordered. He ordered extra side dishes of potatoes, asparagus and creamed spinach and ate those as well. The man's appetite was so prodigious that she had to smile at the memory. Once they were finished, he asked if she would like to take a walk around the city. After looking ruefully down at her heels, they walked first to her office where she put on a sensible pair of flats and out they went, walking over to Burnside, turning left and then going up to Broadway, where they turned and walked up to the Park blocks. The air was crisp and fresh with the chill of fall. Sometimes she leaned on Steve's arm; sometimes he held her hand. Once in the park, shaded from the streetlight by one of the big-leafed trees, Steve asked if he could kiss her. That evening he had the manners of a gentleman. She had seen the more aggressive side of him and she was having trouble reconciling the two.

Ivy stopped trimming the rudbeckia, still with a few of their cheerful black-eyed susan flowers that she put aside for an arrangement in the house. She thought about the way Steve had kissed her -- long, slow and increasingly sensual. For once in her life, she felt scaled to size when he put his arms around her. He gently drew her close, nestling her against him. Afterward he stared at her without smiling and said. "Oh yes, this is about much more than just dinner." They meandered their way back to the parking lot where Ivy had left her car. Finding out that he would not leave until ten the next morning, she offered to pick him up at his hotel, buy him breakfast and drive him to the airport.

Seeing him again that morning let her know that more than the wine the night before drew them together. They talked easily as they sipped lattes and dug into large plates of food at a place called Mothers downtown. All too soon, they were in the car and on their way to the Hillsboro airport where Steve had an FBI jet coming to pick him up. Once there, he wanted her to meet Mathew who she had heard a fair amount about. She watched from the small waiting room while Steve jogged out to the jet and returned with yet another fine-looking agent in his late thirties. Like Brian Tovey, Mathew Heylen was about six feet but more substantial. He had sandy hair and moody sea-green eyes that almost seem to laugh as they echoed his warm smile. Mathew was like a blue spruce, tall and handsome, with many fine attributes that made it a perfect specimen planting as the backbone of a garden. They talked for a few minutes and then Mathew left to go back on the plane.

Steve kissed her again. "I will not say good-by, Ivy, because I am hoping this is only hello." He strode towards the plane, then turned and hastened back, taking her in his arms, swooping her in a waltz-like turn and then dipping her back for another kiss. Those blue eyes of his were intense with warmth.

"What are you doing for Thanksgiving?" he asked gently pulling her back upright.

Ivy let her face grow serious. "Making a big turkey dinner for a fellow I know who is going to be in Portland."

It surprised her that he appeared crestfallen. "It's kind of iffy," she continued, "You see, he travels a good deal and is very committed to his work."

Steve took in the teasing expression in her eyes and realized she was talking about him. "Darn it Ivy. You shouldn't taunt a man like that. If this case is wrapped up by then, I will schedule to be in Portland for the Thanksgiving weekend. If not, let's plan a long weekend together when the case is over. I want to know you better. You are one special woman, Ivy Vine."

"And I am learning that perhaps you are not always a fire-breathing dragon yourself, Agent Nielsen."

Smiling at the memory, Ivy went back to cutting down the perennials. Steve was different from any man she had dated in the way he seemed made up of contradictory parts. The brash, demanding FBI agent juxtaposed with the easy manners of a gentleman; his delight in technology seemed out of sync with an appreciation of fine wines; he was oversized and yet always pressed and neat. While he touched her gently, she worried that he could turn aggressive in a relationship during a rough spot. The long, soft kiss and the tender way he held her were as unexpected as the boyish grin that he rarely showed. Even with her concern, Ivy found she was eagerly anticipating hearing from him again.

Chapter 4

Back east once more, Steve pushed away from his desk at the FBI offices in the J. Edgar Hoover Building. He swiveled in his chair to stare out at Pennsylvania Avenue where the small trees planted in the sidewalk were turning a delightful golden yellow. When he took the early 40 minute walk to work that morning, the chilly air in D.C. made him think of Ivy and their walk in Portland on Friday night. Being with her tantalized his senses and opened him to the smaller wonders of the world around him.

He smiled to himself when he thought about her. She was brimming with intelligence; she was attractive. Heck, she was lovely. Why was she single? Single now for a long time -- a dozen years, but then he had been single for twenty-five years. Ivy Vine. Ivy Littleton. Steve found both the nickname Moll had given her and her real name pleasing. The letters twined around his tongue as he thought of her. She was tall just as he was, but with alluring curves. Like him she had dedicated her life to her career, yet unlike him she was ready to retire. She was noticeably self-sufficient and must have great inner strength. Even so, now and then he could see some conflict that she hid away. It crept out in her eyes before she pushed it back -- not fear exactly, but something was troubling her and that made her even more intriguing.

Why would she find an oversized, ill-mannered man like him appealing? Steve had been thinking about that question on and off the last couple of days. He hoped that he had conjured up some of the charm his mother tried to instill in him. Ivy made him want to behave like a gentleman and become a tender, yet still passionate lover.

She smelled fresh and flowery, reminding him of a wild blackcap patch in summer that he used to frequent as a kid. He had to smile to himself as she could be about as prickery. When they went to her office on Friday night, she put on a soft cashmere muffler hanging behind her office door and lent him one in a navy plaid. He still had it and wore it that morning. It smelled deliciously of Ivy. Silly of him to have kept it, but it made him feel closer to her. How sweetly Ivy had melted into his arms. How yielding she was to kiss and yet she was not passive. Steve realized he was becoming aroused thinking about her. She . . .

Right Nielsen, compartmentalize. You want to know her better. Be realistic. You are on the east coast nearly 3,000 miles away. You need to keep your wandering mind on this case. Besides, nothing worse than an old man in the office pitching a tent. Focus. He shook his head at himself and turned his attention back to his laptop.

Abruptly his thoughts jerked to an image that his mind had captured last night when he and his three senior agents were walking back from dinner at an Italian place a few blocks off Dupont Circle, not far from his condo. They had met up on Sunday night to exchange information on their work over the weekend. The three younger men had fallen behind him, engrossed in a conversation about baseball. Steve strolled ahead enjoying the mild October evening, walking through the first of the rustling leaves of the tree-lined street, past the little front gardens where some window boxes sported chrysanthemums in the bright yellows, burnished bronzes and deep burgundies of autumn.

They were about three blocks from the Circle when he caught a flicker of movement in the shadows just behind and to the left of him on the other side of the street. He cocked his head, saw no one, then turned back to peer fully behind him. It might have been a dancing shadow from a breeze in the trees. He slowed to a saunter, kept his head pointed forward, with his eyes focused to the left, walking more leisurely as if waiting for the three agents to catch up. A block later he caught a movement that might have been a person sliding through the shadows. At the Circle he stopped, turned around and scanned the area -- no sign of anyone on the far side of the street.

He waited for the three agents to reach him and then crossed the Circle. On the other side he checked again, saw nothing out of place, and then suggested they go into the nearby Kimpton hotel for a brandy. As they entered the hotel, he glanced back and saw no one lurking. Maybe it had been nothing. However his sixth sense had alerted him and it served him well over the years.

While he had never had a perp come after him, it could and did happen to FBI agents. It made him wonder who might want him followed. Perhaps that drug lord they went after in Mexico.

The whole operation down in Manzanillo had been odd. How had the perpetrator known they were after him? Why had he baited them into boarding the yacht to catch an actor he had planted there? Was the same perp having him followed? Did someone want to make the DEA, the FBI or himself look ridiculous? Was some mole feeding the perp confidential case information so that he could anticipate the FBI's next move? The very thought went against the ideals to which Steve was committed. Was someone trying to make him appear incompetent to take pressure off themselves? If that were true, the perp would find he had picked the wrong adversary. These questions had been buzzing in and out of his mind since the operation in Mexico. The possible shadow in D.C. the night before brought them into focus. He would keep a sharp watch and see what played out next.

***

Ivy found her mind wandering while she sat at her sleek modern desk between meetings on Monday afternoon. No word from the Big Guy – she noticed that she now capitalized that nickname in her mind. She also said his name to herself repeatedly, as young girls do with first crushes. Steve. Steve Nielsen. After so many years of chastity, she felt that dating could be as it was in her college days, with all those silly flutterings from this man whose masculinity lit her up. That height of his came from his Nordic roots, in the same way that hers came from her half-Finnish father. Steve's hair was dark and silver with a hint of curl and nicely trimmed. His eyes were the deep gray blue of a Norwegian fiord, the way she pictured one in her mind's eye. His eyes alone fascinated her -- he had intense, watchful eyes that became softer, more wanting eyes when he looked at her. In his arms, she felt feminine, secure and desirable.

Once he dropped the brusquely aggressive stance of the FBI agent, his face transformed, becoming more attractive as his expression softened. She liked the way he dressed. His suit had been freshly pressed -- navy pinstripe, almost black. His shirt was starched, white, thick and crisp, worn with large gold

44

signet cufflinks and an elegant silk tie. His black tassel loafers were well worn, yet in perfect condition. She liked a man who took care of his wardrobe and of himself.

Ivy adored the way his smile varied from a slight twinge with his lips curling up to a generous toothy grin. Brian had mentioned that one of Steve's nicknames in the Bureau was "the Boy Scout" and Ivy wondered if it was his grin or his ideals or the combination of the two that gave him that epithet. The subtle smile seemed to come from his heart; the grin straight from his boyhood. Ivy found it refreshing that he still had that grin.

Her mind lingered on their conversations, thinking about his praise of Mathew who he considered his most talented agent, even better than himself which he said with a hint of pride. He talked about Mathew's innate goodness. In talking of Mathew, Steve revealed so much of himself and what he valued -- commitment to justice, devotion to his country, intelligence coupled with common sense. The federal agent was there in his movements, in the eyes that never stopped watching his surroundings except when he gazed at her. How sweet he had been to ask if he could kiss her. Of course, he could be the cleverest actor she had come across. That thought scared Ivy and made her feel vulnerable.

Two days and no word from Steve. Although he indicated there might be days and weeks when he would be out of touch, Ivy hoped she would hear from him. When her office phone rang, Ivy picked it up and answered with her usual business tone, professional yet accessible. "Ivy Littleton."

A little thrill went through her when she heard, "Ivy, Steve."

"Steve! I was wondering if you would find time to call."

"Can you talk now?"

"Give me a moment." Ivy rushed to have her assistant push the upcoming 4:00 meeting to the next day and closed her office door.

"Hi, Big Guy. What has your week been like?" The deep yet soft sound of his voice flowed seductively from her ear down through her body. She squirmed a little in her chair as the warmth in his tones seeped into her. She found herself caressing the navy sleeve of her cashmere blazer, as if she were being touched by Steve.

"I work on a theory that there is little sense in chopping off the pieces of a big operation, because, like the mythical hydra, the tentacles are quickly regenerated, whereas if you capture or kill the brains the whole thing implodes. Not everyone at the Bureau agrees with me, including my boss. He wants to tout victories by count, not by impact."

"Your approach makes sense."

"How are your dogs?"

"They are the cutest little bundles. When I open the door at home and see those happy faces waiting for me, it makes even the worst days better. The cat does his bit too. You like pets?"

"Like them yes. Never home to have one."

"Where is home, by the way?"

"Not sure any more. I keep a condo in D.C., even though I'm only there a few days a month."

"Where was home, then?"

"Eastern shore of Maryland. My Dad was a small town lawyer."

That explained that slight drawl that comes into his voice when he relaxes. "And your Mother?"

"Mom ran an import business for Nordic crafts out of our basement -- sold them to specialty shops in areas of the country with significant Norwegian populations. It let her be home for me and my Dad. They emigrated from Norway right after World War II seeking a warmer climate."

The call lasted almost an hour, with each of them conversing as easily as the previous weekend, sometimes seriously, sometimes bantering. They talked about Portland, about their lives and about technology. After Ivy hung up and opened her office door again, a couple of her staff stood there waiting to give her updates on their projects. Ivy left at six, wanting to be at home where she could savor the glow of talking with Steve.

He told her to expect only an occasional call or email over the next weeks, as his cases demanded his full attention. He did end the call by reminding her about their planned Thanksgiving weekend. If he was a player then he was delicate about it for she sensed no falseness. From years of managing people,

46

her senses were attuned to listening and watching for signs of duplicity. With Steve, she sensed only that he was a good, straightforward man. She remained worried that his forceful life as an agent could spill over into personal relationships. Sooner or later, she needed to voice that worry to him and see how he reacted.

Ivy's life changed from meeting Steve. Now she felt more alive and aware of the world around her. Talking to him filled her with glistening hope. She smiled to herself, silently thanking him for giving her color back. She saw it again now in the trees as they headed towards fall. She appreciated the warm gold and rust-colored flowers at the garden center. She noticed the late pink roses along her driveway waking up to the morning sun, with translucent dew drops caught at the tips of leaves. Moreover she realized that she wanted to laugh more and run with her dogs playing hide and seek with them in the yard. If nothing else came from having met Steve, Ivy would be sorry but also thankful. He let her remember what it was to feel the warmth of a good man. More than that, he had awoken a delightfully sensuous part of her that perhaps had always been dormant, something deep within her. Even so, did she have enough left of herself to offer him? Would he quickly find her to be worn out?

***

A few days later, Ivy was pleasantly surprised to find an email from Steve in her personal inbox. She chided herself for her silliness when seeing his name made her gasp with surprise and delight. He had sent it via a secure service that required her to create a login before the message would be decrypted and available to her. His use of secure email for a personal communication added to the intrigue of the man who was Steve Nielsen.

Secure Email from Steve Nielsen, October 26, 2012

Dear Ivy

When you walked into your offices a few weeks ago, the first thing I noticed was your assurance. You have a regal quality about you, exuding strength and independence, and yet you seem to have a wonderful lack of awareness of how captivating you are. Seeing you again Friday night, it was as if a light came on in that restaurant. Even *after being away from you for a few days, I found that light stayed with me. I realized the glow was coming from inside of me; it needed the right spark to brighten. This may sound a bit crazy at my age -- I am smitten with you. Your outfit Friday night was striking, with your filmy blue blouse that dipped alluringly low in the front. When you smiled as you saw me, I knew flying up to Portland was the right decision.*

Until that trip to your company a couple of weeks ago, I had never been to your City of Roses. I spent some weeks in Seattle a few years ago, working on a jewel smuggling case. Mt. Rainier and the Olympic Mountains struck me with their majestic presence. I thought then that I wanted to return some day and hike out into that wilderness. That was before I saw Mt. Hood's graceful crenellated peak that is like a jutting inselberg out of a Tolkien book. What was it called? The Lonely Mountain? Seattle now plays a distant second to Portland. You have something to do with that.

To be honest, I have never been great at interpersonal relationships, but with you the words flowed like a river between us. Each sentence was laden with meaning, telling each other who we are. Like you, I hadn't dated in years, not once I came out of a long, horrid dead phase in my life. My monk's life allowed me to find my values again. I found ways to chase away the emptiness inside of me, if only through work. Nevertheless of late, with me about the oldest field executive/agent around, I could see the door to retirement. That is a door I fear opening. Beyond it I have only been able to see a void.

I mentioned that for a time I worked in D.C. at the Bureau's headquarters in a very prestigious position that I wanted my whole career and once there I found I missed solving nasty problems and nailing the perps. Working at HQ where I had to use my influence was not my strong point. After about 18 months at HQ, I engineered myself back into fieldwork in a role I defined, heading up an elite squad, or team as I prefer to call it, to handle cases where the perps are located typically in Europe or Latin America.

Originally the FBI focused on domestic issues. However as the world has changed, most of our big cases have international roots or tentacles. The Bureau set up a growing number of Legal Attaché offices around the world to work with the local authorities to help solve cases. When on foreign soil, we act in conjunction with in-country forces under terms arranged by our legats, as we call them.

Tomorrow we are flying to Bern for the final planning to apprehend the leader of this child trafficking operation, save the innocent children held captive, and destroy the network. We will stick with this goal, no matter how long it takes. All my time and concentration will go into this operation. Keep me in your thoughts and be confident that I will return to Portland to see you as soon as I can – with any luck Thanksgiving weekend. You may see an email from me before then or I will call when this operation is over.

(Hopefully) Your Favorite Big Guy,

Steve

Ivy read and reread the email, feeling even more impressed by Steve and the man he was. FBI High Bureau Official, or HBO, was what Brian had called him. She contemplated the dark October sky, seeing the lights across the valley and up on the hills to the south. She turned back to her screen, did a couple of searches and found that the FBI employs over 35,000 people. To be an FBI HBO was an impressive achievement.

Steve seemed to dwarf her. His work made hers, even as the head of an important business unit, feel less significant. With work soon to be in her past, Ivy needed a new definition for herself to stand up to her own expectations and to the scrutiny of a man like Steve. Yet he was a bit one-dimensional or at least that was what he conveyed. Maybe she could help him round out and fill that void that he fears will be retirement. She had similar concerns about herself. If things progressed between them, perhaps together they could define a life after their career years were behind them. She shook her head at herself and pulled her thoughts back. She was way ahead of herself. That night Ivy composed an email back to Steve, but before she hit the "Send" button, Ivy told herself to keep her desires under control. Given her work commitments and pressures, having a long distance relationship that would have to develop in fits and starts might not be so bad.

Chapter 5

Around nine that same evening, Steve and Mathew arrived in Washington by train from New York, using the trip to go over their findings and plans on the child trafficking case. The next day, Steve had an obligatory breakfast meeting scheduled with his boss to update him on his assigned cases. He had no respect for his current boss, thinking him a Bureau HQ lightweight who had never done fieldwork. However he would go through the motions of meeting with him. Steve considered his real boss to be the Director of the Bureau and he talked with him every week or so. Right after the breakfast meeting, Steve along with Mathew, Brian and four other team members, would fly to Bern to prepare for the move against the suspected head of the child trafficking operation, identified as located in Sofia. He liked to work closer to the perps once they narrowed in on a location.

After jumping on the Metro Red Line to Dupont Circle, Steve and Mathew dropped their bags at their condos and hustled out for a late dinner at the Italian place they frequented a few blocks away. Walking back, Steve recalled that night when he thought they might have been tailed and kept a discrete watch in case one appeared again. At one point, Mathew peered quickly over his left shoulder.

"You've seen it too?" Steve asked.

"The tail? Yeah. Thought I saw something the last time we were here."

"You never said."

"Wasn't sure."

"Let's split up. You turn left. I'll go right and then one of us will circle behind the other, depending on what the tail does. Maybe we can trap him between us."

Mathew nodded. At the corner they parted. Steve walked for a block and glanced back. A man in black was creeping along behind him on the opposite side of the street. Steve pulled his gun from the shoulder holster, keeping it under his jacket. He slowed his pace, waiting for the tail to make a move. He risked a glance over his other shoulder. Mathew had turned back and was coming up behind the tail. Suddenly the man bolted straight ahead, ran to the corner, turned left and fled, moving with the speed of a sprinter doing a 400 yard dash. Steve and Mathew each took off running.

Up ahead the man in black turned left on 18th Street heading towards Dupont Circle. Steve wanted to catch this shadow and learn who sent him. The man glanced back, saw him and kept running. Steve yelled for him to stop. The man split left on P Street. Steve pushed himself harder only to see the man dash into the Metro Station. Steve raced down the stairs just in time to see the man in black boarding a train as it left the station. Mathew puffed up behind him.

"Missed him?"

"Yeah."

"No doubt we are being tailed, though."

"Ever see anything in New York?"

Mathew shook his head. "How did he know we were back?"

"Same restaurant. Maybe a waiter or somebody gets paid to tip him off."

"Let's go back."

"They were closing when we left."

"Who do you think it was?"

"Maybe from that drug lord we tried to hit in Mexico." They were walking again back to their condos.

"You been followed before?"

"Not that I'm aware of, except that one time. Let's do a bug sweep of our condos and check our electronic gear for tracking software."

"Usual procedure? I check my place and my gear; you check yours?"

"And then we switch and repeat."

In Bern, the team was reviewing suspect email traffic in and out of Sofia and laying out scenarios for how the arrest operation might happen. Bern was close enough for monitoring and to jet in to the target city when needed, yet distant enough to escape detection. Steve had a one-bedroom suite, using the living room for meetings, as well as for their computers and surveillance gear. Early the second Tuesday, Mathew was reading decoded texts and emails to and from the perps in the surveillance area. Another agent named Trina was working on her scenarios. The plan was for her to lead a meeting with the perps. She seemed to be on a mission with this case and was very intent on having every detail right.

"Check this out, Big Guy," said Mathew. He had taken to using that soubriquet since he heard Ivy call Steve by that name during their brief meeting at the airport.

"Twenty Snežanas and six Zvezdans are ready for new homes. The orphanage is full."

Trina crowded over next to Mathew. "Snežanas are Snow Whites or Virgin Girls and Zvezdans are Stars or Innocent Boys," she echoed annoyingly, as if Steve could forget the perps' sick code words.

"If their orphanage is full, then we need to go in now with our proposal for a new network child porn centers in smaller Midwestern cities," Trina continued.

"Tell us something we don't know," Steve said, lacing his comment heavily with sarcasm. Sometimes Trina could be a blunt instrument on the communications side. She seemed to think with her mouth. It could make her risky in the field. That was one of the differences between her and Mathew. He never stated the obvious.

That morning they worked at role-playing with Steve taking the part of leader of the perps, a woman referred to as Matka in the emails the agents decoded. It meant "Mother" in the Slavic language used by a broad range of peoples across multiple countries in Eastern Europe. Mathew took on the role of the man they suspected to be Matka's next in command, a henchman they dubbed Dragomir, which is a Slavic name composed of the elements dorogo meaning precious and mir meaning peace, making the combination literally mean "precious peace". They liked the irony of the meaning, but mostly they liked the dull, threatening sound of "Dragomir" when they said it.

Trina was playing her role as the lead on their team and Brian was acting as the main negotiator. Brian was stalwart, never making a misstatement and never showing that he had been caught off-guard. His performance made Steve proud. While Trina had been flawless, by the end of the morning she was beginning to glow with nervous perspiration. Steve continued to play Matka as the sophisticated executive, who might be selling fine Slavic art, collectible heirlooms, or gold threaded fabrics for plush interior designs. Instead, the perp was selling kids. He made a lousy Matka, but he could do the conversation.

"Now that we have talked, perhaps you would like to see a sample of the goods." He nodded at Mathew and smiled in the cold way he had learned early in his career.

Brian and Trina were not privy to the next scenario. He wanted to see what they would do. Mathew escorted what appeared to be two teenagers into the room. One was a female prostitute, younger in appearance than she was, flat chested and with short-cropped hair. She portrayed a certain waif-like innocence. The second prostitute was a boyish young man with blond hair cut close at the sides but left long on top so that it tumbled down over his forehead. It irked Steve to test the two agents this way, but it could happen and he had to see their reactions.

He had made sure the two hired prostitutes were not underage by American standards and he interviewed them to be sure they were not coerced into their work. Both were students at the local university who were earning their tuition money with their bodies. The young woman had it all lined out -- how she would graduate in a year without having to take on student loans or government obligations. While it bothered Steve, he had heard worse. It was offensive to him to line them up, but this test could become real. The agents might be expected to try out "the goods" to check their veracity as buyers. The agents did not have to take that test now or during the sting. All he wanted was to see their reactions.

He had outlined three responses the agents might have and still get by during the negotiations with Matka. First, they could go along with the scenario and make use of one of the prostitutes. He did not expect them to do that; it was up to them. Second, they could negotiate away the time with the prostitute and play their role as if they had made use of his or her services. Third, they could say they negotiated the deal but did not sample the goods. Any of the three reactions would be acceptable. Any would work in the field. Steve was there to make the agents ready for what might happen, not to judge them.

He watched Brian and Trina closely. Staying in his role as Matka, he said, "Do you want to sample the goods? I can arrange rooms for you."

He could see the shock in Brian's eyes, but he quickly lowered them and remained silent, perhaps at a loss for words. Trina turned a deep purplish red. Her face became so distorted with fury that she resembled one of the gargoyles on the older buildings around Bern.

"You complete and utter deviant," she spat out. "How could you bring in these kids? They are what fifteen? How are you any better than the slime we're trying to catch? This is going too far. I will have you called before the Bureau for this and I hope they castrate you. You are a sick son of a bitch."

Steve held his silence. Mathew opened his mouth to defend him. Steve gave him a look that told him to be quiet. They had to hear it all. Trina was fired up. This was fail or succeed time for her. She flew at Steve as a ball of rage and frustration. He could have pushed her away, but he wanted to see how this played out with her. First Mathew and then Brian moved to grab her. He shook his head. When Steve failed to fight back, Trina moved away and glared at him furiously.

"What you are doing is all wrong. It's sick. This isn't a scenario; it's not in our casebook. Your mind has become so warped you can't see right from wrong any more. Do you have any idea what's it like to be a child forced to do whatever some sick adult wants?"

Suddenly Steve realized why Trina was furious. He was so stunned by this turn of events that a few moments passed before he said, "No, but you do."

She went silent. Her red face paled as if a bucket of whitewash had been thrown over her. As the rage left her, she sank to her knees on the floor. She began to quiver, rock back and forth and sob, and then she went into a stupor, draped over her knees. Steve's guess was that it was a childhood pose -- a place she went after she had suffered.

It was hard to see a good agent implode. He had pushed and pushed until she broke. He had no idea she had been abused as a child and he had driven her back into that personal hell. If he had known, she would not have been on this case. Now it was too late and he felt dreadful.

They carried Trina back to her room, where Brian stayed while Steve arranged for another agent to be with her. He also called for the hotel doctor. He had only wanted to see what she or Brian would do if a situation like this arose. Unfortunately he went too close to those horrible memories trapped inside of her. It explained why she had been on this case with such a vengeance. He hated himself for pushing Trina too far.

Mathew escorted the two prostitutes out of the hotel. Steve went to the bathroom, brushed his teeth and washed his face, trying to cleanse away his remorse. It didn't work. He went out for a walk to make peace with himself. Once he was calmed down enough to return, he started making calls. He arranged for Trina to fly home the next day. He also contacted the Bureau's Human Relations folks to ensure that Trina received the care and counseling she needed. Finally he filed a report on the incident and added the scenario to the casebook along with a fourth possible reaction.

Now they had a problem. Their front woman was gone. They had to activate Plan 8.5 which was to use a backup for Trina. They thought a woman might play better as the lead with Matka, therefore their contact man was describing a woman as the leader in the overtures to set up a meeting with the perps. Steve considered sound planning one of his strengths: outlining possible scenarios, analyzing the risks, devising backup plans and second-guessing the other side. Nothing in reality went by any of the plans. However after testing out so many instances, the team was ready for close to anything.

Brian came back. While he was rattled, he understood the need to keep moving forward.

"What do we do now, Chief?"

"It's Plan 8.5, but we don't have another female agent who is both up to speed and sufficiently skilled to take that lead role."

"So we switch to a guy."

"Yes."

"Mathew?"

"He'll get five o'clock shadow an hour into the negotiations."

"You mean have a guy play a woman?" Brian asked apprehensively.

"It has to be you. You are thoroughly acquainted with the playbook. We need to keep the lead person as a woman. That is what is expected for the meeting with Matka."

"Me? No way. I have never refused an assignment before. This one, definitely not."

"Any other solution will delay us by weeks -- finding the right agent, bringing her up to speed, running scenarios. Think of what could happen to those kids in that time."

Brian paled. "Hey, I may not be a real macho type, but I am a man like you, Chief. Me dressing up as a woman? That's insane."

Steve's expression conveyed his conviction. Brian remained solemn and sat staring at the floor. Minutes passed. Just as Steve was giving up hope that he would come around, Brian sat up straight and said, "While I don't want to fucking do this, I will. I'll need makeup, clothes, hairdo, training and no wisecracks. What happens on this case, stays on this case. No leaks. No kidding around."

"Deal. Let's get started."

To stay on track, they had only a couple of days to turn Brian into a convincing woman. Steve would shift the negotiations to Mathew to take some pressure off Brian and to let him concentrate on his role as a convincing female executive. Twenty-four hours later, with the help of a junior female agent on our team, Brian passed for a woman. He learned a new walk that was athletic yet feminine. They worked on gestures that women make -- primping, playing

56

with his necklace, licking his lips a certain way. His beard had never been heavy and he could hide his slight Adam's apple with a scarf or a turtleneck. The issue was his deep, masculine voice. Steve lined up a Bureau speech expert to work with Brian on his speech. Once his tones were worked out, they would go back to tweaking roles and doing practice scenarios. Steve planned to lean on their contact the next day to have the meeting confirmed with Matka.

That night Steve was reviewing their risk analysis. Perpetrators are dangerous criminals who often fight to the death to avoid capture. Every mission had risks. Steve considered it his responsibility to minimize the impact of those risks on his team and on the public. He glanced over at Mathew.

"We need a strong lead for our backup team, now that you're not on it," Steve said.

"You remember that Lenny guy from that second case we did together?"

"Lenny lacked finesse."

"Damn it Steve. Have you ever played back yourself in action? When the pressure is on, you kind of lack finesse too. You shoot first and worry about arrests later. You get the job done and you get it done fast, but it isn't always tidy."

"And you could do better?" Steve countered a bit belligerently.

"No, I think with time I might become as good, not better."

Steve battled with that hard stubbornness he had and then he said, "You are already better than I am in action. You're craftier and you're a bit faster. We are lucky to have you."

Mathew smiled at the unexpected compliment. "And Lenny?"

"Yeah, line him up. Have him plan to meet me in Frankfurt when we're ready to do the sting. I will brief him there and then we will fly into Sofia."

***

Almost two weeks had passed where Ivy did not hear from Steve. Work was keeping her in the office long hours and often she was working at home in the evenings as well. Client demands were adding to her stress levels and yet occasional thoughts of Steve buoyed her up. On Thursday, she was delighted to see a secure email come in from him and allowed herself the luxury of opening it while she ate lunch at her desk.

Secure Email from Steve Nielsen, November 8, 2012

Dearest Ivy,

How very often you have been in my thoughts. We have only been together twice, talked a few times and emailed, but like your namesake you are twining yourself around my heart rapidly, completely, divinely.

Before I met you, for about the last year or so, a long-dormant part of me decided to come awake. Everything about you, including that captivating "big town" you live in, reaches out to this new region in me. You are warm, enticing, and verging a bit to the unusual. I think that all the oxygen from the trees in the Northwest makes you folks a bit elfin, yet you seem to have both feet on the ground.

You are a curious mix of sophistication and earthiness. You are soft and yielding yet strong. Womanly but capable and I think you are totally lacking in guile. Still you are mysterious in some ways. I sense that you have unexplored layers and depths and that perhaps I could spend years with you and still discover surprising new twists.

At that moment, one of Ivy's directors burst into her office with the news that a key project manager had walked off the job, crumbling under the pressure and leaving a major client project in trouble. Reluctantly she closed the email to focus her attention on the immediate problem, which became all absorbing as she strove to fill the gap.

***

The next day, Mathew was in his room working on his laptop and thinking morosely about where he was in life when Steve walked in.

"What's up?" he said, spinning around in his desk chair to face Steve.

"One o'clock, we leave. Bubird taking us to Frankfurt. From there we take public transport by various routes to Sofia. Spread the word."

Mathew nodded and turned back to his laptop.

"What's with you?" Steve asked. "You usually jump up and down with enthusiasm when we're ready to move in. Today you look like your pet dog died."

Mathew shook his head. Steve sat on a spare chair in the room.

"Spill it or I'm not leaving."

"Thinking too much. Like how does this happen? I'm sailing along in my thirties, feeling like my life is coming to fruition. Then I wake up one morning, and I hit forty. Suddenly I'm rushing headlong into the second half of my productive life. What do I have to show for the first half?"

"The big four-oh? Yeah, milestone birthdays make you think, don't they? Mathew, you have one hell of a career. You are well educated. You have the ability to go to the top of the Bureau. Maybe even be the Chief one day."

"I wasn't thinking of my career. I am so isolated personally. Sadly no one cares that this is a milestone day for me. My mother never remembers my birthday. At least when my Dad was alive, he would have given me a phone call from wherever his business interests had taken him."

"I'm here and for what it's worth, I do care. Happy Birthday, Mathew. What are you going to do? What do you want to change?" Steve made a mental note to add Mathew's birthday to his calendar so he would remember it next year.

"If turning forty fails to give me the impetus to change my life, what will? My life clock is ticking inexorably that way it does, steadily marching forward. I have to make some life-changing resolutions to find a wife, family, and fulfillment. How do I get there? How do I find someone as promising as this Ivy you met?"

Mathew noticed that Steve blanched a little at the mention of Ivy's name. "Something wrong with you and Ivy, Big Guy?"

"Don't know. Oh crap. I emailed her about what I'm like -- what a demanding SOB I am and stuff. Gave her some examples -- things she should understand about me before we go further. She hasn't responded."

"Maybe she is thinking. Maybe she is busy. Can't believe you did that in an email."

"Yeah, well maybe not the best way to tell her. It's done now. To make things worse, we have to take off and leave all our personal stuff behind in some airport or other."

"Stinks. Why don't you call her before we go?"

"Nah. I'll do that after the action. Right now, I have to focus on those kids. Hope I haven't scared her off."

"If I ever do find someone, how do I hold onto her? Can I do that and maintain this career path? My FBI career is great -- challenging, stimulating, and gratifying. Is it worth the heavy toll it takes on my personal life and me?"

"Guys do it."

"You didn't."

"My life should not be an example for you. Remember that discussion we had about love and marriage a few years back?"

Mathew nodded.

"Take your own advice. Manage it like a project. Commit yourself to having an approach settled in your mind by a certain date."

Mathew nodded. "You're right. Three months. By February 9th, 2013, I will have a path to follow. Every day I will spend at least ten minutes on it. For now, "*Ad Meliora Vertamur*" -- Let Us Turn to Better Things!"

Feeling, if not better, at least glad to have a goal, he picked up his cell phone to alert the rest of the team that they were flying out at one.

***

Going out of Bern, the team split up using the tickets Steve arranged for them, boarding planes for Vienna, Rome or Budapest switching IDs as they went. From those cities, they would then fly to Sofia. Anything that could identify who they really were -- passports, credit cards, driver's licenses, and even personal cell phones, tablets and laptops were left at an FBI office or an airport locker en route. Steve planned to leave his in a locker at the Frankfort airport since he expected that to be his route flying back to the States. Mathew left his in Bern. They had to do the sting in Sofia, handle the follow-on work to shut down the child brothels once they knew where they were, and finish the case wrap-up that was required. Steve rechecked his iPhone at the airport, but found no messages from Ivy. He stopped to check his secure email service. That was empty as well. He put his roscoe, creds, iPhone, iPad and laptop in the airport locker, closed the door, spun the dial and walked away, hoping he would have a message from Ivy when he picked up his iPhone again, but fearing that he had scared her off.

All the agents, except Steve and Lenny, arrived in Sofia on Zero Day minus one. Each agent was down to a suitcase, anonymous laptop, a new cell phone, and leather briefcase. On the surface, they appeared to be business people from the American Heartland. Steve and Lenny were to meet up in Frankfurt on Day Zero and fly out on the next flight to Sofia. Behind the scenes the legats had arranged local forces for the arrest team, the required in-country weapons and technology, and social services to take the children. The first meeting with the head of the child trafficking ring – the woman they called Matka -- was scheduled for late in the afternoon of Day Zero. Only Mathew, Brian and a bilingual agent would attend.

***

Not until early the following Tuesday morning was Ivy able to get back to Steve's email, reading the part she had not read before twice in the early morning quiet of her home.

While I want to see more of you, I have been doing a great deal of thinking and soul searching when I manage to pull myself away from this investigation. Before we go further, you need to better understand me. Ivy, you have seen that as an agent, I can be brash, headstrong, and difficult. While I would never (and have never) become physically aggressive, I likely will always be obdurately demanding when I feel I am in the right. My parents used to tell me that I was their American angel with one devil of a Norwegian stubborn streak.

My work life has been successful even though that is at a cost. I have done and will do whatever it takes to solve a case. I have killed people; they were always the perps; it was always in self-defense, but I pulled the trigger. Can you still smile at me and want to be with me knowing that? Sometimes team members have been severely hurt on missions because I insisted that we solve a case, catch the perps, and end the crimes. Agents have been shot up, nastily wounded and even crippled. Can you gaze at me with those sincere eyes of yours and still want me as you learn more about this tougher side?

I also mess with people's heads. I push them beyond their physical, emotional and psychological endurances. I have ended any number of careers; I have put aspiring agents in situations where they came to think far less of themselves. Working with me shook their confidence down to their toes. Often I go after solving a case so hard, that I fail to see the impact on the agents on my teams. Recently I pushed a good agent on the team so hard that she had a flashback to a bad time in her life and completely broke down. She had to be sent home, take a leave of absence and go into therapy. While I had no idea that she had this ticking time bomb of memories inside of her, I should have seen the warning signs and backed off. Unfortunately this is not untypical of me. I push agents to take on roles that they do not want or are not always ready for. Over the course of my years at the FBI, I have damaged the careers of scores of agents.

Why am I telling you this? Because it is what I do and what I have done for 35 years. Working for the Bureau on cases takes my full concentration; it takes up almost all of my life and my energy. Frankly my personal life has been a disaster. I buried myself in work when my marriage failed. I turned my back on my son, letting my wife and her second husband bring him up.

Now I want to find my way to you, if you will have me. At 60 years old I need to have more of life for myself before it becomes too late. I would like to think that you are interested in me too, but you have to understand what I can be like. You need to recognize that I have this harder side that I built over many years. While I can compartmentalize, it is there when needed. I can be a demanding SOB who always, or so I believe, keeps the end good in mind.

Tomorrow the team flies to our target destination. Take your time to consider what I have told you. It is unlikely that I will be able to pick up a personal call or email in the next week or two or even longer. If you still want to move forward in a relationship with me, call my cell phone and leave a voice mail. If you decide this harder side of me is not for you, then understand I will always treasure having known you, if only briefly.

I feel as if I have come to your door as a charming spook in a white bed sheet on Halloween, then I took off my mask to reveal the ugly ghoul underneath. Ivy, be sure you make the right choice for yourself.

Steve

Ivy pulled a warm lavender wool plaid throw closer around her to ward off the early morning chill. She felt torn between spending time contemplating the message from Steve and work obligations. While they had met the client's deadline the day before, Ivy had other work to tackle that morning. Unfolding herself from the chair and tossing the throw over her shoulders, she decided to go handle the critical items at the office, check in with each of her direct reports and leave work no later than noontime. She had some thinking to do that afternoon and she was still reeling from the excessively long work hours of the last few days.

Chapter 6

In Sofia the session on Tuesday afternoon with Matka was challenging. At least on the surface, Brian was smooth, confident, and cool as he performed his impersonation of a female executive. Even Mathew found him believable -- for sure he had hoodwinked the perps with his short gel nails, hair blown into a feminine style, perfect eyebrows, soft slacks, a set of modest falsies and a sexy, throaty voice. Mathew took most of the negotiations, however he would check with Brian for approval, as he (she) was the lead in Matka's understanding.

With the perps, Mathew talked about how they wanted to start a so-called personal network out of St. Louis and then expand into other cities in the American Heartland. From what they knew so far, the brothels Matka already dealt with were located in the major cities in the United States and Europe. Their proposed enterprise would step that down to the next tier of cities, with a concentration in the Midwest. He described how they would handle security and how they would rely on the still-existing exclusive clubs and organizations for business executives to get the word out, one man to the next. The network would be fronted behind their existing chain of upmarket steakhouses, using adjunct space in the basement or on upper floors. They owned each of their restaurant buildings, allowing them more flexibility in how they managed their businesses. They would offer a variety of services, from upscale women to gay men to more youthful alternatives. Mathew could feel a line of tense sweat forming on his back and under his arms and was glad he left his suit jacket on. Luckily, his face stayed cool and he kept his demeanor serious but not brusque.

Matka had a number of questions concerning their finances and their expected growth rate. Mathew discussed their proposed operations as if he were laying out a business plan, relying on the scenarios they had put together the previous week. At one point, Brian opened his briefcase and took out a computerized line graph that showed their planned growth rate in terms of numbers of so-called employees by age group over the next 12, 24 and 36 months, as well as where they were targeting to be at the end of five years. Matka managed a cold smile as she looked at the numbers. Mathew could see her calculating her revenues on the sale of the children. Dragomir asked a tough series of questions on how they would keep the operations secure and away from the prying eyes of police or local do-gooders.

They were there for over two hours. When it was over and they were back at the hotel, Mathew walked to a nearby park and called Steve in Frankfurt.

"You're on." Mathew said by way of greeting. "Tomorrow at one. We asked to see the so-called orphanage. Got a no go. Brian stood up to walk out; deal off."

"That took balls," Steve said admiringly.

"His action changed Matka's thinking. After a third of the cash is wired to their bank account tomorrow morning, we get to make our choices. Then the next third is due the following morning and the rest will be COD St. Louis. They have a way to bring the kids into the U.S. The process takes two weeks."

"Good negotiating on only a third of a million up front. What are the logistics?"

"Hotel lobby. Tomorrow at one. Car coming for you, me and Ms. London."

Tomorrow they would do the smash-up, kids out and arrests all in one, provided they made it to the so-called orphanage. Once an operation was underway, Steve never liked to play it slow. They had to hope the technology worked, the backup team would be at the ready and they did not encounter too many curveball surprises. Steve made a mental note to reinforce with Lenny that they had to minimize any impact on the kids when the bust in the orphanage went down.

***

Secure Email from Ivy Littleton, November 13, 2012

My dear Steve,

Sorry not to have been in contact sooner -- I saw your email last week, but only read the beginning, which warmed my heart.   I was in the office, crunched for time and wanted to savor the rest by reading it at a quiet time at home. As it turned out that same day our Project Manager for a big client walked out leaving a mess. I had to spend my every waking moment going through papers, making assignments for the team to document the test results and observations properly, reviewing the findings, writing the required report, and so on. We made the deadline to give the client proof of compliance for a large federal contract, so the client is happy. However, now I need to reassess the timeliness and thoroughness of our project reviews my directors conduct.

I went home from those long days of work and little sleep, took a shower and fell into bed. My eyes popped open at four this morning with the memory of your email surfacing in my brain. I read all of it and after comprehending its full contents, I fear my delay was unkind to you. What you had to say about yourself and illustrated with your replays of team activities made me remember times in my career I would rather forget. However I like to think that each of us has always tried to do what is best for the greater good -- in my case, the company and its clients, and in yours, the FBI, the law and the victims of the crimes committed.

You called me guileless. Oh Steve, I have guile. You have seen only part of my persona. I am that person. However, I have other sides too, some of which are less attractive. Ivy Littleton has been a corporate career executive. Corporations have their politics in the same way that the Bureau does. Sometimes I had to take on tasks concerning employees that I would rather not have done. Even though it benefitted the Company, an employee might have been fired, suffered the ignominy of a demotion or slunk out of the building for good because of me. While I never acted without the conviction that it was good for the Company, I wonder what right I had to play judge and to take away a person's livelihood.

You talked about over-challenging agents on your teams. I am not always nice to my staff. I give them a lot of latitude when maybe I should be there as their safety net. Sometimes I want to make a point on their performance; more often I want to see if they had the strength of character to stand up to me. If employees can survive these tests, I can be supportive, even mentoring, but it can be hell for them to gain my confidence.

I can be tough with clients if they demand more than they contracted for, without paying more. I can be harsh with service providers and vendors if they do not perform. No Steve, all too often in business I am not a nice person. How different am I from you? You fight for real causes; at best I have fought to keep a company solvent, people employed and our clients satisfied. Will you still want to see me, now that you see that I have a flawed side in addition to my sometimes hot temper?

I believe that you acted in the best interests of our country, our citizens and your teams as a whole. What was required in the line of duty, I could never hold against you. If anything, I am attracted to you more for your concerns, for wanting to be open with me, and for being the man of character that you are.

I feel shabbier for having revealed parts of my career and myself that do not sit well with me, but you have been so open that I am compelled to be the same. Now I will say what you said to me. Call me on my personal cell, if you want to keep exploring what we started, knowing that Ivy Littleton is a somewhat tarnished version of Ivy Vine.

Ivy

After rereading her reply to Steve, Ivy reluctantly hit the Send button and pushed back from her laptop. She did not want to lose Steve. However he had to be aware of these aspects of her personality and character or he could find out at some later point and be disappointed by her lack of honesty about herself. For now, she would have to wait and hope.

***

The next morning in Sofia, equipped with a hidden wireless microphone that would transmit to Lenny, Steve confirmed that the first third of the million-dollar payment had been wired to the required account. He then met Mathew and Brian (aka Ms. London) in the lobby just before one. He and Mathew carried locally-supplied Glock handguns; Brian had only a small plastic Smith & Wesson hidden in the purse he carried, buried at the bottom under a comb, wallet, lipstick and other paraphernalia that a woman might have. While they did not expect any weaponry to get past the perp's security, they had to try.

Security was a pat-down search by the perp they had dubbed Dragomir. The large hulking man had small black eyes, a square face and pock-marked skin. He checked each of them with his thick hands, removed their guns, and then pawed through their briefcases. When he reached Brian, Dragomir grabbed for Brian's purse to search it.

"No, please," Brian said quietly. The man looked up in surprise.

Brian ducked his head and stammered, "Wrong time of the month." Dragomir opened the purse anyway. It was tall, but too narrow and thin for a conventional weapon, so much less suspect. He raked through the tampons Brian had tossed on top and shoved the makeup around, but didn't get down as far as the little Smith & Wesson lying on the bottom under a slim notebook.

Dragomir then escorted them to the conference room where they had met with Matka the day before. They were in an older two story building in a rundown section of Sofia. The business that operated there was ostensibly an employment agency. After a few minutes, Matka joined them. She had such a cold assurance about her that Steve wanted to backhand her across the face but he held his cool.

"You have the first third of the money," he growled without preamble, having decided to play the pit bull, which was a frequent role for him.

"Yes. It arrived in our account," Matka's English was precise, although it carried a noticeable Slavic accent. She was a stout woman of medium height, dressed expensively with a showy Gucci scarf arranged around her neck, and wearing a plethora of hefty gold jewelry. Her makeup was equally heavy. Her hair was medium length, streaked with silver and pulled back with a bejeweled thick barrette. In an Eastern European way, she had the appearance of a successful executive from the retail industry.

"Let's see the goods." Steve responded impatiently. "We have a plane to catch."

Matka nodded at Dragomir who led them to an elevator. She followed them. They rode down and emerged into a basement lit by harsh fluorescent bulbs. In the bleakly bright room were six barred cells. Each one contained four to six children. Steve estimated that they varied in age from five to fifteen. While most were girls, two cells held boys. He noticed that they were all silent and withdrawn, likely from drugs. Where he could see their eyes, each one was terrified. Steve clenched his jaw, thinking that they should be in school or playing at home, not locked in sunless cells waiting for horrid fates.

He slid his eyes to Mathew and Brian, checking that they kept their faces serious and showed no horror or sympathy. He had drilled them well. Their faces were impassive. Steve then spoke the code words into the microphone that would signal Lenny and the arrest team to make their way inside in silence and alert Mathew and Brian that things were about to grow hot. "We will make our choices."

The three of them walked past the cells where the children watched, cowed and fearful. It was a struggle for the three agents to keep their emotions off of their own faces. As they walked back, the elevator door slid closed and the elevator motor ran, startling Matka and Dragomir. Steve slid his eyes left and right to Brian and Mathew, and then lunged for Matka. Mathew lurched forward to overcome Dragomir who swiftly pointed his gun at Mathew. Brian leapt through the air at Dragomir, throwing himself between the gun and Mathew. The gun went off, hitting Brian in the leg. Mathew wrestled the gun away from Dragomir, pinning his arms behind him. From the floor where he knelt, Brian pointed his small gun from one perp to the other, ignoring the blood running from the wound in his thigh.

Footsteps clattered down the stairs. The backup team burst into the room with Lenny in the lead, submachine gun in hand. Steve's eyes swept over the children, who had taken whatever cover they could. Most were cowering near or under the cots in their cells, making him glad the shooting had not been worse. He stood with Matka's left arm bent up behind her back and his arm wrapped around her neck until he could turn her over to Lenny. Then he knelt down by Brian, whipping off his own tie and using it as a tourniquet around Brian's leg. He yelled for a medic. Mathew shoved Dragomir over to be cuffed, and then searched him for keys to the cells. The two perps stood by the elevators in handcuffs with agents on either side. They would be taken to squad cars parked outside.

"Go with them," Steve pointed to two of the agents. "Call the legats. You know the drill on questioning."

Two medics rushed in and took over Brian. They were surprised to find him talking like a man dressed the way he was. Steve explained the impersonation to them in a couple of terse sentences, then he pulled out his cell phone, dialed and ordered the jet they had on standby to be ready for departure in an hour for Bern, getting a little heated when he met resistance about flying on such short notice. He hung up and sent another agent to pick up their suitcases at the hotel.

"Mathew, handle things here. Do a quick search for where the kids were sent in the past. Then get the files and computer equipment inventoried and packed for shipment. I'll send the jet back here right after we land. I want that stuff transported to the Bureau office in Bern with as much of our team as you judge are not needed here. If you find any locations where the other kids were sent in the U.S., send them to Moll right away so he can start coordinating the takeover of the brothels and rescuing those children. Any in other countries will go to the legats in Bern for coordination. Also see if you can find any backup media on-site or where they might have backed data up offsite so we can access an audit trail of past events."

"You got it. See you in Bern."

"Hard to believe that these kids are the lucky ones." He nodded towards the children in the cells.

A large team of social services workers led by two FBI legats came in. Steve noticed how shocked their faces were when they saw the children incarcerated in cells. Nonetheless they quickly recovered and worked out a procedure to take the children a cell at a time. They would then do the research needed to move them back to their families or into foster care. Two FBI legats would oversee that aspect of the operation. Lenny came back down after ensuring that Matka and Dragomir were cuffed, in a squad car and on their way to be held for trial.

"Lenny you fly with me, Brian and a medic to Bern. From there, I'll dispatch you to the nearest city where we have to free more children."

Lenny sadly regarded the rescued youngsters as the first group filed submissively out of a cell, following a social worker. He gripped his submachine gun resolutely and said gruffly, "Send me to every site you find. No kid should go through this."

All those weeks of planning, all those scenarios Steve had the team practice, all the technology, the agents, and the local arrest team, worked out. Nothing ever went 100% according to plan. This operation came close and their impromptu actions were flawless. Even though he wished Brian had not

70

been shot, Steve was satisfied with the results. Unless something absurd happened in court, Matka would serve her life out in Bulgaria's penal system. As part of the deal that the FBI legats had negotiated with the Bulgarian authorities, Matka's assets would be seized and ultimately directed to local children's programs. The third of the million wired that morning would be returned to the Bureau.

With the arrests made and following their plan, Mathew organized the on-site work effort to do quick scans for leads and then called Moll to be on standby in the New York office to organize local FBI and police teams for raids of the child prostitution centers. They had to act fast so that the local perps would not relocate the children before the FBI teams could shut them down and rescue the children. They also had a team standing by to take phone calls and respond to emails that came in to Matka so that the communications would stay intact, giving them a longer window of time.

Mathew and two other agents flew to Bern that night, joining Steve at the FBI office where they would methodically comb through the computer systems and archive tapes searching for additional information. They distributed copies to agents in New York and Washington to hasten the analysis work. Lenny flew out to join the local shut down teams as if he were a jet-setting action hero. Another team reporting to Mathew would track and arrest the so-called recruiters who stole children from their homes.

Steve stayed with the team in Bern, working around the clock to force fast action on having the brothels shut down, arrests made and children in the hands of social services, using the leverage of his position at the Bureau to gain local cooperation, both within the FBI and with local police forces and governments.

On the following Monday in Bern, Steve had the FBI team assemble in Brian's hospital room where he was recovering from surgery. Working quickly, Steve set up the FBI equivalent of a Skype station on his laptop and hooked it to the TV screen in the hospital room. He had cameras and microphones pointed towards Brian and himself. He was on his cell talking, and then the Director of the FBI appeared on the screen.

"Special Agent Tovey, we are here today to recognize your achievements with the FBI and to honor you for your recent performance in a critical case during an operation in Sofia."

Brian's surprise showed on his face as he scrambled to push himself up straighter in the bed, wincing when he moved his hurt leg. Steve adjusted the camera and microphone, then nodded to Brian to respond.

"It was a team effort, sir. I only did what was necessary in the line of duty."

"That is not what I hear from Special Director Nielsen. Agents often put their lives on the line in the call of duty. You also had to put your reputation on the line. Nielsen, would you elaborate?"

"Yes, sir. Not only did Special Agent Tovey perform his impersonation superbly, as required for this sting and under very adverse conditions, he also had the courage to take a bullet for a fellow agent. Only a courageous man and outstanding agent would perform either one of those valiant acts. Brian Tovey did both during the most important humanitarian sting I have been on."

Steve opened a box and held it towards the camera.

The Director continued, "I find it an honor to present Special Agent Tovey with the FBI Medal of Valor. Usually we make these presentations in Washington, however given your injury, we decided to advance the timing. Agent Tovey when you are able to travel, please come to Washington and get on my calendar. I would like to talk with you in person.

"For the rest of the team, thank you for your many contributions to the FBI and in particular for bringing this case to conclusion. You should take pride in knowing you resolved a critical humanitarian case."

Steve handed the medal to Brian who appeared dumbfounded by the award. Mathew found himself smiling during this presentation. The FBI has four of these types of medals, which are highly prized when awarded. Steve glanced over at him and he nodded his approval. All too often Steve was impervious to what he asked of agents, yet today he found a way to make every agent in the room feel it was worth it.

Mathew noticed that the other agents treated Brian with more respect. No one made jokes about his masculinity or his impersonation. Receiving the award awed Brian, and yet he remained the unassuming man he had always been. Maybe that sting made him more confident in who he was. Mathew discerned that the public recognition contributed, as did the knowledge that he had the courage to save his best friend.

They continued working with local authorities in the U.S. and in other western countries to shut down the brothels and start to rehabilitate the children, although they wondered how a kid finds any kind of life after the kind of experience those children went through. During this time, Steve was often impatient, pacing around, responding snappishly and acting preoccupied, even though he was determined to see it through. Mathew could tell that he was eager to fly back to Frankfurt, pick up his personal cell phone and hear Ivy's reaction to his email. A couple of times Steve tried to break away and fly out, however some new communication or finding would keep him in Bern. Rescuing those kids still trapped in their hellish lives kept him going. Besides as long as his personal cell phone stayed untouched, he still could hope that Ivy had called him. Mathew regarded him with new admiration. He was glad to see Steve wanted to be in a relationship based on truth and trust. He smiled to himself, thinking of Steve's worry about Ivy -- *at Spes non Francta*, but Hope is not Broken.

Chapter 7

Nearly two weeks had passed since Ivy emailed Steve and no call back had come from him. She was holding onto the hope that he was in the field and unreachable, yet she wondered if a sting took this long. In the movies they were always fast-paced with the agents in and out with lightning speed. How long would one of Steve's operations last? Would it have made a difference if she had responded to him the same day that he sent the email? As the days stretched out, she was increasingly worried that he would never call, fearing that he found the Ivy beneath the surface not what he expected.

How foolish she had been not to ask for a response one way or the other. He may have so romanticized her based on their limited contact, that what she revealed in her email might have tainted her in his eyes. If Ivy's life was bleak before she met Steve, how much more desolate it would be now if she had lost him. He set a new standard for her expectations of what a man could be. While they had known each other only a short time, she would have trouble finding another man to step into those big shoes of his. Even though she suspected that he had read her email and the truths it contained turned him off, Ivy still hoped he would call. She began to wonder if she should call his personal cell. She carried that thought with her to bed that Tuesday night of Thanksgiving week and fell into a fitful sleep.

Four hours later, Ivy's cell phone rang. She fumbled for the light and grabbed the phone out of her purse, clicking it on with a sleepy hello.

"Ivy, its S . . ." Line dead.

She dialed him back, hearing only a fast busy signal. Swinging her legs over the side of the bed, she glanced at the clock. Two a.m. -- she entered a quick text, hoping it would go through: "U CLLD? CALL or TXT ME." She waited. Nothing. She tried dialing again. Same fast busy. She was about to email Steve when the tone signaling a new text sounded on her cell: "TKNG

OFF. DP FF. U ME GD. CLL U SEATAC. YR BG." She sure hoped that meant "Taking Off. Departing Frankfurt. You and I are good. Call you from SeaTac. Your Big Guy." SeaTac -- Seattle! He was heading her way. She could feel herself smiling. Suddenly the tiredness that had been plaguing her was gone. She jumped up and twirled in a circle, picking up Druid as a dance partner. The corgis shook themselves awake and wriggled at her feet as she began sashaying down the hall and into the kitchen. Steve would be here in her house this afternoon!

Suddenly her mind was racing with things she had to do before he arrived. Luckily the housecleaners were scheduled for the coming morning. She would have to leave work early and stock up the house with groceries. She went to her wine closet to check her inventory, noting that she should pick up a bottle or two of champagne. Her first order of business was to make a couple of lists – things to get done and all the food and munchies for the long weekend. She decided to make a reservation at the coast for two nights. It would be rainy and windswept, but even so the Oregon coast was irresistibly romantic. All through these thoughts, her heart kept humming – Steve is on his way, he still likes me, he wants me!

***

Steve flew from Frankfurt directly to Seattle, calling Ivy at work as the plane taxied to the gate. He cleared immigration and customs, checked case progress with Mathew and ran for the next flight to Portland, texting the flight number to Ivy as he scrunched himself into the small seat on the shuttle flight, sitting with both legs stuck out in the aisle. Although he had slept for a time on the plane out of Frankfurt, the long weeks on the case had worn Steve out. Even so, his heart buzzed with triumph that he and Ivy had survived their first crisis. He needed the comfort of her calm assurance, he wanted to watch her smile at him and he longed to have her soft yet strong body near him. These cravings for another person were new to him and the dependency made him uneasy, but Steve recognized if he failed to forge ahead with this stimulating woman, he might not have another chance at a broader life.

As soon as Steve called her from Seattle, Ivy scooted out of the office, did an accelerated shopping trip for a full turkey dinner and then zoomed out to the airport to pick him up, weaving through side streets to avoid the backed up holiday traffic on Interstate 84. How wonderful their reunion was when she ran towards him the moment he rounded the turn into the airport walkway where she was waiting. He dropped his bags and engulfed her in his embrace. They stood, hugging and kissing, oblivious to the crowd of holiday travelers pushing their way around them.

After battling the traffic on the drive back to her house, Ivy was in the kitchen putting away groceries. While she was worried that the long weekend could be a disaster if they realized they had nothing in common, the airport greeting was a good start. Hopefully the magical evening and breakfast they shared a few weeks ago marked the beginning of a promising relationship. While she pushed things around in the fridge to make room for the turkey, Steve was out in the living room, coaxing some logs in the fireplace into a steady flame.

"Ivy, Ivy, Ivy," he whispered coming into the kitchen. He pulled her into a big hug, stepped back, gazed at her intensely, and then kissed her so tenderly and so long, that Ivy thought her heart would burst.

"Oh God, holding you is like coming home. You feel fantastic in my arms. My Ivy Vine." He bent down again and nuzzled her neck.

"Steve, I am so glad you made it here."

"You smell wonderful, like baking spices and yet like you too," he whispered in her ear.

He kissed her again, this time more deeply, pulling back reluctantly and leaving her wanting more.

"Why don't you show me around?" he asked. Cleo and Harry followed them as they moved to the front of the house. The two corgis had given him an excited greeting and inspection, trying to figure out who he was and why he was in their house. Steve poked his head in Ivy's office by the entry foyer and then tried out the easy chair in the little library nook off the hall. He checked the bookcase, his hands lingering on the spines of books as if they were treasures. From there, they stopped in the open dining room to pick up glasses of pinot noir.

Opening the door to the little upper deck off the living room, he checked out the distant lights in the misted view, the driveway below and the pots of herbs, smiling when he turned back to her. The house was built into the hillside with the living space on the upper floor which was street level. The downstairs was for the garage and the guest rooms.

The kitchen had a thorough going over as he poked through what she had bought to cook that evening. They walked through a small den that was open to the kitchen where he went out to the larger deck and checked the views in all directions. Down below was the backyard, its walkways dotted with white winter pansies in pots. Steve was quiet, only sometimes asking a question or making a comment.

"Are you always this thorough?" Ivy asked, as he nosed around the big pantry and the laundry room.

"Have to be." Steve stopped then and glanced at her as if realizing that a man on a date usually behaves differently.

"I should explain. First I am curious. I want to see where you live, so that when I'm not here, I can picture it in my mind's eye. For instance, if you say that you are curled up with a book, I'll know what that chair in the library area is like."

"And second?"

"You know that I deal with high impact cases against big-time bad guys. One of them could come after me. While that has never happened, procedure dictates that I have to be prepared. Most importantly, I don't want to endanger you by not being familiar with the layout of your house."

"That's comforting," Ivy said drily. "I suppose you want to see the bedrooms too."

He arched an eyebrow at her, making her blush. She led him down the hall to her master bedroom, letting him step into the room first while she watched him from the doorway. Suddenly Ivy was a bit leery of this big man prowling around her house. After all how well did she really know him? Steve peered out the windows and then stared at her big bed with its curving metal frame.

"Ivy leaves," he muttered. "Her bed is decorated with twining ivy leaves and vines."

His color rose as he realized he had spoken aloud. They each took a big sip from their wine glasses and headed downstairs where the guest rooms were. He checked the window locks and then stood quietly with Ivy while the corgis took a break in the fenced yard.

"They from the same litter?"

"No. If you look close, you will see they are really quite different in markings, body shapes and personalities, however both have big corgi hearts."

Ivy whistled for the dogs, clapped her hands and watched them as they flew past in that romping way corgis have, ready for their dinners. Steve and Ivy sipped wine, ate crab cake appetizers by the fire and talked while she cooked. Steve assigned himself to cleanup and had things rinsed and in the dishwasher almost before they hit the sink. When Ivy could, she glanced over at him and realized that he appeared more tired than the last time she had seen him. She noticed that Steve only sipped a little wine and she asked if the pinot was okay.

"Wonderful. Soft and delicate. Full too. Rather like you, it deserves to be savored." He would have liked to have winked, but it was a skill he had never mastered, so he just gave Ivy a subtle smile. He found it endearing that she blushed a little at the compliment.

"Besides Ivy, I am really tired and I don't want the wine to put me to sleep, so I'm pacing myself."

At their dinner in the open dining room, Steve ate everything Ivy had prepared for him and then finished her salmon and sautéed potatoes too. After a tossed salad of local organic greens, Ivy suggested that they poke up the fire and have dessert in the living room. Steve had two helpings and then sat back, eyeing the rest of the tart. He sighed, pulled Ivy closer to him, and they reclined together, cuddling close without talking. Ivy felt warm and safe in Steve's arms and her earlier concerns drifted away. The evening was turning out as she had hoped. She snuggled closer to him, only to realize that he was asleep with his arm lying heavily over her waist. Her seductive powers were simply not working that night.

She had a bed made up for him downstairs where he could sleep his cares away. She tried to rally him. He woke up, snuggled and kissed her sleepily, then mumbled. "Need hotel. Call car." and he fell asleep again. She managed to pull him to his feet in a semi-conscious state. Moving him was difficult and Ivy knew she would never get him down the stairs to the guest room. They stumbled along the hall and he flopped on her bed. Ivy tugged his shoes off and then with some half-conscious help from him, wrestled him out of his suit, shirt and socks and into bed, pulling the covers over him. That was it -- he was gone into a deep sleep. She hung up his clothes, set the house alarm, put on a lacey nightie, grabbed her robe and went downstairs to sleep in the guest room.

The next morning at about eight, after having the dogs out for their morning walk, Ivy came back into the house. The master shower was running, so she went to brew fresh coffee. Within a few minutes, Steve came out, hair still wet, dressed in a crisp white shirt and suit pants. He gave her a lingering kiss and asked where she had slept.

"You missed a glorious night," Ivy teased him. "I slept in my bed and took full advantage of you."

His jaw dropped in surprise. "You're kidding, right?"

"You'll never really be sure, will you?"

"That was the best and longest night's sleep I've had in years. Usually no matter how tired I am, six hours is my limit. Most of the time I only get four. Did I dream it or did we eat a wonderful pear tart in front of the fire?"

He began snooping around in the kitchen. She moved to pour him coffee.

"When does the turkey go in?"

"Let me get breakfast done and then I can worry about the turkey."

"I thought I might mix up some bloody marys or mimosas or something and we could watch the Thanksgiving Day parade on TV."

"Mimosa for me. Sounds like a plan. We have no schedule today, except relaxing and getting to know each other."

"Now that is a plan!"

They spent the day bundled by the TV in a little den off the kitchen that Ivy called the cozy room with its big windows and warm gas fireplace. Sometimes they would be in the kitchen cooking or pulling on raincoats to walk the dogs. Steve admired their holiday feast when it was ready late that afternoon and ate more turkey, stuffing, mashed potatoes and gravy than Ivy thought one person could hold. After dinner, they took their wine in by the fire and cuddled, this time more passionately until Steve pulled back.

"Sorry Ivy, I'm moving too fast. One step at a time."

"It's okay."

"No, it's not. We are not going to rush this. Besides I am so full of turkey that I can barely move. Let's cuddle and take this slowly."

Even though Ivy was mystified by Steve's pulling back, she curved herself around him, willing for that night to follow his slow lead. This time he slept in the guest room where he had moved his luggage and she crawled alone into her own bed. The next morning he woke her up by slipping into her bed, freshly showered, pulling her close and smiling at her.

"This morning I'm taking my best woman, heck my only woman, out to breakfast at that place she took me to last time and then she is going to spend the day showing me this great city of hers."

"She is, is she?"

He nodded. Ivy noticed that his eyes were warm with anticipation. While Ivy showered and dressed, Steve made coffee and then took the corgis out for a morning walk. As independent as she was, Ivy found she liked the way he made himself useful. Ivy drove them down to the restaurant called Mother's where she had their scrumptious Eggs Benedict and Steve had a large order of buttermilk pancakes with thick marionberry syrup, along with apple pork sausages.

As they sat holding hands and finishing their lattes, Steve surveyed the room and leaned closer to her. "I'm the only suit in here -- no problem finding the federal agent in this picture. Ivy, you have to take me shopping and dress me like a Northwest native."

A couple of hours later after stops at Patagonia, REI and Nordstrom, Steve was laden with packages and dressed like a newly minted Portland arrival. He had been putting things on as he bought them -- striped turtleneck and jeans that miraculously fit his long legs, navy fleece vest and windbreaker, and low hiking boots and socks. In the bags were corduroy pants, more socks, tee shirts, two fleece tops, two sweatshirts, a pair of sweatpants, a rain jacket, flannel pajamas, a wool Pendleton robe and sheepskin lined slippers.

"Will I pass?" he asked

"In about two years when everything is broken in and worn-looking."

"That means you have to give me at least two years."

Ivy smiled at him.

"And I hope longer. Oh jeez, slow down Nielsen." He turned away from her, shaking his head at himself.

As he wanted, that day they toured Portland. While it was wet and the mountains were hidden, Steve enjoyed the views of downtown from Council Crest where they took the dogs for a walk. From there, they drove up to the Pittock Mansion to see its annual Christmas display, thankful that the heavy rain kept the line short. After having cheeseburgers for a late lunch at the Heathman Pub, they rode the Max line around downtown and then took the aerial tram up to the teaching hospital of OHSU at dusk, watching the city lights come on as the short late autumn day ended. At that point, Steve seemed ready to return to Ivy's house. Once inside, he took his packages into the guest room and came back up, dressed like an overgrown kid in his new pajamas, robe and slippers.

Ivy fed the dogs and cat while Steve rebuilt the fire in the living room. As it started burning, he rose and pushed a couple of pieces of furniture out of the way to create a little dance floor. With the kindling now burning well, he added several bigger logs and put the screen in place, then with hopeful anticipation, he went over to the Bose stereo that Ivy had in the library nook, checked her CDs and chose one called "Saxy Love Songs" by Gary Scott, hoping it would set the mood he wanted. Once the music was softly playing, he went around the house, switching off lights, leaving only the glow of the fire and a light by the bed. Dinner could wait.

He tugged Ivy into the living room and held out his arms for her to dance with him. They danced slowly to "The Very Thought of You", letting the music and the fire lull them towards each other. He stopped for a moment and tilted

81

up her chin, kissing her in that long slow way he had decided was the only way to kiss Ivy, who was a gift to be treasured. She moved closer to him, letting her hips move gently against his in a way he found subtly suggestive. Slowly he began to undress her, discarding one piece of clothing at a time and gently kissing and caressing the delicacy of her soft skin. After waltzing her closer to the fire so she would not become chilly, he concentrated on a few special places, like the hollow between her collarbones, the inside of her elbow and the soft palm of her hand, wanting to arouse her without being too direct. At their points in life, they should savor each other. The fast passion of youth was behind them. They could take the time to discover each other with slow lovemaking.

Ivy followed Steve's lead, enjoying his gentle approach. He began humming softly to the music with Stardust now playing as she began to undress him, laying each piece of clothing on a chair before turning back to slide her hands down the long muscles of his arms, then his back, and his chest. She let her hands play lightly on a couple of scars he had, one on the upper arm and one along his right leg. He was so aroused that she struggled to keep to his slow pace. While she yearned to have him inside of her, she also wanted this first time together to be a memory they would recall and cherish during their days or weeks of separation ahead.

When they were both fully undressed, they circled around in a slow waltz until Ivy led Steve out of the living room. He shielded her with his body as they passed the windows that opened onto the view south, folding himself around her. Once in the bedroom, he opened a couple of windows just a little, letting the plantation shutters block any direct breezes and then joined Ivy in bed, continuing his gentle caressing, until he eased her over on top of him wanting to see her lovely, expressive face as their bodies merged.

When he began to enter her, she flinched with pain. He pulled back, reached up and gently caressed both sides of her neck, letting his hands rest on her shoulders.

Embarrassed, Ivy ducked her head and mumbled, "Been a long time."

"We'll take it slow. Long time for me too."

"Born Again Virgins," she scoffed, her smile returning.

82

Steve laughed. As Ivy gently pushed down, little by little, Steve found the sensation exquisite. The pressure inside her eased and she slid down against him throwing her head back in sensual triumph.

"Oh Ivy," Steve said, stroking her thighs where they pressed against him.

Ivy found Steve to be the gentlest man she had ever made love with and yet he brought out a level of passion in her that was new and unsullied. She loved the strength in his shoulders when she leaned forward to embrace him, tracing the muscles down his arms. They kept things slow and easy, appreciating each other, until their passion overcame them, leaving them breathless with its intensity. When he cradled her head against his chest before drifting off to sleep, she realized a missing part of her had been restored, taking its spot in her heart. She pressed her lips against his chest, let her eyes drift shut and nodded off as well.

A couple of hours later, she woke up to hear Steve rummaging in the kitchen and went out to see him slicing the leftover turkey. On a cutting board next to him, he neatly laid out slices of bread spread with mayo on one side and cranberry sauce on the other. Ivy took out some lettuce and prepped it to go on the mayo side. They took the late dinner back to bed, feeding each other bits of turkey that escaped from the sandwiches and drinking big glasses of milk before sinking back down into the covers and into each other's arms.

***

That night Steve found himself awake at 2:00 a.m. Trying not to disturb Ivy, he slipped out of bed and slid on his new robe. The corgis followed him to the kitchen where Steve rewarded them with biscuits before pouring himself another glass of cold milk. Despite the joy that Ivy gave him, his nerves remained jangled. In his mind, he still saw the faces of those children in the cells. The photos of the abused adolescents from more than a dozen brothels they had shut down thus far haunted his waking and sleeping hours. They had moved over a hundred and fifty children and teens into social services organizations in eight countries including in seven cities in the United States.

Moving quietly, he rebuilt the fire. Since the coals still glowed, he added some kindling, blew on it a few times, watched the wood spark to life, and then stacked on smaller logs. He pulled over an ottoman and sat, staring at the dancing flames and thinking about those captive kids and the terror in their drugged eyes. This was his first case involving children. Most of his cases had been against major drug lords, mob leaders, or underground fraudsters. Rarely did he deal with ordinary citizens and never with children.

Sitting alone with his thoughts, tears started trickling down his cheeks, not something that had happened since he lost his parents. He heard Ivy come up behind him with her slippers scuffing across the hardwood floor. She sat down next to him on the corner of the big ottoman, put her arms around him and rested her head on his shoulder, not asking questions, just being there. They sat that way for some minutes until Steve wiped away his tears, got up and put a bigger log on the fire.

"Tell me," Ivy breathed out the words against his back, once he sat back down.

He glanced over his shoulder at her, then back at the fire. "It started during that trip to L.A. The teenage girls we interviewed from the house that was raided were so hard and so evasive. The truth is I don't usually work with victims. Generally we go after the crooks who do money laundering, have large drug rings, defraud major companies, or even smuggle jewels. This case was unusual in that we saw and talked with the abused children. It got to me."

Ivy tightened her grip around him.

"Then there was the whole thing with our agent, Trina, imploding during our case preparation because I pushed her too hard, not knowing that she had been sexually abused as a child. I mentioned that in my email."

Ivy nodded against his back. She relaxed her grip on him and turned him to look at her, placing her hands on his shoulders.

"And then Brian. Shit, I didn't know he had been harassed by the other agents about being too . . . well, too girlie. You know how he has that slight build. I required that he masquerade as a female executive in our sting after Trina broke down. Mathew told me it was Brian's worst nightmare. The whole operation was just one emotional issue after another."

"And the sting itself?"

"Went well, but those children -- the ones we found in Sofia. Oh Ivy, it was so awful. They were in cells. They had been stolen from their families and were in that holding area waiting for appalling fates. Even though they were drugged, the kids were terrified."

Ivy pulled him towards her, trying to take some of his pain away. He found he was crying again. She held him until he stopped.

"Ivy I never cry like this. Cases don't impact me in that way. Not until this one."

"You've opened yourself up a bit by letting me in. Other barriers you put up may be starting to come down too."

He nodded, yet he remained uncertain how to deal with the jumble of painful emotions. Then he pushed himself up, tended the fire and held out his hand to Ivy. Together they walked down the hall and slid back into bed. Ivy turned to face him, gathering him in her arms. He snuggled into her warmth, burying his face in her hair, glad to have her close as she gently rubbed his back. Sooner than he expected, he found himself relaxing into sleep.

***

Around seven the next morning, Ivy slipped out of bed, gave the dogs a quick outing in the yard, showered, and made apple cranberry muffins with a walnut crumb topping. The weekend was different from what she had expected, but in its own way, it was simply idyllic -- fresh, warm, exciting, and passionate, yet comfortable too. Steve appreciated everything, the way a person does when their senses have opened and life is rushing in full throttle. Seeing Steve so overcome with emotion the night before helped allay her concerns about his harder side. Ivy found herself both calmed and re-energized by him as the new day softly sparkled around the house.

By mid-morning when they left for the north coast of Oregon, Steve seemed more settled emotionally. He and Ivy talked further about the child trafficking case as she drove and he found that leaning on her helped him to deal with the horror of the enslaved children. Ivy headed due west on Highway 26 before turning south on the coastal highway. They had an early lunch at a little place in Cannon Beach and then battled their way through sluicing rain and battering wind, driving down Highway 101 to the scenic Salishan Lodge on the central part of the coast. Even with the heavy late autumn rain, Steve found himself drawn to the coast with its rocky shoreline, sudden sandy beaches, curves of cliffs and giant rocks rising out of the water. The more he saw of the Northwest, the more he felt as if he had come home.

With the wet weather, their drive had been slow down to the Lodge and both of them were glad to make it to their spacious room, finding it welcoming with its casual furniture, stone fireplace and warm interior. The Lodge impressed Steve with its quiet setting in the woods overlooking the peaceful Siletz Bay. He liked the layout of the sprawling grounds where they could walk from their room to the Lodge without becoming wet by following the covered walkways. When the rain turned to fog late that afternoon, they strolled along the golf course, veering off onto a rustic path through the woods and coming out to cross a bridge over a pond before trekking on the golf cart path back up to their room.

While they walked, Steve found himself stopping to examine the different varieties of moss, or to crouch down to check out some late mushrooms or simply to inhale the fresh air, bright with oxygen and scented with cedar and spruce. Each new aspect he discovered in the Northwest drew him to its magic, except maybe those big banana slugs. He had greased a few of those under his big feet, as he slopped along though the mud and leaves. Up ahead, Ivy was giving the corgis a boost over a tree that had fallen on the trail. He stopped, realizing that his life was like a physical book. The front cover had been his childhood and formative years. The pages thus far had been his career. He wanted Ivy to help him write the remaining pages -- their future. He jogged a few steps to catch up, took her in his arms and kissed her, hoping that she saw him in her future too.

As they continued on, Ivy pointed out a big old stump amidst tall, younger trees. The stump was massive, soaring up about twelve feet and was nearly six feet in diameter. Ferns and a shrub she called salal grew at the base, while some plush green moss crept up here and there. Small bushes sprouted out of the top, nourished by the slowly decaying wood. Ivy told him the old trees as living specimens were rare now and were referred to as "old growth". This stump was a majestic remnant of the forest as it had once been.

Steve walked forward and put his hand on the big stump's silvered surface, feeling the smooth wood where the bark had peeled off decades ago. He moved around the old tree, trying to not tramp on the ferns. The term "Old Growth" reminded him of himself and the changes he was going through. When he came back to where Ivy was waiting, he thought of the two of them in terms of nature. He was solid and at times immoveable resembling the hard stump and true to her namesake, she was more flexible wrapping around his heart like curling twine. Together they might be called Old Growth and Ivy. He had read that ivy growing in the wild could become invasive, choking trees and plants, but as far as he was concerned, Ivy could wrap herself around him as much as she wanted.

On Sunday morning, Ivy took Steve out on the long spit that separated the ocean from the Siletz Bay. The waves were enormous and pounding the beach hard, leaving only a narrow strip of dark sand next to the grassy dunes for walking as the tide came in. While he stood staring at the waves, Steve noticed that the tops were capped with white foam, so thick it was almost like a whipped icing. When the wave peaked into the wind, the foam was pushed back, streaming out behind the wave like a white fluffy scarf.

Steve wanted to look for shells, but few survived the relentless pounding of the surf. They did gather a few small translucent agates and found one sizeable one that still had most of its white outer coating. Ivy explained how they were likely trapped in rock that washed down the river or eroded from cliffs, went out to sea and then were returned with the outer rock layer more or less worn off. Steve put them in his pocket, wanting to take these bits of the Oregon coast away with him as good luck charms to bring him back to Ivy. They walked back to the car along the quiet road that ran the length of the spit, chasing each other as they sloshed along in the rain and playing with the corgis who scooted around their feet prancing and wriggling with excitement.

From the beach they went to the Salishan Spa where Steve had booked a romantic couples massage. They were a little early and spent some time dangling their feet in the warm water of the spa pool, enjoying the motion of the jetted water and splashing each other with their feet in a way that was both playful and flirtatious. The room they went into at the spa had a fireplace with a quietly burning fire. During their massages, soft music played in the background, while the rain outside drummed its own soothing tune on the metal chimney cap. Afterward, they took hot cups of tea to the lounge area and watched the softly colored waterfowl cruising peacefully on the serene Siletz Bay, ducking down every now and then after some tasty morsel. While there, Steve talked about wanting to see more of the world. Ivy looked at him in surprise, knowing that he traveled most of the time.

"I want to see places as a tourist, not as an agent. You know -- go to the historic sites, take walks in the country, enjoy the food . . ."

Over the years, she had seen most American cities, but usually on business trips where she rushed in and out of town. Her vacations had been travel to spots where she could drop out for a time. "Even coming down here is refreshing, but I know what you mean with going to museums, buying fresh foods at village markets, and learning about the people and culture. Where do you want to go first?"

"Travel to Norway to learn about my heritage. Roam the English countryside. Drink aged malt scotch and wander the Highlands in Scotland. Learn how to slow down in Provence or Tuscany to savor the experience."

"See the rugged mountains in Patagonia."

"Island hop in the Galapagos. Buy a really good camera and take photos along the way."

Ivy smiled over at him, realizing that retirement with Steve, if things worked out between them, might become the best time of her life. Torn between the tranquility of the spa and wanting more intimacy, they soon dressed and departed for their lodge room to be close. The day had been one of tenderness and romance and Steve knew that he wanted Ivy full time in his life, even though he could not yet see how to make that happen.

On Monday it was raining hard again and they spent the morning in their room, reading, talking and packing.

"Steve, are you religious?"

He looked at her in surprise. While he had been baptized and raised in the church, religion had ceased to be a part of his life. "Guess I'm kind of a failed Lutheran. More of an agnostic."

88

"You want to hedge your bets, just in case the general populace is right about having a God to watch over us?"

"More like I just don't know. You?"

"Dyed in the wool atheist. Raised as an Episcopalian, but in high school the question was raised in a debate and I realized that the formal religious stuff did not make sense to me."

"No faith?"

"I have faith," she said, jutting out her chin and looking determined. "In myself, in some of mankind, in the beauty of nature."

"Independent wraith, aren't you?" He pulled her close. "Faith in me?"

Her face grew serious then, "Beginning to. Yes, but then," she said, kissing him lightly on the cheek. "I am foolish enough to hope there are angels."

Steve laughed, knowing he was no angel but he thought of himself as solid and trustworthy. As they loaded up and talked on the drive home, they found their views coincided on most topics, although sometimes they enjoyed debating their differences. They exchanged opinions on alternative lifestyles, on racism and other forms of prejudice, on politics and on their President.

"When I fly back tomorrow, I have to pick up the threads of a case against a major drug lord -- the one who made fools of us during a sting in Mexico. We're working this case with the DEA, but I have the lead on it. It was the damn DEA who got bad information on the perp that last time in Mexico. They claim to have a more solid lead this time around. At any rate, it will be some time until I can return, maybe not until after the holidays. The good news is that if we nab this perp, I can take time off to spend with you."

"How much danger will you be in when you go after the perp?"

"There will be agents all around me."

"That is not what I asked," Ivy said, using her firm business tone.

"Ivy, I am a federal agent. I go after major perps. There's always danger. However I have been doing this for more than 35 years and I'm still here. FBI actions are different than police cases. Our mortality rate is much lower."

"Like how low?"

"Less than sixty agents killed in the line of duty."

"Annually?" she asked.

"No, that is less than 60 agents killed <u>ever</u>. Check our website. Their names are listed there as an honorarium. My teams do everything possible to reduce risk. We stay fit and do target practice. We wear protective gear. We plan extensively. Often a SWAT team skilled in approaching explosive situations goes in ahead of us. We are careful and methodical. We do make a federal case out of it."

She had to smile at his little twist of humor and then reached over to squeeze his hand, wishing she had some extra-human power to give him to repel bullets. How had this man attached himself to her heart so quickly? Their long Thanksgiving weekend had her wondering how she could handle their sporadically developing relationship. She had such a deep passion for Steve. He was so tender, so loving, and so gentle that the desire came from deep inside of her to flow out to him. Never had lovemaking been like this for her. He was an unselfish lover, seeming happy to lead or be led, but Steve was much more than the passion. Ivy delighted in the warmth, the romance, the conversation, the emotional exhilaration and the plain fun of being with him. Tomorrow she would have to deal with his long absence and the worry. For these next hours, he was hers to enjoy.

His car came at four the next morning for his flight back to D.C. and to the drug lord case. He made no promises, except that he would be back, as soon and as often as he could.

"My Ivy Vine," he whispered, holding her in the front doorway while his driver took his suitcase to the car in the pre-morning light. "Can I trust falling this much in love this fast?"

She nodded against his shoulder, gripping him tighter, and whispered. "With me, you can."

"Then how are we going to handle these long separations?"

PART II

Chapter 8

Secure Email from Steve Nielsen November 30, 2012

Ivy my Ivy, staying with you, talking with you, making love with you is so heavenly, that compared to my regular life, it is as if I have changed galaxies, especially during times like these when the days on a case threaten to stretch out into weeks. Every time you turn, every time you speak, I discover something new about you. I may hear a different tone in your voice, or learn your point of view on a topic. I see even the smallest things about you, like the way your left eye crinkles a little more than your right when you smile. I take mental snapshots of each observation to imprint them in my memory and play them back when I dare to let my mind wander to you, which happens far more often than it should.

I am so torn now between my work for the Bureau and spending more time with you that I resent how my work will keep me away so much. This case we are concentrating on started when we traced a money laundering scheme that led us to a suspected drug ring. Sometime in the upcoming weeks, when we have enough intelligence to be effective, we will make our move.

Please believe me when I tell you that I want so much to be with you, especially over the holidays. I will break away if I can, but the stakes are high on this one. For my teams and me, they always are. We are working as much of the 24/7 schedule as our bodies can handle to position ourselves to nail these traffickers. Times like these, I feel as if my career has been in Dante's nine levels of hell, where, no matter how much we battle or how successful we are, we only are able to clean-up some anterooms.

Ivy, while we talk most days or nights and email and text, nothing replaces being with you. I miss seeing you. I miss touching you. I miss our banter and playful moments. Until I can be with you again, you will be in my heart. Yes, I know things are moving quickly between us in terms of hours spent together, but still in all, the word "us" has become very special to me -- I never appreciated that it could be.

Your loving Steve

***

Early the next day Steve and Mathew left for Houston to work out of the local FBI office with a team from the DEA. Steve had Brian and Moll handling follow-up on the child trafficking case where they would finish organizing the evidence and work with the legats on preparing the FBI's case against Matka and the other arrested perps, both domestically and internationally.

The DEA located a warehouse a few miles south of the international airport in Mexico City which they suspected housed one of Astuto's drug repackaging plants. At the site, they understood that the perps were taking in bales of cocaine from Colombia, then breaking them down into small packets for street distribution and boxing those up for shipment. Steve estimated that each 55-pound bale had a street price of $2.5 million, once it was cut and repackaged for sale. The warehouse could contain tens of millions of dollars' worth of cocaine, potentially making it one of the bigger busts in history. However he would only consider it a victory if they also apprehended the head of the drug ring.

Their limited knowledge of the physical layout of the building made planning the sting challenging. From the outside, it appeared to be a long, flat warehouse, with a loading dock and a small parking lot, all surrounded by a chain link fence. Using photogrammetry software with satellite and aerial photographs, FBI HQ derived the dimensions of the building. From the surveillance team's observations, they were aware that the operation ran over three shifts. In their understanding, El Zorro Astuto made unannounced trips to inspect the facility, arriving on any day at any time of day. The DEA claimed that their undercovers had recently sighted Astuto several times in Bogota, but he always managed to give them the slip when they went to follow him. They did have more success in tailing his pilot. For now, they were waiting for the DEA operatives in Colombia to receive word that Astuto's pilot had filed a flight plan from Bogota to the target city in Mexico. They would track the flight and prepare to catch Astuto at the cocaine-repackaging warehouse.

Additional agents were assigned to Steve in Houston from the local FBI office and the DEA, including the same leader from the DEA who they had dealt with on the last operation in Mexico. Having relied on bad DEA info once, Steve was suspicious of any insights brought forward by them that his FBI agents could not verify as factual. That weekend, they poured through the DEA case files on the drug operation in Mexico, its location, the estimated volumes of drugs, how the logistics worked to move the cocaine from Colombia to Mexico and from there, packaged now for street distribution, to various locales in the United States. They could have moved in to shut down the operation at any time, but Steve's goal was to catch this suspected El Zorro Astuto red-handed. He wanted a visit confirmed and then he wanted to apprehend him at the site.

On Monday Steve was waking up from his usual short night sleep when his cell phone rang. He checked the incoming number and saw it was the leader from the DEA.

"Yeah," he said, forcing himself to sound wide awake and a bit grouchy.

"The subject's plane just filed a flight plan to Mexico City." The DEA lead spoke in an overly aggressive tone as his defense about the mistake in Mexico.

"You're sure this time." Steve was careful to make it a statement to be refuted and not a question.

"His creds check out. You know we had the perp under observation for the last six weeks."

"And yet, all you know is that he calls himself 'Astuto'?"

"We've been all through this. Are you joining us or what?"

Steve was in a corner. If he did not go and Astuto showed, it would end his career in a very sour way. If he and his FBI team went and Astuto was again an actor, they would have egg on their face, however they would also have commandeered a warehouse with cocaine and shut the operation down.

"At the airport and in the Bubird at 04:00 hours," he said tersely, clicking off his phone. That gave him an hour to get the Bubird crew alerted, their flight plan activated and the plane warmed up. His team had just enough time to be armed, ready and on board. While the timing would be tight, they could do it.

He hit the speed dial key to alert Mathew and then they would each make a bevy of other calls.

Their flight landed in Mexico City well before dawn, giving them cover of darkness. Once they were taxiing on the runway, they confirmed that Astuto's plane had landed on schedule. They took a fast drive south from the airport to the cocaine repackaging plant. Fearful of a tipoff, Steve only alerted them about the actual sting when their cars pulled up near the site housing the suspected operation.

With the agents all packed into two vans, they stopped around the corner from the warehouse. Their undercover jogged over and confirmed that a limo had entered the site about five minutes before, carrying only a driver and one man. He was fairly certain there were less than ten people inside the target site but several would be armed.

Two Houston-based agents quickly and quietly overcame the gate guard who was left gagged and bound with the undercover. Steve then led the team at a run across the parking lot to a small side door. He stepped back to allow a skilled agent to blast open the door lock. Then Steve barged through and shot the first armed man he saw. Mathew flew by his right side, leading two agents. Shots started coming from several directions, including from above. Running across the warehouse, Mathew was taken down by shots to his left hip and thigh, spinning around and landing hard on his stomach. The two agents with him dove behind a worktable, leaving Mathew stranded on the warehouse floor. He started crawling crabwise towards cover dragging his damaged leg.

Steve fired his submachine gun upwards in an arcing motion aiming for the guards who unexpectedly patrolled a catwalk from 12 feet above that circled the warehouse. He kept shooting back and forth. Mathew managed to scrabble his way about five feet when another shot creased his forehead. He flattened himself on the floor. Steve ran over, still firing upwards, swinging his gun in a wide arc. With his left arm, he grabbed Mathew around the chest, and still firing, pulled him to cover behind a metal worktable that he upended to serve as a shield. He ripped off his tie and bound it around Mathew's upper thigh as a tourniquet, while yelling for a medic. Blood was streaming from Mathew's hip, which he was trying to staunch himself by pressing his hands against the wound. More blood dripped down from his eyebrow from where a bullet had skimmed under the edge of his helmet. A medic ran in and started to tend Mathew's wounds. One of the DEA agents had taken a bullet to his upper right arm. Luckily he was now behind cover. Steve jumped over to him, ripped the sleeve off his shirt and bound up the wound. He glanced around, assessing the situation. Another DEA agent lay sprawled on the floor. Steve was certain he was dead.

Steve jumped back out, blasting away with his weapon and took out the remaining guard on the catwalk, freeing up a couple of agents who had been pinned down behind a worktable. Shots rang out from the back of the warehouse where two agents slid down the wall behind some heavy racks of shelves to corner a pair of armed men.

For the next minute, shots kept ringing out and bullets were flying. Local forces arrived and the two remaining perps surrendered. The man they believed to be Astuto, four armed guards and one DEA agent were dead. Two agents were wounded, along with a worker hit in the crossfire. Steve's gaze swept the warehouse. Only one partial bale of cocaine was visible. He ran to the back of the building, checked behind some racking and a forklift. Aside from that bale, the place only contained packaging materials. Either they were expecting a big shipment that day or Astuto had been tipped off again. The DEA leader went through the pockets of the dead perp they believed to be Astuto. Again what surfaced was a passport for an American with the occupation of an actor. By phone he verified the dead man's identity, with a more detailed check to be run back in the office. Steve stopped and snapped a photo with his iPhone. Something about the dead actor was off. Steve leaned down and tugged at the mustache, which came off in his hand. None of passport photos that they had for the sham company officers in the money laundering scheme had mustaches. Apparently, this perp did not have one either. Was the heavy dark mustache on this actor a ploy to make him seem familiar to the guards or workers? Still, the dead man closely resembled the perp/actor on the yacht in Mexico, although his hairline was higher and he had a small cleft in his chin.

Again it appeared as if the DEA and the FBI had been setup. Did Astuto hire these actors to impersonate him and handle the inspections of his operations or had he learned that the warehouse would be hit and sacrificed the actor? Was the entire warehouse a sham setup? Outside of arranging the plane and alerting the other agencies at the last minute, no one should have been aware of their plans. That left certain possibilities, across the DEA, the Bureau and Border Patrol making Steve again wonder if they had a mole at the FBI or the DEA serving as an informant to the real El Astuto.

Madder than hell at being foiled, possibly by his own government's staff, he ran back to check on Mathew. The medic had stopped the worst of the bleeding and was giving him oxygen and fluids. After conferring with the medic, Steve pulled out his cell phone and forcefully gave commands to have the Bubird ready for a medical evacuation to D.C. Steve would have Mathew airlifted out for treatment along with the Washington-based DEA agent who had taken a bullet in the right arm. Given that the mission was again a failure, Steve decided to take the plane with the two wounded men and a medic, appointing the DEA leader to oversee the cleanup. The wounded worker would be treated locally, held and charged along with the others they captured. The agents would also stick around to try and nab anyone who showed up for the next shift.

The team had taken over what might or might not be a major drug re-packaging plant. The amount of coke at the facility was minimal. Even more, Steve wanted El Zorro Astuto either dead or alive. After that they could shut down his operations. As it was, two good agents had incapacitating wounds and one was dead. He was upset about Mathew whose injuries were serious. Steve worried that the best agent he ever worked with, and maybe the best man he knew, would never walk right again. Standing there as the medic worked on Mathew, Steve realized that he had become more of a son to him than his birth son from his misfit marriage had ever been. This was his time for him to be there for Mathew.

He thought then of Ivy and her concerns about his safety when they were last together. For the first time since his parents passed away, he had someone who worried about him. He had to watch out for her too. It was time to report the incidents of the tail in D.C. For now he would keep his suspicions about a mole at the Bureau or the DEA to himself. Someone was out to make them appear incompetent by laying false trails and offering up hired actors as bait.

The whole setup stunk, making Steve more determined to hunt this Astuto character down, no matter how long it took.

***

For Ivy, December started out bleak and lonely with no visits from Steve. With the dark, wet days of winter, the nights seemed long. She kept busy at home by decorating for Christmas, putting up her trees and bringing out the greens, candles and other wonders of the season she had collected over the years. She had fresh spruce wreaths on the doors decorated with red ribbon with gold backing that flipped merrily in the wind.

Her new replacement at work had been identified and would start on January 2nd, allowing Ivy to move to part-time and then become redundant. While this had been her choice, years of commitment made it hard to step away. Even so, despite the exhilaration from her times with Steve, she continued to feel worn out. She had to retire, regain her health and move on. Her phone began to ring.

"Steve?" Ivy said into the phone, seeing his cell number and lighting up inside.

"Ivy, I'm back in D.C."

"Can you come out?"

"Not right yet."

To Ivy, his voice sounded strained, "Is something wrong? Are you hurt?"

"No."

Ivy heard a long intake of breath.

"Mathew is. He took three bullets, one creased his forehead, one went into his hip, right below his protective vest, and chipped the bone. The third bullet tore up his thigh, shattering his left femur. Ivy, I can't leave him."

"Is he in a hospital in D.C.?"

"Airlifted him here. Haven't been able to reach his mother. She must be off on one of her travels. Mathew is conscious, but his leg, oh god, his leg. I'm so afraid he will never walk right again. He came out of his second surgery about an hour ago. I'm taking time off to be with him."

97

"Do you want me to come out?"

"This perp could turn vengeful. I don't want you close to us here; it might become dangerous, even in D.C." His voice carried a lacing of the menace he felt. "I was thinking of taking an apartment in Portland when Mathew can be transported there. That way I could take care of him and see you too."

After hearing how upset Steve was over the shooting, Ivy wanted to help him and Mathew. At least she could handle the local logistics. "Give me an idea of what you want to spend and I'll check out places in the Pearl District or downtown so you can be within walking distance of shops, restaurants and the Max line for rapid transit."

"Can I get a bus or something to your house?"

"Steve, do you really not drive?"

"I can, but I don't. While I have a license, unless I am totally absorbed in a high speed car chase, I get to thinking about something and oops, I'm a ticking time bomb behind the wheel."

"At least you're smart about it. No wonder you're a city boy. Once we have the location of the apartment, we can check bus schedules. They run at least hourly and stop a couple of blocks away from here."

"I'll arrange medical transport for Mathew. Don't worry about us getting out there, but I sure appreciate you screening the apartments. It'll need to be furnished. The Bureau will pay for this as a kind of safe house. Two bedrooms and a study, as I will work part-time from there. No stairs for Mathew – elevator okay. Also good security on the building. Month to month lease."

"I'll see what's out there."

"Ivy, it's possible that we could be followed. Which means . . ."

"I could be in danger. I figured that out already."

"So I have a request."

"Only one?"

Despite his serious mood, Steve had to chuckle. "Well, four actually. First, you have the security on your house reviewed. Second, you learn self-defense tactics. I can teach you or you can take a class."

"Okay on both." Those were steps she should take anyway, living alone the way she did.

"Three, you learn to shoot and carry a gun."

"No way."

"Then I will stay in D.C. and we will not risk seeing each other."

Ivy was silent for a long time. Steve waited, letting her think it through.

"I am not happy about it, however if you will help me learn to shoot and select a gun I can handle, then okay. You said four things and that is only three."

"If you sense danger, you call me or you call 911 or you drive to a police station – anything that will get you away from that danger."

"No problem, there." Ivy felt a chill go through her. "You live a whole different life, don't you?"

"So ordinary people can live their ordinary lives. That is what the FBI does. We work to keep things safe, or at least to keep the worst of the scum at bay."

"Okay Big Guy, I have some requests too. First if you spot anything, you will alert me."

"Second?"

"Say yes to the first one."

"Yes."

"Second if you leave town, you will tell me."

"Not going anywhere until Mathew is recovered."

"And lastly no bugs at my house. I can handle everything else, even having agents around, but I do not want the house bugged. I will not tolerate having anyone listen to private conversations."

"Yeah, got it."

Ivy jutted her chin out, making her vocal cords tighten as she spoke. "This is not negotiable."

Their conversation left Ivy concerned, exhilarated and apprehensive. Poor Mathew -- her heart went out to him. While she only had an impression of him from their meeting at the airport in October, Steve's high praise of him made Mathew seem more familiar than he was. He was badly injured and he lacked a family to care for him, with his mother too much into her own life even to stay in touch. Nonetheless how conflicted Ivy felt -- saddened by Mathew's injuries, apprehensive about the potential danger, excited by the prospect of seeing Steve more regularly. Living under a possible threat would be a change in lifestyle after all her years of independence. Ivy was not the most patient of women and was certainly a private one. On the positive side, this change would pull her head out of the office. She stared out into the rainy night at the lights on the hills beyond and nodded to herself. She could do this.

Should she invite them to her house? They could take over the downstairs where the two guest rooms were. While she would see much more of Steve that way, it seemed too soon. She needed time alone to deal with the upcoming transition at work, moving to part time and then retiring. It was too early in their relationship. She smiled then, pleased that Steve wanted to be in Portland and closer to her during this time.

***

The day before Steve and Mathew were due to arrive, a group of agents and technicians scheduled time to install a hospital bed and temporary security devices in the apartment Ivy had found in the Pearl District. It was a chilly, blustery day that threatened snow, although so far only a few fat flakes had come down. They did a walk-through of the apartment, drawing up a floor plans and noting access points for the building.

Ivy's life had taken such an unpredictably weird turn that she was unsure it would ever be the same again. Now as she waited for Steve and Mathew to be driven in from the airport, she wondered if that was what Steve had seen in her -- a potential refuge when he needed it. Was she a lonely older woman who was just plain gullible? Was Portland only a place for Steve to hide out from the perps the FBI hunted? Did she really appreciate who Steve was? While she had seen the FBI badge along with his gun and gear, her mind wandered into dangerously negative territory.

100

She walked down the hall, went into the bathroom and took a long, hard look at herself in the mirror. Doubts were crowding in around her, making her feel both vulnerable and more than a little foolish. Had she deluded herself into thinking that she was so special that Steve was falling in love with her? While she had never sensed any falseness in him, should she confront him and ask for the truth? She decided to wait until after Mathew was settled in.

That morning Ivy stocked the kitchen. Knowing that Steve was not a cook, she selected foods that would be easy to prepare, especially for breakfast and lunch. At home the night before she made a big beef stew, a meatloaf and a pot of chicken soup going for comfort food to suit the weather where snow was swirling around outside. Downtown Portland might receive a snowfall or two a year and this year several inches were forecast with this storm.

With the snow now coming down in earnest, Ivy worried about Steve and Mathew's safe arrival. Around noon, Steve called to say they had landed and were on their way. Silly though it seemed under the circumstances, Ivy went around the apartment turning on the Christmas lights she had brought from the Portland house. She put a little tree in Mathew's room to give it a holiday feeling and a larger tree in the living room, as well as some greens, candles and mini-lights here and there. She had baked an apple spice cake that morning and the apartment was scented with cloves and cinnamon.

Mathew, sandy-haired and pleasantly handsome, who Ivy remembered for his laughing eyes, was wheeled into the apartment from a big government Suburban. His haggard face showed his pain, though he clutched Ivy's hand with some strength as he went by, murmuring thanks. She stayed out of the way while Steve and the agents who drove them settled Mathew in. With more drugs pumped into him, he was quickly asleep.

After conferring with Steve, the agents did another inspection of the apartment and then departed. She noticed that they called him "Pete". With Mathew settled, Steve pulled Ivy close, thanking her again for her help. He took in the twinkling decorations and smiled a little. They made him realize that he would have to do Christmas shopping, something he had not done since he lost his parents.

Rather than put it off, Ivy decided to confront Steve.

"Who is Pete?"

"What?"

"You heard me."

"My alias. Guess I should have told you. Even the local agents don't know my real identity or Mathew's. They think we're witnesses to a crime and are in the Witness Protection Program. The Chief set it up."

"To hide you from the perp?"

"Yeah and from, never mind."

"Steve, tell me. Keeping me in the dark will only make me more anxious."

"I think we have a mole at the Bureau."

"Who is tipping off this perp?"

Steve nodded glumly.

"Why didn't you tell me this over the phone? Is that why those guys yesterday kept calling me Mindy?"

"You didn't correct them did you?"

"No. Why didn't they ask for ID?"

"I had emailed your photo. Told them you were a local contact arranging our personal logistics. Your full name is Mindy Madeline."

"You make that up?"

"Yeah. Same number of syllables. My full name is Pete Kampton and Mathew is Ivan Holden."

"Is the lease in that name and everything?"

Steve nodded. "Got all the ids too."

"Do I get phony ids?"

"No. I am trying to keep you untraceable."

"Steve, be honest with me. Is this why you pursued me? To have someone you could hide out with?"

He looked surprised and then sad. "Oh god Ivy. Nothing like that. You are NOT part of this FBI life. If that is what you think, then we shouldn't have

102

come out here. I so want to know you more. I spent the last week working to cover my tracks so that you would not be sucked into this."

Ivy stayed silent for a long time thinking over this conversation -- false identities, her alias, hiding from a mole at the Bureau, Steve trying to shield her from the perp. Steve waited. She noticed that for a man as demanding as he could be, he was surprisingly patient when she needed to think things over.

"How is this going to work? Do we act like friends and see each other now and then?"

"I sure hope not. I checked with the landlord and you can bring the dogs here if you want to spend the night. I paid an extra pet fee. When Mathew can move around, maybe we can come up to your place on weekends or I'll schedule a local agent to stay with him when we go out."

Ivy nodded. "Speaking of the dogs, I need to get them outside. How about I brave the snow now and go home?"

"You coming back?"

"You lighting that fire?" she asked, pointing to the gas fireplace.

"As soon as you're back and I have my woman here to cuddle. Hey, you have any board games or jigsaw puzzles? My parents and I always brought them out on snowy or rainy days."

Ivy laughed so hard that the sound of it filled the room. These twists in Steve's persona kept catching her off-guard. This consummate FBI agent wanted to play Scrabble?

"See you in an hour or so. Why don't you make some sandwiches? I stocked the kitchen. Do we have a secret knock or anything?"

"You make one up. I'll commit it to memory."

He pulled her up and for about ten minutes kept her wrapped in his embrace, kissing her until she was glowing with anticipation of spending the night with him. As she closed and locked the door to her SUV, Ivy wondered if she might be going through a pre-retirement crisis, throwing her lot in with this FBI agent and putting her safe, carefully constructed life in danger. These were not small-time risks she was taking. If things went awry, she could find herself playing in the good guy/bad guy big leagues.

Chapter 9

On Tuesday, Steve received a call from the Director of the FBI, asking him about Mathew and wanting to discuss the case against the drug lord. In Mathew's absence, Steve appointed a fully recovered Brian to head the investigation, putting Moll in charge of coordinating with the other departments which he did well, in spite of or maybe because of his offbeat personality.

As the days passed, Mathew made steady progress. With his bones knitting nicely around the pins in the shattered femur by the week before Christmas, he started to put a little weight on the damaged leg and went around the house with crutches, hoping soon to only use a cane. Steve set up a basic workout area in the living room for Mathew to do the exercises the thrice-weekly physical therapist would leave for him, using a resistance band in more ways than Steve thought possible.

On Friday evening of Christmas weekend, Ivy helped Steve get Mathew into her car and load up what they would need for a long weekend. She drove up to her house, taking a circuitous route for Mathew to see a few of the Christmas lights around the west side of the city, including the landmark martini glass on the side of one building. On Saturday Steve took the bus downtown for a long shopping trip, coming back so laden with shopping bags and packages that it took three trips to bring them in from the cab he used. Most of the packages were casual clothes for Mathew, however Steve bought a few surprise gifts for Ivy, including a lustrous pearl necklace from him and a matching set of pair of pearl earrings from Mathew. The pearls had been Mathew's idea and as soon as Steve saw the single strand of perfectly round pearls with a pale pink luster, he could picture them around Ivy's slender neck.

Back at the house, Ivy hung the three stockings she had rush ordered in personalized quilted velvet for Steve, Mathew and herself, each one hanging on the backs of their chairs in the dining room. On Christmas Eve, she would fill them and ensure that each one sported a big orange, a homemade gingerbread man and a candy cane sticking out of the top. Stockings hung, she then lugged brightly-wrapped and beribboned packages up from the project room downstairs and put them under the tree, including gifts for the Steve, Mathew, the corgis and the cat.

On Christmas Eve, Ivy surprised Steve by making food from his childhood -- a versatile Scandinavian pancake called Ebelskivers. The exact recipe and contents varied region by region in the Scandinavian countries. From Steve's evident delight, she had the gist of it right. Ivy cooked the little round pancakes in a special pan that held seven. She put on some Norwegian folk music she had found on CDs and had the two men sitting out by the fire while she brought out the pancakes as each round turned a delicate golden color. They were drinking wine while Ivy fed them courses of the Ebelskivers, varying the filling each time. She made savory ones with delicate fillings of triple crème brie and smoked salmon, goat cheese and bacon, gouda and ham, or basil and ricotta. Steve ate so many that Ivy had to rummage around in the refrigerator to find additional fillings. By the time that they hit the dessert Ebelskivers with raspberry jam on the inside, Ivy found she could barely get one down.

While enjoying the tasty morsels, Steve kept them amused with stories from when he was a boy, particularly ones where other transplanted Norwegians in the D.C. area gathered at his parent's house, playing traditional music and doing folk dances in the living room. Steve could still do those dances. He hummed tunes and danced, sometimes jumping up in the air, as he illustrated the dance steps, including pivots and what he called svikts. He pulled Ivy over to join him in an arms-over-the-shoulders pivot and showed her how to do the basic dance steps. Mathew could not believe that he was seeing serious Steve Nielsen, FBI executive and agent extraordinaire, cavorting about performing folk dances. He was like a young teen performing for a girl he had a crush on. The more Ivy laughed, the more he would add to his dance routine. She did draw the line on him trying to kick a hat off a stick as the young Norwegians do.

Near the end of the evening, flushed by a number of glasses of wine, Steve finished a dance routine to a round of applause, sank down on the couch, and huffed out, "Call me Sven Nielsen from now on."

Ivy and Mathew laughed.

"No, I mean it. The name on my birth certificate is Sven Nielsen. It means Steven in the Nordic countries."

"Yeah, right." Mathew said.

"I'm serious. When I was born, my parents named me Sven. Once it was nearing time for me to go to kindergarten, they wanted me to fit in and started calling me Steve."

Ivy glared at him with a mixed expression of consternation and surprise. "Pete, Sven, Steve? Is Nielsen really your last name?"

"Of course it is. While I may have other identities, you know the real me."

"How many names do you go by?" she asked a little crossly.

"No more than five at a time," Steve joked. As federal agents, the two men were accustomed to using false identities to protect their real ones.

"Being around you two makes me feel as if I am learning to skateboard and every time I get the hang of it, the sidewalk takes an unlikely turn."

"And that coming from a woman who can't decide if she is Ivy Vine or Ivy Littleton or even Mindy Madeline," Steve taunting her.

She glared at him. Mathew decided to set the record straight. "Ivy, Steve (née Sven) Nielsen really is Steve Nielsen."

"Thank you, Mathew." With her good humor now restored, Ivy went over and pulled Steve up. "Com'on then, Sven. Show me those dance steps."

Watching Ivy and Steve playfully enjoying themselves, Mathew was warmed by a feeling of belonging. The lost little boy inside himself felt less alone and unloved. They made him believe that he was worthy of love. Mathew realized that was a plain truth -- all these years he perceived himself as unloved because he thought he failed to deserve love. He must stop letting his past rule his life. He had to forge his path to his future, secure that he had Ivy and Steve to orient him, as he pivoted and svikted through life. They had become *In Loco Parentis* -- In the Place of a Parent.

Odd as it may be during this healing process, for the first time in his life Mathew felt that he had a family. No father could have tended to him better than Steve did, from the time he pulled him out of the line of fire, through the flight back to Washington, staying with him during the two surgeries and then caring for him during these weeks of healing. In all the years they worked together, Mathew never thought that Steve had that level of devotion in him, much less any form of nursing skills. Mathew did remember that Steve had flown with Brian to Bern, and was at the hospital with him every day, even after Brian's mother arrived to fuss over him.

What a remarkable man Steve was with so many facets to his personality, Mathew mused. He goes from brusque team leader to unrelenting adversary on cases, to gifted analyst, to creative mentor, to caregiver, and with Ivy, to devoted lover. Seeing those extremes consolidated into that one brilliant man was remarkable. Then there was Ivy whose kind heart seemed gladdened at having him around. As a couple, Steve and Ivy lived as if they had been together for years, instead of near the beginning of their relationship. The only downside of seeing them together was that it raised Mathew's expectations for finding his life partner.

This time of recovery was solidifying his decision to leave the FBI. Mathew expected to heal well enough to continue fieldwork but in his heart, he was finished with it. His career had been challenging and rewarding, however now he could no longer give any job his full commitment. Where and when would he find his Ivy? No way could he wait until he turned sixty as Steve had.

He was at such loose ends about his future -- going into business failed to excite him, as did practicing as an attorney. Propping his leg up, he frequently sat staring at the walls, with his iPod on and music playing. He had been reading a book on the vineyards of Oregon that Ivy had given him. When she noticed that, she had given him a couple of more books, one about starting a vineyard and another about Northwest wines. He also began to surf the web to research operating a vineyard.

Reading about vineyards gave him a different life to ponder. Would he enjoy waking up each day on his own land? Would he feel proud that what was growing in the fields was because of his own hard work? Did he have the ability to create drinkable wines, pitting himself against a steep learning curve, against nature, and against established vintners? Was it even in the realm of possibility or was it only a delightful dream? Would he be creating a financial sinkhole and setting himself up for sure failure?

Mathew wished his Dad was alive to discuss the risk of squandering even part of the fortune that he had inherited. His Dad had left the bulk of his money to Mathew, although he set up a generous trust for Mathew's Mother, as well as a substantial charitable foundation that helped fund her causes. Mathew saw himself as obligated to honor his Dad with a legacy of remembrance. After his whole life of living alone, he found it unexpected that he needed parental approval at this late date. He wanted to talk with Steve, but he would be disappointed that Mathew wanted to leave the FBI. He hated to let Steve down, especially now with all he was doing for him. Mathew decided to seek Ivy's advice sometime when Steve was out of earshot. Perhaps she could assist with how to communicate his decision to Steve.

His life clock was ticking. He had set a deadline of February 9th to have a plan to change his life. Did he have it? Leave the FBI and open a vineyard? From that base, could he put his heart into a search for that elusive woman to share his life? Were these objectives achievable? As so often, a Latin phrase came to him to sum up his mental meanderings, this one from Seneca the Younger -- *Non est ad Astra Mollis e Terris Via*, The Road from the Earth to the Stars is not easy.

***

As Ivy drove home from work the following Friday afternoon, she was thinking about her relationship with Steve and where it would head. With Mathew healing, Ivy wondered when the two agents would depart. During this time, she had come to see Steve as the man she wanted. The care he gave Mathew, the way he had settled so considerately into her life, how he put Mathew ahead of the case he was on -- all told her so much about him. The more she discovered about Steve, the more she found to appreciate about him.

108

Mathew had quickly become a part of her life too, a bit like the son she never had. She could not understand how his mother could have only called once and not come out to see him. She almost treated him as an inconvenience. His face lit up when she called, only to be followed by him withdrawing when she dismissed him as not needing her help. Ivy nearly grabbed the phone from him to lecture the self-absorbed woman.

She had just turned off Vista to take the road up to Council Crest, when she noticed an SUV behind her make the same turn. It was a black Ford Cruiser and she had seen it before that day. She realized that vehicle or one like it had been parked across the street from her work parking lot when she drove out. It stood out to her because with its dark shaded windows, it seemed out of place in Portland. She kept her speed a steady 35, then hooked a sharp right away from the road that led to her house, scooted under a little overpass and drove down towards the small Heights Shell station, intending to cross onto Humphrey, follow that twisty-turny road, and if still followed, try to lose the Cruiser in the traffic on Highway 26 while heading back into town.

She stopped for the intersection, waiting her turn in the traffic rotation to cross. The Cruiser pulled off the road about a block behind her, letting a couple of cars pass before moving back in line. Trying to push back her fear, she reached over, moved the car's controls to dial her cell and hit Steve's number. It rang four times with no answer. She left a short voicemail as she let her SUV creep forward to the stop sign. She crossed the road and shot down Humphrey knowing that to lose the Cruiser, she would have to drive as fast as the many turnings of the road would allow. She was almost to Highway 26 when her phone rang.

"Ivy? Did you call?"

"Think I'm being followed. Black Ford Cruiser with dark tinted windows."

"Damn. Where are you?"

"Heading back into town. Didn't want to lead them home."

"Good. Is there a hotel where you can park inside that has an attendant?"

Ivy thought quickly. "Fifth Avenue Suites. Valet parking. All inside."

"Head there. Tell the attendant you may be leaving in a few minutes. Mathew and I will meet you in the lobby. Stay where other people are in the hotel."

"Got it."

"I'm going to give my phone to Mathew. Stay on the line with him. I'll call for a cab and line up a couple of local agents to meet us at Fifth Avenue Suites."

Ivy found she was shaking and gripped the steering wheel harder. The traffic in front of her on Highway 26 was crawling along. She pounded the steering wheel in frustration. It was the holiday week. Traffic should not be so heavy. In the rear view mirror, she could see the Cruiser coming down the entrance ramp she had taken. She waited impatiently as the traffic stalled, then inched forward. Ivy had enough of the highway. For luck, she reached up and touched the pearl necklace Steve had surprised her with and then swerved over on the shoulder, riding it until she could turn off at the Zoo exit, going as fast as she dared through the park, down past the back of the Japanese Garden and then around the Rose Garden. At the bottom of the road, as the light changed she rolled forward to slip down Park Place. In her rearview mirror, she saw the Cruiser nose around the last turn coming out of the park like a stalking panther.

"Mathew, he's still with me."

"You got your roscoe?"

"In my purse."

"Get it out just in case. Slip it into your coat pocket when you are near the hotel."

Ivy waited impatiently by the MAC club as people strolled across the street. She could feel nervous sweat soaking her blouse. Once at the light, she flew as fast as she dared up the street, planning her route as she went -- scoot down Salmon, hook various turns, then cut over to Washington and into the Fifth Avenue Suites lot under the building. Soon traffic slowed and she wound up jockeying her way around. She kept checking her rear view mirror. No sign of the Cruiser behind her.

"Mathew, I think I lost him."

"Great! I'm in a cab heading to the hotel. Slow going -- traffic is a mess. Steve took off running. You okay?"

"Scared, but okay."

"Wait for me in the lobby."

Washington was all backed up but it was her only choice for the remaining two blocks to get to the hotel. Ivy sat through three lights before she could inch her way to the right block. She looked around the cars to see Steve was running down the street to the hotel. She started tooting the horn. He jerked his head around, saw her, changed course and ran for the passenger side of the SUV.

"I think I lost them," she said as he jumped into the car.

"FBI on their way. Portland police alerted. I was so damn glad to see you when I heard that horn. Good idea to imitate the knock we use."

"I couldn't see the number on the Cruiser, but it looked like a California plate."

"How many in the vehicle?"

"At least two."

"Bastards."

Ivy swung into the lot, edged her way down the ramp and stopped by the parking attendant. After giving him the key fob, she stepped out of the car. Her legs were trembling and she had to walk leaning against Steve over to the elevator that would take them up to the hotel lobby.

"Somehow the perp must have linked us to Portland and to you," Steve said.

"Who knows about us?"

"Brian and Moll. I told them our location was top secret."

"Your boss?"

"All I told him was that I would be out of the office and to reach me by cell or email. I told the Chief, but only in general terms."

"Human Resources?"

Steve thought for a moment. "Maybe Mathew's medical services. Maybe that was a tip off on our location. From that, someone could have put two and two together."

"Or Brian's travel records out to meet with you."

"Maybe. He flew in and out of San Francisco; the flights involving Portland went on my personal credit card."

"Too many holes to keep plugged up."

"Yeah."

They were standing near the front desk where they could see the hotel entrance. "Here's Mathew."

He limped up slowly, leaning heavily on his cane. One of the agents who had helped with their relocation to the apartment ran in. For the next half hour, they briefed him on who they really were and gave him a situational overview. Steve placed a call to the Chief who in turn called the Special Agent in charge of the Portland office, giving Steve authority over the follow-up actions. Since their cover was blown, they decided to go to the apartment, pack up their things and move to Ivy's house where they could best protect it and her. The FBI would arrange for on-site agent surveillance there as well as watch the apartment. If the perps knew about Ivy, then her home address would be known to them too. In the meantime, the police would try to apprehend the perps in the Cruiser.

"What's next?" Ivy asked.

"Expect to have an agent tailing you to and from work, shopping or wherever you go. They will have a monitoring van in the garage. I would offer to leave town, but I think you could still be in danger. Alternatively we could all go to another city."

"I want you here and I have to be at the office next week -- my replacement starts on Wednesday."

"Then we stick with the plan, if it is okay with you."

Ivy nodded and then reminded Steve of his promise that any beefed up security at her house would not include any bugs planted inside. Privacy was something she had to have. Right then all she wanted were Steve's arms around her and she realized that sometime in the last three weeks she had crossed an unseen threshold between choosing to be in control though isolated to being loved and dependent. Scared though she was, that thought let Ivy know that she had traveled through one of life's major passages.

On Sunday, they returned to the apartment and finished cleaning it out. Steve had already paid the rent for January, so it would remain under surveillance. While Ivy sorted out the kitchen, the two men cleaned the other rooms, did the laundry and put the apartment back to how they originally found it. On the way back to her house, they picked up groceries and champagne to celebrate the New Year, since they would be staying in for the holiday.

At home Ivy found herself lamenting that her charming house with its views out to the southern hills, its hedged perennial gardens, its warm brick patio, and its gracious, comfortable interior, had become what she thought of as fed central. As usual in winter, the weather was rainy, with occasional dustings of snow that quickly melted as the temperatures rose into the forties during the day. Life outside went on. Inside her home everything had tilted and felt different. It was now an FBI recovery center and a planning center, with agents handling security round-the-clock. She doubted she would ever feel the same about the house again, and yet how much fuller her life was now with Steve and Mathew in it.

Steve did his best to avoid any extra burden on her. He was there each day when she returned from work and opened the back door, having jogged down the steps when hearing the toot of her horn as she passed the house on the way down to the garage. Sometimes using his wireless headset, he was in the middle of a briefing from Brian or Moll, nevertheless he never missed that time to smile at Ivy, kiss her, and carry in whatever she was bringing home. While the black Cruiser had escaped detection and the perps had not yet surfaced, each of them knew it was only a matter of time until their lives would be shaken up again.

Chapter 10

On the 10th of January, the weather in Portland had been showery with occasional sun breaks. After work, Ivy stopped at the local organic food store for a couple of freshly roasted chickens, salad ingredients and other groceries and then headed up the road to her house. The weather up on the hill was mild for January and a foggy mist was starting to rise giving her a feeling of foreboding. When she arrived home, Steve seemed apprehensive and Mathew could not meet her eye. Something was up and Ivy figured it had to do with the Bureau.

"Big Guy," she said, without even a hint of a smile. "I think you had better make us all stiff drinks."

Steve gave her one of his assessing looks, nodded and headed to the little bar by the kitchen. Their habit was to share cocktails or wine before dinner like a regular family while they talked about their days. Ivy could tell this evening would not be a cozy chat over drinks. Steve had a fire going in the living room, but she noticed he had a half-packed suitcase out on the bed. Mathew was near the fire in an armchair. Once he made the drinks, Steve sat at one end of the leather couch. Instead of taking her usual place next to him, Ivy pushed over an ottoman and sat facing both of them.

"Ivy, I had a call today from the Chief," Steve began, as was his style, starting right in without any preamble. "We think we have located the head of the drug operation on a yacht off the coast of Mexico. We are working with the Navy and the DEA to organize a search and capture mission. The yacht is anchored off an inhabited island. The thought is to bring a ship in a couple of miles away to track it if they run. We will approach the boat from the air, rappelling down out of a chopper. Surface vessels might alert the perps to set sail, however the yacht is under a regular flight pattern. Our chopper will swoop in a bit lower."

A frisson of fear skirted around Ivy's heart. "They want you to head up the mission."

"Like I said, it's a joint operation. We'll have lots of support."

"And you've done this before, rappelling out of a helicopter?"

"In training. We'll do a couple of refresher test jumps. The Navy Seals will go first to handle the lines for getting the rest of us down."

"Ivy, it's not as hard as you think," Mathew interjected. "I was scared shitless the first time we did it in training. However you follow a set routine and you're down in a matter of seconds."

Ivy glared at Mathew and then at Steve. "You could get shot up like Mathew. I know it is what you do, but I don't like this one bit."

"If I don't go, Brian will be designated to go in my place. He is not ready for this. These joint operations are tricky enough, without having to rappel out of a chopper, direct the operation, seize control of the vessel, and apprehend the perps before they kill you."

"Why can't another leader go?"

His eyes were solemn. He held his tongue.

Mathew jumped in to further his cause. "None of them are as good as Steve. None I would trust with my best friend's life. Next to you two, Brian is my best friend. He took a bullet for me in Bulgaria, for chrissakes. I can't go with this bum leg. Ivy, while I am reluctant to ask this on top of all you have done for me, please think about it."

Ivy felt boxed in. Choices were tough when they involved duty, loyalty and friendship. What about love? What about the danger to Steve?

"If you get this drug lord, won't another pop up in his place?"

Steve shook his head. "This perp is very strong, powerful, and mega-wealthy. He keeps the logistics of the drug business in Colombia organized. Without him, it will fragment, making it easier to shut down smaller units. When we have gone after him before, all we nabbed were some lesser guys and some actor hired to play his part. It's vital that we apprehend him."

"How can you be sure it's him this time? Him on this yacht in the middle of wherever?"

"Six months ago, the DEA infiltrated. They set up their own little drug packaging operation, headed by one of their people and let him be consolidated into the big ring. He sent an encoded message about this setup. He's been invited for a weekend with the drug lord as a reward for how well his drug operation is performing. We have to arrest this Astuto character and get the DEA agent out."

Ivy was overwhelmed by this talk of drug lords, undercover agents, climbing down a rope out of a helicopter into an explosive situation. The love of her life wanted to play soldier at 60. She needed fresh air and time to think. "I'm going for a walk."

Steve stood up.

"Alone."

"Ivy!"

"Alright, come with me. Do not talk."

Ivy leashed up the dogs and walked for about twenty minutes in the misty air with Steve staying silent at her side. With night settling in, the air had lost the mildness of the afternoon becoming a damp misty cold that crept insidiously under rain jackets and sweaters. Only a couple of people were out with their dogs, their shoulders hunched against the chill. She kept a fast pace until she calmed down enough to think clearly. She was so afraid that this could be the last time she saw Steve and she would have let him go to his death. She had to find some way to make this mission safer for him. Even he had to realize that he was not invincible. Mathew had been his second set of eyes and brain. An idea came to her. She reached over and took Steve's hand and turned around to hustle home, things straight in her head. After walking back into the house, Ivy took a long slug of her Old Fashioned, looking first at Mathew and then at Steve.

"All right. You have my support on one condition."

The two men waited.

Ivy pointed to Mathew and herself, "We get looped into the operation. Steve, you and Brian must have two-way communications with Mathew from when you take off in that damn chopper until you are back on safe ground. I will listen in so I can know what is happening, when it happens. I will sign a code of secrecy or whatever. Most importantly, I want Mathew's brain with you."

"Ivy, we can't do that," Steve took a step towards her.

"Find a way," she said stonily. They faced each other as two strong, determined people in love.

Mathew struggled up, leaning on his three-footed cane and began talking in his smooth, convincing voice. Within a few sentences, he succeeded in getting the stubbornness off Steve's face, drawing him into planning how to do technically what Ivy asked for and how to sell it to the Bureau. Now at least she would be plugged in and having Mathew there by voice would give Steve an extra resource.

Mathew and Steve started making calls. Some technical FBI agents arrived to beef up their communications gear. By midnight, Steve was on a Bubird on his way south. Sometime in the next 24 hours, the team would move in. The local FBI sent another agent over who would take up residence in a van outside the house. Ivy went into work, expecting to take the next day off or however long it took for Steve's mission to be over. She was so worried that Steve could be killed the next day, leaving only memories in her devastated heart. Here she was an ordinary female executive embroiled in an international drug raid. As the old adage says, sometimes you should be careful what you wish for -- Ivy wanted a man of action in her life and she certainly had one.

***

Steve arranged to have Mathew and Ivy patched in shortly before he boarded the helicopter to take off for the yacht. The call came in at three Pacific the next morning, with Steve and the team planning to depart right before dawn. Mathew had on Steve's headpiece and microphone. Ivy had sound only -- even she could see that it would be best for her not to be able to speak, scream or cry into a microphone, depending on what happened.

117

Ivy and Mathew had communications with both Steve and Brian. Moll was also with the team, but not plugged in to their communications. They could hear the officer on the Navy vessel who they referred to only as "Captain". Ivy found it nerve-wracking to hear the hissing interactions at the same time that Steve heard them. Steve made the initial contact and then put them on mute, only switching on the sound when the helicopter took off from the nearby naval craft. All too soon, it seemed to Ivy, they were up and heading to Isla Holbox, a low-key fishing and tourist island off the eastern coast of Mexico near Cancun. The team was mostly silent. The noise of the rotors droned on. Everything was so real, yet it was like being part of a movie. Ivy could see it clearly in her head as a movie done in black and white, everything dim and eerie in the predawn gloaming.

"Target at two o'clock."

"Roger."

"Jump time in three minutes."

Ivy could hear movement, gear being snapped, feet shuffling.

"Commencing count down."

Ivy visualized the chopper sinking low, then hovering with the Navy Seals and the FBI agents lined up to kick off and rappel down. She could picture Steve having to bend over to clear the doorway. Her shoulder muscles clenched tighter when she hunched forward, listening intently. She gripped the arms of her chair feeling as if she were going out of the helicopter with Steve.

They heard rapid counting as each team member rappelled out. Steve gave an "oof "into the microphone when he kicked off and Brian made what sounded like a growl of anticipation. Could they really control the lines well enough to land on the yacht? Ivy's heart was pounding in her chest as they waited for an update. Mathew gripped the edge of the desk, leaning forward in anticipation. A whump and then a muffled, "Fuck" let them know Steve landed. They heard feet running stealthily and then a "Holy Shit" from Steve.

"Report," barked the Captain's voice.

"Target surface deserted." Steve's voice was tight with tension. "Seals heading for the cabin and the bridge."

"Anyone in sight?"

"The undercover. Dead and strapped to the mast. Hold on."

A second passed. Two seconds. Three seconds. Mathew and Ivy each leaned forward, trying to catch any sounds that would tell them what was happening.

Finally they heard Steve yelling, "Abort. Abort Agents. Abort Seals. Abort. It's a trap!"

Feet thudding. Splashes. Steve yelling at the Seal leader to abort.

Another splash. And then another, "Fuck".

"Steve, jump." Mathew yelled into his headset.

They heard a series of explosions, one echoing after the other, loud splashes, and then some sloshing. Ivy was on the edge of her chair, fear for Steve surrounding her heart, listening intently.

The Captain repeatedly demanded an update. "Report. Report. Report."

For Ivy the waiting seemed to go on far longer than it should. Had none of them made it safely away? Where was Steve? Where was Brian?

Again the Captain came on. "Are you there? Report."

Brian came on, his voice faltering, making him restart twice before he could speak clearly. "Agents all in the water, sir. I have one with a dislocated shoulder -- thrown overboard. Two Seals here too that I can see. Maybe more behind some debris and smoke. Shit's on fire all around us, uh, sir."

Mathew went on then. "Steve, where the hell is Steve?"

Brian gave a choked, stressed laugh and said, "He has water in his headset."

They heard a lot of splashing and then a blast of air blown into the mouthpiece.

"Nielsen here. Fuck, I was reporting in. Nothing was transmitting. Can't you give us waterproof headsets?"

"Damages?"

"Vessel destroyed. Damn pricks must have set charges to go off when the door to the cabin area opened. Two Seals likely dead. They failed to jump when I shouted to abort. They were heading down into the cabin. I think that's what set off the charge."

After a long silence, the Captain asked, "What tipped you off besides the dead undercover?"

"The boat wasn't in the best shape -- not what this kind of drug lord would have as his yacht. He would have it spic and span. Real flash."

"Good work, Nielsen. While this was bad, the situation could have been a whole lot worse. Swim around to see if you can find those two missing Seals. Pickup should be in about five minutes. Anything to salvage from the vessel?"

"Bits and pieces. That shit was flying all around; parts of it are still on fire, floating in the water. I hear a siren. Likely the water police are coming out of Cancun."

"We just alerted them."

They could hear swimming, and then some muffled words, a yell of pain and a distant "son of a bitch". Steve must have reached Brian and was helping to hold up the injured agent.

Brian came back on. "Agent's shoulder is back in place, sir."

Steve gave a gruff, "Sorry Stanford."

"You save my life and you worry about hurting my damn arm?" They heard what sounded like Moll in the background.

Then silence, until Steve spoke quietly, "Ivy, one of your angels was riding on my shoulder."

Tears welled up in Ivy's eyes, spilled over and ran down her cheeks. Steve understood that while she was not religious, she did like the concept of angels. That mission was nearly a disaster for Steve and everyone else. Ivy was not cut out for this kind of action and she was safely sitting in her home, thousands of miles away. How did Steve do it?

Mathew spoke quietly into his headset, "We are all thankful for that."

He pushed away his microphone and sagged back in his chair. "Believe it or not, it's easier to be on the ground than to monitor the action remotely. Thank god for Steve and his sixth sense, deducing trouble from small signs. That poor agent. Felipe was his name, though he went by Phil. I worked with him a few years ago on another drug case. Family was from Puerto Rico. Great guy -- gung ho on our country and on his work with the DEA. Awful way to die. Damn, damn, damn."

"And those Navy Seals. Likely not too old. Maybe they signed up for it, but so wrong, so awful."

Ivy felt drained, though her heart was humming, "Steve's okay. Steve's okay. He saved most of the team. He saved Brian and Moll. Steve's okay."

Mathew and Ivy sat silently, their energy too sapped by the chain of events to move. They listened to the communications until Steve landed on board the Navy vessel and went off for debriefing. Mathew struggled to his feet, leaning on his cane. They dragged themselves like two worn soldiers to the kitchen where Ivy began to make an early breakfast, thinking that Steve would call when he could.

***

Late that afternoon, Mathew selected a varietal burgundy from the Joseph Drouhin vineyard in the Burgundy region of France, opened it, poured a glass and held it up to the light.

"Good color, rather a ruby red," he murmured to himself. He twirled the glass, inhaled, tasted and smiled in appreciation. "To produce a wine that will delight whoever is lucky enough to drink it, would be a worthy achievement."

"Why don't you?" Ivy asked hearing the admiring tone of his voice.

"Oh sure, with the work demands I have and this bum leg?"

"The leg will continue to improve. You can hire out the running of the vineyard."

"What would the sense be in that?" he retorted peevishly.

Mathew moved into the kitchen where Ivy was grinding a mix of red, white, green and black peppercorns and then pink sea salt onto some bone-in

121

chicken breasts marinated in lemon, garlic, rosemary and olive oil. He regarded Ivy sulkily.

"Ivy, I don't want to go back to the Bureau, even if my leg fully recovers," he blurted out. "I can't figure out how to tell Steve -- too hard, like deserting him."

She nodded. "So that's what has been on your mind these past weeks. Maybe Steve isn't so sure of things himself these days. He hasn't talked about it, but he has been moodier."

"What should I do?"

"Wait and heal. One day, the time will be right to discuss it with him. Are you thinking of opening a vineyard?"

"Stupid to even think about it."

"Not necessarily. I have an acquaintance who is the owner of a large vineyard that started as a hobby and grew to a successful enterprise. I could see if he will talk with you."

"Thanks."

Ivy thought for a bit, trying to think of other ways to help Mathew. "I remember a special on our OPB TV station that had interviews with the growers in Oregon who started the wine industry here. You ought to do a search for it and watch it. Those folks had a notion that Oregon could produce good wines. Hearing their stories might give you more confidence."

His face showed that he was not encouraged.

"Mathew, you're smart, hardworking, and good at research. You have money from your Dad to invest for the startup. As long as your heart is in it, why not?"

"Thanks, Ivy. Times like these, I wish you had a younger sister."

"Someone is out there for you."

He smiled sadly. "She'll have to like a cripple."

"Oh com'on, limps and canes can be both distinguished and sexy to a woman," Ivy said as she opened the oven door to slide the roasting pan onto the rack.

"Oh sure, right up there with fat old men in tweeds." The glimmer of enthusiasm that appeared when he talked about the vineyard was gone. His expression was glum; he even slouched over.

"That's it, Mathew." Ivy closed the oven door with a little bang and whirled around to face him, hands on her hips. "From this day forward, you are not to act sorry for yourself or have that hangdog, depressed expression. You are still relatively young, you are handsome, and you have laughing eyes that could seduce the panties off any woman you chose. Most importantly, you are capable of doing so much with your life. To spend it morosely, acting as if your life is over, is simply not acceptable."

She turned and started chopping some spinach with more vigor than usual.

"Jeez-Louise." Mathew stared at Ivy in surprise. He limped past her and went out on the deck. Once out there, Ivy heard the first real laugh out of him since he had come to stay. He took an appreciative sip of his wine and stood there -- a man who had a little hope scolded into him.

Chapter 11

That evening, Steve sat on the Bubird that would take him back to Ivy, Mathew and Portland. Even though he would arrive late, he needed to bury himself in Ivy's reassuring embrace. It amazed him how quickly he had become dependent on her. He remembered that night by the fire after the child trafficking case, when she had so gently comforted him and listened without pressing him. While he was tired and he often slept fitfully on flights, today with his nerves jangled from that awful mission, he was glad for the time to sit back and reflect.

He had perceived a couple of years ago that his edge started eroding, haunting him on the last four field missions. His reactions were no longer what they had been. At first he thought he had become soft; he trained harder. He was stronger; he felt fit. Again on the job a year later, he could tell that his reactions were not what they had been. If not for his great teams, he could have been in trouble. While he worked hard to mask it, he was aware of a gradual slippage in his edge. As an agent, he should have retired at 57. However each year he had been extended. He was beginning to see why the FBI has chosen to push older agents out, especially high mileage ones like himself.

Until Steve met Ivy, retirement scared the bejesus out of him. While leaving the Bureau still worried him, he could envision a life with Ivy. He saw a warm home. He pictured the inspiring image of Mt. Hood. He could see Mathew with them for as long as he wanted to hang around. Steve had a foretaste of a place where he could be happy. Moreover these weeks with Ivy, taking care of Mathew and now living in and working out of her house, had been so fulfilling that he had to continue seeing her every day.

What he had not talked about with Ivy was how much the excitement of the hunt was a part of him. The complex cases were like giant multidimensional puzzles with lots of layers and moving parts. Figuring the puzzle out, learning how to out-think its evil makers and then shutting down a dastardly operation were all are so stimulating. The ultimate goal to make the world a better place, or at least save it from deteriorating into a worse one, drove him. Moreover he was accustomed to living on adrenalin surges. While he still craved the feeling of power they gave him, now the adrenalin from the hunt left him sick in its aftermath. That was the way he was now, wanting only to get home to Ivy.

He glanced out at the clouds drifting under the plane. The child in him still liked to see big puffy clouds moving merrily along. They were flying into the setting sun and would have light for some hours as they passed through time zones heading west. No matter that he had flown more than a thousand times, he still found the experience refreshing.

On this mission, Steve should have called to abort the action sooner. Once his eyes fixed on that dead undercover, he froze in place. He never froze. None of the hellish things he had seen in his career had paralyzed him. Yet today he lost all consciousness that he needed to move, to see and to run the damn operation. While it was only for a second or two, when the timeline is in sub-seconds, each moment becomes mission-critical; each moment could make the difference between life and death and between success and failure. He could still see a snapshot of the scene in his mind, frozen in time with the edges jaggedly distorted by diffracted light from the water.

Standing there, Steve had heard a voice in his head. The voice was Ivy's, whispering, "Look at the yacht." It was enough to break him out of that trance. He saw the neglected deck, sensed it was a trap and yelled to abort. That is why he told Ivy one of her angels was on his shoulder. He did not understand how her senses were with him, maybe only a murmur in his subconscious to survive because now he had so much to live for. Had it not been for those whispered words, his yell would have come too late or not at all.

He understood that his field days needed to be over. He wanted to arrest this perp and destroy his drug-based empire. He wanted to be there to shield Brian. Yet he almost got them all killed. As it was, two Seals died. The leader of the Seal unit resented having to report to an FBI agent. Steve thought that was why he kept going when he heard the command to abort. He wanted to show that Steve was only a panicky old man of an agent who had called to abandon ship precipitately.

Steve had recognized his physical deterioration and was too stubborn and scared to face it. Now that Ivy was in his life, he was less afraid and that eased his natural obstinacy. He understood that he could be stubborn, particularly when challenged or apprehensive. His challenge now was to figure out how to spend his days. He needed ways to keep his brain busy, because he feared that if it did not have challenges, it would become neurotic or even paranoid. He had seen agents become like that. He was afraid that all the badness he had seen would collect like too much street litter and blow around in his mind until it drove him insane. Work had let him put the bad stuff away, locked in file drawers in his brain. What if those locks broke down? What if boredom drove him to examine that litter? Seeing those bad memories collectively would be to wade in a quagmire that could be overwhelming.

Determining what to do with his life would be his number one challenge. Ivy was defining a retirement life for herself. He did not want to become so dependent that he stifled her. He had to delineate a life for himself, too. Only then could they map out one together. While these topics would be hard for him to discuss, maybe she could help him out of his own head. Perhaps Ivy could again be the angel on his shoulder. Even so, he worried that this revelation could make her think less of him. He decided to think about it for a few more days.

***

Early the following Friday afternoon, Ivy was out in the back yard with the dogs watching them sniff around to see what creatures might have invaded their space. She was now working four days a week with Fridays off and, particularly with Steve and Mathew in her life, she was liking the change. She was mulling over her relationship with Steve while wandering around the little garden where spring would soon start to make it come alive again. He seemed preoccupied since his return from the mission in the Caribbean. He spent a couple of days filing reports, doing the required paperwork, conferring with Brian by phone, and checking in with Moll about his shoulder. He kept up with the continuing work on the case, however she sensed a difference -- he

126

seemed more withdrawn and thoughtful. She could only hope that he was on a path that included her. Despite her concerns, she sensed that he needed to journey in his mind for a time on his own. She worried that Steve was feeling confined and feared he would leave to return to fieldwork. The way he lit up when he was intent on a case made him appear unready to retire. While she found it hard to imagine him doing anything else, she was not sure she could live with seeing him only the occasional weekend.

Mathew continued to improve. He was diligent about doing his exercise routines twice a day. He still had a significant limp, which he was determined to reduce. The biggest change she noted was his attitude -- he was more cheerful and more focused. He was keeping busy, working at a makeshift desk he made out of a table in his room. He was so intent on researching the vineyard, that Ivy could picture him as a formidable FBI agent.

As she opened the door to the garage to rub off the dogs, she could hear Steve and Mathew talking close by but she doubted they were in the FBI van that was parked in the garage with an agent on duty round the clock. When she stepped back outside and closed the door, she could no longer hear them. A sinking feeling came into her stomach. She unleashed the corgis, letting them roam again in the backyard, then exited through the side gate to walk up and enter the house through the front door. As Ivy slipped inside, she saw Steve and Mathew talking in what was now Steve's office.

She put her finger to her lips and motioned for them to follow her outside. They stood on the street while she explained what she had heard. The deal had been that surveillance was okay, but no bugs in the house. She watched Steve's face harden and Mathew silently clenched his jaw. They hurried back to the house, taking off their shoes and moving quietly. Steve went into his office, opened his big briefcase and pulled out a device that Ivy guessed was a bug detector. He quickly found a bug in the office where he worked. Mathew came out of his room, Ivy's old master bedroom, with a similar device and holding up one finger. They slid around the house, finding four more on the top floor. By now Ivy was seething. They tiptoed downstairs where they found another four bugs, including one in the bedroom that Steve and Ivy now shared. She was more than mad, she was simply livid.

No longer stealthily, Steve jerked open the door to the garage. Mathew and Ivy could hear him yelling at the agent in the van, telling him to shut down and leave. The van doors slammed. They heard the motor start and then the van backed out. The garage door closed. Steve stormed back in, dialing his cell phone and demanding to speak to his boss at the FBI.

He listened for a moment and then he spoke forcefully into the phone. "I don't give a damn if he is in a meeting. Get him on the phone. This won't take long."

After a few minutes, Steve bellowed into the phone. "What the hell are you doing? Spying on two dedicated, experienced agents? We don't do that to our own. Not without reasonable cause. AND YOU HAVE NO FUCKING CAUSE." Steve paused, listened for a moment and then continued in the same angry tone.

"I was very clear about no bugs in the house. Expect a letter announcing my retirement in your email box within the hour."

Steve was silent for a moment then started hollering again. "No damn it, I will not cool off. You have always been a know-it-all-desk-riding jerk. I may be pissed off but I know exactly what I'm saying. While you are waiting for my letter, take your little pin head and stick it up your fat ass, where you can't do anyone any harm." He clicked the phone off and stood glaring at the wall. Mathew stared at Steve with a dawning look of wonder on his face.

"That was eloquent." Ivy spoke with humor in her voice, wanting to break Steve's angry mood. Seeing him so worked up about the bugs made her own annoyance dissipate.

Steve turned the full force of his glare on her. Her devilish look reached through his anger and his mouth began to twitch with amusement. Suddenly the three of them were laughing and holding on to each other. When they finally stopped, Mathew did an imitation of Steve on the phone and they started laughing all over again. Soon Steve was doing imitations of himself. All those weeks of being cooped up and all the tension of the last few days, came bubbling out in their amusement.

When they finally calmed down, Steve regarded Mathew and Ivy questioningly, "What the hell do we do now?"

Mathew wiped tears of laughter from the corners of eyes, "First we all make sure we are armed, just in case. That includes you, Ivy."

"I have to call the Chief to tell him I'm retiring before that sanctimonious son of a bitch who calls himself my boss runs in to tattle on me. Then I have to write that letter to confirm my intention to retire."

"Me too," Mathew said and smiled cryptically at Steve.

"Huh?"

"I have a letter to write to you. I'm resigning from the Bureau."

"Mathew, that's a knee-jerk reaction."

"Steve, I have wanted to leave for months. I hung on because you inspire me."

"Take time, think this over."

"Like you did?"

"Today, that HQ goldbricker I report to and the bugs he had put in this house were the catalyst. I have been in a muddle about my life since I turned 60. No way do I want only to see Ivy only now and then. I've been too damn scared to act, not seeing what to do with my time."

Mathew and Ivy exchanged a glance. She nodded.

"I have a solution for that," Mathew began a bit tentatively. "You're going to be my partner."

"What are you talking about?"

"We're opening a vineyard. We'll be growing grapes for wine and becoming vintners."

"Mathew, we don't know a damn thing about farming or about wine."

"You're wrong. We are great at drinking it."

Steve snorted and shook his head.

"Steve, hear me out. We're top-notch researchers. We learn fast. We work hard. We excel at what we do. You are fit and active and I soon will be again. I can finance it with part of my Dad's fortune. You can take some of the wad you stashed away over the years and build a house for Ivy on the land."

Steve shook his head again, although his eyes did light up when Mathew mentioned building a house for Ivy.

"Give it some thought, Steve. We can do this. I'm talking to a major grower and vintner next week to begin learning the facts. We can check out land and vineyards for sale. Think about it, just think about it."

Steve shrugged. Ivy leaned over, kissed his cheek, and whispered, "Consider it, for Mathew."

Then she stepped back trying to appear more serious than she felt. "Okay, if you are ready to do it, write those letters. And then clean this place up."

The two men were perplexed. Ivy never asked them to clean -- they were both so neat, she never needed to.

"The bugs, dummies, disable those damn bugs. I want them out of here."

"Oh, that's what you meant. We also have to retool the surveillance cameras and the security system so we can do monitoring from here or wherever via an internet connection."

She let the dogs in, toweled them off and then turned to go upstairs.

"What are you doing?" Steve asked.

"Getting armed, icing a bottle of champagne and then making a reservation for dinner. Steak sound good?"

Mathew and Steve exchanged a look and smiled.

"Yeah, big steak dinner." Steve said. "Oysters first."

"Garlic mashed potatoes." Mathew batted back. "Then a cheese course."

"Dripping in calories dessert."

"Different wine with every course."

"Right. Urban Farmer at seven. I'll arrange a town car because we are going to celebrate!" Ivy's jubilance danced out in her voice. She turned and sprinted up the stairs feeling more energized than she had in years.

Over dinner, which was rowdy and only sometimes serious, the two ex-agents tossed around names for the vineyard, jokingly settling on 'Spook Hills'. Steve confessed that he always wanted to be a spy or spook as they were called, but he was too big to be inconspicuous. He gave his agreement to Mathew to

130

support him with the vineyard idea. He stared at his plate thoughtfully and tapped the table a few times with his forefinger. "I have a few conditions, though."

"Expected that," Mathew responded with a shake of his head.

"You take the lead on it. I will support you. I'll do labor. While I will learn about it, this is yours to run."

Mathew nodded. "That will be a big change! What else?"

"Ivy and I are going to travel as tourists. I'm going to start seeing more of the world than hotel rooms and some perp's operation. We're going to spend time visiting iconic landmarks, appreciating different countrysides and learning about a variety of cultures all around the world. And hey, we'll be sampling local wines. Maybe sometimes you'll come with us."

"And?"

"You live with us until you have someone in your life."

Mathew laughed at him. "You drive a hard bargain -- yes to all three."

"Shake on it," Ivy said quietly. From that crazy upside-down, half-serious, half-joking day, the concept of their vineyard was born.

Chapter 12

Steve put his cell phone back in his pocket early the following Monday morning and went in search of Ivy, catching her pulling on her raincoat to leave for work. "We have to go back to D.C., clean out the condos, turn in our gear, get out-processed and all that jazz."

She regarded him with mild surprise. "Should I go with you? I could take some vacation. The dogs and Druid can go to a kennel."

"Safer that way. How about we leave this Thursday, out-process on Friday and spend the weekend figuring out what to do with the furniture, the clothes, and the whole empty, pathetic life. I'll make the arrangements today. Target to have the condos on the market on Monday and we're back here Tuesday."

Mathew walked up as he heard the gist of the conversation, smiling a bit sadly and said, "Almost all my stuff can go to the Goodwill or somewhere like that, except some things from my Dad's house."

"Ditto. I have stuff from my Mom that Ivy can decide if she might want." Steve said. "Whatever we keep can be shipped out and stored until our plans are in place."

"Cars?" Ivy asked.

"Busteeds."

"What?"

"Busteeds -- Bureau vehicles when we were in town. Also called Bucars or BuCs."

"I suppose you call it BuSpeak too, this FBI lingo."

"You're getting the hang of it."

"Is Brian coming down for the final debrief?" Mathew asked. "I want to keep in touch with him, Moll and a couple of others."

Steve nodded. "Let's take Brian and Moll out to dinner one night. Oh, and I have to close a safety deposit box."

He and Mathew exchanged a look. "Me too," Mathew said.

Ivy wondered what the two ex-agents had secreted away. False IDs? More firepower? Surely, they would have to turn all that in.

"Let's book into that Kimpton across the street from our building. That way we can dive right into stripping the condos."

***

They spent Friday morning in Washington picking up packing materials and starting to box up Mathew's place. Each of the men's studios had the sterility of a hotel room. The only furniture Ivy found worthwhile was what they had taken from one parent's house or the other. Early that afternoon, Moll arrived to stay with Ivy while Steve and Mathew went for their out-processing and debriefings at the Bureau. After receiving strict instructions about not opening the door to anyone but them and being careful to have her gun handy, Ivy concentrated on boxing up Steve's condo where she sorted his things between Portland and Goodwill. Moll helped as best he could with his arm still in a sling.

That night the five of them walked over to an upscale, comfortable place called Restaurant Nora, where an undercurrent of the city's energy seemed to crackle in the room. Champagne was flowing and the three younger men were in good spirits, although Ivy thought that Steve appeared a little on edge. Brian broke the news that he and Moll were leaving the Bureau in the next few weeks to start a forensics audit business.

"What the hell?" Steve said. "You have great careers ahead of you -- each of you."

"The truth is," Brian said, "I've succeeded with you and Mathew, the best agents in the Bureau, because you shielded me in the field. However I can do this forensics stuff. Moll and I started talking about it when you had us audit your code on that first case with you. Since then, we've spent whatever free time we had learning more.

133

Moll seemed uncomfortable. "Face it, I'm a desk jockey. I froze up so bad on that last mission that I'd be dead if you hadn't pitched me overboard."

"Every agent freezes up sometimes," Steve said somewhat gently.

Moll shook his head. "Every time for me. I'm more of a brain than a body."

Mathew was surprised that they had been silent about their change in career; on the other hand, had he ever talked about leaving the FBI? "The Bureau might hire you back as consultants."

Steve was still frowning, but then he nodded. "Yeah, believe it or not, I'm in good with the head of technology. I can put in a word whenever you want me to."

"We were thinking banks." Brian said. "They get stuck with big penalties when a money laundering case comes along. We could help them head it off, find the issue and help them take it to the Bureau. Likely by taking the initiative, any fine would be reduced or eliminated."

Moll was hunched over his plate and edging his silverware around, lining the pieces up in a neat line. "Maybe both banks and the Bureau. Have a diversified client list. We figure that 'London and Stanford', as you like to call us, have solid credentials and great experience. What about you two? Going to consult? Be vigilantes for third world governments?"

They all laughed and then Mathew leaned back, holding up his head with mock pride, "Become farmers. Plant pinot noir grapevines. Sit back and watch them grow. Then Steve is going to roll up his pants and squash the grapes with his big feet."

Lots of laughter followed that comment.

"Seriously, we will start a vineyard and learn the art and science of making world class wines. We have a line on some land that is located smack dab on a ridge between two great vineyards in Oregon. A couple of viniculture experts will check it out for us and we will have an appraisal performed. If not there, we'll find another location."

"A night of surprises. Well, go for it guys. Who would have thought? Harvard and Georgetown becoming vintners. What are you going to call it?"

"Spook Hills," said Mathew, finding it impossible to keep a straight face. "Make people think we were jet-setting spies instead of plodding federal agents."

They laughed some more and toasted each of their ventures; their spirits were high and heads in the restaurant turned towards their table trying to figure out the cause of the revelry. Steve ordered another bottle of champagne and asked for fresh glasses. After it came and their glasses were full, he stood up from the table and then knelt down next to Ivy, taking a small box from his pocket.

"Ivy, will you take this officially retired FBI agent for your husband?"

He opened the box. Inside was a sparkling emerald-cut diamond set in white gold, with smaller diamonds in the band. The box was from Tiffany. Ivy was speechless.

"Say yes, Ivy." He took her hand, slipping the ring on her finger. A thrill of happiness ran through her. This fascinating, tough, seasoned man wanted to spend the rest of his life with her!

"Yes, of course, yes." She bent over to kiss him. "It's just a total surprise. When did you get the ring?"

"When we closed the safety deposit boxes today," he pushed himself back up and slid into his chair. "Mathew and I did a shopping trip in early December."

"You wanted to get engaged back then?"

"During our Thanksgiving weekend, I realized I wanted to meld my life to yours. While we felt so right together, I had things to work out about the Bureau and me. That is now behind us. Haven't you sensed that we would be spending the rest of our lives together? Like we reached out across the proverbial space-time continuum to find each other?"

The rest of the evening passed in a champagne and red wine haze. Moll amused them with scraps of memories of times at the Bureau. Steve and Ivy kept looking at each other and touching each other. Their knees would brush each other's lightly or they would caress each other's fingers in light motions. Ivy kept staring at the ring and then at him, wondering at this latest twist in their relationship. When they walked back to the hotel, the mild late January evening twinkled around them as if lit by summer fireflies. The last week had been a time of new beginnings for them all. After the stresses of the last couple of months, on top of the work pressures of the last few years, Ivy was ready for a fresh start.

Despite his joy at securing Ivy's commitment to marry him, Steve had a sense of ominous concern. The walk back to the hotel was only a few blocks. Out of the corner of his eye, he saw a figure on the opposite site of the street, slipping from shadow to shadow. When they stopped at the corner, he risked sneaking a peek back, but saw nothing. Mathew, Brian and Moll trailed along behind them. Mathew gave a barely perceptible nod, confirming that they had a tail. In the hotel lobby, where Brian and Moll had also booked rooms, they parted for the night.

"We're going to the bar for a while," Mathew said. "Have a brandy or something. Watch the night unfold."

"Maybe get lucky," Moll said, looking around the almost empty lounge. "Though that seems unlikely. Still by D.C. standards, the night is young."

"You guys got protection in case you do get lucky?" Steve asked, looking at Mathew, who would understand he was talking about guns, not condoms.

"Always. You trained us well. See you for breakfast."

Ivy laughed and tugged Steve towards the elevator, wishing the three younger men a good night. Steve smiled at her, glad that he had three well-trained agents as friends to do a stakeout around the hotel. Mathew would brief Brian and Moll who would contact hotel security, show the FBI credentials they still carried, share their concerns, and start a methodical check of the hotel while Mathew kept watch on the entrance. On this night of all nights, Steve wanted Ivy to remain unaware that someone, FBI or a perp, was following them.

***

As soon as they returned to Portland, Mathew and Steve dedicated themselves to learning about becoming vintners. The property Mathew found vetted out well. He agreed on a price with the current owner and quickly set a date for closing. Steve found a smaller adjoining property on the same ridge that was half planted with wheat and half with an old, mostly sick, walnut grove along with three strips of evergreens. After spending a couple of afternoons sipping a single-malt scotch with the crusty old owner of the property, Steve was able to convince him to sell. Mathew's land came with a tumbling down house and two rotted outbuildings, which he wanted to restore even though they were so ramshackle that he worried they might have to tear them down.

Ivy enjoyed observing how Mathew and Steve worked when they set an objective. Through cajoling, tough stances, and persistence, they scheduled the closing on both properties far faster than she would have expected. They went out one afternoon and bought a big metallic charcoal Suburban to use as their vineyard vehicle. With Mathew now able to drive, he and Steve spent their days meeting with various folks to evaluate the land, run tests on the soil, verify the presence of a good underground water supply, have perk tests performed for two septic systems, work with their attorney to ensure the land was unencumbered, and so on. For several weeks, every day they would drop Ivy at the office and then run down to Dundee for one reason or another. Sometimes Ivy thought they simply wanted to make sure the land was still there.

The third Sunday in February, after days of work on acquiring the land for their vineyard and pursuing building permits, Steve pushed his chair back, put his feet up on the desk and sat staring out into Ivy's perennial garden that was already displaying some spring flowers. Steve knew he was very fortunate. He had a new venture to learn about wine, farming and viniculture with a partner who was like a son to him. He would receive a nice pension from the government. He had the most marvelous woman to share his life and now he was designing the house that they would live in for the rest of their days. He wanted it to be a house that Ivy would treasure and where they would be comfortable. The spot he picked for it was on the top of a knoll on the property he was buying, a little downhill from the walnut grove. The very fact that he would own some land made him proud and excited. He jotted down a list of features from this house of Ivy's in Portland to include in the new house, such as a little deck for morning coffee and a library nook. He wanted to surround the house with rambling gardens, the way the Portland house was. They would need big closets and lots of storage. Ivy had more stuff stashed away in this Portland house than Steve thought one person could accumulate. From what he could tell, she actually used it all now and then throughout the year.

Funny that Mathew, Ivy and he were each only children. His parents were good to him, yet they strict too. Even though Ivy had grown accustomed to spoiling herself, her heart was so generous that he could handle her little peccadilloes like over-shopping. Mathew could be somewhat persnickety. He made fun of Steve for his obsession with what he called the three 'nesses -- cleanliness, neatness and crispness. However Mathew was a dilettante about food, cocktails and wine. On the other hand when out with the team, Mathew used to chow down Big Macs or sub sandwiches like any of the other agents. Each of them had their little oddities.

Steve's thoughts turned back to the house. After being cooped up in office buildings all their lives, he wanted lots of windows on every exterior wall, along with multiple outdoor spaces with decks and patios. The windows had to open to catch the fresh country breezes. Sometime if things went well on the vineyard, Steve would add a narrow indoor lap pool where he could swim to keep in shape and sometimes skinny-dip with Ivy when the water would reflect the resplendence of the moonlight or the magic of a rare snowy night. He bet the night skies would be expansive and filled with stars at the farm away from city lights.

While Ivy would select all the finishes, Steve wanted to surprise her with the overall design. What a delight he was finding it to have a wonderful woman to indulge! Back when Mathew told him he had to believe someone was out there for him, Steve had been skeptical. Time had proved Mathew right. Taking those years to find his personal values again had paid off big time. Steve was no longer the desperado that Mathew once called him.

Sometimes he still worried about the Bureau. Not having caught Astuto bothered him. The perp had setup elaborate traps sacrificing two trained actors to act as his doubles, two expensive yachts and one cocaine operation. He continued to worry that the tail they had in D.C. might show up in Portland like those other thugs had who followed Ivy. Weeks went by and no one appeared who seemed out of place. Still it was troubling. As time went on without any incidents, Steve could feel his vigilance slipping. He often had to remind Ivy to carry her roscoe and Mathew had become so absorbed in the vineyard startup that he was losing his agent's edge. Could they simply walk away from those perps? Was he no longer considered a threat now that he was retired?

***

On the last day of February, Ivy was waiting in the Suburban with the two corgis and watching for Steve and Mathew to emerge from the title company's offices. Suddenly the door burst open and the two men came out, grinning as happily as two boys who had found new bikes by the Christmas tree, making her glad that she had packed a celebratory picnic complete with iced champagne.

On that dewy afternoon, they wandered around their new properties, sampling the picnic, sipping wine and talking. Mathew mapped out his plan for the fields of grapes, with trial plantings to go in as soon as possible. They paced the fields, talking about which direction the rows were to go and how to contour the rows to the land. On the steeper slopes, they intended to plant grass between the rows to help with soil retention. They talked about doing that with all of the fields, although Mathew wanted to consider certain cover crops, like a short variety of sunflowers.

With a fresh bottle of champagne in hand, Steve led Ivy to the knoll he had chosen for their new house. She listened intently to his plan to build it into the bank of the hill. He pulled out the sketches of the house and preliminary copies of the blueprints. She stared in amazement at the plans. The back would be mostly windows facing southwest to catch the sunsets, as well as views of the Coastal Mountain Range. The vistas were nothing short of stunning even on that misty afternoon. That day the low mountains had lingering snow at the upper elevations where they ran in a line of curves and sudden sharp outcroppings, blocking some of the excessively wet and windy weather from the coast.

Since Ivy had advanced her retirement date at work and was now a full time retiree, she was looking forward to working on the vineyard. They planned to lease a couple of trailers to live in at Spook Hills until Steve's house

139

was built, although they would commute on weekends to the Portland house. Ivy envisioned a peaceful year, filled with hard work and the satisfaction of having portions of the land cleared, plowed and planted. It was exactly what she needed to heal her overwrought nerves and work the stress out of her body.

The day their first tractor arrived, Ivy found the two men to be quite comical -- a new sports car would hardly have been as thrilling to them. They took turns driving it, playing with the bucket and using the attached post-hole digger. Ivy was afraid Steve would tip the big tractor over as he headed off up the hill grinning in that boyish way he had. Thankfully the tractor was well balanced and he made the round trip without incident.

Spring was passing actively and happily. They went to bed each night tired in a good way. Neighbors and wine growers stopped by to see what they were doing and offer suggestions.   Once a week, they visited one of the nearby tasting rooms to sample the wines, talk to the staff and learn about making wines. Mathew also took a few hours each week to visit other growers, seeking leads on vines, suppliers, methods and approaches. He was a great listener and with his genial manner, he quickly made himself welcome.

Mathew was excited to receive the first small shipment of potted pinot vines from Sonoma and he was expecting a second small delivery of bareroot plants from a vineyard in the Burgundy region. He was like an anxious parent worrying over those plants, eager to finish prepping the fields where they would be planted.   While the soil had been too wet to work completely by tractor, with a combination of machine and handwork, they managed to do the early planting.

The night after the vines were planted, a heavy rain came in around midnight. Mathew was up and out of his trailer with a big flashlight, checking to be sure his fledgling vines were not washing away down the hill. Steve and Ivy heard him leave his trailer and pulled on their rain gear to join him. The first growth on the potted vines drooped pathetically in their rain-drenched, muddy environment. Nevertheless they were clinging tenaciously to the hillside, taking the worst the rain was giving them. All three of them were up at first light to check the vines again. They had an area eroding down near the bottom of a field where they needed to improve the drainage, but other than that, the field and the vines were holding up. The heavy rains had passed on, leaving only a characteristic Oregon misting dampness. For the first time, Mathew understood the satisfaction of working with live plants, creating an environment where they could thrive, and then nurturing them through the early weeks of rooting and growth.

As April progressed, construction began on the new house. Steve was bursting with excitement over this new project. He had gone from being a man with little to lose to a man who had a bounty to live for, and yet his sixth sense refused to stay quiet. He would be working at the house construction site with the contractor and suddenly feel eyes on his back. He would whip around, check the neighboring hills, look down at the road and scan the land in the valley. Once he caught a glint of sun on glass in the distance. While it was most likely a passing car going up to a neighbor's house, the glint could have been light bouncing off a pair of strong binoculars or even a high-powered riflescope. His sixth sense had never failed him. Why was it sending him danger signals here in their bucolic setting? Was he turning into one of those aging ex-agents who sometimes plagued the Bureau with false reports of some perp hunting them? He sighed, willing to take neurosis over the actuality of someone spying on them.

Chapter 13

On Saturday the fourth of May, they were having a quiet afternoon at the Portland house. Ivy was in the kitchen preparing a bone-in pork roast for the oven before prepping a carrot cake. Down the hall in the office, Steve and Mathew were batting around plans for next steps on the vineyard. From what Ivy could hear, they were outlining the sequence of fields to be prepared and planted. True to their analytical mindsets, they had divided the land into strips laid out on a blown-up plot map that showed contours and elevations. Each field was numbered. They planned later to rename them by the date, source and variety planted, such as "2013 French Gamay". She could hear them arguing over whether to include the name of the source vineyard or grower. Steve wanted to include it; Mathew wanted the grapes to become Spook Hills varieties, since much of the character of their wines would be attributable to their terroir.

When Ivy turned to get the flour and other dry ingredients for the cake out of the pantry, through the glass door to the big deck, she caught sight of a man dressed in black climbing over the deck railing. The deck was elevated on the second story. He must have shimmied up one of the posts that held up the deck. She froze as she watched him swing his second leg onto the deck. He turned, saw her and pulled a gun. It took all of her survival instincts to force herself into action. She grabbed her gun off the counter, dove for the floor, landing hard against a cabinet, screaming for Steve.

She could hear him pounding down the hall, yelling for Mathew to cover the stairs. A shot rang out by the deck and the door crashed open. Gunshots sounded from the front of the house; glass shattered. Ivy could hear the corgis barking as they raced out to the kitchen. Two more shots rang out when Steve flew in. Ivy heard a crash in the cozy room. More shots came from out front and then a car screeched away.

Mathew raced into the kitchen moving fast despite the limp from his damaged leg. Steve ran past Ivy into the cozy room with blood dripping from his arm.

"What the hell?" Ivy scrambled up, grabbed a dishtowel and ran after Steve to press it on his wound. Mathew scooped up her keys, yelling "Corners Better" and flew downstairs to the garage. Steve was fumbling with his cell phone one-handed, then hitting speed dial.

"Retired Agent Steve Nielsen. Shooting at 1279 Council Peak Lane. Call the local police. One intruder dead." He stopped and listened.

"Former Agent Heylen in pursuit of the other perps. Get out on Council Crest Drive, Fairway Drive, Vista, and so on. Get a fucking chopper in the air if you can. Yeah, I'll hold."

He turned and said. "Ivy, call Mathew on his cell. Stay on the line with him no matter what."

"Your arm!"

"Tie the damn towel on and leave it – it's only a scratch. Find out if Mathew saw which way they went."

Ivy grabbed her cell phone and hit Mathew's number on speed dial. She was shaking so much she doubted she could have dialed his full number.

"Mathew, have you seen them?"

"Yeah. Kind of dumb shits at driving. Skidding around so much it slows them down. Black Toyota FJ Cruiser -- again. They headed down Council Crest, and then took that road toward Vista -- I hope they stay away from Fairmount Drive with all the people who walk and bike there. Great, they turned left onto Vista and now, dammit, left again onto Dosch."

Steve grabbed the phone and relayed messages back and forth until the FBI had them all patched into one line with the local police connected as well.

"Chopper in the air. Portland and Beaverton police setting up roadblocks. Agents coming quickly from Portland."

"Confirmed."

"Agent Heylen, are you armed?"

"Handgun."

"Keep your distance but don't lose them. If they go anywhere near ordinary citizens, you may have to jump in. Local squad cars are coming as fast as they can behind you and in front of you. Once they catch up, they will pass and you are to stand down. Understood? We want you live at five for testimony."

"Got it. Police car in sight. Pulling over."

"Good work agent. Do not follow. Repeat. Do not follow. Turn around. Drive home. We have two squad cars heading to your house in case others are after you or these perps double back."

The squad cars pulled up and Ivy answered the door cautiously, pulling the two corgis away from the police officers. One joined Steve on the phone in the kitchen and three staked themselves out in the house. She grabbed leashes for the dogs to keep them out from underfoot. FBI agents also arrived.

Ivy called the head of the Neighborhood Watch on the landline, briefed her, and asked her to do a call down of their neighbors, telling them to stay put. With that done, Ivy grabbed the first aid kit and assessed how bad the scratch on Steve's arm was. While not deep, it was bloody. After cleaning it up and bandaging it, she checked on Druid who was awake and safe, watching the action from his favorite chair.

In a few minutes, Mathew returned, identified himself to the officers and joined them in the kitchen where Steve still had his cell on speaker. The perps made a sharp left turn into a little neighborhood called Dosch Estates and were winding their way back up towards Sunset Boulevard. The police were moving roadblocks into place, employing a device called an X-Net, which Steve explained to Ivy as having spikes and fibers to slow the vehicle down by puncturing its tires, then wrapping around the tires to impede forward motion.

"Chopper overhead. I'm going to drop down and try to scare them to a stop."

"Watch it. These guys are heavily armed."

They heard bullets hitting the helicopter.

"Bastards have submachine guns. Going back up."

"Approaching Sunset. Don't let them go around the X-Net."

"Ah fuck, they flew across Sunset and skidded onto a narrow neighborhood road heading uphill. Chopper stick with them. Lots of twists and turns ahead."

"Any outlet?"

"Yeah. They can drive up to Fairmont or double back to Sunset or Dosch."

"These guys are fucking crazy. Driving these streets way too fast. They clipped a parked car and bounced off a curb."

"Stick with them. We're getting roadblocks in place and clearing cars and pedestrians out."

"Holy Cow!"

"What?"

"They missed a turn, ploughed into a garage and went over the edge of a steep drop-off into the woods. Holy Shit! The car exploded. Those perps aren't going anywhere now. Man alive. It's a fireball."

"Damn," Steve muttered, "I really wanted those guys apprehended alive and held for questioning."

They spent the next hour filling in the police and the FBI agents, giving them background information on who Steve and Mathew suspected the perps were -- revenge drones from the elusive drug dealer. So far no one had reported any pedestrian injuries. The police got a contractor to come out to seal up the door to the deck and the shot-out windows with plywood. Ivy called the Neighborhood Watch woman again to give her an update. Agents guarded the house and a van was now visible in the driveway near the garage. Police officers were patrolling the neighborhood. Between the two forces, a 24-hour rotation schedule was established. Finally technicians wrapped the body of the dead perp in a white body bag and took it away.

As evening approached Steve, Mathew and Ivy with an agent trailing closely behind them, took the dogs out for a walk. When they rounded the second curve in the road, Steve began laughing.

"What on earth are you finding funny?" Mathew asked crossly.

"I may owe this Harry dog my life."

"What do you mean?"

"When I ran into the dining room and stopped to take aim, the perp who came in the back door just got into position to shoot me. Luckily as he went to pull the trigger, Harry flew up and went for his ankle. It was enough to throw off the perp's aim. Who would have thought that fun-loving fur-ball had it in him? Cleo was right behind Harry, only I shot the perp before she could get a piece of him too. I had no idea that those two corgis would ever do anything like that."

"They're small, but not stupid," Ivy said, her voice still shaky.

"I have a whole new respect for corgis." He grabbed Harry's leash, pulled him to a stop and bent down to give him a big hug. Harry gave him a slurp on the check with his soft pink tongue. Steve reached over and cuddled Cleo too when she came over for her share of the praise.

"That will raise some eyebrows in my deposition. Attack corgis to the rescue! What a pair of little protectors -- they have some bite behind their bark. Now I understand, Ivy, what you meant when you said they had big corgi hearts."

She smiled at him weakly. Nightfall was approaching, bringing low, heavy clouds that promised rain, already beginning as a dense curtain of damp air. Although it was only 7:00, the early evening was dark as dusk. She peered worriedly down the darkening streets that seemed to presage further danger and said. "I think we should go back inside; the corgis have finished."

Steve nodded and they turned back. Once in the house, Ivy returned to prepping their dinner. Earlier she had turned off the oven, but now put it back on to let the pork roast finish. Working in the kitchen, with its big sets of windows over the decks, made her feel vulnerable, even though Steve stood at the sink to keep guard. She started grating carrots for the cake, hoping that normal activities would channel her fears into a more positive direction. Mathew turned on the outside lights, and then took up a post in the hallway where he could keep surveillance on the front door and the stairs. Harry lay by his feet, ostensibly sleeping, but Ivy could see that his eyes flicked nervously between the stairwell and the door. While likely nothing more would happen that night, they had to act as if they could be under siege again at any moment.

***

Even two weeks later, Ivy was finding it impossible to sleep other than in fits and starts. Her nerves, still not recovered from her stressful work life, were unraveling. She kept forgetting what she was doing or where she was going. Her attention span disintegrated to where she could no longer read or concentrate on much of anything. She would jump at the slightest sound. Every time she left the house, it was with Steve or Mathew. Since they only made day trips to Spook Hills, the Portland house had become more of a nightly prison than a relaxing place of comfort and joy.

A contractor had replaced the shot-up door and windows and then painted the door and woodwork. The chair the gunman fell back on was out to be reupholstered and the rug had been cleaned. Even though physically the house was almost back where it was before that dreadful day earlier in May, those few minutes replayed in Ivy's nightmares. She still saw the man as he climbed over the railing. She saw him sprawled dead in the cozy room.

All seemed back to normal, except for the agents who stayed around the house -- two of them outside on surveillance 24/7 on a rotating basis. Police squad cars frequently circled the neighborhood, showing force as well. Even with the added protection, Ivy worried about when the next strike would take place. The FBI focused a team on tracking down the head of the drug ring with Steve receiving periodic updates. They conducted a raid on a Colombian drug shipment site, but so far Astuto evaded them.

The following week, they started staying again at Spook Hills to catch up on work on the vineyard and to push the contractor's crew to work longer days on the house. Steve hoped that the change of scenery would restore Ivy's peace of mind. He felt so guilty for having brought the attack at the Portland house on his beloved Ivy. If she had never become involved with him, she would be as feisty, confident, and radiant as the day that they met. Now she barely had color in her face, rarely smiled and jumped at the slightest sound. He hoped that with time she would find her way back to herself and to him. For now he would comfort and protect her.

On the fourth night at Spook Hills, Ivy broke down during dinner, trying to hide her sobbing by retreating to the bedroom area of their trailer. Only after a couple of hours, could she stop crying and shaking. That night she slept very little and was up making coffee well before dawn. Over a breakfast she barely ate, Ivy told Steve that she had to make a change. She was jumpier than ever at the farm -- every sound, every gust of wind, every flash of light made her think someone was outside, trying to break in. Going back to the Portland house with its memories of the intruders was out.

To Ivy, they were so exposed at Spook Hills. She could no longer stay there, waiting for the next attack. She felt compelled to drop out of sight for a few weeks or months, mend her shattered nerves and rebuild her inner strength. Steve wanted to accompany her but for her own self-respect, she had to heal on her own. She suspected that he would have her followed, no matter what they agreed.

Ivy viewed herself as selfish and cowardly to run away, but her life had changed so radically in the past year, culminating in the shooting at the Portland house. She needed time alone to regroup. Even though most of those life-changing events were positive, altogether on top of the accumulated years of work pressures, she had reached a point where a complete breakdown was inevitable. Her nervous system was short-circuiting. She did not want to leave Steve or Mathew. She wanted Harry, Cleo and Druid with her for comfort. Still, she had to be practical. For her own safety, she would need to travel incognito and change locations frequently. Her three little protectors would have to stay at Spook Hills.

Once she decided what her undercover appearance would be, she had photos taken, Steve arranged an alternate set of IDs through the Chief at the Bureau that were overnighted to her. She crammed her hair under a short fluffy silver wig, wore a different style of glasses and packed only casual clothes -- all things she could leave on a moment's notice and be Ivy Littleton again. Her new name was Anna S. Foley from Boothbay Harbor, Maine. The "Anna" was her middle name, the "S" stood for Stephanie, the female version of Steve, and the "Foley" was her grandmother's maiden name on her mother's side. The familiarity of the names comforted her. Steve hoped they were not too traceable.

148

Leaving Steve at the downtown hotel when he dropped her off was the hardest thing Ivy had ever done. That tough man had tears streaming down his face and she could only give him a hug and one last kiss. If she let her own tears start, she was afraid they would be unstoppable. To be any good for him again, she had to retreat like a battered female fox going underground to lick and heal her wounds. She forced herself to walk away and then exited through the front of the big hotel, found a taxi and went out to the airport.

She had a new debit card and two new credit cards as Anna S. Foley. Steve funded an account in her new name via a trail of other accounts he set up at various banks under an old false identity that he had kept when he left the Bureau. Mathew coached her on how to check for being tailed, how to lose a tail, where to go for safety, like a police station, and to always map out where the next one was. She had a new cell phone, a new laptop and a new iPad that Steve ordered for her. Steve bought a new iPhone with a new number for himself that Ivy was to use instead of the old one. She left with only a small rolling duffel bag, a light expandable briefcase, and her purse. In her jeans, tee shirt, windbreaker and walking shoes, Ivy had the appearance of any other newly minted retiree off to see the world.

Chapter 14

Steve slumped in a deck chair outside their trailer at the vineyard, staring vacantly up at the house construction site. With Ivy's departure, the light she had given him went with her. His emptiness was worse now from having his life so illuminated. Without the glow that she cast, everything around him was dull as if thickly tarnished. Steve knew she had to make a change to get relief from the life-threatening trauma that he had brought to her. He recalled how lovely, vivacious and spunky she had been and however unintentionally, he had made her into a shadow of herself. Her lively spirit that challenged him had disappeared.

He was thankful that Brian agreed to be her secret protector. Since that first traumatic experience against Matka last fall, he was becoming skilled at disguises. Steve wished Ivy had let him go with her. He believed she blamed him. She became remote and then left him downtown, not shedding a single tear. He felt so guilty -- he had driven her from her home and her life. She had to leave behind her dogs and her cat, as well as her clothes and identity. The only hope Steve held onto was that she had taken her engagement ring, strung on two gold chains around her neck and tucked out of sight. A small part of him clung to the belief that its closeness to her heart would bring her back to him. While Mathew insisted that they continue work on the house, it seemed a feeble task with her gone. Never had he been so bereft, not even after his parents died. How would he go on without Ivy?

That same afternoon, Mathew was working at the construction site and thinking. He had to burn off some frustration with Steve or his temper would get the best of him. Steve was driving him so crazy, he could take the tractor and send it right off the hillside with Steve on it. In the days since Ivy left, he had folded up. He showed no interest in anything -- not the house, not the vineyard, not even food. Almost overnight, Steve had become an old man. It was beyond Mathew's comprehension. Less than a year ago, Steve worked extremely long hours on challenging cases, and while he was always demanding, sometimes crotchety and occasionally impatient, never did he buckle under pressure. Steve had to appreciate that Ivy's love of him would compel her to come back. How could he have so little faith in what she felt for him?

Mathew used to think he was important to Steve. Here he was, trying to start a new business, struggling against a steep learning curve, dodging bullets for chrissakes, worrying about the next attack, taking over building a house, and Steve picked this time to stop contributing. What about me, Steve? Remember me? Your almost son?

He was digging the footing for a retaining wall on the slope behind the house. The local soil was called Decaan Basalt and was high in iron oxide which glowed a deep brick red in the sun as he turned it over. He dug hard in his frustration even though his muscles protested. Maybe the truth lay deeper. Maybe the issue was not only Steve. Perhaps it was also within himself. He had that same sense of abandonment as when his parents flew off to different parts of the world, leaving him to wander through their big, empty house with only a housekeeper for company. Ivy was gone. Steve was not there for him. They were in their own worlds and here Mathew was, reduced again to the little boy left alone at home. Well damn it, this time he was not staying silent. Steve was going to hear about the impact he was having. Mathew stopped to catch his breath, leaning on the shovel. At least dealing with his emotions had the digging job almost done.

Was this core loss from his childhood ever going to let him grow into the man he wanted to be? *Manet Cicatrix*, The Scar Remains. He went back to digging. He had to trust that Ivy would return. He had to believe that kind of love existed. What would Ivy do if she were here? Mathew thought about the two times he had seen her angry -- the time she and Steve argued over the mission in the Caribbean and the time right after that when she sent him out of the kitchen with a kick in the butt. The same image came to mind. Ivy standing, hands on her hips, and speaking in a harsh tone that was so unlike her. Each time she brought Steve or him to reason. Mathew guessed that every now and then, each of them needed a hit on the back of the head to move along on their journeys.

Maybe this was his time to do that for Steve. He had to believe that Ivy would come back to him. Mere bullets could not tear their great love apart. Steve had to realize that Mathew mattered too. While he could give this time away to Ivy to grapple with her fears, he needed Steve contributing at Spook Hills. He threw down the shovel and stomped from the jobsite down to the trailers. The digging made him hot; he pulled off his chambray shirt as he strode along and wiped the sweat off his face with it, streaking the pale blue shirt with the damp red soil. Steve was sitting outside, not moving. Mathew stopped and stood in front of him. Steve slowly looked up.

"Enough." Mathew said, striving to remain calm. "Ivy will come back. You have to realize that."

Steve went back to staring at the ground and shook his head.

Mathew could feel his temper rising. "Damn it. This is about believing. Remember believing?"

"She is gone. I did this to her. Me. I brought the danger into her life."

"Ivy needs time. Get that in your stubborn head. She loves you. She became overwhelmed. She was scared."

"She doesn't call. She said not to call her. I email every day, but only every few days, when she changes cities, do I receive a short email that she left the last one."

"Get over it. She loves you."

Steve gazed off into the distance, still shaking his head.

"For the more immediate issue -- remember our partnership?"

Steve gazed at him without interest.

"Damn it. We are in this vineyard together. You have a house to build for Ivy for when she returns. What the hell is wrong with you? You told me that I am like a son to you. I matter, Steve. I am trying to get this vineyard going and keep your house on track. I can't do it all. Maybe you don't need me, but I sure as hell need you."

Mathew threw down his shirt and stomped back up the hill. Having no reaction from Steve was far worse that having him become angry. He was mad and unhappy that he failed to get through to Steve and worse, he was unsure what to do next.

***

Ivy stood at the rail on the Bar Harbor ferry crossing Frenchman Bay to Winter Harbor, Maine. Even though she cared little about where she went, she hoped that new experiences would refresh her senses. The day was cloudy with a stiff breeze coming off the steely gray of the Atlantic Ocean. As the white boat intrepidly moved towards the distant shore, small waves hit its bow, giving off a stiff spray. She barely noticed the movement, lost as she was thinking over the weeks since leaving Steve.

She had plotted her initial course that first day by getting on a plane to Salt Lake City. From there, she bought a ticket to San Francisco and stayed at a Kimpton hotel she had used years before when traveling on business. For two days she hid in her room, ordering from room service and either staring mindlessly or crying. On the third day she left her room and walked out of the hotel to buy a second pair of walking shoes. After three nights she checked out, rented a car and drove up to Sonoma, choosing lodging at random. From there she drove to Sacramento, stayed a couple of days in a modest hotel downtown and flew in two hops to Phoenix, using different airlines, and then drove up to Sedona where she stayed at a resort, taking the smallest of their rooms.

Every day for that first week, she cried for hours until she was drained of emotion. She spent a week in the Sedona area, going out occasionally to sit and stare at the rock formations. That second week she was so tired that she slept more than she was awake. She napped for a few hours during the day and slept 8, 10, 12 hours at night. At the end of the week in Sedona, she flew to Boston and drove up the coast of Maine, stopping at two different inns as she went, winding up in Bar Harbor at the end of the week, which was where she was now, still sleeping long hours. She only ventured out to walk the short sand beach near her inn or to sit on the rocks above the coast. One day she drove up Cadillac Mountain, blending in with the other tourists. She wandered around, bought a coke and drove back to the inn where she was staying.

She sent a short secure email to Steve after she left each town. She was too drained to do more. While she felt rotten to be so uncommunicative, she had to rebuild herself in her own way. Every day Steve sent her a secure email, full of tender thoughts.

She saw a man she thought was Brian a couple of times. Having a highly skilled FBI agent trailing her gave her comfort. He would be reporting to Steve every day about where she was and what she did. Steve needed that lifeline to her, in the same way she needed one to him. However, only she could rebuild her inner strength. If she failed, then Steve would be better off without her. She could not tie him to a shattered shell. If she could not come back to herself, then she had to find the strength to end their engagement.

***

Steve watched Mathew go off up the hill. He had never lost patience with him like that before. Mathew was working double shifts between the vineyard and the house, keeping the vineyard workers and the builder's crew organized. One of the workers was a young Hispanic fellow named Fred, short for Federico, who followed Mathew around like a lost kid eager to find his place in the world. Even he had noticed how badly off Steve was. He overheard a comment Fred made to Mathew that "Big boss, he no happy. Better he drive tractor. Wreck things."

Steve wanted to believe that Mathew was right. He must not give up hope about Ivy coming back to him. Maybe the time for that would be when she did not come back. Brian reported in daily with details about her solitary wanderings, although at the beginning she disappeared inside her hotel rooms for days at a time. Only trays of food appearing at the door or left outside mostly uneaten indicated she was there. Now she had flown to Maine and was staying in Bar Harbor. Brian was seeing her more, sitting on the cliffs, staring at the ocean or walking the beach in town. Steve wanted to fly to be with her even though he knew if she needed him, she would call. Did she detest him for the danger he had put her in? Was she afraid of him as well as the perps? What else could explain her long silences?

Again Steve told himself that Mathew was right. He must not despair. He must put his head into building their house for when Ivy returned. He would put in every security gadget available -- cameras, alarms, motion detectors, sound surveillance inside and out -- anything to help her feel protected. Above all Steve wanted to make it an "Ivy home". What was it Mathew had said once about her Portland house? Ah yes, the expression he used was "*Utile Dolci*" -- combining the useful with the agreeable. Steve decided to decorate the little balcony off the master with metal railings designed like twining ivy and think up other embellishments that would delight her.

He stood, picked up Mathew's shirt, shook it out, folded it neatly and turned to walk up to the house construction site. He would take Mathew into Dundee that night so they could talk over dinner and update their plans. He would have him order a great bottle of wine and they would have steak. Mathew always enjoyed a perfectly cooked steak. He smiled a little remembering the steak dinner the day they left the Bureau. That steak was so full of flavor and tender. When Ivy returns, he would take the three of them to the same place again.

As Steve recalled what Mathew said about needing him as a partner and as a friend, some warmth seeped back into him. They had been a team for some time now. Mathew had never let him down. He had believe that long term, Ivy would never let him down either.

"Get it in gear, Nielsen," he muttered to himself as he trudged up the hill. "You must have faith. What kind of pathetic old man have you become not to believe in the most enchanting woman you ever met? You must believe that Ivy will come back to Spook Hills, back to her new home and back to you."

***

After five empty days in Bar Harbor, Ivy drove the expressway down to Boston and flew to London, registering at a small hotel where she had stayed several times before. From there, she rented a car, drove down to Cornwall and sat by the sea, thinking of all those Rosamunde Pilcher novels she had read long ago with her simplistic approach to romance. No one snuck around her corners of Cornwall shooting with intent to kill. The aura of Pilcher's ghost would have to be her protection on the rocky coast with its dramatic cliffs and hidden sandy beaches.

Following three days in Cornwall with its summer weather turning hot, on her birthday of June 15th, Ivy drove back to Heathrow, turned in the rental car, took the train into the city, and stayed overnight in a trendy hotel. The next morning, she checked out and took an early train to Edinburgh, surprising herself by enjoying a hearty Scottish breakfast in the dining car. As she savored the simple tastes of thick, ham-like bacon and English-style scrambled eggs, she realized her appetite was coming back. More than that, she wanted Steve. She could envision him sitting with her on the train, sharing what should be a vacation adventure with him.

After a couple of days in Edinburgh at a small, quiet hotel, she took a train to Glasgow, overnighted in a non-descript tourist hotel and drove to Portree on the Isle of Skye where she moved into a bed and breakfast. As she walked around that rugged, windswept isle, she could feel herself coming back together. The shattered sensation that had been haunting her was retreating. Bit-by-bit parts of her essence were refinding each other and knitting new, and hopefully stronger, bonds. Her nervous system was becoming more reliable, her heart had ceased its sporadic fits of pounding, and that elusive part of her that must be her soul crept out of wherever it had been hiding, making her feel more complete.

She spent a week wandering the rocky coastline and seeing the Isle of Skye. One day, she hired a local guide to take her hiking into the highlands. Walking the cold, wind-blown path up the side of the mountain to a hidden loch, she discovered that she needed Steve more than she feared the bad guys. The time had come to do more than send a short email.

Secure Email from Ivy Littleton, June 27, 2013

My Dearest Steve,

I have left Scotland after spending some days in Edinburgh and then more than a week on the Isle of Skye, roaming its highlands and rugged coastlines. While you have never been out of my thoughts, by the time I boarded the train from London to Edinburgh, some of my depleted reserves had returned and I had the energy to daydream about you.

Until that time, so little of me was alive that the part of my brain that dreams had no ability to function. I can appreciate that these weeks have been devastating for you. However you must know in your heart that when I am sufficiently healed, when I have my inner strength back, and when I can no longer stand being apart from you, that I will return.

In my mind, you sat across from me on the Edinburgh train eating a full Scottish breakfast. You walked around that historic city with me, reveling in the twisting, scenic streets, the views, and the sheer Scottishness of it all. You snuggled with me at night, warming me with your love. You were on the Isle of Skye as I roved the Highlands and braved the winds on the coast. At night, I let my thoughts linger on memories of you kissing me, holding me, and becoming as much a part of each other as it is possible to be. Those thoughts and memories have helped to heal me.

I fear I have let you down, the way I crumbled so seemingly easily. What you don't know, because I could never talk about it and made every effort not to show it, is that work had stolen my life. When I met you, years of continual stress had so worn me down, that my life had become one gray series of days to plow through. Oh yes, I kept up a facade, but inside I had nothing left to give. Then you came and made the world have color again. My blood began to hum in my veins. Suddenly I had positive forces to bolster me up. However only time without the negative grind could repair the underlying damage and time was what I was not to have.

So many things changed so quickly -- you and Mathew moved in. FBI agents were staked out in the garage and following me everywhere I went. You and Mathew left the FBI. You bought Spook Hills together to make it our new home. You proposed, giving me a new life. I retired and thought that working with you on Spook Hills, I could recover. Then all too quickly, that peace was shattered. As soon as I had a glimpse of that man on my deck at the Portland house, the threads that were holding me together snapped, flew about the room and lay in shards around me. I could no longer keep up the pretense that all was well with Ivy.

Please believe that I did not leave because of you. I left for you. I left for us. I left for me. I had to find what was left of me, pull the shattered pieces back together, put as much heavy-duty glue as possible in the cracks and plug up the holes so that I can be strong again.

I cannot tell you when that will be -- next week, next month, next year. I only can tell you that it will be. I hope that you still love me enough to be there when I can come back to you. You are the center of my world that has kept the essence of me breathing.

With all my Love,

Ivy

P.S. Give Mathew and my dear corgis and Druid hugs for me and remember the feel of my arms around you, as I cherish the memories of the warmth of yours around me.

***

Steve pushed back from his laptop after reading Ivy's email. He closed his eyes and let out a deep breath, one that seemed like he had been holding since she departed, leaving him standing and crying in the lobby of the Heathman Hotel. She still loves me, he whispered. Now he better understood what caused her to crumble. While he was sorry that she had not told him at the time, he well understood having a misplaced sense of pride. She still loves me, he said out loud, no longer whispering. He could feel the joy spreading outward from his heart, filling him up. He wanted to be with her. While he wanted at least to call her, he understood that this opening up had been hard for her. He remembered when he first met her, he had noticed a flickering emotion that would creep into her eyes -- fear, conflict or a troubling memory -- and she would quickly push it back out of sight. Now he understood that even then she had been fighting to hold herself together. He had to give her the time to rebuild in her own way. Perhaps if she found she was not the only one with issues, it would make the healing process a little easier for her.

Secure Email from Steve Nielsen, June 27, 2013

Oh, my darling Ivy, how precious having you open up is to me! I have been living in a quagmire of guilt and despair, fearful that my crazy life had driven you away from me forever. I have been so worried that not only had I put you in mortal danger, but also I had robbed you of your home, your peace of mind, your health, and your strength.

To hear that you still want me and to understand that more was happening with you than I appreciated have combined to raise my spirits. For the first time in weeks, my inner self has a chance of becoming whole again. You had woken up parts of me that were in hibernation. Having felt those parts come alive, I no longer wanted to revert to the half-man I used to be.

If it is any comfort, let me tell you something about me that I held back from you. Heck, I held it back from myself for a long time because I refused to admit that age was catching up with me. My reactions started slowing down. While not a lot, it was enough to make a difference in situations where split second timing is required. The last four missions I was on only went as well as they did because of the teams I had, the planning we did, and support from other units. That last one, the one on the yacht, was the worst. I damn near got us all killed. I never had the courage to discuss it with you -- I was so afraid you would think less of me. When we are together again, I will tell you how it played out, but that was the reason I told you one of your angels was riding on my shoulder.

If we learn nothing else from this time apart, we should learn to be open with each other. We should not hide what is troubling us from pride, from fear of appearing diminished in each other's eyes or from the terrifying thought that our honesty about natural human changes would drive us apart. We must have more faith in ourselves and in each other. While the love we share is as ethereal as the gossamer wings of a butterfly, it is also stronger than any substance we know.

If one of us is unable to talk about a troublesome topic, thought or emotion, then let us commit to sending each other emails now and again. They can be love letters or confessions of inner doubts or soul searching we are doing or reminders to each other of who we are. I have spent years searching for you. We must not allow our overgrown senses of personal dignity to get in the way of deepening our love.

Take as much time as you need, my dearest Ivy. If you want me, I will be there by your side as fast as a jet can transport me. Until that time, I will be at Spook Hills, making the land we bought into a home for you to fill with love and happiness. When you are ready, we will enjoy each other and grow old together.

Ivy, my Ivy, I love you more than I ever thought was possible,

Steve

***

Ivy took a circuitous route back to Portland, first staying in London at a modern hotel for a few days, testing her newfound strength. Early on the fourth morning, she checked flights online, found one with some open seats and packed, planning to take the train out to Heathrow, buy a ticket at the airport and fly from London to Washington D.C. From there she would book a flight to Denver and then another one to Portland.

Once in Portland, she found a vacation rental of a studio apartment in the Pearl that she took for a week. In the apartment or out walking, still in her disguise, she spent three days making sure she was confident in her decision to rejoin Steve. The next day she planned to leave for Spook Hills by a roundabout route to shake anyone who might try to follow her. She wanted to surprise Steve. He needed to understand that she would not leave again. Wandering and being away from him were not how she could live. She was determined to stand by his side to face whatever might lie ahead and not take this coward's way out. She had to get her nerves under control; she accepted that. Now it was time to be there for Steve.

She was full of joy at the prospect of seeing him. She found she was eager to see Mathew too. She wanted her corgis and cat around her. Now was the time to pick up the threads of her old life at Spook Hills. Her heart was suddenly so hopeful and full of promise that she wanted to leave right away, however she had been cautious over the past weeks. She could be watchful for another day, or two, or even three, until she was safely back with Steve.

PART III

Chapter 15

Mathew sat near Ivy's and Steve's beds at the hospital in Portland. Neither one had fully regained consciousness after the shooting at Spook Hills and their surgeries. A bullet hit Ivy within minutes of her arrival back at Spook Hills. She woke up on and off but was too disoriented to talk. Steve lay in the bed opposite in a coma after losing a great deal of blood when he was shot twice as he spun around to fling himself in front of Ivy after the first shot hit her in the shoulder.

With each of them lying in front of him, Mathew wondered if he should be out trying to catch whoever was responsible for this travesty, but he felt compelled to stay with Steve and Ivy as their personal guard and friend. FBI agents were on duty in the hallway; they covered for Mathew in the room when needed. The Bureau had a team after the perps with Brian and Moll acting as consultants, making Mathew glad that the Bureau took care of their own, even former agents. This was his time to be there for his two friends, even though he felt useless just sitting there and waiting. While he could not make them better, Mathew could help them when they woke up. He prayed he would get that chance.

He was so saddened and angered that Ivy and Steve had been attacked so viciously and devastatingly. Similar to the shooting at the Portland house, this shooting had all the earmarks of a vendetta, where the attackers also went after Ivy first. He was thankful that Steve and Ivy did have their reunion, even though it only lasted a minute. At least they had that to hang onto. Mathew had to believe they would both recover and live to get married because their hearts were so intertwined.

He noticed that Ivy had moved again. This time her eyes were open and she was trying to sit up. He jumped out of his chair and rushed to help her.

"Steve?" she asked weakly.

Mathew nodded over to the next bed. The nightstand hid Steve's face from Ivy's view. She began to struggle to get out of bed. He gently pushed her back and rang for the nurse. Once she had fussed over Ivy and checked the IV and monitors, the nurse left the room. Ivy whispered. "Is he sleeping?"

"He's in a coma, Ivy. The doctors aren't sure why. He lost a great deal of blood."

"Have to see him. Touch him."

Mathew nodded, moved the IV and monitor trolley and helped her sit up.

"Where do you think you're going?" The same nurse bustled back in with a refill for one of the substances going into Ivy.

"To see Steve."

"Lay back down," the nurse ordered Ivy. "And Agent, don't tell me this is protocol. You get back to your post in that chair."

"I have to see him," Ivy said in what was supposed to be a firm voice, but it came out as a rustling murmur.

"Please nurse," Mathew interjected. "These two have the most incredible bond. They are engaged to be married. Ivy might be able to reach him and bring him back to us."

The nurse gave him a steely glare, then handed Ivy two pills and a paper cup of water. "Take these."

As she left the room, the nurse turned to Mathew. "That medication will start working in 10 minutes. Right now, I am going on break. When I come back, I expect to see her exactly as she is. And you," she said sternly, "You had better be sitting in that chair like their guardian angel. A doctor will be in shortly."

As soon as the nurse's footsteps faded, Mathew scooted over to the bed, gently pulling Ivy up. She helped as she could even though she was weak and only had use of one arm. Once her feet were on the floor, Mathew supported her by her waist, taking most of her weight and helping her shuffle over to Steve's bed.

She reached down to take Steve's hand, leaned over and began calling softly. "Steve, Steve, wake up. I need you. Come back. Come back to me." She stroked his cheek and kept calling him, but he lay there as impassively as he had since his surgery. Tears ran down Ivy's face and Mathew could feel her sagging heavily against him. He slowly moved her back to her bed, settled her under the covers and arranged the IVs and monitor cables. She closed her eyes, lying there with a very troubled expression on her face. Mathew took a tissue and wiped away the tears on her cheeks, pressed her hand and went to sit down, making it back right before the nurse's footsteps approached.

The nurse checked both patients, nodded at Mathew and left. Every few hours Mathew helped Ivy over to Steve's bed. Several nurses yelled at them and threatened Mathew, but he would give them a charming smile and say that they needed Steve awake to question him about the shooters. One by one, through a mixture of charm and persistence, he wore the nurses down. Each time Ivy was getting stronger when she woke up, always wanting to be near Steve. The nurses began taking the monitors and drips off.

Towards dinnertime on the day she first woke up, Ivy whispered her concerns about Steve. "What will we do if he doesn't wake up? What if he has brain damage from the blood loss?"

"He will come back to us, Ivy. He has a great constitution and he is fit. Inside of that body of his, he is healing. Give him time and try not to worry."

"This is my fault. I shouldn't have come back."

"Ivy, this shooting would have happened sooner or later. If you did not come back, Astuto would have sent some goons after just Steve and me. The Bureau is on it. The bastard will be caught, even if I have to rejoin the FBI to do it. You stay calm and heal for Steve. He will need you when he wakes up."

The next morning, Ivy put on make-up and fixed her hair as best she could with one arm. Color was starting to return to her face. Mathew could not help but smile watching her primping.

"From the first time I saw you together at the airport last fall, I was struck by how you would lean towards each other. I have seen you in the same room

163

standing or sitting several feet apart, yet leaning towards each other. You are so drawn together."

"You're exaggerating."

"A compelling force pulls you together. If you get within a certain distance of each other, you are always in physical contact. Never before had I understood Aristotle's comment that love is composed of one soul inhabiting two bodies. You two illustrate that concept."

"Actually I think that love is a merging of two souls into one. We are each too independent not to have individual souls."

Mathew was glad to see that despite her injury and the drugs she was on, that Ivy's mind remained sharp and even argumentative. However the conversation and the primping had tired her and she slid groggily back against the pillow. Mathew went over to make her more comfortable and watched her go to sleep in a few seconds. He put her makeup away, then went over and talked to Steve for a bit, but had no response. Could Steve hear him and either could not, or given his stubbornness, would not react? He went over to his backpack, took out the electric razor he had brought with him and gave Steve a shave. Every day the hospital staff bathed him. A physical therapist came in the afternoons to exercise his legs and right arm. His hair needed a trim, but that was more than Mathew could do.

Mathew wanted to pick up lunch for himself, and judging by Ivy's disgust with the hospital's food the previous evening, he would get some light fare for her too. He asked one of the agents in the hall to stay with Steve and Ivy. Maybe he would try putting food under Steve's nose. If Ivy failed to wake him, maybe food could.

***

Once back, he called Brian to see if the investigation was turning up anything, then he settled back with his lunch. The hospital staff brought in food for Ivy, but she went on sleeping. Steve did not move. Around one, a nurse woke up Ivy and told her to eat. She drank the milk on the tray, poked at the yellow gelatin, but left the plastic-looking cream of chicken soup alone. Once the tray was taken away, Mathew opened a second bag and handed her a

164

carton of the good Mama Leone's chicken soup from Elephant's Deli, knowing it was a favorite of hers. She took it gratefully and began eating.

"There's some pudding too. And an oatmeal raison cookie for after your next nap."

She smiled and nodded. "You're a lifesaver – I'm starving. Mathew, tell me what Steve was like when you worked together at the Bureau."

Mathew thought about where to start and decided it may as well be at the beginning. "Back when I was at the FBI Academy in Quantico, Steve conducted a guest lecture series about what prospective agents should expect on real cases. He would depict situations from cases he handled as much as ten years before where he made each situation come alive with details. He talked without notes, going for two hours at a clip. His memory was astounding.

"After about an hour to describe the situation, he made the lectures interactive, asking us what we would do, drawing out comments and questions. At first only the show-offs raised their hands. He never shot anyone down; he explained why whatever scenario, let's say 6.3, had weaknesses or risks. He always had the scenarios numbered and remembered the numbers -- we checked the case histories."

"Is that standard protocol at the FBI?"

"Not the way Steve did it. He placed a particular emphasis on planning and on examining as many possibilities as he and his teams could think of, particularly before going in for an arrest."

"He is so logical."

"And uber-organized. Anyway by the fourth lecture, I gathered my courage and responded with what I hoped was a scenario outside the box. While I was naive to think I could impress him given how green I was, I wanted to succeed where others had failed. His reaction was different as he listened; he stopped for a moment, looked hard at me, and then explained the fault in my solution that created too much risk, but he didn't recite a scenario number. Steve made redacted PDF copies of the case files he cited, including all the planning scenarios, and made them available to the students on a server -- a relatively new approach back in the '90s. After class, I checked the case study and my scenario wasn't listed."

"That's interesting."

"I didn't know if it was feeble or if I had actually come up with a possibility that this superhuman agent and his team missed. Years passed before I learned the answer. All of us prospective agents talked about him. He had a reputation as the most successful agent, team leader, and FBI executive in the business. He also had a rep for being about the meanest SOB too. No, mean is not right word. Most demanding, that was it. Never have I known Steve to be mean, unless the situation -- the scenario -- required it and then he directed his angst towards the perps. At the Bureau, rumors about him so enhanced his reputation that it became an aura. He was *sui generis*, a sort of demi-god to us as students. Seeing this living legend in our classroom took our already high goals for ourselves and moved the bar up."

"Did he have any nicknames besides 'the Boy Scout'?"

"Yeah, one was 'Drittsekk'. I am sorry to say that is Norwegian for asshole or more literally 'shitbag'. Yet another was simply, 'B.A.', which could be for bad ass or big agent, depending on the circumstances."

"Like the 'B.A.' one."

Mathew continued. "When it came time for me to graduate from the FBI Academy at Quantico, my first choice of assignment was the International Operations Division where Steve then was. He had made such an impression on me that I hoped to test my worth by working for him, but the Bureau assigned me to my second choice, the Criminal Division in the New York office.

"On the job, I buried myself in each case and in my free time, learned about cases with international roots. From New York, the Bureau transferred me to D.C., where my boss had earmarked me to move into management. I set the record straight that all I wanted was fieldwork. Within a few months I was sent to Dallas, by way of annoyance I think. From there, the Bureau transferred me back to New York -- six years older and with significant chapters of experience behind me.

"Sometimes I would hear about cases Steve was on and I saw him in the office a few times, but that was it. In 2007 in New York, we began working on a case that involved drugs from Afghanistan, money laundering, and suspected funding of terrorist activities. From the money-laundering point of view, it was not unlike the case we picked up last year involving this Astuto character. The trails were leading to Turkey, which might have meant a drug cartel, but the path the money took was off. The money routed from the U.S. through France, then Spain, then Bermuda and then Cairo and there it sat from everything we could tell. Most money schemes associated with laundering had the money re-invested or withdrawn. We found it puzzling; we were stalled. Then guess who showed up to take over the investigation?"

"Steve," Ivy said in a whisper.

Mathew nodded in confirmation. "The very announcement that he was managing the case caused a flurry of speculation in the office and generated more than a little apprehension. I was worried that I might fail to measure up to his standards. His aura had not faded. In fact the intervening years had enhanced it. The rumor was that he always ran the perps to ground, usually quickly, but even if it took months, he would get them. He never forgot a case or a perp or an agent."

"Like he will never forget Astuto," Ivy said as she leaned over in her bed to look at Steve.

"On the day Steve took over, we had to assemble at seven in the morning. He walked in, introduced himself and then had us go around the room giving our names. Unbeknownst to us, Steve had researched each member of the team. After each person said his or her name, Steve recited some notable action from the agent's record. Ten of us were on the team. He had no notes. All the information was in that incredible brain of his.

"When it came to me, he stated my class year at the Academy, the case I had responded on and a new scenario number. That is when I realized that I had come up with a new and valid twist on that classroom case. At the end, he announced the leaders for four sub-teams. I was to head up the Scenario Planning Team. He expected us to choose our teams on a round-robin basis. Brian was also in the New York office although not assigned to this case. I chose him for the team because he can be a good sounding board, a solid data man and a meticulous organizer. The next agent I asked for was Moll. He would bring the creative twist we needed. I could have chosen one to two more agents, but those two were my team; it felt right. I noticed a lifted eyebrow from Steve when I shook my head, refusing to take a Round three selection. It made me apprehensive about my decision to keep my team small."

"This is great stuff!" Ivy said. "Keep going."

"He moved us to rooms with a different layout than most Bureau operations. The suite had four workrooms, one office and an open space, which he soon filled with a long table and a trio of computers and projectors. Our workroom had two computers per agent, each with two flat screens; every room had a projector. That meant that in my room, we had 12 flat screens, plus the projector. Since this was to be a paperless operation, the room lacked the traditional flipcharts or printers or even scrap paper. The only concession to creature comforts were water coolers, but every morning Steve had pastries or bagels and coffee delivered for us and late every afternoon, he had some sort of snack brought in. Often he also had lunch delivered and sometimes dinner. The suite had landline phones in each room; it had its own security system and full-time armed security guards.

Steve introduced us to his electronic casebook that he had designed and created long before the Bureau had one as comprehensive. Every day all of our drafts, findings and work papers had to be stored in his casebook system to ensure secure backup and easy recall. Every night he read what we checked in. I sometimes wondered when he slept."

Mathew paused and looked over at Ivy. He watched her pick up the pudding container and begin to lick the inside of it to get the last smears of her dessert. Clearly the only thing wrong with her appetite was the taste of the food in the hospital. He got up, poured some ice water for her, cleared the debris from her table and sat back down.

"Was he really that fearsome?" Ivy asked.

"He was tough. He had high standards. We heard that if agents failed to measure up to what he wanted, he booted them off the team. In addition he was so darn big and smiled so seldom that he seemed intimidating, at least until an agent worked with him for some time.

"As an aside, the Bureau implemented a big system for electronic files last year called Sentinel at a cost of, no joke, over $400 million. It took almost seven years to develop, well eleven, if you count the first false start. Steve wrote his system in 2000 and kept updating it as technology evolved. Admittedly the Bureau's system is much broader in scope and serves the whole of the FBI; Steve's only served his teams. I have used both -- his was better from an agent's perspective, containing exactly what the team needed for each case. Steve is simply brilliant at understanding how to use technology to get the job done."

Ivy smiled and nodded. "I can see that. He is very technical, yet practical too. He could have been an industry leader if he had chosen a career in software development."

"Never thought of that, but I bet you're right." Mathew paused and took a drink from his own water bottle before continuing.

"You know anything about Steve's personal life?" Ivy asked.

Mathew looked at her, debating if Steve would want Ivy to know about the dark time earlier in his life.

Seeing his hesitation, Ivy said, "Only what you're comfortable telling me."

"For a time, years actually, Steve was really empty inside. What I am going to tell you is about the time before he became what we all jokingly call an FBI monk. Has he talked about that time?"

"Only that he went through a bad time in his life. He has said he would talk about it but he hasn't, at least not yet."

Mathew wondered if he should proceed but decided that since it long predated Ivy, he could go ahead. "At night some of us would meet up at a nearby bar. Sometimes Steve would join us. From what the rumor mill said, often in the evenings he went to various hotel bars, ordered a drink and waited. From what we heard, most nights some woman would hit on him. Well, that was the rumor.

"Near the end of the first week after Steve took over the case, a couple of agents on the team put on disguises and followed him. Within 20 minutes, a tall woman with short brown hair came into the hotel bar, glanced around, walked over and started talking to Steve. Less than an hour later they went out together but at the door Steve stopped, turned around and strode back to the table where the two agents sat in their disguises. He gave them one of his glares and told them to get back to work. He was unmerciful on those two from that day on. He questioned every suggestion they had; they never researched their work well enough. He made sure they would never follow him again."

He noticed that Ivy was laughing and was glad she was so good humored about this disclosure of how Steve had once been. "Starting the first week, Steve had us take physical fitness tests and do shooting drills like those that at the Academy, only these were harder. At seven every morning he began the day with a discussion around his code of operation, the Bureau's code or basic truths. Anyone who was late was subjected to what we called 'the stare' from Steve. Late twice and he or she had a private session with Steve. No one was ever late a third time, not even Moll who was the least morning person on the team. At 7:15, it was on to business, including information sharing, critiques of our casebook contributions, etc. Trust me, Steve could be very pointed in his evaluations, but not belittling.

"At the start of week two, Steve dropped several agents from the team for not making the grade. From this point forward we ate together, we drank together, and we worked together. We worked 12, 14, 16 hours a day, every day of the week. When we drank together, Steve would often repeat the same pickup routine but now openly.

"One night we decided to place bets on how long it would take for some woman to hit on Steve. Some variation in our demeanors betrayed us to him. He was walking out with a tall thin blond, when he turned back, walked over to our table and held out his hand. He made five hundred bucks from us that night. We left the bar shamed that we had failed. If we couldn't to fool him, we would be unlikely to fool a perp."

A doctor and nurse came in, interrupting Mathew's story. They checked Steve first and then Ivy. After they left, Mathew studied Ivy's face still feeling concerned that she might be upset over hearing about Steve's practices in those days, but all she seemed was interested.

"I was never desperate enough for one-night stands," she said, "But I had my share of dates and relationships. So much so that I became tired of it and stopped dating for several years. Until Steve. He was different."

170

"He told me once that the dead time started after his parents died. He felt he lost the last ties he had to a personal life."

"How sad for him. How very, very sad."

Ivy sagged back against her pillows. Mathew stood up, moved her tray table away and helped her slide down for a nap.

"More to the story?" she asked fighting to keep her eyelids open.

"Yes, later."

Chapter 16

Around four that afternoon, Ivy woke up again, refreshed her makeup, checked her hair and asked Mathew to help her get over to Steve. He remained as immobile as before. Ivy stayed with him for some time, talking and holding his hand. Then she decided to sit in a chair until dinner, such as it would be, was brought in.

"Let me hear more about Steve."

After all the hours of sitting in the hospital, having Ivy to chat with was a welcome relief. Mathew gladly resumed talking. "That third Friday night into working with Steve, only the two of us were left in the hotel bar -- Steve and me. We began talking about love and marriage. I told Steve that I believed someone special was out there for me; but that I needed to earn the right to unconditional love.

"I stretched out my legs and waited, wanting Steve to say something. Finally he started talking about his parents, how together their marriage was and how much he was a part of their lives. He told me that he knew people joked about his boyish Beaver-Cleaver grin and then said that his childhood home was a lot like the Cleaver house only with a Norwegian twist. He always assumed he would grow up, find Miss Right and live happily ever after like his parents had.

"I remember that he paused then and looked off across the room at nothing in particular. He tilted his head slightly back and forth a couple of times, as if debating if he should disclose more. He then talked about how he was a failure at relationships and how he had so much trouble carrying on a conversation with the women he went out with that he gave up and went only for what he called 'the wham-bam-thank-you-ma'am' sort of deal."

"Interesting. We never have trouble talking. Well, sometimes we have trouble owning up to the things that bother us the most about ourselves, but other than that, the words flow between us."

"That's because you are a lot like Steve – kind of light on the chit-chat, but intense on more meaningful conversation. Anyway I asked about his marriage, hoping I wasn't prying too much. Steve shook his head and told me that his ex-wife wanted the D.C. social life, so she divorced him and quickly married an influential lobbyist making tons of money. Then he asked about me and what I was after in life.

"I talked about how I wanted a woman with enough life experience to put the man inside me ahead of my face, my brain and the fortune I inherited. I wanted to build a life with her that brought us so much joy we could never leave each other. However I had to get me figured out first. All those years when my parents were traveling their separate ways, I was with nannies and housekeepers or in boarding school. All that aloneness took its toll. A heavy shroud was so enmeshed in my heart that casting it off felt impossible. Intellectually I understood what I needed to do, however the pathway remained illusory. In the meanwhile, I planned and dreamed.

"I'll always remember what he said next -- he wished he had enough hope and faith to dream."

Mathew looked over at Ivy. Her face was very sad and he could tell that while she may never have felt the degree of isolation that Steve experienced, she understood it well enough.

"He did a funny thing then," Mathew continued. "Steve ordered two glasses of milk and a plate of cookies. Then he smiled that open grin of his and I marveled at the dichotomic nature of the man. He could act so world-weary and in a flash, despite being a man in his fifties, he would turn into the wholesome kid next door. When the cookies came, he split one in half, dunked it, chewed slowly and asked me how I thought a man could get un-disillusioned.

"I found it odd that Steve with his aura of invincibility was having this conversation with me and seeking my advice. He was so commanding on the job and had a powerful magnetism that attracted women to him. It was only then that I appreciated his weaknesses when it came to more sensitive interpersonal relations. We talked about paths to finding more of ourselves, opening up our hearts and pursuing a woman romantically, as a life partner and as an equal.

"When we finished the cookies and milk, Steve asked me if the other agents and I often talked about this sort of romantic idealism. I responded with something to the effect of, 'Yeah, we do sometimes. And you and I just did. El Desperados.' "

He became somber when I used that epithet and I worried I had gone too far. Steve settled the bill in silence and we parted, each of us looking thoughtful. The next morning our break came in the case, leaving us with no time for follow-up conversations. However I never saw him pull the pickup act again.

Ivy stretched in her chair. She was smiling. "He is so appreciative of me. No wonder. All those one-night stands. All those wasted years. Thank you for telling me more about him. What else?"

At that point, Ivy's dinner came in. It looked like turkey and gravy and smelled better than Mathew might have expected. Either that or he was getting hungry. Ivy tasted it, looked pleasantly surprised, and started to eat. He continued talking.

"The next morning was a Saturday in mid-July. Steve was in his office and from what I could tell, he had been there most of the night. He canceled our morning meetings, which was something he hadn't done before. He appeared to have gone for a swim and as always was in crisp, pressed clothes -- even on weekends he wore a suit. He was banging away on the keyboard like an oversized rock star on a set of bongos. If he had been less intent, it might have been comical.

"Around 11 he burst out of his office, shouting excitedly and calling us to our meeting table. While we hustled over, Steve phoned in a lunch order. From that time right up to lunch, he ran a computer model he had built showing scenario after scenario, which shifted banking transactions over time and between accounts, selected from the broad spectrum collected from the banks in our database. The model kept sets of running totals at the top of the

174

screen, showing comparisons to the accounts where the money sat in Cairo. On the left he displayed a table of anomalies -- outlier transactions that did not adhere to the pattern.

"Steve pointed at the screen and explained that the money transferred out of a certain group of twelve accounts showed staggered totals that over each three-week period, exactly matched the money that came into other accounts we identified in Cairo. The pattern went back through the most recent six-month window he had selected and likely further. Moreover it was continuing day after day. This money transferred out was systematically flowing somewhere and it was our job find out where."

Ivy pushed a piece of floppy bread aside and drank some of the milk from a carton on her tray. "He built that model from scratch?"

"Yeah. It was a combo of code written in C and Excel. He embedded Excel in a window, so he could more readily show the detailed transactions in a drill down. He put one team on tracing the money after it left the twelve identified accounts in Cairo. Another had to go back in time to see how long this money-laundering scheme had been active. He assigned my team the daunting role of auditing the computer model he built and resolving the outlier transactions -- the ones that did not fit the pattern that he had found.

"My understanding of program code is not great. I can read straightforward logic but the more advanced techniques lose me. Luckily Brian had taken advanced classes and had performed several program code reviews on cases. In addition Moll had become quite expert at database structures and at searching and manipulating data.

"Steve told us the location of his code and granted us read access permissions. He instructed us to set up our own library and to start with a clean copy of the database of banking transactions, in case he had gunked up the data. His eyes glittered with excitement. This was the first time I had seen him totally focused on the hunt -- his intensity was a bit scary. An hour later having come down from his high of discovery, he left. He was back in the early evening, again with his hair wet and in a fresh set of clothes. He called us together for an update.

"Brian had been leading the code review and at my insistence, he was to report the results. When he stood up to present our findings, his voice quavered as he started to speak. He reviewed the procedure we followed and discussed how we tweaked Steve's code, since it did not seem to be running properly.

"Steve's face went pale. His shoulders sagged. He motioned for Brian to continue.

"Brian inhaled deeply and said something to the effect of, 'The results are even cleaner. Those code changes reduced the outlier anomalies by about 80%. We are close to having it nailed.' Brian paused, and then added more quietly, 'Your model was brill, Chief, really brill. That's one for the book.' He reddened and sat down, surprising himself with his temerity.

"Steve sank back into his chair with a slow satisfied smile that had a hint of pride. Then he stood up, walked around and shook Brian's hand, something he only did when an agent exceeded his expectations. He nodded at Moll and at me still with that smile. After each team had accounted for their activities, Steve gave us his big toothy grin, nodded and said, "Been a great day for us -- a breakthrough day. Let's call it a night. Drinks and dinner on the Bureau. We'll hit it fresh in the morning. I'll get a table at that upscale Italian place down the street – the one called Val d'Orcia. Be there at 8:00.

"I noticed his use of 'us' and I was to find that Steve always credited victories to the team and if blame came down, he took it. I remembered that at the Academy we considered him superhuman. After a couple of weeks of working with him, I realized we only had an impression. The reality was far broader and deeper than any of us grasped. He was demanding; he could be impatient. On the other hand he was insightful, technically adept and committed. He led by example and he was a great mentor in all the ways that counted."

Ivy squirmed in her chair. Mathew rose, moved her dinner out of the way and helped her over to see Steve again. As they walked, she said, "We have never really sat like this and talked about Steve. It gives me a very different perspective on him. Let me spend some time with him. When I'm back in bed, maybe you can tell me about this case against Astuto until I nod off. Then you better go, have dinner and get some sleep. Are you staying at the Portland house?"

Mathew said, "Not exactly. I shower there, but I have been sleeping here."

Ivy looked at him in surprise.

"And I will continue to do that until you both are released into my care."

She pressed his arm and smiled her appreciation. Tears welled up in her eyes, though she quickly wiped them away as she bent down to kiss Steve. Once she had settled herself back in bed, she asked Mathew again to tell her about the recent case against the drug lord.

"Okay, but first there is something I want to say. You and Steve are so good to me. You treat me like an equal and yet like a son too. You let me lead when I want to; you act as my sounding boards. You even give me a good swift kick in the pants when I need it."

Ivy laughed a little, remembering the time in the kitchen when she had lectured Mathew.

"Most of all, you give me a wonderful example of a loving relationship between two strong people. More than ever, you make me want to get married, have a home and start a family. You gave me a refreshed *raison d'être*. I have more to say but that will wait until all three of us can be drinking champagne, lying back in the sun, gazing down at our embryonic vineyards and our homes-to-be, up on those high knolls we call Spook Hills."

Ivy leaned forward and stared with concern at Steve. He remained as motionless and unaware as before.

"We have to believe that day will come Ivy. We have to. Remember what Virgil said, *Amor Vincit Omnia* -- Love Conquers All Things." Mathew said softly.

Ivy nodded but continued to regard Steve anxiously. Mathew decided to talk about the drug lord to distract her from worrying about Steve. Just to be safe, he scooted his chair closer to the side of Ivy's bed so he could talk in a less-carrying tone.

"So this case against Astuto . . . we became embroiled in it because of money laundering; in fact the patterns were similar to the 2007 case, but

177

involving different banks, locations, accounts and companies. This time we had much improved software and the knowhow to find the blueprint for the transactions relatively quickly. Someone was storing money in accounts in Colombia, for now letting it appear like a long-term investment, spread into mutual funds, stocks, etc. In total, the same amounts from different accounts moved systematically out of Colombia."

"Do you think it was a copy-cat crime or just coincidence that the pattern was the same?"

"Since it was such a good scheme in the 2007 case, we filed that part of the evidence under seal at the Court."

Ivy thought for a moment and said. "Therefore the scheme from the 2007 case should not be available to the public. So either Astuto reinvented the scheme or . . ."

"We have a mole at the Bureau. Steve was worried about that though he kept it quiet. He only mentioned it to me after we departed."

A look of deep concern crossed Ivy's face. She pulled up the covers a little higher, as if she were just then realizing the power of the perp they were dealing with.

"You sure this is the right time to talk about this Astuto character?" Mathew asked.

"I need to know." Ivy's body language might look as if she were feeling vulnerable, but the determination in her face told him she meant to hear it all.

"We began unraveling the owners of more than 150 suspect accounts across the 14 different banks involved in the transfers. Each account belonged to one of 25 companies in six countries. The final destination, except for about 30% siphoned off in Zurich, was a series of accounts at three banks in Turkey, which is not one of the best countries at cooperating in these money-laundering investigations. We couldn't tell if the money was used to buy drugs coming out of the Middle East, passed on to terrorists, or stockpiled for some other purpose.

"We now had to bring in the FBI's Joint Action Task Force that dealt with terrorist activities, the DEA, and several other agencies, making for slow going at the beginning. This was in addition to working within the Department of Justice, and with the Treasury Department which included the Office of Foreign Assets Control. We began to have far more help than was productive. Several agencies began lobbying for control of the case."

"Bet that made Steve happy," Ivy said quietly. She had slipped a little lower in bed but was listening intently.

Mathew laughed as he recalled that time. "Steve started shaking things up at HQ to either retain control of the case or move him to another matter. He did this with his characteristic charm and aplomb. We could hear a number of heated conversations echoing out from under the door to his office. No agency wants to give up control of an investigation but taking all aspects together, this operation belonged in the FBI.

"In the end the Bureau appointed Steve to head a joint task force for the field operation of apprehending the perps. About five team members joined our core team to serve in the additional coordination roles. Steve brought in a senior HQ type to oversee them -- a position he sarcastically referred to as the Coordinator of the Coordinators or the C.O.C. which he sometimes pronounced as 'cock'. He added twice-daily standup briefings with the C.O.C. and his project team leaders to make sure we all stayed synchronized."

"The 'C.O.C' -- love it. Be a funny title on a business card."

"Yeah. We had to keep the other departments organized and in communication. Anyway back to Astuto -- of the 30% of the money siphoned off in Zurich, about half stayed in the account. The balance went into an account for a benevolent trust called, 'The CCE Charitable Foundation'. Its alleged purpose was to fund security and safety programs in poor neighborhoods with concentrations of Latinos in the United States. We went after more detail. Steve charged my team with researching the myriad of shell and sham operating companies that owned the money laundering accounts. We were seeking commonalities in ownership, officers, signatories, type of business, location -- anything that would lead us to the top of the pyramid. Moll set up a database to house these characteristics. We analyzed it for congruities and disparities based on both actual and fuzzy searches -- you know, those "sounds like" type searches."

179

Ivy nodded. "We used those a lot at my company searching client data. We kept expanding the degree of fuzziness until we would reach the point of diminishing returns."

"Us too. Nothing popped out though. We tried matching spellings both forward and backward. We translated names between Spanish and English. Out of ideas, we sat down with Steve to identify other approaches. He suggested various methods of encoding. We tried dropping letters and shifting letters from front to back. Steve suggested we try to find patterns in the abbreviations of the company names. After numerous dead ends, we discovered that they all abbreviated to Spanish common names of animals or plants or insects -- all native to Latin America."

"That's odd. Makes me wonder why," Ivy said quietly.

"We also scrutinized the names of the officers, signatories, etc. After running into a bunch of blind corners, we found that if we took a list of common Spanish first names and paired it with a list of common Spanish last names from each end of the alphabet, we could create the officer names by age of the company. The second name on the list would be the reverse -- the first name came from the end of the alphabet and the last name from the beginning, the third would be taken from the middle and then the pattern would repeat itself. For example, the first company, which dated to the year 1998, had the following three officers, Presidente: Adan Zermeno; Vicepresidente: Vincente Alvarez; Secretario: Luis Martinez.

"The companies were registered in Spanish-speaking Latin America, including Colombia, Mexico, Argentina, Venezuela and Cuba. Many of the companies listed shipping, tourism, or investment management as their type of business. Several listed ships as assets. As we researched, we found these ships to be very expensive yachts. We began to investigate the operations of these companies and attempted to verify the existence of the named officers. As we obtained copies of specimen signatures from the banks for those individuals who could authorize bank transfers, our graphologists or hand writing specialists identified three patterns in the penmanship. This was our most exciting discovery to date. We then checked to see if any of these names were linked to travel to or from the United States. About a dozen had been, three fairly frequently. Six held U.S. passports. We acquired photographs from

180

the passports on file. Photo and signature analysis revealed that they likely belonged to two individuals using multiple identities. In fact, the two men bore a remarkable resemblance to each other and might even have been the same person, although one had a scar on his forehead, which possibly was applied with makeup or hidden by it. Unfortunately, no fingerprints were on file.

"We were dealing with a mastermind who had set up a brilliant web of financial transactions and likely had a mammoth drug ring and other illegal operations behind it. We began an intensive action to run this man to ground. After some weeks of networking and searching, we finally received intelligence through the DEA that the perp was on a yacht off the coast of Manzanillo, on the southwest coast of Mexico.

"Steve picked his field team of six. Brian, Moll and I were on it. We now reported to Steve full time. It made me pleased that the four of us were working together. Steve's choices told me what he valued, including performance, commitment, attention to detail and creativity. Right when we planned to move to Guadalajara to prepare for a possible raid in Manzanillo, the judge signed the data order in the child trafficking case, so off I went to Guadalajara and as you know Steve, Brian and Moll appeared in your offices that same Monday morning.

"On the morning of the fourth day, we planned to board the yacht with a small team from the DEA and with support from a Mexican SWAT team."

"So that's why Steve left after the first day," Ivy noted.

"Yeah. Turned out the actual sting was easy, since the crew was small and mostly unarmed. All we caught was an actor traveling under a U.S. passport hired to be the double of the owner of the yacht, a man who paid him and who he knew only as El Zorro Astuto. We arrested and questioned the crew hired in Veracruz where the yacht was registered under one of the Astuto corporations. The actor and the crew accounted for all the prints we found on the yacht. Either the real Astuto had never been there, or he had the yacht wiped clean after his last visit.

"We were stalled. Our quarry appeared to have gone underground. The flow of funds into the accounts in Colombia stopped also, and the phony passports were not used again. Thanks to you, we had a lead to follow on the child trafficking case and we shifted our primary attention to it. During this time, I never saw Steve do the bar scene, outside of a drink with the team, although we did share a number of plates of cookies. He told me that he began his life as an FBI monk a few weeks after we talked back in 2007. The asceticism made him cranky as hell for about six months and then he was clearer-headed and lighter-hearted. He kept swimming, often twice a day. We joked that he was trying to freeze it off."

"Glad that didn't happen," Ivy said sleepily.

"I can't say he became less demanding, but he was different, even more focused and yet, sometimes somewhat dreamy. So why is all this important to you, Ivy? Because you should appreciate how much it meant to Steve when he met you. As far as I know, he had been sexually abstinent for five years and emotionally isolated perhaps all his life. He did personal soul searching. If a man had to find his dream ahead of me, I am glad it was Steve. With luck, I still have some time in front of me. You should also recognize how damn excellent he was at his work and how hard it was for him to leave the Bureau. Now we have to nail the bastards who did this to you. This vendetta has to end. We will catch them, even if I have to rejoin the FBI to do it."

Mathew stopped talking. He had been staring into space, unaware that Ivy like a little girl had drifted off to sleep during her bedtime story. No matter -- he could repeat the last part in the morning. He gazed over at Steve who lay in his bed as he had for days now. Mathew said a prayer for his recovery. Although he was not an overly religious man, unlike Steve and Ivy, he believed in some omnipotent power. He prayed that Steve was *Vulneratus non Victus*, Wounded but not Conquered.

He rose, stretched and pulled the covers up over Steve. This man had saved his life in Mexico. Even without that, they had bonds of friendship and they had their new vineyard partnership. He bent and kissed him on the forehead, then went over and did the same for Ivy. He was meeting Brian and Moll for a late dinner. After that he would shower at the Portland house where they were staying, put on fresh clothes and come back to the hospital for the night.

Chapter 17

The next afternoon Ivy was released from the hospital and, guarded by Brian and Moll, went to stay in the Portland house. Early the following morning when Mathew turned away from Steve's bed, he saw or thought he saw a little fluttering in Steve's hand. The nurse came in to check his IVs, followed by a doctor to go over his incisions and his chart, and finally a physical therapist arrived to exercise Steve's limbs.

During this time, Mathew watched Steve closely but he could not detect any voluntary movements. Once the room was quiet, he stood by Steve's bed watching him. He called his name; nothing happened. He reached down, gripped his hand and called his name. He felt a slight grip back. He gripped harder and called his name more loudly and urgently. Steve's eyes opened. He focused on Mathew, frowned and tried to speak. Mathew raised the back of the hospital bed, helped him to sit up and gave him some water.

"Ivy, where is Ivy?" He spoke slowly in a gravelly undertone.

"She was released yesterday afternoon. She should be here soon. Moll will drive her in."

"What time is it? And where the hell am I?" he asked hoarsely.

"9:45; you're at Providence Hospital in Portland."

"I was out overnight?"

"Steve, today is Thursday."

Steve looked confused. "But it was Sunday when Ivy came back to Spook Hills. Is she okay?"

"Yes, thanks to you for shielding her. She went through surgery to have the bullet removed that did get her. Her arm is in a sling and she'll have weeks of healing and recovery ahead of her, but she should be fine."

"And me? Damn, my whole left side aches, shoulder, chest, even my butt."

"You were hit twice. Like Ivy, you took one in the shoulder as you spun around to protect her. It passed through your upper shoulder muscles and slammed into your collarbone, making it crack. They had to operate and pin it together for stability. When you dove over Ivy, you turned the other cheek, so to speak. Luckily you are enough of a lard-ass that the bullet passed through and came back out before it hit the pelvis. As it was, you lost a terrific amount of blood. I was trying to plug up the bleeding on you and Ivy while waiting for the ambulance, but it kept seeping out."

"You sure she's okay?"

"Don't worry -- she'll be fine. She's been here to talk to you and hold your hand several times a day ever since she could get out of bed."

A little smile spread across his face. "I heard her. She sounded far away. I wanted to go to her but I was too weak."

"Let me tell you, there was so much blood on me that the medics thought I was hit too. Likely you were weak from the blood loss."

He nodded and moved his mouth a bit as if he wanted to say something. "Toothbrush? Mouth is like the floor of a Metro station."

"Steve, I think I should get a nurse."

"Not yet. Help me brush my teeth. I want to kiss Ivy when she arrives without smelling totally repulsive."

Mathew rummaged in his backpack and brought out Steve's Dopp kit, handed him his toothbrush and toothpaste, poured more water and found a pan for him to spit in.

Steve brushed his teeth, checked that he was shaved, fell back against the pillows, closed his eyes and appeared to have returned to his coma state. Mathew hit the buzzer for the nurse. The nurse examined Steve and shook her head, scolding Mathew for not calling her right away. She bustled off to alert the doctor on duty.

Mathew decided not to tell Ivy that Steve had been conscious and sentient, feeling that she should be the one to wake him up. He was pleased he had

184

been awake and seemed clear-headed. A half-hour later, Ivy walked in with Moll and frowned at Steve.

"Why is he sort of propped up?"

"I thought the change of position might do him good."

She gave Mathew a funny look, then bent over and kissed Steve. Slowly Steve's eyes opened. He saw her and smiled. His eyes went from unfocused to having that warm glow they had every time he saw Ivy. Using his good arm, he edged himself closer to her and signaled for water. After he drank, he was alert again as he had been before. He held Ivy's hand, stared at her and began crying. Ivy held on to Steve as best she could -- two victims of a battle.

This time Mathew did ring for the nurse. Outside of healing from the bullet wounds and surgery, Steve appeared to be in good shape. He did complain of dizziness and a headache, but said it was nothing much. Three different doctors came in over the next half hour. Each one appeared puzzled by how alert Steve was.

Tests were scheduled on him for the afternoon but from that morning on, he recovered quickly. His headache became less frequent and less intense each day. He still slept a fair amount, but he did not appear to return to his coma state. Most telling in his recovery was that several times a day, either Steve or Ivy would send Mathew out for things to eat -- cheeseburgers, milkshakes, lattes, garden salad, chicken soup, cookies, muffins, pie, ice cream, more ice cream. Not only did they send him out, but Ivy had very specific shops for each item. Clearly neither of them had taken a bullet to the gut.

***

On the morning after Steve woke up, Ivy was ready to talk about the shooting. Steve was half-sitting up in bed, taking most of his weight on his right side. He appeared to be both alert and interested.

"Tell us everything you remember," Mathew said.

Ivy thought for a moment, "How far back?"

"Let's go back to the night before."

185

"You know I had returned to Portland and sublet a studio on a week-by-week basis in the Pearl?"

"Brian told us," Steve said. "Took all my self-discipline not to grab a car and drive to Portland."

Ivy and Steve held each other's gaze. Mathew could see that unspoken words were passing between them in an invisible stream. He waited and then cleared his throat. Steve nodded at Ivy to continue.

"On the fourth day I drove to the airport, returned the rental car, went to the Alaska counter and bought a ticket to Seattle. From there I passed through security, sat down, went online, canceled my flight to Seattle and booked one to Spokane that was going out about the same time. I had my boarding pass downloaded to my cell phone and then went to the gate and boarded. Since I only had carry-ons, luggage was not a problem.

"Once in Spokane, I rented another car and drove to Walla Walla where I stayed overnight at the historic Marcus Whitman Hotel. I watched my rearview mirror closely to make sure no one was following me. I never spotted anyone. From there, I checked out at four in the morning, got into my rental car and drove back to Portland, rotating between the Oregon and Washington sides of the Columbia River whenever I came to a bridge, again checking the rearview mirror the whole way, especially when I changed sides of the river.

"In Portland, I returned the car to Avis, went into the airport, picked up some bottled water, walked back out and rented a car at Hertz. Still checking to see if anyone followed me, I drove to Hillsboro, picked up lunch, ditched the wig and fluffed up my hair. Then I took back roads in an unplanned, circuitous way until I arrived at Spook Hills. Never did I sense that I was being followed."

"Did you see any cars as you neared the vineyard?" Mathew asked.

She searched her memory. "A delivery truck for bottled water turned on the Archery Summit dirt road."

"You remember the name or brand?"

She frowned for a moment.

"Something Glacier. The sign was blue and white. The truck was turning as I came by."

"Did you see anything right before the shooting?"

"My back was to the shooters; I was hugging Steve. Hugging him and crying." They looked at each other at the memory of it.

Mathew smiled, having watched them from the living room window.

"Wait! I pulled back to see his face. He had on those mirrored sunglasses he wears sometimes. I saw a little flash -- a reflection in the sunglasses and then a shot. Pain, Steve pushing me down, more shots, Steve landing on top of me."

She shook her head. "I must have passed out then."

Mathew nodded, surprised she remembered that much.

"Mathew, where were you?"

"Inside the house. I followed Steve when we heard your car pull up, but then stopped because I thought you two should have a few moments to yourselves. Now I wish I hadn't. Once the shots started, I ran out, gun drawn and firing. They took off and I ran for you two, calling on my cell for the ambulance and the police, telling them to alert the FBI. I put the phone on speaker and tried to staunch the bleeding, but you two were making a big donation to the Red Cross. Steve had taken off his protective vest when he was working in the sun on the balcony by your master bedroom. He forgot to put the vest back on when he saw you."

"What about the others?"

"It was Sunday. No one was working. You remember Fred, the diligent Hispanic kid?"

Ivy nodded.

"He works directly for Spook Hills now. Anyway a few minutes before he stopped by and I asked him to go check on a leak we had patched in the irrigation system the preceding day."

Steve looked a little guilty. "I ran over a valve. Mathew wanted to be sure the patch was holding."

"Silly the things I remember -- as I stepped out of the car and saw how much the house had come along, all I could think was Steve having enough faith in our love to go on building it, even though I had disappeared. That time away taught me one thing -- it was far harder to be alone, than to be here with you." She reached out and took Steve's hand.

"So nothing while you were gone? Nothing to make you think you were followed?"

"Oh I was followed all right. Brian is good, but not good enough to get by me."

"You saw him?"

"His appealing Brian smile gives him away. He was a woman in line behind me in a Portland, Maine Starbucks. He was a beachy sort of guy in sunglasses and a cap worn backwards, pumping gas into his car and joking with a local in Bar Harbor. He was man with dark auburn hair two rows behind me, flirting with the stewardess on the flight to London. Think I spotted him a few other times. I always notice perfect eyebrows on a man too. I found it comforting to have him with me."

Mathew thought for a moment. "I wonder what that flash was. A car door opening, reflecting the sun? A signal of some sort?"

Steve shrugged and then said. "Sometimes working outside at the house, I felt as if someone was watching me. Once or twice I saw a glint, like from a mirror or glass, but then I thought I was just being paranoid."

"You have that great sixth sense. Bet it was someone with binoculars or . . ."

"A high-powered rifle sight," Ivy said, understanding someone might have stalked them for weeks.

They looked at each other, knowing that from now on their best defense would be themselves.

"You're a great friend, Mathew. Thank you for being here and for caring for us."

"Oh heck, we're family, aren't we?"

Ivy smiled at him, nodded and asked, "Where was Brian by the way? Why wasn't he following me to Spokane and back?"

"You would have made a good agent. He lost you in the gate area at the airport, so he took a chance and boarded the plane to Seattle right when they were shutting the doors. He tracked you later, but he was always one stop too late."

"I changed my hat and jacket in the Ladies room before going to the Spokane gate. Now I wish I hadn't. Maybe Brian would have been there to stop the shooters."

"Or maybe he would have been shot too. Don't second-guess yourself, Ivy. You did what you thought was best."

"How did they know I would show up at Spook Hills at that exact time?"

"Triggerfish," Steve muttered.

"What?" Ivy asked, looking at him a little worriedly as if he had just spoken gibberish.

"Tracking device. I figure that they planted a tracking device or software in your cell phone, your laptop, or your iPad -- something you would have with you." A little guiltily, he added, "We did too. We call those tracking devices 'triggerfish'."

She nodded. "When? How?"

"I installed ours before you left. Remember when I told you I wanted to check the setups? They were in case Brian lost you on a line of sight basis. The tracker is software that transmits and logs positional data on a server. Sophisticated ones like ours can be set for how often to transmit and where. That's why you never saw Brian tailing you in the car."

"I should have expected that -- you two will forever be FBI agents," Ivy said, shaking her head and chuckling at the same time. "But when did the bad guys do it?"

"Were there times when you left things in your room? Like when you went out for a walk or to go shopping?"

"Wouldn't Brian have seen the guys go in to the hotel room or apartment or wherever?"

"Not if he was out following you."

"Damn."

"I'm surprised that security software on your PC didn't detect it."

"Is that detection software on my iPhone or iPad?

"Likely not -- I'll check. Those devices would be more suspect. If they are on, they are connected."

"But I have passwords on them."

"Certain devices can pick up what you key -- typically through a window. Do you store the passwords anywhere?"

"Not those. Numerics. In my head."

"Common numbers?"

"My Dad's Birth Month and Day."

Mathew looked at her questioningly.

"Damn again. It should have been a random number."

"Some agents do the same thing. I don't. Steve doesn't. We should have told you. I'll verify the tracking software, but that's likely how they knew when you would arrive at Spook Hills. We'll make sure it gets removed. "

Steve spoke up then. "The other possibility is that they were tracking you by the new credit cards as you used them. Looking back on it, someone at the Bureau could have known about that ID I kept and when it went active, he or she put a trace on the money I transferred to pay your bills."

"You mean the mole? Mathew told me your theory."

"Yeah. As at the Portland house, this shooting was like a vendetta. I think El Zorro Astuto wants to make me suffer. The bastard wanted me to see you die. He wanted me to have to bury you. Then some other time, he would have me and Mathew finished off too. We must have killed a key person in his ring during the raid in Mexico."

Ivy adjusted her sling, and then did her best to square her shoulders and appear capable. "What do we do now? Go after him?"

Mathew regarded her with surprise, glad to see she had the spunk to fight. "First you two heal. Let the Bureau go after him and give us all protection."

"And if they don't conclusively get him?" Ivy asked. She could only put one hand on her hip, but she still stood in the aggressive posture she used when riled.

Steve got a stubborn look on his face. "Then we activate the Spook Hills Gang."

"That the one you have to either limp, or have the use of only one arm, or both to get into?" Mathew asked, glancing pointedly from his own bad leg, to Ivy's shoulder, to Steve still in the hospital bed.

"The very one -- luckily brains count the most in any operation."

Chapter 18

The next day Mathew wheeled Steve out to the Suburban, settled him into the back seat with Ivy and headed for the vineyard, deciding that despite everything, they should be there, continuing their work on the house, the vines and the fields. Brian rode shotgun and Moll crammed himself into the way-back, gun drawn, but on the floor next to him. When they stopped at Spook Hills, Ivy immediately struggled out of the SUV to go around and help Steve. Not only was Steve wearing a brace for his pinned collarbone, but he had his arm in a sling and he limped painfully along on a cane. Still he managed his big grin when the corgis ran to greet them. Fred came out of the new house with an equally wide smile on his face and lugging the cat, Druid. Despite feeling drained by the trip to Spook Hills, Steve wanted to give Ivy a tour of the house. He leaned heavily on his three-footed cane, trying to limp around the pain in his backside.

As Mathew surveyed the area around the house, he realized that Fred had continued working on it, interfacing with the contractor and laborers. What a godsend that young man turned out to be! Beds were dug for the landscaping and footings were ready for the planned serpentines of rock walls. A curving front sidewalk had been painstakingly laid out and dug down the required 14 inches, with first gravel and then sand put in place. Aware of how particular Steve was, Fred left an area exposed so the depth of the base layers could be checked. Cobblestone pavers were stacked nearby on pallets, used by the workers as they paved their way up the walk. Steve had picked the pavers out, going for natural split-granite in shades of blue-gray to make a pleasing combination with the stone for the garden walls.

Out in the vineyard, the vines had grown since Mathew saw them the previous Monday during his quick trip back to the trailer for a supply of clothes. From behind the house, he could hear the sounds of drills and screwdrivers as work continued on the long roof deck over part of the lower level. This will be Steve and Ivy's home, Mathew thought smiling to himself, and it will be mine as well for a time. His eyes shifted over to the site that would be his house one day. A couple of carpenters were restoring the old barns. While he was eager to see the work completed, he was all too aware that they still had to contend with El Zorro Astuto.

As they walked into the house, the Director of the Bureau called Steve on his cell phone, asking how he and Ivy were. When he said he would check back in a week, Steve wondered what he had in mind. Maybe he wanted only to see how their recovery was progressing. After all, he had long been one of Steve's supporters. Somehow Steve doubted it would be that simple.

The day was warm and the air smelled of summer. Mathew noticed that both Ivy and Steve were taking in big lungfuls of the fresh country air, as if trying to get the hospital smells out of their nostrils. Ivy found it unbelievable how the house had taken shape in the weeks she had been away. The wood siding was on, the rock facing was in place on the front of the house and on the chimneys, the roof was on and the windows and doors were in. What had been an empty shell was starting to look like a home. She reached over and kissed Steve on the cheek as they moved through the house, gingerly stepping along the temporary boards that made a path out to the roof deck where Steve proudly showed off the ivy-patterned railing, which both surprised and delighted her.

Steve and Mathew were hard drivers about having the house built and the vineyards planted. Ivy was glad to be back for the remaining work on their Spook Hills house. Without her, Steve might have never stopped adding security gadgets, balconies, patios, crown moldings, wainscoting, cornices and other architectural gewgaws. His thoughtfulness was touching, even though he verged on overdoing it.

The owners of a neighboring vineyard stopped by to check on their personal progress, the construction of the house, and the growth of the vines. When they asked about the shooting, Mathew explained that he and Steve were formerly with the FBI and they believed that the shooting was a vengeance move by a suspected drug lord. Their neighbors nodded and apparently spread the word to the other vineyard owners, as they found they were regarded warily yet sympathetically, with a couple of neighbors stopping by with casseroles and soups.

Following the shooting, Ivy could face the devil that was after her. What kind of cowardly act was it to shoot two people in the back? Now she carried her gun with more determination. That shooting removed any lingering conflicts she had about harming the perpetrators. She had been fortunate that Steve was there to shield her with his big body or those next two shots would have killed her. As it was, his act of love could have cost him his life.

Ivy realized during her recovery that she had loved Steve for herself far more than for him. She had loved as a selfish woman who needed her life to change. Now she could love him because he deserved it so very much. She resolved to cast aside centering on herself and reach outward to him, although hurt as they both were, expressing how they felt physically would be limited in the near term.

***

The rest of July and August were devoted to healing and working on the house as best they could. The second week of September, Ivy, Steve and Mathew spent a couple of days in Portland, picking out smooth Brazilian cherry flooring, dense golden tan travertine from Peru, sedate slabs of granite in shades of brown with a little gold coloring running through, paint colors in moody hues, as well as sinks, commodes and appliances. With those essentials ordered, Mathew went back to Spook Hills.

Steve and Ivy stayed on to select furniture and carpeting. They would need area rugs to create warmth on the hardwoods and tile throughout the house. First they did a walk-through of the Portland house, with Steve making a list on his laptop of what Ivy wanted moved down to Spook Hills. A few pieces of furniture, some of the art, four rugs, kitchen things, china, pottery, holiday decorations, her clothing and her personal things would be moved. After they were finished, they took Brian and Moll out to lunch to talk about their startup enterprise. That afternoon, Steve took a set of plans for the new house that he had automated on his laptop and created a layout for the furniture so they could see what they were missing.

A small table, an antique sea chest, and a big painted hutch from Steve's mother would go into the new house, along with pieces of her Nordic pottery and a few other ethnic pieces from Norway. The furniture was decorated in the patterns and colors of the traditional Norwegian rosemaling style, which would add points of interest. Ivy planned to use old photos from Steve's family and hers to create a collage on one wall, leaving space to add their own memories. Her challenge was to blend the styles to be part of a whole, rather than an eclectic muddle. As she discussed these ideas with Steve, he added them to the layout.

Ivy decided that the new furniture would be her contribution to Spook Hills. She began to wonder what she should do with the Portland house. As long as Brian and Moll wanted to stay there, she would leave the rest of the furnishings. At some point, the two men would want to get on with their own lives by moving back East and she would likely put the house on the market. For now they were concentrating getting the software, practices manual and marketing materials ready to start their new business, as well as consulting back to the FBI.

While still not 100%, each week found Ivy and Steve stronger and able to take on more tasks. Luckily Steve was more patient about the shopping process than Ivy had expected he would be. As long as they stopped for coffee or tea breaks and tried a new spot for lunch each day, he was happy to be out with her, updating their computerized room layout after each purchase. Their evenings were spent either at one of the Portland restaurants or with Ivy preparing a simple meal at the Portland house. Either way, they kept evenings as their time to talk and to be together. While Ivy was sorry that Steve now had scars that marred the sinuous flow of his shoulder and chest muscles, she saw them a mark of his love that he had shielded her with his body.

On Friday, they headed in separate directions, each with an agent tailing them. Ivy went to shop for dresses for the party after their planned wedding -- not classically bridal, but something long, striking and flattering. She found a dress in a moody emerald satin with shadowy tones that could be special ordered in her size. While the back was high, the neckline in front was so décolleté that Ivy was glad it came with a matching wrap. She thought that the ensemble would be becoming, while avoiding the younger person's bridal image.

Mathew returned to Portland that evening to bring them up-to-date on the house and vineyard over dinner while at the same time Brian and Moll flew back to New York to prepare for a meeting with a prospect bank on Monday. Ivy chose the long-standing, but periodically re-invented Genoa Restaurant where its quietude would be perfect for conversation. They ate their first course slowly, listening to Mathew talk about progress at the house that week, most notably the front walkway and the curved patio off the conservatory by the kitchen that dropped down to a lower-level walled garden, as well as the remaining wallboard and some of the trim.

Their server brought their pasta course while Mathew gabbed away enthusiastically about the vineyards and how the vines became appreciably bigger each week, with larger leaves, longer branches and stouter bases. Earlier in the year, the few grape clusters that appeared had been removed to encourage growth in the young vines. Mathew was filled with amazement at how hardy the vines were and how tenaciously they clung to the hillsides. Over salads, the conversation drifted to El Zorro Astuto and their concerns about when he would have his gunmen attack next.

"What if he is a twin?" Mathew asked. He glanced a little guiltily over at Steve. "While I was waiting in the hospital, I got access to Sentinel and read through your case notes."

Steve regarded him with surprise for a moment and then nodded. "Not impossible. Odd that twins in business would operate as if they are one person in two bodies."

"Fungible," Mathew said almost to himself. "Not a word you usually apply to people, but they could have developed a relationship so tight that it works for them and they have become almost interchangeable or fungible."

Ivy noticed that Mathew had such a fascination with words, seeking the *mot juste*. His affinity for Latin and Greek words came from his private school background. Sometimes along with his fussiness, it made him seem a little effete, although no one would question his masculinity. Steve and the FBI had kept Mathew grounded, pulling him away from his wealthy background into reality.

"I remember you saying that Astuto named his companies after animals, plants and insects native to Colombia. Correct?" she asked a bit tentatively, as if to talk about the perps was to invite trouble.

"That's right and the fictitious officers had Spanish names taken methodically from lists of common names." Mathew said.

"How very peculiar. Something childish about it all. Clever, but childish," Ivy ventured.

Steve's eyebrows lifted. "Say more." He put his fork down with a morsel of golden beet, a sprig of arugula and toasted pine nuts still on it, giving Ivy his full attention.

"Think about it -- the names of the companies and officers, the fascination with yachts, the use of the actors and the copycat strategy with the money laundering. It almost sounds like a made-for-TV movie. You know how they are often rather obvious."

"The guy is clearly smart. Brilliant even." Mathew said frowning. He was having trouble fitting childish approaches with a successful and deadly drug lord.

"Maybe it's a case of arrested development," Ivy commented speculatively. She had been conjecturing about Astuto in the back of her mind.

The two men went back to eating, but Ivy could see they were mulling over what she said.

"Could be a post-traumatic stress disorder," Mathew said after he finished his insalata with asiago and lightly grilled prosciutto.

"What if?" Ivy stopped and looked down. "No, maybe I've watched too much TV."

"Say it," Steve commanded.

"You said there were three different sets of handwriting on the signature specimens you found, right?"

Mathew nodded.

"But only two faces, very similar faces, appeared on the passports?"

"Yeah."

"What if three of these guys exist-- a set of twins who do the field work, oversee the operations, buy the yachts, hire the actors, whatever, and a third one, another brother?"

"Keep going," Steve leaned forward, listening intently.

"Let's say they all grew up in a rough environment, where something dreadfully shocking happened to one of them. What if he then became reclusive, making his own world where he could control everything?"

"Even his brothers?' Mathew asked doubtfully.

"Maybe they are all really smart, but grew up poor, took to the streets at a young age, started small time drug dealing. The rough life could have bound them together closer than family ties alone."

"But they protected the brother, except that one time when some awful thing happened," Steve said, supporting Ivy's theory.

"Let's also suppose the kid educated himself and began planning how to have the good life. Perhaps he became reclusive to the point of never going out . . . what's that syndrome?"

"Agoraphobia." Mathew interjected, "From the Greek word *ageirein*, meaning 'to gather' and *phobos* meaning 'fear'."

"That would mean his source of information was the TV, except what his brothers might tell him and today what he accesses on the Internet."

As he warmed up to the idea, Mathew appraised Ivy admiringly, "He's sounding more like he grew up in the States, but everything points to Colombia."

"Exactly -- as if he watched drug crime scenes on American TV," Steve said.

Ivy shook her head. "Sorry guys. Too far-fetched. Let's drop it."

"Keep going," Steve said intrigued. "We're up against a brick wall on this case. This is a fresh perspective and it fits -- it explains certain aspects that have been bugging me. With every encounter with these perps, I sensed a familiarity about it. Things too clean. Too organized."

198

"Like a stage set?" asked Mathew.

Steve nodded, pushing back a little in his chair as their entrees arrived.

"This theory would also explain how the wire transfers were initiated -- one guy in a back office handling the money, while the others are out managing the revenue-producing drug operations." Mathew said between forkfuls of elk and potatoes.

"Twins -- that's why one guy in the photograph has a scar and one doesn't," Steve said.

The restaurant had emptied while they had been talking quietly at their corner table. Their places were cleared and dessert was coming out -- Ivy's was something prettily described as Hazelnut Crunchy Ciococolatta. They waited for their server to move to the back of the restaurant before continuing.

"We'll need access to local police records and newspapers in a wide variety of areas for a 10 year period -- five years on either side of our guessed age of 45 for this perp." Steve commented, as he took a big forkful of his dessert.

"Hey, you're not serious about this theory, are you?" Ivy asked looking from Steve to Mathew.

"I agree with Steve. We need a fresh start," Mathew said. "If we can get access to the records, why not? I bet it will be a big city with a large Spanish population, like Miami."

Steve tapped the table with his forefinger the way he did when an idea was percolating and he wanted action. "If we had access to the Bureau experts, we could see if they can figure out their genetic heritage. They don't have that typical Colombian appearance. They are only a little swarthy, blue-eyed and tall. They look Spanish -- not like they have much in the way of genes from indigenous peoples, at least based on the actor or actors we shot."

"At least one may not have been an actor," Mathew said, thoughtfully. "Can we get a genetic test run on the perp killed in Mexico City and the actor from that ship in Manzanillo?"

"We'd have to get the Bureau to order the body exhumed. Families hate that. All we may find is that they don't match." He smiled over at Ivy. "You are now an honorary agent. Our thinking was stymied -- all the pieces were in front of us, but we weren't seeing how they might fit together. This theory fits the unexplained aspects of the case that have been niggling at my subconscious. We may find the truth to be quite different, but I like this new direction."

Now Ivy better understood the effect praise from Steve had on his teams of agents. Pleasing him professionally and not only personally felt like a real achievement. Noticing the way his eyes had begun to shine reminded her how alive he became from the excitement of the hunt.

Upon their return to Spook Hills the next morning, the now former Director of the FBI called Steve. Since the shooting, he had been checking in with Steve every week on their healing process. They were walking around the outside of the house, admiring the paths, walls and patios that had been finished while they were in Portland. Ivy could envision wide planters with silvery lamium, the fuzzy gray foliage of lamb's ears, trailing flowers of verbena, white Johnny Jump Up pansies and geraniums in various shades of pink all growing around trimmed boxwoods. Pots of herbs would grow happily in the sunshine on the back garden patio. Here and there, Mathew left a half cobblestone out of the patio so that Ivy could dig down and plant a small ground plant, like thyme or Irish moss or maybe Corsican mint. Most of these plants could go in this fall to form their root systems over the winter and be flowering by spring.

They stopped and Steve put the call on speaker, letting the phone rest on the waist-high wall. While the two men talked to the former director, Ivy wandered off to check out the stone pathway to the lower level, staying close enough to catch the drift of the conversation. The Chief had just stepped down, but he indicated that he was serving in a consulting capacity during the transition and had specific responsibility for few issues -- one of which was apprehending Astuto and another was to determine if the Bureau and/or the DEA had one or more moles. His call was the perfect time to talk over their new theory with him. While he was unsure which current FBI HBOs, senior agents and staff could be trusted, he wanted to deputize Steve and Mathew as consultants to him for the investigations. The Chief promised it would be a desk job only with no fieldwork. He would use SWAT teams for that. Steve signaled for Ivy to join them.

They would have no real peace until the FBI had taken Astuto into custody or killed him. As long as it was a desk job only, Ivy could support the work. She nodded her agreement. Steve explained their hunch that they were in search of an incident in a U.S. city, involving a teenage or maybe preteen boy from a family with a set of identical twin brothers. The Chief agreed to open channels for them to search for old cases in likely neighborhoods in the United States. Records would vary, depending on how rural the locale was. If their guess was right, they could narrow the years to about a 10-year period.

Steve indicated he would want to add a few other former agents or others as consultants. While the Chief did not exactly give him a blank check, they could tell he was not against expanding the operation, knowing that Steve kept his team sizes on the conservative side. They discussed ideas about the possible mole or moles at the Bureau, which was of the utmost concern to the incoming Director, and their suspicion that a link existed between the mole and Astuto. Steve was instructed to set up a consulting group that fronted as a surveillance company in the D.C. area and to submit all invoices through that company to generate less attention. They also agreed to use alternative names for anyone working on the case to disguise their identities.

Ivy's stomach clenched during this discussion. Nevertheless she was determined to be part of the consulting team. Like it or not, they were back in the FBI's business, as if Steve and Mathew had never really left. As long as Astuto or perhaps this unholy trinity of three brothers was out there, they never would be free. Ivy had qualms about the work and she expected to have some sleepless nights, but the weeks of travel reconciled her to this life, and the additional weeks of recovery from the shooting had steadied her nerves. While the shooting itself might have put her into another tailspin, instead it strengthened her resolve to be with Steve. She loved him and she needed to assist him in whatever ways she could.

Steve and Mathew could teach her how to perform the necessary online research. In addition, she would handle the mechanics of time collection, billing, and record keeping. She would now be part of their conversations. She only hoped that when the pressure came back on, Steve would not hide information, thinking that would protect her.

Chapter 19

Steve sat back in his chair, shifting his weight off the still-tender left side where the bullet had passed through his derriere. They had turned the main bay of Mathew's barn into an office. The old barn had big sliding doors on either side that the carpenters had repaired and set on new, modern tracks. On most days, they left the doors open to catch the breezes in the afternoon. Even with the chilly morning air, they had pleasant working conditions with views of the coastal range on one side and the drive up to their houses on the other.

While the new approach they had from Ivy was pure conjecture, it felt right to Steve and when he got that feeling, he had learned to trust it. The research was tedious -- the type of thing he would put newer agents on, but the Bureau had taught him that you did whatever it took to catch the perps. They were concentrating first on larger cities with significant Hispanic populations, breaking up the search geographically, with Mathew and Steve taking Florida, which had the largest concentrations of Cubans and was where Steve suspected the brothers would be. Ivy took New York and Brian and Moll were splitting up the western states. Unfortunately only some of the archives from 20 years ago were available online. The work was slow going.

Steve shifted in his chair again. Sometimes he worked standing up, moving his laptop onto a big box on his table, so he could use the keyboard and thumbpad without bending over. He gazed at Ivy. She was as intense as a fox after prey when it came to research. She would get going on something and the whole world around her seemed to disappear. Steve could see that she would have made a great agent, perhaps even giving him stiff competition.

Steve liked to watch Ivy at work. He loved to watch her anyway, but this intensity about her was new to him. Every day when they kissed good morning, he was so grateful that she returned and that she survived that dreadful shooting. She had a vengeance now that Steve suspected was not

202

previously in her nature. He could only hope that after they caught Astuto, her frequent smiles and laughter would return.

She was such a gift to him. He brought so much danger to her that the rest of his life might not be time enough to make it right. He owed her his vigilance and so much more. She was making him more whole than he had ever been, leading him to open doors and rooms within himself that he had never known existed. When this case was over, he would make her life with him as perfect as it could be. While in Portland, he bought their wedding bands to compliment her engagement ring, and he purchased a gold bracelet with a heart of rubies embedded on top as a wedding present. Steve wondered if Ivy had given any thought to their wedding. His guess was that she had it all planned in her head.

He gazed out the barn door. The tree company they hired was starting the removal of the walnut trees on his property. Walnuts produce a toxin called juglone that will kill grape vines, so the sooner the project was finished, the better. Nevertheless Steve hated to see the old trees go. They agreed to keep a few healthy walnuts in a mini-grove at the top of the hill and have them pruned and treated. They would then surround them with a three-strip buffer -- sweet woodruff that is juglone-tolerant, and then grass to picnic on and then lavender. Ivy told him that the sweet woodruff would become a circle of white lace when it bloomed in the springtime.

When Mathew first suggested this whole vineyard business, Steve thought he would find it dull and unchallenging. However the more they delved into it, the more they found they had to learn. Instead of sitting around bored as he expected, Steve found himself drawn into it. Wine was such an intriguing combination of feminine and masculine aspects -- the delicacy of its bouquet had nuances absorbed from the terroir juxtaposed to the masculinity of the vines and barrels. The flavor of the grapes can improve as the vines aged becoming more knobby. Steve found it to be like Ivy and him -- as they aged, she softly mellowed and he grew gnarlier.

Every time he thought about Astuto's men going after Ivy, his resolve was renewed to see him, or theoretically them, brought to justice. First it had been an FBI money laundering case, then pursuit of a perp who had outwitted him, but since Ivy took a bullet, Steve's resolve to exact revenge was as fierce as that of his legendary Viking ancestors.

***

On the second Wednesday of October, Mathew drove Ivy and Steve up to Portland to pick out backsplash tiles for the kitchen and to select the lighting fixtures, drawer pulls, cabinet knobs and other doo-dads for the house. Ivy had a good idea what she wanted; Steve tallied what they ordered into an electronic list.

They went to three shops on the east side of town before moving over to the west side. Steve wandered off and selected, piece by piece, a box of luscious chocolate truffles at Moonstruck Chocolates. He then ordered three cayenne-spiked Hot Chocolates that he brought back to Mathew and Ivy who were engrossed in choosing a pot rack at Williams-Sonoma. Since it was after five before they finished, they picked up a couple of gourmet pizzas and salads at the nearby Pizzicato and left for Spook Hills. Both Steve and Ivy nodded off on the drive back, proving that the day of shopping was more tiring than a workday.

After eating dinner, Mathew strolled up to the house to check on progress. The deliveries of the kitchen cabinets and appliances were scheduled for the next day and he wanted to be sure that they had room to store them. Fred was still at work going over the newly installed hardwood floors in the living and dining rooms with a big buffer mop. He jumped when he heard Mathew's voice, put the mop aside and walked over nervously. "Glad you back, bossman," Fred said. He always called Mathew 'bossman', in the same way he called Steve 'the big boss', but this time he said it without his usual broad smile of greeting.

"What's up Fred?" Mathew noticed that he was so jumpy that he could barely stand still.

"Something bad. New field."

Mathew's heart sank into his stomach. Were those white burgundy bareroot grapes they planted sickly? He asked, but Fred silently motioned him

204

outside. They walked down the hill to where the grapevines were catching the last rays of sunshine. The young vines had every appearance of good health.

"What is it, Fred?"

He dug the toe of his boot into the soil. Mathew waited.

"They came."

"Who came?"

"The bad hombres. They say they kill my family, then me."

Mathew sucked in his breath, held it and then blew it out heavily to dispel the surge of anger that threatened his normally cool demeanor. Fred was such a great kid and now he was in danger and worse, so was his family. "Let's walk and check the vines, like we have something here to be concerned about. We'll talk as we go. Try to act normal, in case they are somehow watching. What did you do?"

"Said I think about it."

"And?"

"Jesus, man. They put a gun to my head. Almost pissed myself. I was alone here."

"We left an agent. Where was he?"

"Went for some lunch in town. Told me to stay inside."

That negligent agent had to go. After another deep inhale and exhale, Mathew bent down to examine one of the plants, dug a bit in the soil and then motioned Fred down.

"And you agreed to work with the bad hombres?"

"I nodded at them. They punched me in the gut a few times, like for the joy of it."

"Americans?" Mathew asked, standing back up and walking.

He shook his head. "Spoke Spanish, but not my Mexicali Spanish."

Mathew nodded and bent down by another plant. "Would you recognize them if you saw them again?"

"Si. Them I no forget."

205

Mathew regarded him sympathetically. "What do they want you to do?"

"Report you guys. Tell them when you all gone again. Gave me a special cell phone."

"Where is it?"

He nodded up at the house. "Afraid it transmit, like on its own."

Fred was proving himself to be both cautious and loyal. Mathew started rooting around in the ground. Fred joined him. The soil held warmth from the afternoon sun, making it feel comforting between his fingers. Mathew thought fiercely -- my vines, my land, and my soil -- that fucking perp will not take this away from me. He felt as protective as the homesteader who first settled this land.

"My family?" Fred asked worriedly.

"Let's wake up Steve. We'll get FBI coverage for your family or maybe have them relocate somewhere. Why didn't you call me?"

"Afraid the phone, you know, bugged."

They checked a few more plants, and then walked back up to Steve's trailer. Mathew had to knock repeatedly before Steve came to the door. Apparently he and Ivy had resumed their nap. Steve was barely awake standing there in his crooked boxers.

"Get dressed. Bring Ivy."

He went to speak but Mathew shook his head. Once Steve and Ivy stumbled out of the trailer, both armed and with their protective vests on, the four of them walked back down to the field, where they continued the random examination of the plants and soil as their cover, while repeating the conversation Mathew had with Fred.

"Fucking bastards," Steve said. Ivy nodded agreement.

"We need different agents here. Set up a rotation with agents out of various offices. That agent never should have left Fred alone. Maybe he's dirty or has been threatened too."

"Or just stupid."

206

"My family?" Fred asked. "I got you guys, but they have nobody. Since he drink, my papá, he not the best, but Mama and my little sister -- how we help them?"

"They all need protection. They could come here," Ivy suggested. "Or would that put them in more danger?"

Steve was weighing the options. "More dangerous all clustered together. The Portland house is out, as it is a made location. We'll get a couple of agents out to their house and hold it at that. Fred, you will need to go over there tomorrow and explain the situation. Mathew, see if Brian and Moll can do a stakeout tonight outside Fred's parents' place."

"Maybe they go back to Mexico to stay with family?" Fred asked. He always said Mexico like the native he was, although most of the time, he tried very hard to speak English as Americans spoke it. However when he was scared, his English became more choppy.

"Perp operates in Mexico. Too hard to cover them down there," Mathew observed.

Ivy said firmly, "Secure their place for your Mom and sister. Your Dad goes into rehab."

"He no go. We try."

Steve looked grim. "He'll go."

Fred said wistfully, "He was great papá. Taught me stuff. Good with knives. Then he drink, drink, drink. Go loco."

Steve lifted an eyebrow at the knife comment. "What about knives?"

Fred gave a half smile and made a flipping motion with his right hand. "Throwing. He taught me."

"You carry one?"

"Yeah, switch blade. I'm a, what you say? Pig-Squeaker?"

"Pip-Squeak," Ivy said.

"Si," Fred said, laughing at himself. "Pip-Squeak. Why you guys so good to me? I'm nobody."

Steve regarded Fred with a friendly smile. "You're somebody to us. Somebody pretty darn special. Your loyalty is a gift."

Fred's eyes filled with tears and he quickly knelt down by a vine. The light was fading and they were about to lose their reason for being out in the field.

"From now on, you sleep in Mathew's trailer. Bedroll tonight. We'll get a sleeping bag and mat tomorrow. We'll also order a protective vest for you and a couple of more knives, along with a shoulder harness and a leg strap -- always good to have extra fire power, or knife power in this case."

Ivy regarded Steve with surprise.

"We'll set up a target in the barn for him to hone his skill with a knife. Might come in handy. Let's go in. We're beat and we have to get up early to call the Chief."

They started walking uphill back to the trailers. Mathew dialed Brian on his cell while they walked. The evening air shifted softly around them, but the gathering gloom and this latest threat made the night ominous. Mathew so wanted to be able to walk out among his vines without worrying about somebody opening fire. He wanted peace and a place to belong.

"Oh, and Fred," Steve said, turning to look him in the eye. "You will report to those rats, as if you are cooperating."

Fred gazed worriedly from Steve to Mathew, who nodded somberly at him. Fred thought for a moment and then made a little walking motion with his fingers, followed by a quick snap together of his hands.

"That's right," Steve said. "We'll set a trap. We have a rat infestation."

With that, they trooped back up to their trailers. Fred and Mathew headed for Fred's trailer to get his blankets so he could be somewhat comfortable on the floor in Mathew's trailer. Before they parted, Steve gave them one of his stern looks. "From now on, nobody and I mean nobody, goes anywhere alone. Not to the house, not to town, not to the fields, not even to take a crap."

This was a grim new twist. For Astuto to pick on a young man like Fred showed a lack of scruples that bad perps had. That not speaking Mexican-style Spanish was interesting. While it still left of big world of Spanish speakers, it confirmed their new theory that Astuto was Cuban. Mathew wondered what

208

Steve had in mind for the trap -- likely nothing yet, although he would have a plan by morning.

Fred took some time settling down in his bedroll but after twenty minutes he was sound asleep on the floor. Mathew checked for his own knife under his pillow and then glanced over at his gun on the ledge by his bed. He decided to reposition the trailers the next day to get them closer together with fewer sides exposed. They would also need to start searching delivery vans. He fell asleep making a mental list of changes for their protection and for the security of their vineyard as well.

***

On Friday afternoon, Ivy found herself unable to concentrate on the research. The weather was surprisingly warm that day and she was a bit sleepy as the October sun streamed in through the barn doors, bathing her in its golden light. She was finding that their lives had a schizophrenic quality as they lived in the shadows of the contrast between their bucolic vineyard retreat and their work to catch this possible triumvirate of drug lords. Steve and Mathew found incidents in the Miami area that met some of their criteria, but none involved twin brothers and another sibling. They had exhausted the online systems in major cities and were researching an additional five-year span on either side of their target age for Astuto. Ivy was beginning to think this theory was pure conjecture spun out on wine and good food and no more than that, but Steve was determined to explore all aspects. She admired him for his commitment even though the work was certainly tedious.

The two men were planning some kind of trap for the 'bad hombres' who went after Fred, but they were not sharing it with her. She decided to see if she could provoke a reaction from Steve.

Secure Email from Ivy Littleton, October 11, 2013

Steve, I have tried to have this conversation with you about what you are planning to thwart an attack by the perps, but you always play innocent or laugh it off. Consequently as you suggested while I was traveling, if we cannot talk about a topic then we will email each other. I sense that you and Mathew are planning some maneuver that you are hiding from me.

If you do not trust me enough to make me part of your plans, I can accept that. I will be hurt, but I can understand. If you think you will protect me by keeping me in the dark, then you are very wrong. I worry the most about what I don't know. If you are contemplating something so dangerous that it will not get my buy-in, then maybe you had better give that some thought. You are not back to 100%. Mathew still has a slight limp that limits his agility. You need to leave the dangerous missions to active agents. Do you really want to leave me a widow before you even marry me? If you cannot tell me what you are planning, let me know how dangerous it will be. You owe me that.

By the way, we have to catch these creeps so we can set a wedding date. Our house should be ready to occupy by the first of December. I so want to have the celebratory party when we have our new home decorated for Christmas. If we are lucky, that evening will be a little cool and you can take me on a magic carpet ride by the fire in our bedroom on the new sheepskin rug, as well as spend time christening our new bed.

With impatient love, Ivy

<u>*Secure Email from Steve Nielsen, October 11, 2013*</u>

Ms. Vine, around four this afternoon, you and I will leave Fred and Mathew behind, take a walk up to our little grove of walnut trees to have some 'us time' sitting on the grass up there. I will tell you then what we are planning. Could I talk you into bringing along a thermos of hot chocolate and some cookies?

Mathew and I do trust you, but we want to get this scheme worked out in our own minds before we let you poke holes in it. I have setup a secure casebook, which includes scenarios for trapping rodents. If our plan holds up to the "Ivy Test", I'll give you access to the casebook.

Wow, Ivy -- I may need to order some Viagra to keep up (so to speak) with your plans for our wedding night. I can't wait to get out of that trailer and feeling fully fit again. I think we should start doubling up on our exercises -- uh, at least the ones from physical therapy.

Lovingly, Steve

<u>*Text from Ivy to Steve, Same Day*</u>

C U LTR. NO V DRG. TK U AS U R. LV IVY

***

Mathew too was reaching the end of his patience with living in his trailer. Having Fred sleeping on the floor and sharing meals with him did not help. Even though Fred was a great kid, living together was too cozy for comfort. If Mathew even belched, Fred would laugh. Just that day Mathew had seen a pretty woman on a bicycle down on the road. He and Fred were out for a periodic survey of the property, sampling the soil by the end of the driveway where they would do a late planting of a different variety of white burgundy grapes once they arrived from France in the next couple of days. The woman on the bike looked over at Mathew, smiled and gave a wave as she went by. She even glanced back over her shoulder at him.

Mathew could not imagine why. He had a two-day stubble, his shirt was grimy from wresting with the bucket on the tractor and his baggy shorts were anything but flattering. She was maybe thirty with long, dark, straight hair blowing out behind her. Riding as she was in cutoff jeans, a tee shirt and old-fashioned sneakers, she made a pleasing image. She had a nice figure, tall and slim. Mathew wondered who she was, where she lived and if she happened to be single. This was not a good time for him to get involved. He wondered if there would ever be one.

Fred teased him about the woman. He did an imitation of Mathew with his jaw dropped open for Steve and Ivy. Mathew liked Fred, but he noticed every little thing and lacked an internal censor on making fun. Even so, something about that pretty woman captured his attention and he decided to find out who she was.

Chapter 20

The next morning, as each of them was again wondering if their theory on the three brothers was a dead-end, Steve let out a yell of victory.

"Hey, quick! Check this out. Mathew, get the lights."

He jumped up to connect his laptop to the projector that they had rigged up to shine on an improvised screen made from an ironed white sheet hung on the barn wall. Mathew slid the barn doors shut. They had enough light from the windows to operate and still see any projected computer images.

The police records of an abduction of a ten-year-old boy came up on the screen. Steve juggled the windows on his laptop to display two other pieces of information -- a news story and a county birth certificate. The short news coverage read:

Miami Herald, The (FL)

October 8, 1985

Section: Front

Edition: Final

Page: 22A

Missing Boy Found Near Death

Miami Herald Staff Report

The missing boy, Eduardo Fuentes of Hialeah, abducted 10 days ago has been found alive and is under treatment for broken bones, burns and lacerations in Palmetto General Hospital in Hialeah. When he was walking home from school, a roving drug gang out of Miami kidnapped the boy. He was held captive in a house used for drug packaging in the Opa

Locka area. The reason for the boy's detention is unknown. Police sources indicated that he had been subjected to extensive physical abuse inflicted over the time he was missing. He was also suffering from water and food deprivation. The house was deserted when the police arrived after receiving an anonymous tip. They found the boy locked in a closet, bound, gagged and near death. They also discovered the remains of a drug operation. They continue to search for those responsible.

His mother and brothers appreciate the community's support in the search for the boy. They ask for prayers for his recovery.

Copyright (c) 1985 The Miami Herald

"If this is Astuto, it means that he is only 39," Steve said excitedly. "This incident of extreme duress happened when he was 10. Assuming he started working on the drug operation when he was 20, in less than the same number of years he was able to put together a powerful drug cartel, set up effective money laundering schemes and become very wealthy, although to what extent can only be guessed."

"You find anything on his parents?" Ivy asked.

"Dad died at 50 from lung cancer, if I found the right obit." He fiddled with the windows and up popped the obituary. It sure sounded right based on the survivors:

". . . Alejándro is survived by his wife, Marista (née Machado), and his three sons, Cristo, Cruze and Eduardo.

"And the mother?"

"Died in 2008 of complications from an aneurism. Here's that obit."

Marista Fuentes had been living in Coral Gables. The three sons were listed as survivors. A private memorial service had been held and the mother buried next to the father in Hialeah.

Mathew was staring at the screen. "Wait a minute. Those names -- Cristo, Cruze and Eduardo. CCE. That was the name of the charitable foundation where the money went after it was siphoned off in Zurich."

"Bingo!" Steve shouted with a grin of triumph. "Now to factually link them to known crimes, and then run each one of them to ground."

He leaned back in his chair, gazed up at the rafters and allowed himself a moment of victory before rocking back down and saying. "Finally, we may have something concrete on who these perps are. Thank you Ivy. Your creative thinking that led us down this path. Your work and contributions have shown sides of you that otherwise might have remained hidden from me, such as your tenacity, your dedication to what has been tedious work, and your determination to see it through."

Then he turned to Mathew. "Mathew, I so appreciate that you stayed with this when you would rather be into your new life, out in your vineyards, and starting the plans for our wine production facility. You stuck with this even when you thought it was a dead end. Heck I even was beginning to think we were off track."

Steve brought up a blank word document, inserted a table and they began brainstorming next steps and assigning tasks. While they were putting up the task list, he called Brian and Moll to see if they would leave on short notice for Florida to handle research on the ground. They also had to search for links between the Fuentes and the drug and money laundering companies they had identified. Mathew found it interesting that the mother's obit failed to mention any daughter-in-laws or grandchildren.

"We have to catch them or we will spend our lives waiting for the next blow." Mathew clenched his jaw so tightly with determination it started to hurt. "Let's hope this leads somewhere."

"It will," Steve said. "All the right signs are there. How about dinner out tonight? Brian and Moll are on their way down, so it can be us three, the two of them and Fred."

"Steve, I'll stay here. I don't think we should all be away at one time."

Steve frowned and said. "Damn. You're right. How about we order in and two of us go pick it up? It's not ideal, but we'll make it fun."

While they were a long way from nailing the perps, they had a possible direction. Once they could find the current location for one of the Fuentes, they would confirm that they had found the right three brothers. For now, they had to get their names run through the available government databases to see if they could find more information. They each wanted this hunt done and over to get on with their new lives. Now the hard part of the case began -- finding the brothers and proving that together they constituted El Zorro Astuto.

***

Out in the barn, Mathew and Fred pushed the worktables together. Ivy went through boxes and dugout a long tablecloth and napkins, and then she and Fred went out to gather late wildflowers, which they strung into a sort of vine of white, yellow, blue and fuchsia woven along the center of the table. Steve pulled chairs up to the table, put champagne on ice and placed glasses in a picnic basket, while Mathew chilled bottles of pinot gris and chardonnay and set out bottles of pinot noir.

Once Brian and Moll arrived, they took some crostini that Ivy cobbled together along with the champagne up to the little walnut grove. They toasted their success and then called in an order to a local restaurant, which Mathew and Brian drove down to Dundee to pick up, including entrees, salads and desserts. Once they returned, they laid the food out on the table in the barn, eating picnic style out of the cartons and sharing bits with each other. Moll added music, drawing from the eclectic collection on his iPod that he hooked up to small speakers, which often included perky Celtic dance tunes and more gentle tones of a solitary harp.

Fred was much taken with Moll, egging him on during dinner to tell his outlandish versions of work at the Bureau. In particular, Moll's fatuous imitations of Steve gave everyone much needed entertainment. For the first time since the shooting at the Portland house, Ivy laughed whole-heartedly and that made the dinner special for Steve. The evening cooled down as they ate, talked, drank and laughed. By ten o'clock, they were ready for bed, with Moll and Brian opting to bunk down in Fred's trailer and drive out early to catch their flight to Miami. Once they completed the investigative work in Florida, Steve planned to spring their trap for the hired guns of the perps. The scheme they devised would be simple to carry out, nicely devilish, and they hoped foolproof.

***

On Sunday afternoon, Ivy took herself on a walk through the house, reviewing the computerized layout of the furnishings that Steve created and verifying that it would all work together. The floors and tiling were almost completed. The exterior and landscaping were all finished. Mathew and Steve had been great at convincing the contractor to do work simultaneously where the housing inspection process would allow it. She was looking forward to being out of the trailers and into her new home with Steve, but they still had Astuto to contend with. So much was riding on what Brian and Moll might find out in Florida.

Perhaps her favorite space in her new home would be the inviting glass conservatory with its grey-blue split granite pavers, situated between the garage and the kitchen. While Steve's idea was for her to grow herbs for year-round use, she also planned to put a couple of oversized chairs and ottomans between the pots of herbs, along with a serving table for afternoon tea or glasses of wine.

Steve planned a workout area downstairs by the lap pool, with enough space for a few pieces of equipment, some free weights and a couple of mats. While he had been hesitant to spend the money on himself for the lap pool, once Ivy indicated she would use it to stay fit in the winter months, his reluctance vanished. She still thought of it as Steve's pool, but she liked the prospect of skinny-dipping with Steve in the moonlight. She breathed in deeply, enjoying the new smell of the house, using the moment to renew her resolve to help find and apprehend the three brothers.

***

Two days later while they were working in the barn, Steve laid his cell phone down on his desk and motioned Ivy and Mathew over. Brian had called from Florida and he and Moll were on speaker.

"Okay London. Mathew and Ivy are here. Repeat what you told me."

216

"We found a mailing address on file with the Mother's will and other papers," Brian said, sounding breathless in his excitement. "It is the same for each of the three brothers -- one Post Office box in Santa Fe, New Mexico."

"That's unexpected!" interjected Mathew.

"One of you book a flight to Santa Fe to go undercover," said Steve.

"Already bagged a flight Chief," came Moll's blasé voice.

"I'll arrange with the Postmaster to add you to the postal staff. Work there until the Fuentes mail is picked up, then follow whoever comes in. I will overnight tracking devices to you along with some software via the Postmaster. Get the tracker on the vehicle of whoever picks up the mail. This will be a no contact situation -- only surveillance. Understand?"

"Yeah."

"Don't get spotted. We do not want to tip off the perps. Make yourself blend in -- take a short term apartment; buy clothes like the locals, etc."

"He's already reverting to the surfer look here in the Miami sun," Brian said with a laugh.

"Good. In the post office, we will set you up as coming from a smaller location that is rapidly expanding due to new housing developments. You will be there to learn the ropes of how a larger postal unit operates. Only the Postmaster will be informed that you are FBI. Don't let anyone suspect which mailbox you are watching. Be prepared for this to take some time. The mail could be picked up in a day or a week or a month or longer."

"Got it, Chief. Worse places to cool my heels than Santa Fe."

"Brian, did you drive by where the Mother lived?"

"Not yet. Will do that next. Do you want me to talk to neighbors?"

"No. Let's not draw any attention. What else is left?"

"That's about it here Chief, unless you have other ideas."

"Fly out today, but go to a city outside the Northwest and stay overnight. Then catch a flight for here."

Ivy smiled at the way Brian and Moll called Steve "Chief" when they were on a case, in the same way that Steve always referred to the Director of the FBI as "The Chief". She decided she would do the same to see how Steve would react.

***

On Thursday they sat in the darkened barn. Brian had rejoined them and they were going over what they accumulated about the Fuentes so far. Their research turned up some very old crimes on the twins dating to when they were in high school. Most were minor issues like carjacking, although one drug dealing charge was on file against Cruze when he was a minor, for which he served a year in a juvenile detention center. After that, nothing new turned up. None of them had passports under their birth names. DMV records in New Mexico and Florida failed to show any driver's licenses, making it likely that they used false IDs inside the United States as well as when traveling internationally.

Brian had copies of the photos of the Fuentes twins from their high school yearbooks, but could not find one for Eduardo. They would have the Bureau age the faces in those photos electronically and then compare them to the phony passports. While the United States now requires fingerprints on visas for non-U.S. citizens to enter the United States, obtaining a regular U.S. passport lacked this requirement. Forged documents would be required to get the passport or the passport could be forged as well. Bogus passports were trickier these days with online verifications to the federal database, but still possible to obtain.

"Chief," Ivy said with quiet authority. "Can we discuss the plans for the sting here at Spook Hills?"

Steve frowned at her. "I thought we did that, but okay. We are adding five agents who we trust to spring the trap, assembling a team of "Rent-A-Goons", as borrowed agents are called at the Bureau."

"Where will they be?"

"Standard protocol will put them hidden at strategic spots here in the barn, the old house and our house."

"If the perps think anyone might be here, isn't that where they would expect them to be?"

218

"If they know how the FBI works."

"So why don't we take an unexpected approach?"

"Something tells me you have an idea worked out. Just come out with it Ivy."

"Next week is Halloween, right?"

Steve's impatience was beginning to show. "So what?"

"And we are Spook Hills?" Ivy knew she was irritating Steve but she was hoping that by springing her idea on him slowly, she would hook him in.

"Dammit Ivy. Quit the dance and come out with the idea."

"We dress up the agents as ghosts. Put them out front, but as stationary objects."

"Don't be ridiculous. That's not how we do things."

"But maybe this is how the Spook Hills Gang does things. Throw something at them out of the box. Like we are so blissfully ignorant that the perps may hit us that we can be light and silly by having Halloween decorations out."

Mathew started laughing. "Set up some of those cornstalks too -- you know the ones like a teepee?"

"The Amish call them shocks of corn," Brian noted.

"Why not put out a big pile of pumpkins?" Steve scoffed, not amused by the ideas.

"Great! We can put some broomsticks outside of the front door too!" Ivy said, ignoring his attitude. "After all, the witches and warlocks will be inside the house cooking up a brew of their own."

Mathew looked over at Steve. "Com'on Big Guy. Let's put the Spook in Spook Hills."

"This is a serious operation, not some damn Halloween party. We go forward as planned." Steve glared at each of them in turn to emphasize his point.

Disappointed and irritated with Steve, Ivy turned back to her laptop, mumbling. "It's a good scenario and it goes in the casebook."

Exasperated, Steve stood up and limped outside. Fall was advancing and the days of rain could start at any time. He shook his head, annoyed at Ivy's idea and at the way Mathew and Brian had supported her. He looked down the driveway to where it curved near the road. The new sign for Spook Hills, in distinguished black and white with silver highlights, was in place along with two curving stone walls flanking the sides of the drive. They were made from the same grey stone they used on the house; each wall ended in a pillar of stone with a large black carriage lamp on top, looking inviting but dignified.

Even though he had discarded Ivy's idea, in his mind's eye he found himself picturing the agent-ghosts down there along with the shocks of corn and piles of pumpkins. He looked over at the unfinished house and then behind him at the barn. If they could do it so that the ghosts really did not look like live agents, it was damn clever, though a bit childish just like some of Astuto's tactics. It also solved a problem of where to hide agents to cover the perps' escape route. He wondered if they could pull it off.

He went back into the barn, aware of the lingering annoyance in the air. No one looked at him. He opened his laptop and went over the planned scenarios, noticing that Ivy had added the embellished version of her option. The Spook Hills Gang could have its own ways of doing things and maybe that involved some flair.

"All right Scenario 5.1 it is. Ivy, you are in charge of the ghost and ghoul costumes. Use Brian and Mathew as your models and get Fred to construct an internal stand for the agents to lean against for support since they could be out there for a two or more hours.

"Mathew, you take the corn shocks. Brian, you get the brooms and the pumpkins, then work with Ivy and Mathew. At the end of the drive, I want two agents standing together by one wall, another one by the sign. Two more will be up here flanking the barn doors. However if the costumes fail to make an agent look like an ethereal, stationary ghost, the plan is off the table."

"Boo!" Mathew yelled. "Let's get cracking. Where the heck do I get the cornstalks?"

220

Steve looked over at Ivy. She had a little smile on her face but said nothing. It made him wonder if she had already ordered the supplies she would need for the agent-ghosts. How did she know he would go for her plan? It was risky. It was unorthodox. Where had this devil-may-care streak in her come from? Was this the same shattered woman who damn near had a nervous breakdown last summer? In the business world, had she always walked a little too close to the edge until it wore her down? One day he would understand the riddle that was Ivy but until that time she would catch him off-guard, and he was okay with that. She had so many layers and aspects to her that for the most part functioned well together. He felt so one-dimensional by comparison and so far behind her in his personal development. He had courage and intellect and he had opened his heart to her. He hoped that over time he would come to know more facets of himself, but that was for after this case against the Fuentes was resolved.

In case the house was watched, the Rent-a-Goons would arrive the morning of the operation, each one packed into a big box, like any of the many deliveries coming in. These boxes would be put in the barn and unpacked, giving the agents access to a microwave and fridge, as well as a jobsite-johnny. Lenny from the Sofia operation was now retired and on the Steve's list of agents, lending substance if it came to a firefight. While they planned an intriguing setup, if the perps decided not to move in, they would have to plot another strategy. To keep the plan secret, the active FBI agents assigned to them at the farm would not be privy to the plan and the agents they were bringing in would only be briefed once they arrived and were hidden in the barn.

Chapter 21

About two the following Friday afternoon, when Ivy, Mathew and Steve were visibly outside working, from inside the house Fred nervously made his phone call to the perps. Steve attached a recording device to the cell phone, so they would have proof of the conversation if needed.

"Hello, this Fred."

"About time."

"The guys, they stick around, only out one, two at a time."

"When?"

"Tomorrow. They go to wine thing. Portland. They leave noon. Back by four."

"All of 'em?"

"Not me and not our assigned agent." Fred was so nervous, the phone almost slipped out of his hand. He tightened his grip.

"Okay kid. You get yourself out to the old barn. Stay there."

"Uh, one thing."

"Yeah?"

"Furniture delivery between noon and one. Go in house."

"Got it."

The day of the setup started right on schedule with the borrowed UPS van arriving at 10. The boxes containing the agents were carefully unloaded into the barn. Once out, Steve briefed the agents on how the operation would proceed. One agent in regular clothes would stay in the barn to protect Fred or to rush the house if needed. The others would be disguised in long, flowing white, silver and gray gowns made of layers of a shimmery material and donned over white coveralls. Each one was made to look like a spooky Halloween ghost. Among the agents, there was some laughter and then some soft grumbling about how to keep the eyeholes lined up, but the agents soon realized that Ivy had made headbands with Velcro that solved that issue. Each one first climbed into white coveralls. Fred had constructed a stand inside each outfit that consisted of a platform, a vertical back post and horizontal shoulders, which the agents could lean against, with their feet on the platform giving them balance. Steve checked them out, gave his approval and walked away, smiling to himself and feeling pleasantly surprised that Ivy pulled it off.

Once suited up, two ghost-agents were wheeled outside on a handtruck and put in front of the barn, on either side of the sliding door. Three ghost-agents were laid on a trailer along with the corn and the pumpkins. Mathew used the tractor to tow the trailer down to the front with Steve, Mathew, Fred and Ivy holding all in place. Once at the bottom, they first put out the corn shocks, then the pumpkins, and finally the ghosts. The greatest challenge was keeping their laughter under control, especially when lifting the robed agents onto the handcart to get wheeled into place. Now they truly were Spook Hills. Brian took a few photos of the finished setup. A light breeze was blowing, adding to the effectiveness of the long, tattered, spooky costumes.

By noon the agent-ghosts were at their posts. "Operation Spook Hills" was underway. Ivy, Mathew, Brian and Steve jumped into the Suburban and waved goodbye to Fred, reminding him of the furniture delivery. In the rear view mirror, Mathew watched him walk out to the barn, his shoulders hunched with worry.

The exchange at their neighbors was fast. Brian sealed the other three into the boxes and then he was sealed into one himself by the two local agents posted at the neighbor's. One agent put three dummies in the Suburban and drove out, heading for Portland. The other agent drove the truck with the boxes, circling around and driving up to Spook Hills. From inside the boxes, they could hear Fred come out and open the back door of the delivery truck. They could either feel or hear him sliding each box onto the hydraulic tailgate, and then lowering the boxes down. Fred and the agent-deliveryman wrestled the boxes into the house using a handcart. The agent left to drive the truck to Dundee, ready to return when called. Fred tipped over each box on its side, pulled off the tape and quickly Mathew, Steve, Ivy and Brian crawled out, staying low to the floor. They kept well away from the windows and crept on their hands and knees to get into position. Fred then hurried out to the barn, where he would wait with the agent posted there.

By 1:00 everyone was in position. Ivy was in a protected area on the floor of the kitchen behind what would be the big island. Brian was in the stairwell, ready to sprint upstairs or down, depending on where the action took place. Mathew was on the lower level where he could guard the sliding glass door to the patio. Steve had the front entry. They waited.

At 1:30 a black Toyota FJ Cruiser sped up the drive. Steve knocked on the floor twice, signaling that the action was about to start. Five hoods piled out, three with submachine guns and two carrying incendiary devices. Four of them circled around to the back of the house, which meant they planned to enter downstairs. Mathew and Steve had displays of temporary security cameras on their iPads, allowing them to watch the perps as they crept around the house. Steve signaled over to Brian to duck downstairs to join Mathew. Like at the Portland house, the perps shot the door lock off the lower level entry.

When Steve knocked on the floor, Ivy called the FBI who would alert the local police, as well as send additional agents staged nearby. Steve saw the perp who stayed out front start to plant explosive devices around the house. Brian and Mathew waited for the intruders to get inside and then opened fire. The man out front ran for the Cruiser. Steve jumped to open the front door and shot him in the left leg. The perp crawled into the car and backed at top speed down the drive. From his position by the sign, Lenny whipped up his submachine gun and opened fire on the car's tires. The action was over in less than five minutes. They had one dead perp and two wounded ones. Each member of Steve's team was unscathed. The plan could not have gone any better.

Agents and police screeched up the drive, followed by ambulances and a fire truck -- no one was sure why the fire truck was there. The Cruiser had plowed off the road into a ditch that ran along the edge of their property. Lenny kept his gun on the perp. Steve jogged down the drive limping a little, pleased that the cobbled-together team performed expertly.

224

The local agents carefully packed up the explosives the perps had brought, along with their weapons. Steve had their own firepower secured. He would always defend his lovely Ivy, his home and his friends. That was his role during Operation Spook Hills -- to stand and protect. It was a new role for him. He had always been the aggressor in FBI actions, but he found the new role better suited this time in his life.

Once the perps were taken away, they set out a buffet on the worktables in the barn and Mathew opened wine for the agents. Each of the agents in the ghost and ghoul outfits had their pictures taken, both standing in position and with weapons out. They also took a group shot of the whole team in front of the barn. Fred was placed front and center in the photo as their honorary agent, due to his key role in the operation. Between the success of the set-up and the comic twist of the agent-ghosts, a party atmosphere soon developed.

Steve liked using Astuto's own tactics against him in the childish approach with the agent-ghosts. Now with this threat behind them at least for a time, they could turn their full attention to running the Fuentes brothers to ground. Steve wondered when that mail in Santa Fe would be picked up. He so wanted to be moving forward in his relationship with Ivy and bring delight into her life instead of danger.

An FBI team out of L.A., handpicked by the Chief, would do the interrogations. Back at Spook Hills, they would see the transcripts after each session and could call in questions, allowing them to be at the vineyard in case a second round of attacks took place. Since the operation left Fred's family too exposed to stay where they lived in Dayton, Steve arranged a safe house for them in Salem. His Dad was still in alcohol rehab and according to Fred, he was doing well. Everyone hoped that this was one good thing that would come out of the menace of the Fuentes.

***

The next Wednesday morning out in the barn, they were slogging through more research when Steve's cell phone rang.

"'Chief. Moll here. A man who fits our description of a twin picked up the mail. I hi-tailed it out the back door and jumped in this old dusty pickup truck

I bought. Just pulling on a plaid shirt and cowboy hat so he won't realize I'm from the post office. What now?"

"Is he outside yet?"

"Yeah. Line of sight. Carrying a plastic tub of mail. Opening the door of a white van. Texas plates. Could be a rental."

"Follow carefully and at some distance. Do not let him think we're onto him. I'm putting you on speaker."

Steve laid his cell on his desk and motioned them over. "Moll's got what looks like one of the twins. He's following."

"Subject turned into a shopping center. Parking. Locking up and heading to the supermarket. I've got these great sunglasses that have a camera in them. When he comes back, I'll try to get a photo."

"Give him two minutes in the store, then walk casually over to the van and plant the tracking device. Once that is in place, get the hell out of there to a vantage point. Be as far away as you can."

They waited, listening. They could hear Moll slide under the van and then a quiet, "In place." A car passed. They could hear Moll's boots on the pavement.

"Shit. Must have pre-ordered. Here he comes with a loaded shopping cart."

Moll's footsteps kept the same slow pace. Then he stopped. "Think I got a shot of him. Groceries stowed. Van locked again. He's going into a deli. From what I could see, the van already contained a dozen big boxes loaded towards the front."

"Get back to your truck and find the tracker on your laptop," Steve instructed.

They heard Moll walking back to his pickup, humming some country western tune. With the tracking device transmitting, Moll could follow the van at a long distance to avoid getting spotted. They heard his truck door open and then shut. He started the engine. They waited, still huddled around Steve's cell phone

"Photo on its way to you," Moll said. His normally casual voice was tight with tension.

"Tracker transmitting?" Steve asked, fiddling with his PC.

"Yeah. Got it on screen. You can pick it up too."

Steve clicked his mouse a couple of times. The mapping software came up and they saw a little flashing light staying still.

"Great work Moll. Stay cool now. Keep out of sight. Remember, we don't want him to even think we know about him."

"Got my cowpoke hat on partner," Moll said in his joking way. "There's a shotgun in the gun rack and I'm sporting a three-day stubble. Picked up some old jeans and shirts at the Goodwill. If this pickup gets any dustier, it will choke and grind to a halt. I look so local, even the locals are envious."

Ivy was smiling to herself at the thought of Moll acting like a good old country boy.

"He's moving." Steve kept his voice steady although even long distance, his abs tightened from the thrill of the chase. "Hold where you are."

"See him. Turning this way."

"Hang loose. Look away from him. No eye contact as he goes by."

"Got my hat tipped over my face, elbow out the window, and an eye on the screen on the seat."

"Let the subject run solo."

"Went by without looking towards me."

They waited and watched the map and the blinking light of the tracking device as the van made its way out of Santa Fe.

"Heading south towards an artsy town I explored last weekend called Madrid."

"Take off now but don't rush it. Stay out of sight of the van."

The four of them watched the van's progress on the map and exchanged words now and then with Moll.

"Madrid coming up. What should I do?"

"Pull into a side street. Stay out of sight."

"Okay Chief. Wish to hell you were here."

"No action today. Surveillance only. Keep your distance."

"He stopped. Going into a burger joint I ate in last weekend. Good burgers with chili and sweet potato fries."

At the barn they stayed quiet, so tense that it was hard to breathe. Steve opened the email that Moll had sent with the photo of the Fuentes twin. While the shot was a bit fuzzy, to their eyes the man was identical to the passport photos from the money laundering companies. This appeared to be the man without the scar on his forehead. Steve would have the Bureau run their facial recognition software for more certainty.

Moll stopped humming. "Heading to the van with a bag of take-out. Man would I like another one of those burgers."

The flashing dot start to move again. This was such a critical time. If they lost him, it might be another month before they could repeat the action.

"Heading northwest, up by the town cemetery."

"Follow. No closer than a mile and more if the road opens up or goes straight. Watch the screen. Signal could weaken out where you are."

"Turning left."

"Hang back. There aren't many houses here according to Google maps."

"There's like nothing here but dirt roads and some trees that are barely a step up from sage brush."

They watched the progress of the red dot over Google maps.

"He turned right onto a washed-out, long driveway."

"Stop and hold. Pull you hat down low on your face. Get out, head to the opposite side of the road from the house and make as if you are taking a leak. Do not look at the house. They might have some long distance surveillance gear."

They heard the pickup door open and then slam.

A couple of minutes passed. The door opened and shut again.

"Had you on mute. Leak done."

They exchanged a look and shook their heads -- only Moll would have actually taken the leak.

"Drive straight on. Do not pursue him. Do not even turn your head towards that driveway."

"Roger."

"Go about the right speed for the road. When you can, get back to a highway."

"Okay."

"What's at the apartment?"

"In Santa Fe?"

"Yeah."

"Goodwill clothes -- that's it. Got the creds, roscoe, laptop, surveillance gear, duffel and the three eyes with me."

"Three eyes?"

"IPod, iPad and iPhone."

Steve laughed. "Perfect. Drive to the Albuquerque airport. Grab a flight out to Seattle and have the Bureau office there verify that no trackers are on any of your electronic devices. Buy some new clothes and leave the Goodwill ones in the trash. Once you know your gear is clean, get back as soon as you can. Great work, Moll! We'll get an agent to empty out your apartment and sell off the pickup. Call when you board at Albuquerque."

"Got it, Chief. Can't wait to bunk down again in Fred's trailer. Never thought a trailer would sound good to me. More as the trip progresses."

Steve ended the call and placed his hands on his keyboard. "Let's get back to work," he said calmly, although inside he was jumping up and down with excitement over finding a location for one or more of the brothers.

"But Steve," Ivy protested, "When do we move in?"

"When we can prove this is the perp we're after."

"What more do we need?"

"Think about it. We have a theory. We have hunches. We are seeing links. We need definitive proof before we move in."

"What if we can't get more proof?"

"Ivy, what if we are wrong? We would risk harassing or even shooting innocent people. We can't do that. We don't do it. I want these clowns at least as much as you do. However, we must have a solid case. We might be the Spook Hills gang, but we're still FBI, not some renegade vigilantes."

Ivy glanced over at Mathew and then at Brian. Mathew nodded. Brian shrugged and nodded too.

"I get it," Ivy replied reluctantly. Then she smiled at Steve, appreciating that his stance was one reason she loved him. He personified those three words in the FBI seal and motto -- Fidelity, Bravery and Integrity. She so wanted him to send a SWAT team in that day and have it done and over. However he was right -- innocent until proven guilty.

"I'm going to find the name of the property owner," interjected Brian.

"I'll review those interrogation sessions again from Operation Spook Hills. We have to find a way to make one of those guys crack," Mathew said.

"Is it possible . . .?" Ivy began tentatively and then stopped.

"What?" Steve said a trifle impatiently.

"Nothing."

"Ivy, remember -- no wrong questions and no bad ideas. Half-baked ones, maybe. But that is why we work together -- to take ideas as far as they will go."

"What if those guys from Operation Spook Hills are telling the truth?"

"That they have no idea who paid them for the job?"

Ivy nodded. "Are there rings of thugs that are organized and paid by central dispatch?"

"What makes you think that?" Steve moved away from his laptop where he had started working and scooted over to her in his rolling chair. The air was becoming chillier in the barn and Steve had on one of the striped turtlenecks and fleece tops they bought the first long weekend they spent together. To Ivy, he was sending out delightfully masculine vibes. She was amazed that at 63, feelings of desire could spring up just looking at Steve. She had to struggle to bring her mind back to their conversation.

"Ivy?"

"Oh, uh, the Cruisers. Like a fleet of limos. Lined up for the next job."

"You think each contract fee is so large as to cover a new Cruiser for as many times as they wreck them?"

"Too far-fetched, huh?"

"Too damn perfect. Mathew," he said scooting back to his own work area.

"Get info on large sales of black Toyota FJ Cruisers. On it, Chief." Mathew said without raising his head.

"Kruiser Killers," Steve muttered. "National network or maybe west coast. I'll get a run on cases in the last two years where the perp drove a black FJ Cruiser."

"Might want to check fleet sales," Ivy ventured.

Mathew shifted his eyes over to her and rolled them. "On it. What are you doing?"

"Checking carjacking rates on FJ Cruisers," Ivy responded quickly. "All colors. They could always repaint them."

Ivy saw Steve do his classic one eyebrow raise at Mathew and they gave a little nod to each other that confirmed she was adding value in their research work. Ivy focused on her laptop, determined to find something useful to further their case against Astuto.

***

While Steve kept his cool on the outside, inside he was brimming with exhilaration now that they found a likely location for Astuto. Brian's research yielded ownership information on three adjoining blocks of property near Madrid totaling about 500 acres, including one with a house on it and one with an entrance to a defunct coalmine. Maybe the three Fuentes planned to retire there, with each brother having his own plot of land. Steve found the existence of the mine interesting as an escape passage or a storage area. He checked online resources and found that the town of Madrid had a thirty square mile coal-rich area that petered out over 100 years ago. Lead and turquoise were also mined in the area.

A company named CCE Mining Interests owned those three blocks of land with the same style fictitious names of officers as were used in the money laundering. They were getting warmer, but they still needed some definitive tie of the Fuentes brothers to the CCE ventures or the money laundering companies or the drug operations. Steve wanted several solid links as hard proof that would hold up in court. He hoped the photograph match turned out positive.

Brian started looking for maps of the mineshafts and tunnels to see where they might run on the properties. The mines could supply one or more back doors for Astuto. Steve was pleased with Brian's initiative and deductive thinking. He was happy too with Moll's work trailing the man who was likely one of the twins. He stayed cool and should not have drawn attention to himself. Steve looked around the room. He had a great team to work with -- they had honed their skills until they were best of the best.

Steve was pleased with Ivy's work too. She had moved them onto a new line of thinking about the hired killers that Astuto had sent after them. Her mind worked differently than theirs. She was equally logical, yet she sometimes saw different possibilities. He was glad she was part of the team and not solely because he loved her.

Chapter 22

On Sunday, Steve, Ivy, Brian, Moll and Mathew took a much-needed short break and went over to the nearby Domaine Drouhin vineyard for a wine tasting. There in the tasting room helping with the guests and pouring wine was the dark-haired young woman Mathew had seen that one day on a bicycle. She wore a simple red dress and a cardigan sweater -- to his mind she looked both classic and classy. Mathew talked with her for a time until the tasting area became so busy she had to return to work. This time he was close enough to see that she wore a wedding ring. It turned out she was the niece of a neighboring vineyard owner and had what Mathew could only call an arrogant drunk of a husband who was there drinking wine. They lived in California where he was a professor at UCLA, but they were up for a long weekend to celebrate her uncle's birthday. When she was in the area, she helped at various vineyards.

Finding this attractive woman only to discover she was not available was maddening to Mathew. He sensed that under her demure demeanor, she was intelligent, caring and hardworking. Her name was Callie Straun, but born Callie Lindquist. Her uncle was the man who steered them to the land that was now Spook Hills. Something about her resonated with Mathew. She had a darling little girl of about 8, with the same long dark shiny hair. If only Callie were divorced or even separated, he would pursue her. He told himself to be encouraged at finding her since it might mean he could find someone else equally attractive to him.

Mathew turned his attention to a nearby conversation where Steve was talking with the vineyard tasting room staff. He heard Steve mention the nuances of the 2010 Laurene wine, but noting how young it was. He asked about the types of barrels used, what percentage of them were new, what types of yeasts went into in the fermentation and numerous other questions. Most of

233

that information was on their website, but Steve was trying learn what more he could at the event.

Steve's great mind remained like a sponge -- he retained every fact he learned about wines, how they were processed and what the growing conditions were for the grapes (even, if he could get it, the original source of the vines). He kept a quick index of specific characteristics of vineyards, their wines and critical attributes in an Excel spreadsheet, which he planned one day to turn into a wine-tracking database. At some point Mathew knew that Steve would distill all the data he was collecting into patterns and the creative side would find a way to take that information and make it productive.

Ivy fit in wherever she went simply by smiling in her charming way. Moll and Brian moved from group to group, trying to find out if any of the younger women were single. So much kept going on hold, while they tried to solve the case of the Fuentes brothers. Ivy and Steve's marriage, Brian and Moll's business startup and his finding a social life each had a lower priority as they tried to progress their case. The situation frustrated the hell out of each of them. When the five of them were standing together again, he decided to introduce the topic of where he would live.

"I'm thinking about buying a condo in the Pearl District so I can start a social life this winter," he said by way of introduction.

Steve experienced a pang of regret. "I thought you would live at Spook Hills for a time."

"I will most of the time but as soon as this case is resolved, I need to get busy searching for my Ivy." He raised his glass to her. Steve nodded in understanding.

Brian turned to Ivy and asked a bit apprehensively, "What are your plans for the Portland house?"

"When you and Moll move out, it will go on the market."

"What if we want to stay?" he asked quickly. "Would you sell it to us? Maybe Mathew will want a share of it too."

"I would take a share in that house," Mathew said eagerly. "Having healed there, it feels like a real home to me. Be a great alternative to a condo."

Moll was nodding. "We'll buy whatever you don't want of your stuff, though I may need to trade out that single bed I've been snoozing solo in. Hopefully soon, I will have someone to rub along with now and then."

Ivy was a bit dumbfounded by the offer on her house. She knew the men were waiting for an answer. She glanced at Steve. He kept his expression neutral. The decision was hers. "Sure. Great solution. We'll work out a deal. I do want some things from there. I have a list."

The three younger men laughed and Mathew said, "Of course you do."

"What do you mean?" Ivy asked perplexedly.

"You couldn't be involved with the Big Guy and not have lists. Disorganization, sloppiness, and carelessness are simply not tolerated. However I suspect you had those licked before you met Steve."

Ivy nodded and held out her hand. "Com'on, let's make the house sale official."

They did a four way shake on the deal. Mathew felt that for the first couple of months, Steve and Ivy should have the new house at Spook Hills to themselves. He would move back to the vineyard by spring and use the Portland place as a pied à terre on weekends or whenever. The house's proximity to both uptown and downtown Portland would give him easy access to gathering places for attractive women between 25 and 40. Brian and Moll were eager to help in the search, which meant they wanted to find dates for themselves. They had already identified a few possible venues like the Art Museum where a Museum after Hours series provided a gathering place for professionals interested in supporting the arts. That was as good a place to start as any and likely better than most for the three of them.

Mathew wished he could have Steve's luck – by chance meet the woman for him. He was so fortunate to have found Ivy, as if the magic between them drew them to together at that point in their lives. Sure beat the bar scene, but then Steve did his share of that earlier in his life. Even with the rocky road Ivy and Steve were bouncing down because of the Fuentes, their love continued to deepen and become stronger as their knowledge of each other expanded.

Mathew thought of Ivy as one in a million and maybe even one in ten or a hundred million. She was so right for Steve -- kind enough to spoil him, yet intriguing enough to keep him fascinated by her. The miracle was that she loved him. Steve was changing because of his relationship with Ivy and was becoming more balanced, more fun and more overtly caring. Mathew glanced across the wine tasting room at the woman named Callie Straun, his eyes meeting hers for a moment. She smiled and for that moment he stood transfixed as if they were the only two people in the room.

***

The following Tuesday, Steve violated his own rule by taking a stroll alone up to the little walnut grove. It was right before lunch and he needed to think. They were getting close to moving against Astuto, but he wanted multiple definitive links that would stand-up in trial when it came to that. Based on the photographic evidence, they could arrest whichever twin it was as he traveled into or out of the country the next time he used a known false passport, but that would still leave one to two brothers free. Steve's goal was to catch at least two of the brothers together, preferably at that house near Madrid, New Mexico.

The agent sent to pick up Moll's things and sell off the pickup reported that it did not appear as if anything had been disturbed. The agent scanned the apartment and the truck for bugs and tracking devices. They came up clean. Steve hoped that meant their surveillance went undetected.

Mathew found about twelve companies that were buying or leasing black FJ Cruisers, but three were rental companies, which they ruled out for now. Eight of remaining nine were likely legit companies, using the Cruisers for construction, tour guiding, and local rentals. One was more interesting. That company operated out of Miami and Los Angeles and could be one of Astuto's own companies, judging by its name and officers. Steve was sending one of the retired agents who helped with Operation Spook Hills to do local research and surveillance.

Steve let his gaze wander down the rows of young vines, now dropping their leaves for winter, enjoying the orderly way they contoured with the curve of the hill. His gazed at the coastal range of low mountains in the distance. How could they link the Fuentes factually to the shootings, the drugs, the money laundering and all those bogus companies? Collectively, they had to be smarter than the Fuentes. The brothers were clever, but not insuperable.

236

Old Growth & Ivy

Maybe they needed a big map of everything they had or suspected on the Fuentes to make the connections. What did Mathew say the other day, one of his many Latin expressions? Steve turned to walk back down to the house, searching his memory. Oh yes, it was *Causa Latet, Vis est Notissima,* The Cause is Hidden, but its Force is well Known.

Steve discovered that right after he retired, his boss had the request terminated that obtained electronic copies of the bank account transactions on the suspected Fuentes money laundering accounts. After conferring with the Chief, the request was reinstated that morning, with the data now flowing directly to Steve through secure bank data sites. The Chief found it interesting that Steve's old boss had so quickly cutoff the flow of the records to the FBI. Steve planned to add any new transactions to an historic copy of the database that contained the transactions up to the point when the data stopped coming in. Brian and Moll were using the software they developed for their nascent business to comb through the bank data, trying to find new patterns. They found multiple short bursts of activity, showing that the Fuentes were still doing money laundering, but in a random way. The money involved was transferred to countries where the banks can refuse to cooperate in supplying their records during investigations, most notably Ecuador, Turkey, Algeria and Ethiopia.

On a daily basis, they were reviewing long distance surveillance photos on the house where the Fuentes brother went. Other than his departure two days later, no one showed up, except that several times a week, a FEDEX or UPS truck made its way up the rough driveway to the front door. Unfortunately the driver left whatever package or packages were to be delivered inside of a Spanish-style portico, which blocked views from a satellite shot of whoever opened the door to collect the package. They requested delivery information from FEDEX and UPS for the last five years to trace the sources of the packages. Steve saw this as a fertile endeavor since it might be one of the ways that the Fuentes moved cash money.

Even though they were traveling to visit one of their prospective clients, Brian and Moll were already building the database to house and analyze the UPS/FEDEX delivery information, beating Steve to it. Instead of making him feel useless, he took pride in their resourcefulness. Before he departed, Brian

237

had obtained available records of the mines in the area of the Fuentes properties. Ivy took over doing additional research. As he walked back into the barn, she looked over at him.

"Steve," she said, pushing herself upright in her chair. "Is it possible that that the Fuentes created an underground bank where they are stashing cash?"

Steve nodded. That thought had occurred to him as well.

"I'm researching how to determine if the mine shafts and tunnels are still intact. Maybe we can use geological soundings to check for hollow spaces."

"Interesting thought. We would have to be careful not to draw any attention to the area, but we also might be able to use the tunnels to enter Astuto's house, trapping him."

"Won't he have security and explosive devices in place?"

"Likely. We'll need a specialized team skilled in counter-surveillance. Do more research on the geological soundings and then let's talk again."

Ivy squared her shoulders and went back to staring at her laptop. Geological soundings were definitely a learning experience for her. Movies and TV did such a compressed portrayal of FBI work. They failed to provide a picture of how tedious it is, how much time the research takes, how many roadblocks are in the way, and how many false paths ate up time. Movies only concentrated on the high points, squashing all the action into what seems like a few short days. Since they were limiting how much they tapped into resources at the Bureau, their work was particularly slow going. Ivy was trying to understand how to trace mineshafts and tunnels with technology that was outside her base of expertise. Databases, analytical applications, and audit systems were all things she understood. However, seismic soundings and the use of robotic technology to map out mineshafts were new to her.

She felt so fortunate to see Steve in this role. He was a great leader with many natural management skills in his repertoire. He gave each member of the team a good deal of leeway. He challenged each of them while suiting the tasks to their talents, like letting Brian and Moll run with the data analysis and putting Ivy and Mathew on research.

Ivy's thoughts wandered away from the case. The work on the house was progressing well, with the painters starting work downstairs. Ivy was envisioning a Christmas wedding with the party held indoors. In the center of the lower garden, they planted as large a noble fir as they thought would take root, which Ivy planned to keep decorated with small white lights year round, adding and replacing strands as needed.

She was exercising daily to keep her anxiety at bay. Mathew was right when he told her that being part of the operation was less stressful than she might have expected -- Operation Spook Hills taught her that. Nonetheless the continuing worry about when the next strike might happen was taking its toll. On the bright side, she was aware that Steve was secretly planning a trip to Europe for the holidays. Ivy caught him closing a document on his laptop called something like "Holiday Europe -- 2013". She pretended to have been looking elsewhere to let him surprise her. How pleasant were these interludes where they could dream, plan, and hope for another life! Without them, she feared they each might despair. They could see this new life in front of them – one that they each seriously wanted and perhaps desperately needed. Yet the threat and danger of the Fuentes brothers lay between them and their goals.

Chapter 23

Brian and Moll were briefing Steve, Mathew and Ivy the next morning on their analysis of the FEDEX and UPS data. At first their findings took a backseat to showing off the software they developed. Their slick browser-based interface displayed the data like Steve's models, but they dressed it up with color-coding and a stylized dashboard, creating a sophisticated interface that made the data instantly accessible. It also had an artificial intelligence engine built into it that helped in finding patterns and cataloging results. The software used a brilliant color scheme with galactic shades of deep blues, bright turquoise and neon yellows. Whenever a given task would take time in a very large database, a variety of options were given to the user to present partial results as they became available or to start a totally different process while the first one was working.

"Chief, check out these major trends in the deliveries to the Fuentes," Brian said trying to contain his excitement.

Ivy wheeled her chair over to see the projection more clearly and was sitting next to Steve, disturbing his concentration with her proximity. Having her close and smelling the delicate natural scents that she wore distracted him. Today she softly exuded cloves and oranges.

Using an electronic pointer, Moll started talking and indicating areas of the screen. "For a man living alone and isolated like Eduardo, getting deliveries takes some of the pressure off his brothers -- and he has a lot of stuff delivered. First we made a table of shippers that we flagged as likely legal, like Dell, Amazon, Saks, and so on. We took out the shipment transactions from those shippers and any return boxes back to those shippers, placing them in a separate table."

"Next we sorted the remaining transactions by count," Brian chimed in. "Many were onesies, twosies and we pushed those into another table for later research if needed."

Moll picked it back up sounding far more polished than usual. "Then we sought patterns in the remaining data with repeating deliveries. Ninety percent of them were from four companies named in the Fuentes style. You see them here, highlighted in turquoise. For the past three years, two to six times a month at random times, overnight packages were delivered to the Fuentes home from four companies located in Las Vegas, Miami, Corpus Christi and Reno."

"Any pattern to the size or weight of the packages?" Steve asked.

"Good question," answered Brian. "All are standard large UPS or FEDEX boxes that always stay well under the required 20-pound limit. We estimate that if they were shipping dollars in twenties that they could send around $25,000 in a box or in hundreds around $125,000."

"So $130,000 to nearly a million a month," Mathew quickly calculated. "Not big dollars for drug profit, but on top of what is likely still laundered through banks or stashed elsewhere, not a bad cash reserve. Shipments of cash would give credence to Ivy's theory that they have constructed an underground bank in those mineshafts."

Steve noticed that Ivy was frowning at the data. That puckered brow meant she was thinking. "Ivy what are you scowling at?"

"For the transactions you eliminated, have you matched the source delivery addresses with actual company addresses where they have operations?" she asked Brian.

"What do you mean?

"This may be farfetched, but these guys are devious. Could they have set up a company, or several for that matter, that appears to be a retailer, even say something like Amazon.com, and pretend to run a distribution center using that company's logo, packaging look-alikes, and so on, but are actually sending money to themselves?"

Mathew started nodding. "That would make it much easier to ship money, have it appear to be books or whatever and go undetected."

Moll picked it up. "Possibly more money back to the First Consolidated Bank of Fuentes? We'll get right on it."

"I'll request data on international shipments _to_ those four companies and all shipments by FEDEX, UPS and DHL _from_ any of the suspected Fuentes companies," Steve said. "If the international information pans out, we should have grounds to get the legal authority to inspect packages as they appear in the delivery companies' systems. If not, then we have to figure out how the money is moved into the U.S. With such a tight network as the Fuentes run, I am guessing they wouldn't trust the cash to underworld carriers. Moll, you see any packages in the Fuentes mail in Santa Fe?"

"Small ones, like bubble wrap brown or white ones. Maybe a half dozen. I do wonder, though if those boxes I saw in the van contained more moolah-roo."

"They must inventory the shipments between each other by phone or using the shipper email alerts." Ivy said. "We should check that out."

"Right," Steve said. "Now we have enough basis to gain authority for a stealth cell phone interception device that we can have moved into the hills nearby.

"It intercepts how?" Ivy asked, her expression curious.

"It puts out a stronger signal than the local cell tower and the calls go to it first. It will grab the calls, record and transmit them to us while it also sends the call on to the local tower."

"Devious. I like it. No land line wire taps?"

"We haven't found any evidence that they have a landline."

"Can we get text, email and Internet access, as well as voice?"

Steve nodded.

"Why haven't we already done it?"

"Very sensitive legal area -- invasion of privacy," Mathew interjected. "That's why we have to show probable cause and get the legal authority."

"Jeez, it's a wonder the FBI ever gets a case solved."

"Frustrating at times, however we do get them solved. Believe me, we would rather move more quickly but we have to adhere to due process," Mathew said, using his attorney voice. "We are part of the Department of Justice."

Ivy made a face at him. Steve continued with her train of thought.

"Everything about the Fuentes operation points to their management of the logistics of the drug trade. They are moving the drugs between countries and cutting down bulk shipments in bales into boxes of packets for street distribution through middlemen. That's what we saw during the raid in Mexico. That would mean they are paid in big dollars for each sale of drugs. Likely the twins handle collections, or now maybe just one twin. They may do some of the transport of the cash using hidden compartments on the yachts."

"Maybe they moved in when Pablo Escobar was gunned down in Colombia back in 1993. Didn't he and his gang handle the so-called logistics?" Moll wondered aloud.

"Who?" Ivy asked.

"Major drug lord," Steve responded. "Had most of the government and police forces in Colombia on the take. A special task force hunted him for years, finally running him to ground in his home stomping ground of Medellin, Colombia. Yeah Moll, I think that is highly likely. The Fuentes stepped into a vacuum, used the Escobar business model, grabbed as much as they could handle and then expanded from there. Likely they are not quite as big or all-powerful as Escobar, but they are keeping a major part of the Colombian drug trade organized."

"By the way," Brian said, "The pattern of where the packages came from changed right after you raided the drug repackaging plant in Mexico City."

"How so?"

"Fewer packages. More use of Miami and Corpus Christi."

"Bingo. Could mean that we killed a Fuentes twin in that raid and not an actor." A cold smile of satisfaction spread over Steve's face.

"Let's get busy," he said. "I'll call to get the international data. Moll, you and Mathew research those retailer packages. Ivy, brief me this afternoon on geological soundings and the use of robotics in mineshafts. Brian, listen in and then review the maps of the known mine tunnels on the property. I want to sound knowledgeable when asking for a surveillance team to go exploring -- stealth mode, of course."

Ivy smiled at Steve and scooted her chair back to her desk leaving a lingering scent of her perfume in the air. He inhaled, taking a sensory snapshot of the scent. They had set a tentative date of the second Saturday of December for the wedding, getting a caterer scheduled and invitations designed for the celebratory party. Steve wanted all that to happen on schedule and then they could move on with their relationship as husband and wife. He had a need to make that commitment and he thought Ivy felt the same way. Given his stubborn nature and her sometimes hot temper, they would have their squabbles, but he knew that this relationship of theirs was one that would last.

***

Mathew worked with Moll and Brian to review the data in their database, analyzing it with the dashboard they built. He found their software to be even slicker than he originally thought. He could see that once they had a couple of banking clients under their belts, their business was going to take off. Mathew considered asking to be an investor. With that notion, he realized he was thinking like his Dad and maybe that was okay, as long as he made time for a strong personal life and family.

He noticed that the relationship between Ivy and Steve was changing and deepening. He wondered what caused the change. Maybe it was because they were mostly recovered from the shootings. Whatever the cause, Steve now regarded Ivy with even more love than before. He acted as if he could not get enough of watching her. Their separation last summer and then the tragic shooting at their reunion had brought them closer. He could almost see the invisible strands that bound their hearts together.

Mathew forced his thoughts back to the case against Astuto. Ivy's conjecture might be right about the bogus fulfillment companies. They found what Moll called an Amazon.com twinner company in Corpus Christi. The agent that Steve sent to check out the site found a small office suite, which only contained empty cartons and tape with the Amazon.com, cases of blank white

244

paper and a funky sort of drill press. The office was unmanned. As Steve would say, "Bingo." They added shipments from that warehouse location to their suspect shipper list.

The data on international shipments was due to arrive the next day from DHL, quickly to be followed by UPS and FEDEX. Brain and Moll were eagerly anticipating getting their hands on the international shipment data. Since their prospective first client had postponed their startup until January, this data analysis for Steve was a good filler project for them. Until this case Mathew had never appreciated what great data hounds those two were, much less understood their hidden talents for analytical software design and programming. He enjoyed watching them transitioning from FBI agents into businessmen. The tool they developed appeared readily adaptable to many types of transactions. After this was over, they needed to sit down with Ivy and Steve, brainstorm uses for it and broaden their horizons on marketing.

Working with a designated group of legats in D.C, Steve verified that all the required paperwork was prepared to obtain the necessary legal authorization for the package inspection, the cell traffic interception and the mine shaft exploration. As soon as they had the analysis of the international shipment data, he would move to get the necessary search warrants and court orders. Mathew noticed a change in how Steve was working. He acted more trusting of each person's ability and he delegated more. This approach let the team perform around him while he pulled the threads together and handled the critical work with the FBI Legats. His mind was just as sharp, but Mathew could see that he was sharing the responsibility for results more with each team member.

They continued to track the twin's movements in and out of the United States under as many false identities as they knew about. Eduardo appeared to stay at what they dubbed "The Bunker" in New Mexico. The delivery trucks rolled up the driveway a few times a week. Other than that, it was as if no one lived there. Yet someone must. This was the toughest time on a case, when they were close, but not close enough to act. They had to follow the sage advice from Virgil: *Durate et Vosmet Rebus Servate Secundis,* Carry on and Preserve Yourselves for Better Times.

***

Finally by the second week of November, Ivy was relieved that Steve judged they were positioned to obtain the legal authority they needed to advance their case against the Fuentes. The international delivery data arrived in three drops to the secure server they had setup. Moll and Brian attacked it with all the single-minded intensity of two wolves after their quarry. They worked all night, waking Steve, Ivy and Mathew at five in the morning to share the results.

All five of them were jubilant! The international data showed regular shipments from various Astuto businesses that they identified in Colombia and Mexico. They matched the timing of those packages to the locations of the twin(s), based on their alias passport data, as he or they moved in and out of the United States. Mathew, Steve and Ivy verified the data and the findings to be certain their facts were right. Once they confirmed that all was in order, Steve authorized the legats in D.C. to take forward the requests for intercepting packages to the Bunker, for setting up the cell phone traffic monitoring and for exploring the mines on the Fuentes properties. Once they had the judge's approval, they could proceed with each initiative.

A couple of days later, upon obtaining the legal authority and with Ivy and Brian on the line, Steve called for the team of FBI agents and federal geologists he had lined up to mobilize for exploration of the mines. One of the shafts to the tunnels went to the surface on property adjacent to the land owned by CCE Mining. Fortunately that mine entrance was out of sight of the Bunker behind a series of land undulations. The cover story for the exploration team was a reported gas leak in the area. New Mexico has the third largest natural gas reserves in the nation, making it a plausible cover story. While most of the reserves are located northwest of the Santa Fe area in a region called the San Juan Basin and in the southwest corner of New Mexico in the Permian Basin, the cover story was at least plausible.

Now that she was part of the investigation, Ivy found herself as energized by the thrill of the chase as Steve was. He designated her as the coordinator for the mine exploration work, which meant she was on call 24/7 as the team worked in shifts round the clock stealthily exploring the mine tunnels, staying wary of security devices as they edged underground onto the Fuentes land.

246

Ivy had been cautioned that if they encountered a major cave-in, they might have to call the operation off. The team could deal with small ones by making their way over and around rubble and shoring up the roof or top of the tunnel as they went. It sounded dangerous to her, but the team leader was confident in their precautionary measures.

Steve found himself walking back and forth outside of the barn. Even though it was raining lightly, the moist air was welcome after the dry summer and fall. At last the case was moving forward! He loved it when the pace accelerated on a case. They were now in the chase. Once the phones and video calls quieted down the day before, he called the team together for a meeting over dinner. Mathew and Moll had driven out to pick up meals like they did when they celebrated their break-through on finding the Fuentes in Florida. This time they camped out in the nearly-finished house with the comfort of the furnace running.

He was so proud of Ivy. She functioned now like any other agent, participating in the meetings on equal footing. She teamed up well with the former agents, but took ownership of her task on the mine exploration. Steve watched how she worked with the three former agents, trying to learn from her team-player style.

Steve had a hunch that the traveling twin would return to see Eduardo for Thanksgiving weekend, keeping up some semblance of family traditions. If his hunch was wrong, he would keep adjusting the timeframe until they could pounce. He would not move in until at least two brothers were together in the Bunker. That evening, they laid out the schedule for the sting. Ivy asked if they were traveling to New Mexico. They tossed that around for a while and agreed that Ivy, Brian and Steve would go to a hotel in Santa Fe if all proceeded as they expected, with their rogue agent Lenny joining them. Steve would need to be close to the action, but he did not want to leave Ivy. Mathew would stay at Spook Hills with Moll and two trusted agents from Operation Spook Hills to defend their property, just in case another strike was scheduled. However they would be in phone and video contact with the Santa Fe team. They now had a wooden gate reinforced with bars of titanium installed on the driveway. Although the perps could crash through it with an armored vehicle or they could go around it, at least the gate would present a deterrent.

Every day brought new updates. The cell phone authorization was signed that morning. Steve had the equipment lined up and a team out of Los Angeles ready to put it in place that night. All wireless traffic to and from the Bunker would be picked up by a surveillance van hidden off the road. When they did the installation that night, Steve would have audio to the team leader and receive camera shots of the setup. The team installing the equipment would give him access to the recordings when they were intercepted going in and out of the Bunker.

They hoped to have the search warrant to inspect the Fuentes FEDEX, UPS and DHL packages the next day. All they needed was one package containing large amounts of cash, but Steve wanted to have several inspected packages from different carriers so that they could establish a pattern. The teams inspecting the packages would be local FBI agents briefed to make certain each package appeared untouched after their inspection.

Provided they could obtain these additional forms of evidence, they would then have stealth teams sweep the Fuentes properties undercover at night to devise a strategy for bypassing security detection devices. Once those plans were in place, he, Ivy and Brian, would fly to Santa Fe, to meet up with Lenny and an FBI SWAT team assembled from the Albuquerque and Los Angeles offices. With all of Steve's requests going through the Chief, he was getting all the cooperation required, and he knew he could be darn demanding.

Today the Chief privately told him that his secret probe had identified two FBI men and one woman as potential moles. In an unusual move, he had brought in undercover CIA operatives skilled in computer systems analysis to identify any moles. The CIA operatives were reputed to be performing an information security audit on Sentinel. The suspects included Steve's old boss, an information security guru and a supervisor in charge of interdepartmental data requests. This info on the moles was so top secret, Steve could not even tell Mathew or Ivy about it. Inwardly he felt justified in the contempt he had for his old boss. The evidence the CIA found was in their unusual computer access authorities, some of which were later over-written, but caught in the simultaneous off-site backup of the security tables and audit trails.

The CIA was now tapping into the suspected moles' bank accounts, their tax filings, and other personal financial information, seeking evidence of excess funds. It would be a sorry day for the FBI if there were three turncoats, but it was essential to identify and arrest the moles. Apparently the DEA would come under similar scrutiny in the coming weeks. Since the arrests were not yet made, the activities of the Spook Hills gang had to remain covert.

That night Mathew was working in his room in the new house, setting up a docking station for his laptop, adding speakers, a large screen monitor and gaming gear. He was torn between wanting to be with Steve and Ivy in Santa Fe for the sting on the Fuentes and defending Spook Hills on a contingency basis. Steve had guaranteed that he, Ivy and Brian would be well away from the actual sting when it went down, but Mathew found it hard to imagine Steve sitting on the sidelines. He suspected that Steve would be in a Bu-Van fully equipped with audio and video so he could monitor the team and ensure that the Fuentes were brought to justice.

Once the Fuentes were in custody, the operation and files would transition from the Spook Hills gang to a regular FBI team out of the D.C. office that would, in Steve's lingo, do the mopping up. They would seize the assets, comb the records and computer equipment, shut down operations internationally and prepare the case for prosecution. While it was probable that the Spook Hills gang would have their depositions taken and perhaps be called upon to testify, for the most part they would be out of any case follow-up.

Mathew thought about his FBI career. He would miss the intellectual challenge along with the assurance that he was serving his nation. He would miss the teams, even though with having Steve, Brian and Moll close by, he would still have the best of the best. However that part of his life would be over. He would have the memories, a slightly bum leg as a reminder and most importantly, great friends as he moved on with his life.

The waiting on the Fuentes case made him tense. He felt as if he were suspended in a pool of viscous liquid, where no matter how hard he struggled, a strong current within the pool kept him away from the shore where his future lay. He could see it there in front of him. He could close his eyes and visualize the future he wanted in his mind's eye but the Fuentes brothers' devious minds and drug cartel stymied his progress.

Chapter 24

With the electronic gear in place, the team was now receiving the traffic from the Fuentes cell tower. Communications between the brothers happened at least once a day. Cristo was the twin in communication with Eduardo and thus far, only Cristo. The conversations moved between English and Spanish. Steve set Fred up with a laptop at his safe house to translate them into all-English transcripts. Generally the calls were reporting collections and deliveries -- a summing up of stops by city. One particular conversation, which was the longest one, surprised him and the team:

> Eduardo: "Cristo, tell me about the negotiations today."
>
> Cristo: "Arrogant fuckers. These people are ready to slit my throat and take over. Now that the first meeting is finished, I'll use my phone from the yacht."
>
> Eduardo: "Good. I have lost one brother this year. I don't want to lose you too."
>
> Cristo: "Losing Cruze was so hard. I miss him, Eduardo. He was my best half."

Steve noticed that Cristo's voice sounded choked up when he spoke of Cruze, whereas before his voice had a harsh edge to it.

> Cristo: "To confirm, the deal is that they wire half the money to the account in Cuba. When that is verified, a courier takes them keys for the hangars, planes and yachts in Colombia, but not the locations."
>
> Eduardo: "Did they go for the $100 million?"
>
> Cristo: "No. Cheapskates. They laughed. I said that was the price or no deal. They want the financials."

Eduardo: "Send them the portfolio I gave you. No names."

Cristo: "Sending it to them electronically tomorrow."

Eduardo: "Then they bite or we move on. It is a steal at $100 million. We will shut down and pull out rather than give it away. Stay cool, my brother."

Cristo: "These dudes worry me. I think I should change locations."

Eduardo: "Move the yacht up to Corpus Christi. Easier to escape then. Too dangerous so close to Mexico. Do it tonight."

Cristo: "You have all the contacts, locations, pickup sites and drop sites organized?"

Eduardo: "Four lists in your folder on the server – hold onto them until the second half of their payment is confirmed. Is the doppelganger out and about in Bogota?"

Cristo: "Sure is -- regular flash party man, this one."

Eduardo: "All the better. When this is over, we send him to party heaven."

Cristo: "What are we doing about those fucking FBI vigilantes?"

Eduardo: "I have thought about that, Cristo. We do nothing until after this sale is closed. Then we hit them hard, wipe out the house, the barns, and the fucking vines. All of it. All of them."

Cristo: "And then we retire."

Eduardo: "Maybe dabble with the banks. We will see. Soon it will be goodbye drug world. Hello CCE Ventures."

Cristo sniggered.

Steve sat back and thought. He found the way they spoke of their drug operations as a regular business with financials and portfolios to be ironic. Did they really envision themselves as a couple of entrepreneurs? Listening to the actual voices, Eduardo's was high pitched for a man. He sounded asthmatic too. Steve wondered if his voice box had been damaged when he was held captive all those years ago. Cristo's voice was more masculine with a little Spanish inflection in his speech. Steve had the team listen to this conversation as well as read the transcript. With hearing their voices, the Fuentes became more than mythical figures.

Steve was interested that they wanted out of the drug business. He put his feet up on the worktable and leaned back. We will be happy to help them out of the drug business. In fact, we will help them out of all the businesses they have. He still wanted to find cash in those packages. That would be the proverbial nail in the coffin. He checked at his watch. Ten a.m. -- time for an update from Ivy and Brian on the exploration of the old mine tunnels.

"Chief," Ivy said with that little glint she had in her eye whenever she called him 'Chief', as if she found it amusing to report to him on this case.

"The geological team has progressed underground to the Fuentes property," she continued.

Brian put up a diagram of the mines on the projector. "The red solid line shows their path. Where it is a dotted line, they had to clear rubble, shore the area up and continue. They have a probe that goes ahead of them -- a little robot with a flexible wheel base that can climb over uneven ground and small rubble."

Steve nodded after tracing the line of the tunnel in the air with his forefinger, committing it to memory.

"I had them send this photo of the robot. Here are some shots of the mine too. You can see that these tunnels are old and crude. The timbers shoring them up are not in the best of shape."

After reviewing the photographs and the slow progress into the mines, Steve began to worry about the planned sting.

"Yesterday they encountered a big cave in," Brian said when Ivy flipped up another photo of the tunnel. "After checking the area for potential hazards including noxious gases, they started to clear a hole through it. They shored up the ceiling of the tunnel and then moved the rubble along the sides of the mine to eliminate carting it up to the surface."

Steve watched him nod over to Ivy and he realized they each had a look of suppressed excitement.

"Early this morning, about a hundred feet after the big cave-in, they found this!" She flashed up a photo of a newly constructed steel and cement wall reinforced with steel beams. Both Ivy and Brian were smiling triumphantly. Steve stared at it, scarcely able to believe his eyes.

"Bingo. Pay Dirt!" He grinned back at them, elated that their hunch on the tunnels and the bank was proving likely. The Fuentes escape tunnel or some underground chamber had to run behind that new wall.

Mathew had been watching from his worktable, but now got up to stare more closely at the photograph on the screen. "What does the geo team do now? Cutting through that wall will set off alarms. The noise alone could do it."

"Have they taken any soundings of the area?" asked Steve.

"Yes. There is an empty space on the other side of the wall, but the metal may distort the waves, so the readings could be off. Here's what they have so far." She put up a diagram that showed the possible path of the tunnel on the other side of the wall. It was running northeast to southwest.

"Put that original mine map back up."

Steve studied it and quickly Ivy flipped up an overlay showing where the explored tunnel came in and where the soundings indicated the Fuentes tunnel might run, at least for a short distance.

"I'll get the stealth team set for tonight. They will go on the Fuentes property from around here." He pointed to an area of back acreage. "They will search for security devices, cameras most likely, and figure out how to redirect them or avoid them. This will be recon only."

"And our mine team?"

"Let's not push our luck. Have them put in monitoring cameras. Then they should clear out and return to base camp in Albuquerque, but stay at the ready to go down that shaft on the Fuentes property. Likely that will be in good repair, although it will have tons of security."

He stared at the mine map with the overlay and smiled at them. "Great findings! Give my appreciation to the geo team. It's all coming together! Now we need a few packages of dough."

"Chief?" Brian asked.

"Yeah?"

"I think Moll or I should be there when the packages are opened. We have to be sure it is done right, photos taken and sealed back up so that each package appears undisturbed."

"Not sure we can do that with the timing."

"We can if we get the info when the package first enters the system. We can then be on location in the carrier's hub city. We intercept as it comes into the hub, inspect the package and send it off as scheduled. Using the hub city gives us time to get there and keeps us away from any potential local spies near the Fuentes."

Steve nodded. "As long as it is easy to coordinate."

"The fraud divisions for the carriers are all over this -- very cooperative. For packages that originate internationally, we'll get to the first U.S. city where it will hit."

"Want a Bubird on standby in Portland?"

"Really?" Brian's normally masculine voice squeaked he was so surprised. "You can do that?"

Steve raised an eyebrow in response.

"Dumb question. Of course you can. I meant you would do that for us? Much easier and faster. Then we can jet from hub to hub as the delivery info comes in. We may have to split up, but we'll work that out. Uh, how do I schedule the plane?"

"You'll have a number to call to arrange the next flight. Give as much warning as you can in case a backup flight crew is required. Call me with any problems or if you need a second 'Bird."

"Got it Chief!"

Steve glanced over at Ivy. Then and as always when he let his mind wander from work, he felt a lurch of happiness at having her nearby. "How about spending Thanksgiving in Santa Fe?"

"Sure," she said with a grim smile. "As long as we're there to cook a couple of turkeys."

Steve nodded. Since they would be holed up in a hotel or in a surveillance van, they would not see any action first hand. However he had to be there for the pre-sting preparations to ensure that the arrest operation went as smoothly as possible. Once it was over, he wanted to look the Fuentes in the eyes when they were taken off to be incarcerated and he wanted to see what Moll dubbed, "The First Consolidated Bank of the Fuentes."

***

Steve reminded Ivy of a man doing a jigsaw puzzle, picking up pieces, finding where they fit, and then methodically completing the picture. He was systematic about it, tracking it all in his head. He also understood new information quickly and stored it away. After the short briefing Brian and Ivy gave him on exploring mineshafts and tunnels, he sounded like an expert. Hearing him on the phone that same day, discussing what type of team he wanted and relentlessly pursuing his timeframe, made Ivy sit back in awe. Seeing him in action, Ivy better appreciated that he was one of the greats in his business -- the FBI.

As Thanksgiving neared, Ivy felt like a cat walking on a narrow ledge, unsure if she should have her claws out or not. Every nerve was taut. With the mineshaft exploration, she had made a real contribution to their case against the Fuentes. Their plan was to fly to Santa Fe on Tuesday. Ivy could see that Mathew was torn between being with them and protecting their home and his precious vines. While he opted to stay at Spook Hills, he would be in phone and/or video contact with Steve. This land and vineyard are his future -- this was where he needed to be.

***

The recent team meeting left Steve satisfied with their pre-sting plans. He had his list to verify arrangements with all the teams. The best news had come in that evening. So far, Moll and Brian inspected four packages sent by FEDEX from Corpus Christi via the FEDEX hub in Fort Worth. Inside each one were two reams of paper. When they carefully removed the paper that sealed each ream, they discovered a few sheets of paper on top, then below those sheets was a stack of paper where the inside had been cut out, creating a hollow rectangular block. Inside that block were stacks of currency. Another few whole pages were on the bottom of the stack. From the outside, it looked like any other ream of paper. Two such reams fit into the UPS box side by side with a little space for packing paper. The packages weighed between 10 and 12 pounds. Three stacks of hundreds (U.S.) had been in each ream in three boxes. Three stacks of Mexican 500-peso bills in each ream were in a similar box. In total, ten such boxes had been dropped at five FEDEX and UPS locations in the city. The drops followed the receipt of large DHL boxes originating in Mexico at the warehouse address of a Fuentes company branch, also in Corpus Christi. The DHL boxes had been shipped from Mexico the same day as the phone conversation about the sale of the drug business they had picked up, right before Cristo left for Corpus Christi.

Ivy's hunch was right about the masquerade mailers. Two of the boxes examined were the same size as the express delivery boxes, but were in plain brown cardboard, taped up with Amazon.com tape and had express delivery slips and stickers applied. While they would have to alert Amazon's fraud division, Steve decided to delay that until after the sting under the guise of the need for secrecy.

If he stepped back to examine the evidence they had collected thus far, he believed they had more than enough to justify a search warrant and make the arrests. His next step was to review the evidence with the Chief. In his organized manner, he summarized their findings in a document that he would use to memorialize the conversation. Under each item, he detailed their proof and how they had obtained it. This information was in their regular files. Nevertheless he always pulled it together in one place when he went forward for arrest warrants. The sting had to be accomplished now and with no mistakes. He wanted zero potential that the perps could wiggle out of the charges. He tapped the desk a few times with his forefinger, confirming his opening statement to the Chief. It was time to make the call.

Not until Tuesday morning at six west coast time was Steve able to reach the Chief. He approved the search and arrest warrants on one condition -- that Steve himself would be part of the arrest team. He could be surrounded by agents. He could have an advance SWAT team, he could be in an armored tank or whatever he required for his personal safety, but the Chief wanted him there because he trusted him to get the arrest done right. Steve knew he would have trouble getting this change past Ivy. Across their little trailer table, she passed him a mug of morning coffee. He thanked her and looked her in the eyes. He had to be straight with her.

"Ivy, can we take a walk? I need some air."

"In the rain and the dark?"

"Yeah."

She regarded him appraisingly and went to pull on some clothes. Steve had to smile when she tucked her silken nightie into her sweatpants and pulled a heavy fleece top on over it. Ivy was a mature, feminine woman, yet at times she could be cutely girlish too. He pulled out their rain jackets and a flashlight. They walked out of the trailer, letting the corgis run ahead of them and because it was their special place, they automatically turned to walk uphill to the grove of walnut trees. Both of them were silent as they trudged along in the dark.

They were most of the way up when Ivy took his hand and said, "The Chief wants you to head up the team and make the arrests."

"Yes."

"Because he trusts you."

"That's about it. He said I can have any number of agents around me, a SWAT team in front of me, even be in an armored tank, but he wants me there."

"What if the land around the house is mined?"

"The SWAT guys will sweep it as they go. I'll be behind them."

"What if, don't laugh, but what if they have the house rigged to explode if they have intruders?"

"The team will scan for that too."

"So there is no risk to you?"

"Ivy, there is always some risk. These are armed and dangerous perps."

"Then I go too."

"What? No way."

"Steve, you have become my life. If you go, I go. If you get blown up, then I may as well go too because the world will be a dark place without you."

Steve's heart melted hearing those words, but he had to be realistic too.

"You could stay for Operation Spook Hills because it was totally my operation. This one will have regular FBI teams -- the SWAT team, a team of agents out of Albuquerque and the team who will take over the case after the arrest. We can't have a civi there."

"Civi?"

"Civilian -- non-agent citizen."

"Steve, I am 63 years old. I could die on my next plane trip. I could get cancer and go in six months. You get clearance for me and we go together wearing all the protective gear we can."

They reached the top of the hill and took shelter under a walnut tree that still had some of its leaves. Rain was coming down lightly but steadily. In the breaking gray dawn, their nearly completed house sat rather majestically in the dark mist below them. Mathew's old barns and little ramshackle house, partially blurred by rain, made a scenic picture in the dim light.

"We should put a little gazebo or something up here," Ivy said, glancing around.

"Treehouse. Give us a vantage point." Steve took her in his arms and held her, this woman of love, magic, intelligence and courage. His heart felt so full. They would have no real peace while the Fuentes were free. The minutes slipped by. Even with the partial foliage and their rain jackets, a wet chill was settling in. Still holding Ivy, Steve pushed back to look her in the eyes.

"We live through this and I will build you a gazebo, treehouse, or whatever you want up here. At the sting, you can be outside in an armored assault vehicle with a trusted agent. You can have audio. Once the arrests are made and the house is swept for explosives, you and the agent can come in."

She thought for a time. While she did not like this option, she had to respect Steve's judgment.

"Deal," she said reaching up to kiss him.

258

The kiss was long, slow and deep. Steve pulled back reluctantly. "Now we need to brief the guys."

They walked down the hill quickly and headed to Mathew's trailer. Steve tracked down Brian and Moll en route to the airport in Indianapolis. With them conferenced in on speaker and Mathew listening live in his trailer, Steve went through the situation with them. For a full minute, the three former agents were silent, mulling over this change in plans.

Mathew said quietly. "I'm in. We'll get agents from Operation Spook Hills to guard the house and vineyard. Lenny comes with us."

"I'm coming too," Brian interjected. "We're a team."

"Ah hell," Moll drawled, "Just don't dislocate my shoulder again."

Ivy and Steve tried to discourage them. The three men were adamant that they would be part of Steve's team. Steve was going in and he would have his top agents with him, with the love of his life nearby. Steve thought each of them wanted to be sure that this case would be truly finished and that they were all witnesses to it.

"All for one and one for all," Ivy said quietly, using the oft-quoted Musketeers slogan.

"*Omnes pro uno, Unus pro omnibus*," Mathew echoed in Latin.

Steve had to look away. Tears of gratitude and deep feelings for Ivy and for those three men welled up in him. How much he had changed or how much he had never seen before! Never had he realized how deeply Mathew, Brian and even Moll were committed, not just to the Bureau, but to himself. He decided that Moll would stay with Ivy in the assault vehicle. His blasé attitude would help her through the tense period of waiting until the operation was over. Inside Moll might be tied in knots, but he would keep up that cool exterior and humorous attitude. Mathew and Brian would go into the Fuentes house with him and Lenny, hot on the heels of the SWAT team.

***

They flew out that day on a Bubird to Santa Fe and then spent that evening briefing the SWAT team and the leaders for the mopping up teams. The next day Steve grilled each team on their plans. Even with the fast pace of the last couple of days, back in their hotel room that afternoon Ivy could tell from Steve's demeanor that all was in place. He was edgy, but not worried about details. Ivy thought he was mostly apprehensive about her, as well as Mathew, Brian and Moll.

The surveillance team confirmed that Cristo followed the same pattern around mid-day as the day Moll followed him. He was now in the Bunker with Eduardo. Ivy wished they did not have to wait another 24 hours to move into position. It would only serve to increase her nervousness. However she had to respect Steve's experience and trust his judgment on timing. She gazed over at him where he was sitting at the desk in their hotel suite. He was staring at his laptop but he was tapping the desktop with is forefinger the way he did when he was thinking. He seemed to be going through a checklist in his brain.

He took out his cell and dialed. After a few preliminaries, she heard him say to the Chief. "Authorize it. We go in tonight."

He was silent for a minute, listening. "Roger." Then he hung up and turned to face Ivy. "We put our gear on in the van."

He dialed again, telling Mathew to round up Brian, Moll and Lenny and to be ready to go in 15 minutes. She knew that one call would launch another bevy of calls. Ivy regarded him with awe. The element of surprise was sure working on her. She jumped up, pulled her devil-may-care hair back into a rough ponytail, put on her shoes, secured her gun in its shoulder harness, and tossed on a hoodie. Just like that, she was ready to go.

"All our personal creds stay here. I'll run them down to the hotel safe," Steve said. His eyes had taken on that cold intensity she remembered from when they had first met. For the next few hours he would be again the redoubtable FBI agent and not the Steve Nielsen she had come to love.

Ivy handed him her wallet after fishing out a few twenties, just in case. She slipped her lipstick in her pocket along with the money and then inhaled deeply hoping that a mythical guardian angel would be on each of their shoulders. At that moment Steve surprised her by taking her in his arms and holding her close, then he kissed her forehead and whispered, "For the rest of our lives. For us."

Chapter 25

The four agents had been around Steve long enough to be aware that once everything was in place, he would authorize the sting. Within fifteen minutes of his call, they were all in the surveillance van with him and Ivy. Moll took the wheel, heading down the highway to Madrid. He turned right north of the town onto a back road that circled above the Fuentes property, meeting up with the expanded team where the mineshaft work had taken place. Once there, they switched into an armored assault vehicle. Their plan was for the SWAT team to get through the front door of the Fuentes house, clearing security devices and neutralizing explosives as they went. Moll would then drive the assault vehicle up. Steve, Mathew, Brian and Lenny would jump out, run into the house and make the arrests. At 6:00 p.m., the late fall evening was just beginning. A little sliver of the moon shone hopefully in the sky, but did not give much light, which suited their need for a stealthy approach.

The SWAT team had its strategy planned to surround the house for an assault, with a second small team going into the mineshaft and down the tunnel at the back of the Fuentes property. It would be slow going at first as security cameras were disabled, the land scanned and agents moved into position. Every ten feet or so an agent would be positioned flat on the ground outside the house. Once everyone was in position, the SWAT team would blast their way through the front door. As soon as the SWAT team was ready to enter the house, Moll would drive their assault vehicle up. Steve, Mathew, Brian and Lenny would pile out on the run. Lenny would be in the lead and they would make their way into the house right behind the SWAT team.

Moll cruised around to the bottom of Fuentes driveway, lights out, turning off the motor and letting the assault vehicle stop quietly on its own. The SWAT agents were already making their way up the drive on foot, cautiously sweeping the ground and shrubs as they went. They were moving low and

261

slow and then crawling. Agents fanned to both sides of the house, surrounding it and cutting off any possibility of the Fuentes escaping through a window or a back door. The house sat silently in front of them with only a single shard of light showing through a crack in the window coverings. They waited through the long minutes that ticked by, seeing only shadows moving here and there.

Steve was watching the action through night binoculars, noting how the security devices were disabled and cameras blacked out. He looked impatiently at his watch -- 7:00. Right before they were ready to power through the front door, the SWAT leader signaled the van. Moll drove up fast and the four men jumped out, leaving Moll to manage the audio connection with Steve and to guard Ivy. Both Ivy and Moll sat at the alert, guns drawn.

The SWAT team was quickly in the front door and running. Steve's team gave them one second and then Lenny burst in followed by Steve. Brian fanned a little to the right, Mathew to the left, running half-backward to make sure no one was sneaking up behind them. They all had weapons drawn. Ahead of them, they heard, "FBI! Put down your weapons. You are under arrest."

They jogged through the living room and into a wide arched doorway to the dining room. Cristo was on his feet. Eduardo sat at the table with the remains of their meal around him. Cristo had his gun out and showed no sign of lowering it.

"Drop it Cristo!" Steve bellowed as he ran in, barreling past Lenny and confronting the two Fuentes brothers.

Eduardo said in that asthmatic high voice of his, "Cristo, I can't . . ."

Cristo spun quickly to face his brother, getting off three shots, then swinging back and shooting Steve twice in the chest before the agents gunned him down. It took only a couple of seconds from start to finish. Cristo had been smacked back against a heavy sideboard. Eduardo was half-slumped off his chair. The two Fuentes were dead

Steve was thrown backward, clutching his chest through the protective vest, his face shocked and his mouth open. He keeled face down onto the floor. Mathew stood aghast, paralyzed with fear that Steve's protective vest had failed. Brian quickly knelt down next to Steve, yelling for medics. He rolled him over and tore open his vest. No blood, but no heartbeat either.

Brian grabbed Steve's headset, "Ivy. Moll. Get in here. Steve is down."

Two medics ran up and began to work on Steve, giving him cardiopulmonary resuscitation -- chest compressions and assisted breathing. They moved methodically yet fast. On their faces, the concern was visible. Steve was not responding. He had no detectable heartbeat or breath.

Ivy and Moll ran in right when one medic pulled out small paddles to attempt to shock Steve's heart back into action with a defibrillator. The two medics worked rapidly, aware that their time to bring the big agent back to life was short. Ivy dropped down by Steve's head, putting her hands on both sides of his face and calling his name. Steve remained unresponsive.

Within seconds, the defibrillator in voice mode instructed, *"Stand Clear."* Brian pushed Ivy back and took her hands off Steve.

"Hit the Red Shock Button," came the next command.

One medic checked the pads and the defibrillator controls, then he nodded to the other one who pressed the shock button. Steve's body barely convulsed and he didn't come back to life. They all stared at him, unable to believe what they were seeing.

"Shock Dispensed."

The medic checked for a pulse and shook his head at the other one.

"Analyzing Vital Signs."

The machine checked for a heartbeat and gave another *"Stand Clear."*

Ivy began calling Steve's name, her voice shaking in fear and desperation. Mathew dropped down beside her. The medic checked the paddles again.

"Hit the Red Shock Button."

The medic nodded, Mathew pulled Ivy back and a second jolt hit Steve.

"Shock Dispensed."

Steve's body again showed a minor reaction, but no sign that he was alive.

"You may touch the Patient. Check Air Passage. Check Breathing."

The medic checked Steve, but did not detect any breathing.

"Begin CPR."

The two medics began a second CPR routine, checking Steve's breathing intermittently. The medic doing the chest compressions was counting quietly to be sure he was getting well over the required 100 pumps per minute. Seconds ticked by, stretching to a minute. The medic kept up the steady chest compressions.

Ivy looked bewildered. "This wasn't supposed to happen. He was supposed to be safe. How could he be ... "

Lenny said guiltily, "He barged past me. It's my fault he was hit."

Mathew shook his head. "Not your fault. He was like a steamroller coming in here. None of us could have stopped him. He was so used to being in the lead, I'm not sure he even realized that he charged ahead to take over."

"5, 4, 3, 2, 1; Stop CPR," came the voice from the defibrillator.

The medic stopped the chest compressions and checked the unit.

"Stop Now, Hands Off the Patient."

The medic moved back slightly.

"Analyzing Vital Signs."

A moment passed.

"Stand Clear."

Ivy stared in horror at Steve who remained unresponsive.

"Hit the Red Shock Button."

Steve's body convulsed slightly more this time.

"Shock Dispensed. Analyzing Vital Signs."

They waited.

"No Shock Advised."

Ivy looked wildly from one medic to the other, not understanding, then she stared back down at Steve. Was he dead?

No! She saw movement. He was breathing on his own! His head jerked once, but he did not seem conscious. The medic pushed an oxygen mask on his face.

"He may not come back right away. Some go into a coma state," the medic said quietly, glancing quickly at Ivy.

She took hold of Steve's head again, caressing his cheeks. Steve's eyes fluttered open, and slowly focused. He tried to sit up but the medic pressed him back down.

The medic listened to Steve's heart and gave a huge sigh of relief. "And sometimes, they come right back."

Ivy was cradling Steve's head in her lap. She asked the medic what happened.

"With these vests, the impact of a direct hit to the chest can make the heart stop, even though the protective vest keeps the bullets from penetrating the body."

The bruise on Steve's chest showed that the two bullets had been a direct hit. Mathew leaned over and pressed first Steve's hand and then Ivy's. He scrambled back to his feet, watched Steve for a few moments to make sure he kept breathing, and then nodded at him. As much as he wanted to stay, Mathew now had to take on Steve's role.

More SWAT team agents swarmed in, securing the inside of the house. Although it was evident that the Fuentes brothers were dead, Mathew first checked their bodies. Steve would have personally verified that each one was deceased. Mathew counted -- Cristo had at least ten bullets in him. That would be one for every agent in the room, plus a couple of extras, likely from Lenny. Eduardo only had the three that Cristo had fired. Both men were definitely dead. That done, he moved behind the SWAT team, stepping deeper into the house and seeking the door to the basement or the old mine tunnel. In the kitchen he met up with the SWAT team leader and the senior agent from the D.C. office who would take over the case, exchanging information on Steve and on the search of the house.

SWAT agents methodically secured each area by searching for and disabling any explosive devices before the other agents could enter it. Brian ran back to check on Steve, while Moll continued on with Mathew. Steve pulled off the oxygen mask and weakly asked Brian for an update. Then he broke loose from Ivy and the medic, pushed himself up against the wall, got his cell phone out and called the Chief, updating him on the situation. His voice was unsteady as he reported in.

Ivy grabbed the phone from him and told the Chief that Steve was hurt and that Brian or Mathew would be giving him more details. She handed the phone to Brian who ran it to the kitchen, talking with the Chief until he met up with Mathew who was waiting by a set of blast doors that the SWAT team had just secured. Beyond them, a winding staircase led down to a lower level that was likely completely underground. The SWAT team was proceeding cautiously down the steps, sweeping for explosives.

The medic forced Steve to take more oxygen. Steve stayed in a sitting position, holding his chest, uncertain what to do next. Ivy examined the darkening bruise that was dead center on his torso. She buttoned his shirt back up and partially fastened the vest back in place. Steve grimaced with any touch to the big bruise. The medic draped a blanket over his shoulders.

"Have to see the bank," Steve said weakly. Ivy nodded and told him to wait until the agents had it secured. Moll ran back to check on Steve.

"Is there an elevator to the basement?" she asked. Steve had come this far; he needed to see bank.

"Yeah. The ninjas are clearing it now."

"Ninjas?" Ivy echoed, a bit puzzled, "We have them too? I thought they were Asian."

"BuSpeak for a fully equipped SWAT team member."

Ivy asked the medic to get a wheelchair or a stretcher or something to move Steve through the house. He wanted to get Steve in an ambulance, but she told him that could happen later. The medics found a rolling chair and helped Steve onto it. Steve grumbled and said he could walk, but Ivy shook her head.

"I'll get you downstairs in the elevator, but you go on that chair with both medics," she ordered. "As soon as you see the bank, you are off to the hospital."

The medics forced Steve to keep using the oxygen and kept a heart monitor on him. Slowly they rolled him into the kitchen, found the elevator, pushed him in, and then rode down with him. Ivy and Moll took the stairs.

The basement appeared to consist of one large room filled with computer gear, an array of flat screens, a huge wall-mounted TV, a line of arcade games, a pool table and a one-lane bowling alley. On the far wall was the kind of door used on bank vaults, surprisingly left ajar. In front of them, the team of agents started to secure the computer equipment for transport to the FBI Albuquerque office it would be thoroughly analyzed.

A SWAT agent was going over the vault door, checking first for incendiary devices, and then examining the locking mechanism. Six team members made their way cautiously into the vault, scanning for additional explosives. The team coming in through the mine tunnel was holding beyond the back of the vault, having encountered the same type of door, which was locked.

Inside the basement the six of them waited, listening to the team inventory the computer equipment, checking out the telecom links and reviewing the surveillance control panel. The Special Agent from the Albuquerque FBI unit, in conjunction with the new team leader from the D.C. office, directed the activities. Every few minutes, one or the other of them would confer with Mathew. Ivy stayed with Steve. Once she sensed his frustration at being sidelined on the chair, she had him pushed up next to Mathew.

The agent examining the vault door turned and nodded that it was safe to enter. Mathew stood back and told the medics to roll Steve in, wanting him to lead them into the vault. Right behind him filed Ivy, Mathew, Brian, Moll and Lenny. They all stared at the rows of metal racking that lined the perimeter of the vaulted room which Mathew estimated to be about fifteen feet square. Around three quarters of the shelves housed long flat metal boxes stacked five high on each shelf.

Taking Moll and Brian with him, Mathew walked over to check out the metal boxes. Each one they opened was packed with currency. The total in the box and the type of currency was written on the outside. They quickly saw three foreign currencies, but most were U.S. twenties and hundreds. On a far rack were thicker metal boxes. Brian went over to check those out. Each one contained stacks of gold bars. Several cartons, labeled "Dell" were sitting on a handcart.

After conferring with the team leader from Washington, they decided to keep the far door to the tunnel closed and locked. Photos were taken of the vault and its contents. The new D.C. FBI team leader initiated the inventory, starting with one of the Dell boxes. It contained gold bars packed in styrofoam. Each bar weighed 27.5 pounds. Doing a quick calculation, Brian guessed that each box held 20 bars valued currently at $1,300 per bar. There were ten boxes, likely what Cristo drove in with that day -- something over a quarter of a million dollars. Emptying the vault would take a number of armored cars to transport all of the cash and gold secured there.

Ivy gazed around the room in awe, then knelt down next to Steve and kissed him on the cheek. "You have done well, Nielsen."

"We, all of us," he said hoarsely pointing around the room at the SWAT team and at the other agents. "Did the right thing and did it well."

Mathew conferred again with the head of the Albuquerque office and the new team leader from the FBI. He took some quick photos with his iPhone, emailed them to the Chief, and called him again. After his update, he handed the phone to Steve who spent a couple of minutes talking with the Chief.

As a group, the six of them made their way back upstairs and out to the assault vehicle and the waiting ambulance. They watched as Steve was loaded up and Ivy jumped in beside him, along with one of the medics and to their surprise, Lenny leaped in with his semi-automatic weapon in hand, squashing himself against the wall. As the ambulance pulled out, Moll climbed behind the wheel of the assault vehicle and made sure Mathew and Brian were settled in before starting the motor.

"Man, I thought the big guy was a goner," said Moll, as the reality of what had happened washed over him. "I always viewed him as like immortal."

Mathew nodded, his heart still aching from the horrifying sight of Steve totally gone, sprawled on the floor. He closed his eyes and said a quick prayer of thanks. He was so relieved that their business with the Fuentes was over. They would switch back into the van and then proceed to the hospital in Santa Fe. Mathew leaned his head back against the jump seat feeling hope and joy seep into him. It might be all wrong to be part of killing two perps and then drink champagne afterward, but that was exactly what he intended to do once Steve was settled in the hospital.

***

Two days later, Mathew was again sitting in a hospital room waiting for Steve to wake up. This time it was okay, since Steve would be released around noon after having a myriad of tests run on him the day before. Ivy sat by Steve's bed holding his hand. Lenny sat in the corner, gun out. The two of them had spent two nights there, refusing to leave Steve even though he was probably out of danger. Lenny blamed himself that Steve pushed past him and had been shot. In atonement, he planned to stay at the farm for a couple of months in case some belated goon squad showed up.

Steve would have a painful chest for some time but his heart was beating steady and strong, although he did seem tired. Mathew had seen to it that they were packed and ready to fly out for home. The Bubird was scheduled for 2:00 p.m. to take them back to Portland, with the lead medic from the Fuentes operation riding with them.

Chapter 26

Life became a blur of activity after the trip to Santa Fe. Even so, Ivy could still see Steve lying inert on the floor with the Fuentes brothers sprawled dead behind him. She had only glimpsed the Fuentes faces -- two nice looking men who chose a life of underworld power, profit and ultimate ruin. Eduardo, who Ivy thought was the brains of the operation, or El Astuto as he called himself, was almost ghostlike with his pale skin that never saw the sun. The way the whole house had been tightly shuttered and draped made Ivy wonder if he ever opened windows or went outside -- perhaps he did at night when he would feel less risk of detection.

They moved into their new home as soon as it had its Certificate of Occupancy. Mathew returned the rented trailers except one that Lenny commandeered, which they moved inside the barn for added shelter. Even though Steve still had pain and fading bruising, he insisted he was fit for their wedding, celebratory party and honeymoon. Their days were devoted to unpacking and setting up the new house and then decorating it for the holidays. Mathew worked with them daily on the house. Moll and Brian split their time between helping with the party preparations and getting ready for the startup of their first banking client at the beginning of 2014. Their contract was in place and they received an advance sample of the client's data to test out.

Fred moved with his family back to their home in nearby Dayton, although he worked at Spook Hills most days. He chose to live at home at least until his father, who so far remained sober, found steady employment. Ivy hired his mother to come to Spook Hills weekly to keep the house sparkling. With a ready smile like her son's, quiet demeanor and attention to detail, she was a welcome weekly addition to Spook Hills.

Ivy sent out the invitations for their party the day after they flew in from Santa Fe. The acceptance rate was surprisingly high for the holiday season, both among Ivy's old friends and business associates and among their neighbors here in the wine country. Mathew helped her with a list of agents who Steve worked with over the years and most of them accepted as well.

They decorated the house with Ivy's evergreen trees placing one large one downstairs in the games room, small ones in the library and Mathew's rooms, a full size one in the upstairs living room, a tall whimsical one in their bedroom and a small one in the kitchen. Two days before the party, they added fresh greens and holly, festooning the mantels, doors, and tables. Ivy had the stairway bedecked with holly and magnolia garlands, making them come alive with fluttering red and gold bows and flameless ivory candles flickering on each newel post.

Outside they placed little white lights on the garden walls, the square boxwood topiaries, the spruce tree, and at Steve's insistence, another live blue spruce was delivered for front of the house, which they planted and then decorated with the same white lights and with a star on top. He surprised Ivy by placing an angel sculpture on the roof deck with a halo of soft blue lights and a hidden spotlight to remind them to look out for each other.

Finally they reached the eve of their wedding and party. Ivy rechecked the plan for the day. Their civil ceremony was scheduled for eleven the next morning. The caterer was due to arrive around noon to set up for their guests. Steve wanted certain specialties as part of the appetizers: three types of savory Ebelskivers made fresh at station in the upper and lower living rooms and what he called Smørbørd, which consisted of open-faced Norwegian sandwiches with a base of Grovbrød, a whole wheat Norwegian bread. He also asked for a tray of Norwegian caraway-flavored Akevitt served the way it was traditionally, at room temperature and in tulip-shaped glasses.

Sometime when the party would be in full swing, Mathew offered to lead a champagne toast to Steve and Ivy. He had a surprise planned, but he was not even letting Ivy in on it. Ivy knew she was lucky that it was Mathew planning the surprise. If it were Moll, anything might happen -- he might set off an exploding Santa Claus on the rooftop deck. Moll surprised Ivy during this time by following her around to learn the way she did things and asking

271

innumerable questions about even mundane tasks like setting the table. He handled the setup of all the white linen draped mini tables tucked in corners around the house for their guests to enjoy an informal, yet filling dinner of lemon chicken, asparagus, and a creamy stacked potato dish called Dauphinoise. For dessert, the caterer was making a tower of white, milk and dark chocolate truffles.

Ivy's emerald green dress shimmered sleekly around her, just as she had envisioned. In the master bedroom, she had a long silky nightgown in pale blue to wear on their wedding night. Due to Steve's injuries, they had been sleeping chastely together, but she hoped Steve would feel up to changing that soon. By this time the next day, she would be Ivy Littleton Nielsen. While the road to this occasion has been more rough than long, she hoped that now she could grow the relationship she started with Steve, a man of wonder and character. He filled her with love and kept her life elevated out of the ordinary. What fun they expected to have growing old together here in this house, working with Mathew on their vineyard and traveling as the mood hit them.

***

The next afternoon, Steve looked himself in the eye as he neatly worked the knot into his black tie. Following the short civil ceremony late that morning, he was now a blissfully happy, married man. He found he was smiling without meaning to and humming along with the Christmas tunes Ivy had on the CD player. For a time, he feared their wedding day would have to be postponed. They did get it all together, thanks to Ivy's careful planning and a few stars aligning for them. Even with his chest feeling like it had been blown open and stitched back together with a crochet hook, he helped where he could – arranging things in drawers, unpacking what seemed like thousands of ornaments, testing lights, setting up timers and doing the easier decorating. They worked as a team to have everything ready for what he hoped would be a stupendous party that afternoon. The house glowed spectacularly the way Ivy adorned it both inside and out with all those little white lights.

He stopped for a moment to think. They had a house that was quickly becoming a home! Every now and then he would stop in one room or the other and marvel at the house he had designed and Ivy had decorated. As much as he was looking forward to their honeymoon trip, he was eagerly anticipating settling into this home with Ivy.

Luckily the weather cooperated for December with only a light mist that softened the glow of the lights as night drew on. In addition to decorating shrubs and trees, Ivy had Fred lay out nets of lights flat on the patio to give what Mathew called a "mille fleur" effect as the day darkened into evening. Steve half expected to see a wood sprite flittering around out in the gardens, it was so otherworldly out there. Ivy clapped her hands in delight when she saw the angel sculpture he had placed on the roof deck, with its crown of blue lights. This transition was bringing out hidden parts of him -- enjoying decorating for the holidays, for example. Who would have thought he would be sneaking out to buy an angel sculpture or a big blue spruce tree to decorate?

Mathew had been his best man that morning in their private civil ceremony at the house, with Moll, Brian and Lenny serving as witnesses. After it, they toasted with champagne and ate a light lunch the caterer had prepared, and then they went off to change for the party. Steve was going to surprise Ivy by wearing black tie. They say men are their best in formal attire and he wanted to appear as good new husband material. He knew he was not a handsome man, but he wanted to look his best for Ivy.

A few minutes ago, she had given him a heavy gold bracelet as a wedding present, which actually fit around his big wrist. On the back of the clasp was an engraving of twining ivy. Luckily for him, she found the heart bracelet he gave her adorable and put it on immediately, letting the rubies wink seductively against her silken green dress. Steve was glad the revealing dress came with that wrap she slid on, because it definitely showed more of her assets than he wanted their guests to see. Jeez Nielsen, he chided himself. Let her show off, for chrissakes. He grinned at himself in the mirror, delighted by the loveliness of his new wife. It had taken over 60 years to get here, making their relationship all the more amazing.

***

Twenty additional agents, retired and active, who Steve had worked with over the years, arrived en masse about an hour before the other guests so Steve would have time to talk with them. Fifteen minutes after their arrival, a long, black limo came up the drive. Steve looked over at Mathew questioningly, but all he did was shrug his shoulders and head to open the front door.

Mathew had arranged for the now former FBI Director, aka the Chief, to fly out for the reception. When two black-suited men and a somberly dressed woman showed up at the front door, all the color left Ivy's face. She seemed to think they were going to open fire or carry Steve off or something dreadful. They filed in with the Chief in the middle. He shook a surprised Steve's hand and kissed Ivy on the cheek, then led their second wedding toast -- the only nod to the wedding Ivy would allow at the party. Mathew had a short speech prepared and then the Director spoke for about ten minutes.

All the FBI agents, retired, inactive and active, lined up in a big semi-circle for the toast in the living room. The ceremony made Steve so touched that tears welled up in his eyes. The Chief used the occasion to present each agent, retired and active, who participated in the Fuentes case sting with special FBI recognition, ending with giving a public service award to Fred for his role in the Spook Hills sting, awing both Fred and his family.

The Chief stayed long enough to sip his champagne, try a glass of Akevitt, eat some food and speak to each of the agents. Overall he was with them for just over an hour, but what an hour! He commended Steve on his career and praised him for the recent success on the Fuentes case. Now Steve felt that he was truly retired from the Bureau and free for the future with his amazing new wife. While the first hour would remain imprinted on Steve's memory, the celebration continued until eight that evening, when Ivy closed the door on the final guest, flung herself down on the couch and flipped her shoes off, gratefully taking a glass of ice water.

Both of them were too tired to do justice to their new bedroom that night (and one of them might have had too much Akevitt), but they made up for it in the days following. Steve found it to be a wonder every time he made love with Ivy that she could be happy with him. He wanted nothing more than to spend the rest of his days ensuring that her life with him would make her glad to wake up each morning.

The three of them were to leave for London the following Thursday. Mathew would spend Christmas with Ivy and Steve at a fancy country manor in the Cotswolds and then he would travel on to Burgundy for wine tasting and learning in that great region, visiting large and small producers. They planned to meet up again in Florence for the New Year celebrations and then Ivy and Steve expected to spend a couple of weeks drifting around Italy, before returning home in mid-January. Steve was happily anticipating this time with Ivy, playing tourist and living his life as fully as he could. Next summer he wanted to take a long trip to Norway to learn more about his heritage and meet up with the remaining relatives he had over there. He hoped Ivy would enjoy that journey with him as he reached back to find more of himself.

Finally Steve was confident that he was progressing down the path of positive answers to those three questions that had previously made him feel so empty: *'In the end these things matter most: How well did you love? How fully did you live? How deeply did you let go?'* He had found his heart and he was more in touch with his soul. Yes, this was a time of personal growth. He closed his eyes and made a wish for the future.

'Ivy, my Ivy, keep me whole, keep me sane, and keep me happy.

You are my center, my life.'

Epilogue

To Ivy & Steve, In Celebration of Your First Christmas Together

I am so thankful that you wanted me to join you in celebrating your first Christmas as a married couple! Here we are at this wonderful manor house that is both relaxed and formal in that distinctive style the English have. I could be a character in the Downton Abbey series, having dressed for dinner and enjoying a glass of bubbly in the lounge.

Ivy and Steve, you remain my inspiration. Today we give you this tribute -- a collection of photographs from your wedding day. Moll, Brian, Fred and I took them as the day progressed. We worked last week to assemble an electronic photo album to mark your wondrous occasion. Intertwined in this volume, you will find shots of Spook Hills, the vineyard in its first year, your house under construction, and more Christmas lights than the North Pole. We hope that this compendium will give you lasting joy and that it will be but the first recorded chapter of your lives together. Perhaps one day, Brian, Moll and I may each have reasons to start our own volumes.

As for me, I must rely on your friendship while I venture out, take risks and hope that I can find a love as strong and shimmering as yours. During my search, may your lives at Spook Hills and on your travels be joyous and fulfilling. I look forward to finding a woman to make those parties up in the little walnut grove a foursome, as we launch our own great love.

Until that time, I remain your "star boarder" and honorary son. You will always be my inspiration and my life guides.

Eis quos amo, "For those that I love"

Mathew E. Heylen

The End